Best wishes,

Robert K Brown

Sonnets

A Novel

So through the night she uses each pained breath
To pray she'll soon receive the gift of death

Sonnets

A Novel

Robert K. Brown

Sonnets
A Novel

Manufactured in the United States of America

For information, please contact:
Brown Books Publishing Group
16200 North Dallas Parkway, Suite 170
Dallas, Texas 75248
www.brownbooks.com
972-381-0009
A New Era in Publishing™

ISBN-13: 978-1-933285-79-5
ISBN-10: 1-933285-79-6
LCCN 2007903044
1 2 3 4 5 6 7 8 9 10

Dedication

To Mary Lynn—my Muse.

Acknowledgements

Writing a book is a solitary endeavor. Publishing one, on the other hand, is most definitely a team effort. I was very blessed to have a wonderful group of individuals provide direction, support, and encouragement throughout the process.

First, I want to thank Ed Stackler of Stackler Editorial Agency, not only for the initial editing but for his patient and constructive tutoring. Without his coaching, this dream would have never been realized. My sister and brother-in-law, Dianne and Clay Querbes, refused to let this manuscript sit and collect dust. They provided a loving push when I needed it, and introduced me to a true innovator in the publishing industry. Milli Brown (no relation, unfortunately) and her entire staff at Brown Books Publishing Group continue to amaze me with their insight, creativity, and diligence. A writer could not find himself in more capable hands. To my wife, Mary Lynn, and our beautiful daughters, Kelley and Courtney, my eternal gratitude for always believing, even when my own faith had crashed against the rocks. And finally, I want to thank my mother, Marjorie, for instilling in me a life-long love of literature that has helped define who I am.

Even with all this help, there is one area for which I take full credit. Any mistakes, and I am sure there are many, are mine.

Robert K. Brown

**A sonnet is a moment's monument,
Memorial from the Soul's eternity
To one dead deathless hour.**

—Dante Gabriel Rossetti, The House of Life

Sonnets

Sonnet No. 1

She walks the night with yearnings undefined
Her auburn hair reflects the harvest moon
Toward which she gazes with a look designed
To capture hearts and make emotions swoon

By day she reads auditions to the Muse
Reflecting passions of the poet's heart
But nighttime brings the darkness to confuse
And, with the twilight, tortured feelings start

So into evening's dark embrace she falls
As love forbidden in the day awaits
She listens for the voice that gently calls
To justify the joy her heart debates

And so her heart will plunge into the night
And grant her restless soul its final flight

Eliot

Prologue

The kiss, although unexpected, was warmly welcomed. Margaret Fenwyck was lost in the moment—face upturned, eyes closed, a glass of wine in each hand. She had held high hopes for the evening, but she had not expected it to start like this. She certainly was not expecting what happened next.

Two hours earlier Margaret had bid everyone at the newspaper goodnight and hurried out into the crisp October air. It had been six o'clock, a splendid full moon already visible above the campus clock tower across the street. A good omen, she thought as she walked briskly up Main Street, nodding pleasantly at those whose eyes she caught. There were many, because Margaret Fenwyck was an attractive woman. Her hair fell about a delicate face in sun-streaked, reddish curls, and she sported a perfect hourglass figure, kept firm by her frequent workouts at The Slim Gym. Tonight, however, she passed the health club without a second thought and entered the wine shop next door. There she purchased a Kendall Jackson chardonnay, already chilled, and continued the four-block walk to the small but cozy house she had recently rented for a surprisingly affordable fee.

Margaret's original misgivings about trading the fast-paced city life of Atlanta for the tranquility of a small, north Georgia college town had been unwarranted. She had landed the job of arts and leisure editor of *The Smythville Gazette* at least ten years earlier than she could have risen to a similar rank at a large newspaper like *The Atlanta Journal-Constitution*. And while the *Gazette's* circulation was admittedly a fraction of that enjoyed by the Atlanta paper, its readership was atypically intellectual for that of a rural town. Smythville College could take the credit for that. The private liberal arts school attracted not only a relatively sophisticated faculty and student body, but also a variety of upscale restaurants, art shops and bookstores to serve them.

One of two fervent hopes that Margaret had held when arriving in Smythville eight weeks earlier was that she would make her mark at the newspaper quickly. She thought she had found a way to do that with a project she'd just announced—one that had the potential to become a permanent feature in the paper. It was essentially a poetry contest, although Margaret preferred to describe it as a "showcase for local talent." Each week *Gazette* readers were invited to compose and submit an original poem. The arts and leisure editor, with the help of Melissa Turner, her assistant, would select the one deemed best for publication in a new, weekly column called *Risk-A-Verse*.

She and Melissa had spent the entire afternoon reviewing the first round of entries, finally deciding that the winner would be a simple but properly constructed Shakespearean sonnet entitled *Sonnet No.1*. Like many poems, *Sonnet No.1* was abstract enough to allow the reader to draw his or her own conclusions as to its true meaning, and this one had particularly spoken to Margaret.

The aspiring poet had not included a full name, address or phone number, simply signing the submission with a single name—Eliot. Actually there had been several anonymous entries, which didn't surprise Margaret. Poetry was, after all, about feelings, and it was not unusual for people to feel insecure about expressing their innermost emotions in a public forum. Whoever he was, Margaret hoped Eliot would submit more compositions, because she felt the poem demonstrated a raw talent that was worth developing. And sometimes all a person pursuing a new endeavor needed was an initial success to fuel his confidence and feed his desire.

Desire. The thought of that word sent shivers of anticipation through Margaret as she hurried toward her house, anxious to get everything in place for her eight o'clock rendezvous. Desire had been the subject of Margaret's second harbored hope when she moved to Smythville. Actually, it had been more a concern than a hope—a fear that her love life might suffer in such a small, conservative town. But one day, shortly after arriving in town, she had found herself gazing into the most mesmerizing brown eyes she had ever seen. And even though neither of them had actually spoken of anything other than what would be expected in a polite, social exchange, the eyes had said it all. They had told Margaret that the interest was not hers alone.

Her anticipation of their first time alone together had increased exponentially by the time she hurried across her short walkway and up the three steps to the front porch. Retrieving her mail from the slightly rusted mailbox mounted on the wall, she fumbled for her keys, unlocked the door, and let herself in.

After putting the wine in the refrigerator, she hurried into the bedroom to undress for a quick shower. On a hopeful whim, she stopped to put fresh sheets on her bed. She selected her outfit for the evening, a low-cut emerald green dress that always turned heads, and laid it neatly on the bed. After also laying out her matching bra and panties, she stepped into the shower and turned on the hot water.

Later, after she had showered, dressed, and reapplied her makeup, Margaret stood in front of the full-length mirror and surveyed the image staring back at her. She was proud of what she saw. She felt that if she couldn't entice those bewitching brown eyes with this body in this outfit, they just couldn't be enticed.

She hurried about the process of making the final preparations for her date's arrival. Magazines were neatly arranged, her favorite Norah Jones record inserted in the CD player, and a crystal dish containing smoked almonds placed on the coffee table. She even opened the wine, not wanting to take a chance of fumbling with the corkscrew and broadcasting her nervousness in the presence of her date.

She would have liked a glass of the wine to calm her nerves, but willed herself to wait the remaining ten minutes until eight o'clock. Instead, she busied herself with a final inspection of the house and then checked her reflection one last time in the antique mirror behind the sofa. Finally she heard the sound she had been waiting for, the distinct creak of the top step to her porch, followed by footsteps approaching the door. A moment later the doorbell rang. She paused briefly, not wanting it to be so obvious that she had been anxiously waiting a mere few feet from the door, then took a deep breath and opened it.

As she stood there peering into those eyes she had thought about all day, she noticed that her favorite song was now playing on the CD. Perfect. This was the moment for which she had been waiting, planning, hoping—the moment when everything could change.

Margaret made meaningless small talk as she retrieved the bottle of wine from the refrigerator with trembling hands, glad she'd had the forethought to remove the cork earlier. She carefully filled two glasses and carried them into the living room, leaving the wine bottle on the kitchen counter. As she extended her left hand to offer one of the glasses of wine, she got her first surprise. The kiss was gentle, yet ripe with the promise of passion. She closed her eyes and savored it, like a wine connoisseur relishing the texture of a fine Bordeaux. So focused were her senses on the lingering kiss that it took a few seconds for her to become aware of a strange, muffled noise, a staticky yet somewhat melodious sound that she had not noticed before. Puzzled, she pulled her head back slightly and opened her eyes. "Do you hear that?" she asked.

The ice pick was so quickly and deftly plunged into her chest that the long, sharp point had already pierced her rapidly beating heart before she felt the first twinge of pain. But when the pain came it took her breath away, rendering her incapable of screaming in response to the agony and shock. Her legs began to quiver and twitch but she did not fall, held upright by her assailant's strong hand.

It was all over in a matter of seconds. But just before her body went limp, just before she took her last shuddering breath, her dimming eyes opened for a final, agonizing moment. The pain was so great that she could not summon the breath to speak the word, but her eyes asked the question as her lips mouthed the single syllable.

Why?

Chapter 1

O n wings of dreams her memories are borne
To soothe my soul 'til I awake to mourn."

Thus concluding his final sonnet for the evening, Drew Osborne closed the book and stepped back from the lectern. The audience, now applauding in the courteous but subdued manner of the intellectual elite, appeared to be made up predominantly of Smythville College students. He noticed a few older faces as well, mostly women, and probably members of the Smythville Literary Society, which had sponsored this evening's poetry reading and whose members fawned over the slender, sandy-haired professor as if he were the reincarnation of Lord Byron.

For the past forty minutes, he had read from his one published volume of verse, *Sole Searching—Reflections of a Lone Heart.* Published the previous year, the book had established his reputation in the ever-shrinking circle of poetry readers. Although the book's modest sales were gratifying, they did not generate much income—for Drew or his publisher. The owner of Troutman Publishing, a small, New York house that specialized in the subject of love—everything from poetry to romance novels to sex manuals—had contacted him after reading some of his sonnets in *The New Yorker.* While impressed enough by his verse to publish a small collection, what she really wanted was for

Drew to write a novel.

"You just ooze romance, darling," she had said at least a dozen times. "Why don't you put that talent to use in a way that can make us some *real* money?"

As the applause subsided, Lucille Chambertin, President of the Smythville Literary Society, clasped Drew's hand warmly and, eyes brimming, whispered, "That was wonderful, just wonderful."

She then stepped to the lectern as the applause began to die down and spoke into the microphone in an aristocratic southern accent. "I believe that all of you now understand why we in the Society feel so very fortunate to have this immensely talented young man here as a member of the college faculty and our community. We have refreshments set up in the foyer, and Dr. Osborne has graciously agreed to stay for a while to chat with you and answer any questions you might have." She cast an admiring glance at Drew. "Thank you again, Dr. Osborne, for a truly enriching and inspiring reading of your lovely sonnets."

The audience signaled its agreement with another round of polite applause, and then began to slowly migrate out to the awaiting refreshments.

Drew retrieved his worn leather satchel from behind the lectern and dropped his book into a side pocket. "May I escort you out to the refreshments area, Mrs. Chambertin?"

"I'd be honored, Dr. Osborne."

Arm in arm, they exited the lecture hall and began to make their way across the foyer toward the long table laden with punch, coffee, and an assortment of cookies. Before they could even reach the table, Drew found himself circled by a dozen or so members of the audience, mostly students, who were apparently anxious to make points with the most recent addition to the faculty.

"Dr. Osborne, would you autograph my copy of your book?" An attractive, dark-haired young woman, obviously a student, thrust the slim volume toward him.

"I'd be happy to," Drew said as he put his satchel on the floor and reached into his coat pocket for a pen. "What's your name?"

"Celeste. Celeste Holbrook. I'm in your freshman comp and lit class."

"I thought you looked familiar," Drew lied as he wrote in her book. There were over one hundred students in that class, and they met at eight o'clock in the morning. Most of the time, he felt fortunate just to arrive alert enough to stay focused on his lecture. Reaching the point of actually being able to differentiate the students would take a while.

"I have a question about the last sonnet you read," she said, as Drew handed back her signed book.

"Mourning Light."

"Yes. It's beautiful. All of them are," she added a bit awkwardly. "My question is whether the use of the words *mourning* and *mourn* in the title and final line were supposed to also suggest the time of day."

"Yes, the homonyms were deliberate."

"But isn't loneliness more traditionally associated with the darkness of night?"

"Absolutely. But what I wanted to convey was that this man's grief was more real—and therefore more painful—in the light of day. His only escape from the visual reminders of his shattered life was when the darkness of night hid them from his sight. And, of course, during sleep when he could actually dream of being reunited with his lost love."

Another voice to his right suddenly entered the conversation. "Was that poem based on a personal experience?"

Drew turned to see a petite blond woman with a pixie-style haircut and large, tortoise shell glasses resting on a small, upturned nose. Her bright blue eyes burned with an intensity that seemed incongruous with her youthful, doll-like face, as if she were a child who had just heard a naughty secret.

"Yes," Drew replied with no elaboration. He then excused himself and stepped over to the refreshment table. With his back to the room-

3

ful of people, he sipped a glass of sickeningly sweet punch. A moment later, he sensed a nearby presence, and then felt a gentle touch on his arm. The voice that spoke to him was a soft whisper, but he recognized it as belonging to the blond woman with the glasses.

"It appears I struck a nerve, Dr. Osborne. I apologize."

He managed a pained smile. "I should be the one to apologize. I'm afraid I sometimes let my feelings show a little too much."

"If you weren't a man of feeling you couldn't be a poet. Not a good one, anyway." She extended her hand. "I'm Melissa Turner from the *Gazette*. I believe Margaret Fenwyck spoke with you about the article we're writing for the Sunday arts and leisure section."

"Yes, I was flattered. Please, call me Drew."

"Sure. Do you mind if Margaret or I call you tomorrow to get a little more background information?"

"No, not at all." Drew looked around the room. "Is Miss Fenwyck here? I was hoping to meet her tonight."

The smile seemed to melt from Melissa's face. "No, she must have had a family emergency or something. She didn't come to work today, and she wasn't home when I called her."

"I hope everything is okay," Drew offered, unable to think of a more appropriate response. "So you're the only one here from the *Gazette*?"

"No, I brought Andrea Warren with me. She's our local news editor." She pointed toward a tall, slender brunette engaged in conversation with an even taller bald black man sporting a single gold earring. "That's Andrea. Would you like to meet her?"

"Sure."

They walked over to the couple as Andrea laughed heartily and flirtatiously touched her tall companion's arm. She turned toward Drew as he approached, and he found himself facing a woman who, in her three-inch heels, nearly matched his height of slightly over six feet. She was tanned, lithe, and obviously athletic—striking, yet not what he considered beautiful in the classic sense.

Drew acknowledged the towering black man before extending his hand to the woman. "Pardon me for interrupting, Charles, but I wanted to meet Miss Warren."

Her handshake was firm and she looked him squarely in the eyes as she smiled. "It's a pleasure to meet you, Dr. Osborne. Your poems are beautiful. Haunting, actually."

"Thank you." He then turned to face Melissa, whose diminutive frame contrasted sharply with her taller associate's. "Melissa Turner, this is Charles Alexander, Professor of English Literature. Charles, Miss Turner works in arts and leisure at the *Gazette*."

"So you're here to ensure Drew's celebrity status in Smythville," Charles said with a wink, although his tone suggested the remark was not entirely in jest.

Melissa peered up at him, her eyes flashing behind the thick lenses of her glasses. "Do I detect a trace of intra-departmental jousting, Dr. Alexander?"

Charles chuckled as he glanced at Drew. "No, just a good, old fashioned case of jealousy, Miss Turner."

Melissa smiled. "Due to Dr. Osborne having been published?"

"Actually," Charles said, "I've been published too. It's just that my textbook on nineteenth century English novelists doesn't quite make the ladies swoon the way Drew's sonnets seem to do."

"No, but your book does have a distinct advantage over mine, Charles," Drew said with a sly smile.

"Oh, and what would that be?" Charles asked, his bald head creased in a quizzical frown.

"Certain people are actually *required* to buy yours."

The group laughed and continued to engage in polite chatter until Drew said he still had some work to do on his morning lecture and had best be taking his leave. As he was shaking hands with the two women and telling Melissa he would be expecting her call the next morning, he felt a tap on his shoulder. He turned to see Celeste Holbrook, the student whose book he had autographed earlier.

"Excuse me, Dr. Osborne, I had another question about one of your poems." A hopeful smile revealed perfectly matched dimples.

"Well, actually I was just leaving. I have to go back to my office and finish preparing for my morning class. I need to make sure my lecture is worth you taking the trouble to drag yourself out of bed so early."

"Oh, I have no trouble getting out of bed for you," she said, blushing crimson. "For your class, I mean."

Drew felt his ears burning as Melissa and Andrea exchanged winks and Charles rolled his eyes.

"So you're a student here?" Melissa asked, breaking the awkward silence.

"Yes, a freshman." Celeste introduced herself, shaking hands with each person before turning back to Drew. "Since you're leaving, I'll walk along with you and ask my question."

"That's okay," Drew said. "I can stay another minute or two."

"No, I really don't want to hold you up. I know you're very busy," she said. "Besides, your office is right on the way to my dorm."

Realizing he had no gracious way to refuse, Drew reluctantly said his good-byes before heading for the door with the beautiful young student at his side. He knew it was probably his imagination, but he would have sworn that every eye in the room was on them as they stepped out into the darkness.

Chapter 2

By ten o'clock the following morning, Melissa Turner's concern over not hearing from her boss had escalated in status from gnawing anxiety to biting panic. She had known Margaret only a couple of months, but that was enough for her to know that this was highly unusual behavior. Something had happened.

She had tried phoning Margaret's house after returning home from the poetry reading at the college last night, and had already placed five more unanswered calls this morning, one every half-hour since she had arrived at the *Gazette* office at seven thirty. Now, as she hung up the phone from the sixth unsuccessful attempt, her worried expression telegraphed itself like a powerful radio signal to the co-workers around her.

Andrea Warren came over and sat on the corner of her desk. "Still no answer?"

"No." Melissa looked up, tried to summon a smile, and then aborted the attempt. "This just isn't like Margaret. Even if her mother was back in the hospital she would've called by now."

"Well, she knows that everything here's in good hands."

"Yeah, but yesterday was a particularly important day, getting the first installment of "Risk-A-Verse" ready for today's edition. And I know she was looking forward to meeting Professor Osborne."

Andrea smiled. "She'll definitely be disappointed that she missed that. Especially when we tell her what he looks like."

"He is cute, isn't he? And his poems are so romantic."

"Cute, romantic and single. If he remembers to put the toilet seat back down, he's pretty close to being the perfect man."

Melissa finally allowed a smile to escape, the corners of her eyes crinkling behind the tortoise shell glasses. "Maybe I should volunteer to meet with him each week to review the finalists for the column. A little extra quality control never hurts, you know."

"Your commitment is exemplary," Andrea said. Turning serious, she asked, "So what should we do now? Call the police and report Margaret missing?"

"I don't know." Melissa glanced nervously toward the office in the corner, the only enclosed office at the *Gazette*. "I suppose I should talk to Mr. Moss, see what he thinks."

"You might want to wait a while longer. I don't think he's had his second cup of coffee yet."

Melissa shook her head as she stood. "No, I'll see him now, before he gets caught up in meetings. Getting yelled at isn't nearly as bad as sitting here worried sick and doing nothing."

A few seconds later she was standing outside of the senior editor's office. She straightened her skirt, took a deep breath, and rapped on the door.

"What is it?" a deep voice bellowed from within.

She opened the door and stepped inside. "Mr. Moss, I need to speak with you a moment."

Bernard Moss peered over his bifocals with the intensity of a falcon preparing to swoop down on a defenseless field mouse, and then leaned his heavyset frame back in his swivel chair. It groaned under the strain. He ran a hand through his thick white mane and pointed to a chair. "Sit down." It was a command, not an invitation.

Melissa closed the door behind her and sat in the designated chair. "I . . . I'm very concerned about Margaret," she stammered.

"I haven't heard from her in over forty hours. This isn't like her. Something must've happened."

"Maybe she had to go away unexpectedly. Doesn't she have family in Atlanta?"

"Her mother. And I know she's been ill. But even if that were the case, Margaret would've called by now."

Moss picked up his phone and punched a speed dial button. "This is Bernard Moss. Let me speak to the chief."

Melissa could not help but smile. The *Gazette's* senior editor always went straight to the top, even when dealing with the Smythville Police Department. It was one of the privileges of rank not just at the newspaper, but in the town itself. Moss' great-great grandfather on his mother's side, Colonel Antoine LeMay Smyth, had founded the town and the *Gazette* in 1868, and his descendents had been running both ever since.

"Lou, it's Bernie," he said, his gruff voice only slightly tempered. "My new arts and leisure editor, Margaret Fenwyck, hasn't been in for two days. I'm thinking she may have had a family emergency down in Atlanta, but she should've called in by now. I need you to check with the highway patrol and see if there's been any serious traffic accidents between here and there since Tuesday night."

He listened for a moment, and then looked at Melissa. "What kind of car does she drive?"

"A white Toyota Camry," she said.

"White Camry," he repeated into the phone. "And why don't you send a couple of your boys over to her house to look around? She's renting the McGregor house on Sage Street."

Moss shook his head. "No, I don't have any reason to suspect foul play. You're in Smythville, not back up there in Philadelphia. It's just that a woman living alone could have an accident or fall off a damned ladder or something. Just send somebody over there, okay?" A moment later he said, "Thanks, Lou. Call me as soon as you know something."

He hung up and looked at Melissa as if surprised to see her still sitting there. "Is there anything else you want? Some time off? A raise?"

Melissa blushed in spite of herself. "Are you offering?"

"No. Get back to work."

She stood and reached for the door. "Thank you, Mr. Moss."

He said nothing, dismissing her from his hallowed presence with a brusque wave of his hand.

Police Sergeant Howard Mullins parked his squad car in front of the small frame house on Sage Street and quickly surveyed the scene. A white picket fence enclosed a small yard, which was covered with red and yellow leaves from the giant maple tree in the right corner. A detached single-car garage which, like the fence, could stand a new coat of paint, sat on the back of the lot to the left of the house.

By all outward appearances, everything looked perfectly normal, but Mullins knew from twenty-two years of experience that normal outward appearances sometimes belied grievous abnormalities within.

He turned to his new partner, Art Schaeffer, a twenty year-old rookie who looked as if he were still waiting for his first shave. "You check out the garage and the doors and windows on the back of the house. I'll check the front."

"Okay, Sarge. What am I looking for?"

"Any signs of forced entry, or anything else to indicate the lady didn't just go out of town, which is probably the case. If her car's not in the garage, it's a pretty safe bet she went off somewhere and either had an accident or just hasn't gotten around to calling anybody at the newspaper yet."

"Got it. Be back in a sec." The young cop got out of the car, placed his cap on his head at a jaunty angle that he had probably perfected after countless hours in front of a mirror, and headed toward the garage.

Mullins smiled to himself as he made his way through the gate and up the walkway to the front steps. Over the years he had seen many rookies suffering from the same romanticized, grossly inaccurate notion of police work that afflicted young Schaeffer. The kid seemed perpetually poised for any signs of criminal activity, and seemed disappointed when none materialized. Mullins knew that realism usually accompanied experience, and the reality of a cop's life in a small town like Smythville was that serious crimes were few and far between. He wondered how long it would take before Schaeffer realized that was a good thing.

He paused in front of the door, and then rang the bell once, twice, and finally a third time it rang with no answer. There was no sound of any movement inside. Mullins tried the door and found it locked. He opened the mailbox and saw a magazine and a few bills. The lady was obviously not at home, and had been gone for at least a day.

Schaeffer emerged from the right corner of the house and joined Mullins on the porch. "The back door and all the windows are locked up tight. There's a light on in one room."

"Well, a lot of people leave a lamp on a timer when they go out of town," Mullins pointed out, but he was beginning to experience a tiny, instinctual spark of apprehension.

"There's a white Camry in the garage," Schaeffer added, as if it were an inconsequential afterthought.

Mullins' spark burst into flame. Car in the garage, mail in the mailbox, light on in the house. Any one of those could be easily explained, but not all three. Something's wrong.

Mullins rang the doorbell again, a long, sustained buzz, but knew there would be no answer. His pulse quickened and the fine hairs on his freckled arms were standing at attention, as if suddenly charged with static electricity.

Sensing movement to his left, he turned to see Schaeffer lifting one foot and then the other, inspecting the bottom of each shoe. "What the hell are you doing, Art?"

"Looking to see if I stepped in something," the rookie said, wrinkling his nose. "Don't you smell that?"

"I don't smell anything." Mullins then stepped to where Schaeffer stood by the living room window. There, he could detect a cloying, musky odor, like decaying mulch. He bent down and smelled that it was stronger, seeming to emanate from a sizable crack in the lower right window pane.

He reached for the radio strapped to his belt. "Headquarters, this is Mullins. Come in, Sarah."

A female voice responded. "Go ahead, Howard."

"We're at the Fenwyck house on Sage. The house is locked, yesterday's mail's in the box, and the car's in the garage. And we smell something. We're going in."

"Roger. I'm standing by."

Schaeffer looked confused but, hearing Mullins say they were going in, he unsnapped the strap over his service revolver and nodded that he was ready. Mullins used his nightstick to break one of the leaded glass panes that bordered either side of the door, and then reached his arm in to release the lock on the inside knob. He opened the door and they stepped inside.

"Police. We're coming in," he shouted. There was no response.

The odor in the foyer was stronger, but not overwhelming. It seemed to be coming from the living room to his left. As he stepped into the room, Mullins glanced toward the small kitchen to his right. An opened bottle of wine sat on the counter. It was about half full.

Schaeffer brushed past him and stepped cautiously into the living room. His eyes widened before he spun around and ran out the front door onto the porch where he vomited loudly. Mullins took a couple of steps to his left and saw her. She was seated on the sofa, her right hand in her lap, the other dangling over the armrest. Several flies performed an aerial ballet around the handle of the ice pick that protruded from the fold of her ample cleavage. Her eyes were open, staring into the room as if she were waiting for an invisible guest to answer a perplexing question.

"What do we do now?"

Mullins turned to see his ashen-faced partner standing in the foyer, staring in apparent disbelief at his first murder victim. "We touch nothing," Mullins said. "And we call the chief."

He lifted the radio to his mouth and pushed the button. "Sarah, it's Howard again. Get Lou on the line. We've got a situation here."

Chapter 3

I t was the appointed time. The only light in the room was the ghostly blue glow emanating from the laptop computer screen. Eliot entered the commands to bring up the "Instant Messaging" screen and anxiously began to type.

Select Screen Name: Eliot

Enter Password: Sonnets

Send Instant Message To: Melpomene

Eliot: Are you there?

Melpomene: Yes, I'm here.

Eliot: I did it . . . just the way you said.

Melpomene: And?

Eliot: Exquisite! Looking into those emerald-green eyes and seeing life's glow fade slowly away. Like watching a passing soul.

Melpomene: Only a poet could realize the splendor of that moment.

Eliot: It was exactly as you said it would be. A wondrous feeling of power . . . purpose . . . truth.

Melpomene: Just remember that your actions have little impact in and of themselves—you salvage one wretched soul among millions. But those actions transform your poetry into truth.

Eliot: And you are my inspiration . . . my Muse.

Melpomene: Have they found her yet?

Eliot: Oh, yes. What a thrill it was to stand by the hearse with all those nervous, gawking people, watching as Margaret's body seemed to float across the lawn in her black, plastic cocoon.

Melpomene: A marvelous image. You know, the ancient Greeks believed one's soul left the body in the form of a butterfly.

Eliot: And now I'll always think of Margaret in that way. It seems funny now that I'd thought her different. But her motives were impure. In fact, they were vile.

Melpomene: But you rose above your disgust and saved her from herself. There are more like Margaret, more who need your special gift. You must continue to develop it.

Eliot: I know. I want to. I want my poems to speak truth.

Sonnets

Melpomene: They not only speak truth, they portend it . . .
make it happen. That is your mission . . . your purpose.
You must find another worthy subject. You must write the
words that speak of truth, then commit the deed that makes
them so.

*Eliot: Should I . . . so soon? Wouldn't it be wise to
wait a while?*

Melpomene: Are you questioning my judgment?

Eliot: Of course not. It's just that . . .

Melpomene: Perhaps the time has come for you to strike
out on your own. Maybe you think it would be better if I
just went away.

*Eliot: No . . . don't! I can't do this without you. I
need you.*

Melpomene: It doesn't sound that way.

Eliot: But it's true. What must I do to prove it to you?

Melpomene: Write me another sonnet.

Chapter 4

D rew knew he was dreaming but was powerless to stop it. He knew where the dream would take him and wanted more than anything to not go there. To be able to awake just once before it ran its tortuous course would be a blessing, a merciful reprieve. Perhaps the time would come when he would be so lucky. But it would not be tonight.

The dream was so real, so vivid, that it was like watching film clips of the actual events. He and Kate arriving in Cancun for a long Easter weekend. The harrowing taxi ride to the Marriott Casa Magna, followed by a passionate christening of their oceanfront room. Lying in bed watching as she sat naked, painting her toenails and finger-nails a bright fluorescent pink.

Afterwards, a swim in the pool, Pina Coladas in the shade of a giant beach umbrella, holding hands as they walked along the sunset-painted beach. He could almost taste the spicy dinner at the tiny, romantic cantina, and hear guitar music floating in the background like smoke in a gentle breeze. He could almost feel the pulsing bass as they danced the night away at Senor Frog's, their sweating bod-ies craving and consuming more tequila shots than any sane person would dare.

A room service breakfast of toast, coffee, and aspirin, and another round of lovemaking. A walk to the beach on shaky legs. Wading into the crystal-clear water as the warm waves caressed their bodies. Blue sky, green water, white sand. Red flags.

They had the ocean to themselves. Floating, drifting, holding each other. Laughing, kissing, fondling. The shore becoming more and more distant, the sounds of beach frolic becoming lost in the lapping of the swells and the gentle roar of the wind.

Drew tiring first, suggesting they head back to shore. Kate, the stronger swimmer, challenging him to a race, and giving him a generous head start. Him taking off in a mad, frenzied splash, moving his arms and steadily weakening legs as fast as he could but feeling the current fighting his progress. As if strong, watery hands were restraining him, making him work harder, sapping his strength.

Finally, nearing exhaustion, reaching the point where the waves were breaking as they rushed to the beach, delighting a group of children playing in the shallow surf under the watchful eyes of their parents. Realizing that Kate should have passed him by now. Struggling to his feet, finally able to touch bottom, turning to look for her just as a wave broke over his head, knocking him five yards in, then tugging him eight yards back out. Standing again and scanning the surface of the water. Searching frantically for Kate. Seeing nothing. His gut tightening. Fear and a deepening sense of dread consuming him. Another huge wave washing over him, dragging him along the sandy bottom, scraping his shoulder on a patch of coral.

Standing again. Shouting her name. Seeing something on the surface a hundred or more yards away, then losing it, wondering if he had really seen it at all. Screaming for help, for the lifeguards. Seeing the fear in the eyes of the bewildered children, and the protective, suspicious looks of the parents as they grabbed their precious human bundles and whisked them away from the unidentified danger.

Being knocked down by another wave, then feeling strong hands clawing at him, fighting to hold on. Kate? Had she somehow sneaked up on him beneath the surface of the water? Was she playing a game?

Then looking into the huge brown eyes of a muscled young Mexican holding a small plastic board with a rope.

Yelling, "Not me! Not me! It's Kate! She's out there!"

Watching the lifeguard swim effortlessly beyond the breaking waves, pulling the plastic board behind him. Feeling other hands grabbing him, pulling him toward the shore. Falling, gulping salt water, standing again. Looking. Praying. Crying.

Watching as the lifeguard returned to shore. Alone. Watching as the patrol boat arrived and covered the area again and again in ever widening circles. Minutes, hours, lifetimes passing.

The hotel doctor. The hotel management. Police. Questions, condolences, false hopes. More questions.

Back in the room, lying on the bed, still unmade from their morning love, the sheets still reeking of her sweat and perfume. A knock at the door. A Mexican policeman, hat in hand.

A ride through the falling darkness. Lights everywhere. Music playing. People laughing.

A squatty, white building. Down to the basement. The pungent smell of formaldehyde and disinfectant. Long tables. A form on the nearest one, covered by a sheet. A protruding hand quickly covered by the policeman. A glimpse of fluorescent pink.

A fat man in a white lab coat stepping to the table, grasping the sheet. Looking at Drew. Questioningly. Accusingly. Pulling the sheet back to reveal the face. Her face, but not her face. The color all wrong. The hair all tangled. Purple, bloated lips. Bruises on both cheeks.

Suddenly the eyes open. The purple lips part. Water dribbles from her mouth as she prepares to speak.

Drew bolted upright as the scream was forming in his throat. He choked it back and gasped for breath. He fumbled for the lamp switch and then looked at the clock on the bedside table. Four thirty. He lay back on the wet sheets, staring at the ceiling, scared to close his eyes. Afraid he might fall asleep again.

After a few minutes, he swung his feet over the side of the bed. He took a few deep breaths and then stood, walked into the bathroom, and splashed cold water on his face. As he raised his head and opened his eyes to look in the mirror, he prayed this would not be one of the mornings when he saw Kate's reflection behind him, her bloated lips slowly mouthing a silent accusation.

For once, Drew did not have to rush into his eight o'clock class at the last minute. In fact, this morning he was the first one in the lecture hall. After the dream, his normally treasured solitude held no appeal. He wanted, needed to be around other people, to simply smile, nod, or extend a casual "Good morning" to another living soul, and to actually hear words emanate from moving lips.

Most of the students who filed into the room seemed surprised to see him there so early, having already discerned his arrival patterns over the previous six weeks. Drew responded to their inquiring looks with a shrug, a wink, or a surprised-looking glance at his watch, as if his early arrival were a grievous mistake. He elicited a few laughs, engaged in some polite, meaningless banter, and decided he should start making an effort to arrive early on a regular basis. He knew there were some bright young minds in this class, and this was a good way to get to know them better.

He began his lecture promptly at eight, and was just introducing the topic of the day when the door at the back of the amphitheater opened. Drew paused in mid-sentence, and looked up to see Celeste Holbrook, the student he had met at the poetry reading two nights ago, stroll nonchalantly into the room, slurping loudly as she sucked the last of a carton of orange juice through a drinking straw. Seeming to suddenly realize that, except for the noise she was making, the room was otherwise quiet, then seeing the professor standing by the chalkboard smiling up at her, she blushed the color of a ripe cherry. Murmuring something unintelligible, she hurried toward the nearest unoccupied seat. Several of her classmates seated on her row quickly discovered that their heads were in the erratic flight path of her back-pack as she scrambled past, mumbling frantic apologies.

Drew could tell that the young woman was terribly embarrassed, but he could not resist the temptation to make a joke at her expense.

"Miss Holbrook, you should be aware by now of my obsession with punctuality. I'll overlook this episode, but please be more mind-ful of this fact in the future."

The rest of the class now abandoned any pretense of polite self-control and erupted into raucous laughter. As the room slowly qui-eted, Celeste appeared to regain her composure. Staring at Drew, she cocked her head to one side.

"Who are you, and what have you done with Dr. Osborne?" she asked in an accusing tone.

The hall again exploded into laughter. Drew joined in this time, relishing the rare, light mood in which he unexpectedly found himself.

"Touché," he said with a smile, and then continued with his lec-ture. He wrapped it up about fifty minutes later, reminding the class of the quiz on Monday and wishing them a good weekend. As the lecture hall emptied, he put his books and notes back in his satchel and proceeded to erase the chalkboard.

"Dr. Osborne?"

He turned to see Celeste Holbrook standing by the lectern, a shy smile accenting her pretty, debutante-next-door face.

"Yes, Miss Holbrook?"

"I wanted to apologize for disrupting your class this morning. I didn't think I was any later than usual, and wasn't expecting you to be so . . ."

"Punctual," he said, completing the sentence for her. "Don't worry about it. I was just kidding, you know. In fact, I hope I didn't embarrass you too much."

"Oh, no, not at all. I was embarrassed, all right, but not by any-thing you did. My mother always warned me about slurping my drink through a straw. Now, I realize I should've listened to her."

"We'd all probably be better off if we had paid more attention to what our mothers told us." Drew dusted the chalk off his hands, picked up his satchel, and started for the door. Celeste followed.

"Actually," she said, a coquettish smile curling her lips, "it was kind of flattering to have you remember my name in front of the whole class."

"I'm not sure I understand why that would be flattering," Drew said as they emerged into the lobby of the Liberal Arts Building.

"Well, you know," she said, her face pointed forward but her eyes glancing in his direction, as if she were too embarrassed to look at him directly. "You being the newest member of the faculty, and a published poet and all. It's . . . it's sort of like having a celebrity for a teacher."

Celeste followed him into the stairwell as he prepared to climb the two floors to his office in the English Department.

"Believe me, Miss Holbrook," he said, "the celebrity afforded to poets, published or otherwise, is virtually nonexistent."

"Maybe in the world at large, but it's a pretty big deal to those of us in your class. Poetry is a lot more exciting when it's taught by someone who actually writes the stuff."

"Thanks for the compliment . . . I think," Drew said, as they emerged onto the third floor and stopped outside the entrance to the English Department office suites.

Celeste suddenly frowned, as if disappointed that their walk and their one-on-one conversation was about to end. "Uh, actually there was something I wanted to ask you."

"Yes?"

"I'm having trouble understanding some of the symbolism in the poems we've been studying, especially Coleridge. I want to do well on the test Monday. Do you think I could get some extra help?"

As Drew was about to reply, Charles Alexander appeared through the doorway, grinning slyly when he saw Celeste. "Morning, Dr. Osborne," he said with saccharin politeness and a subtle wink.

"Good morning, Charles," Drew said, then turned his attention back to the young woman who was standing just a little bit closer than he thought was necessary. "Of course. Go see Jennifer Alsop, one of the graduate students. Tell her I sent you."

Celeste made no attempt to mask her disappointment. "Oh, you don't work with students yourself?"

"If it's necessary. But this is something one of the grads can handle as well as I can, maybe better. I'll see Jennifer in her class at eleven. I'll tell her to expect you this afternoon."

He again felt the door opening behind him, and stepped aside to allow Dr. Ainsworthy, the department chairman, to maneuver his substantial girth past them. The elderly professor looked at Drew, glanced at the young woman, and then ambled down the hall.

"Well, look, I have a lot of work I need to get to," Drew said. "Be sure you go see Jennifer. I expect you to ace that quiz on Monday."

He turned and hurried through the door before she had a chance to respond. A few minutes later, he came out of his office and was picking up his messages from Judi Carr, the department secretary, when Charles walked back through the door, still grinning.

"Gosh, Mom," he said in a mocking, childlike voice, "she followed me home. Can I keep her?"

Drew shot his tall, black associate a look that indicated he was not amused. "Give me a break, Charles. Don't you ever have conversations with any of your students?"

"Sure I do. But I don't recall having any students that followed me around like a love-sick puppy."

Seeing no point in continuing a futile battle of wits, Drew turned to Judi, who seemed a little embarrassed by the sarcastic exchange between the two professors. "Judi, I never got that call I was expecting yesterday from Margaret Fenwyck or Melissa Turner. Could you please call the *Gazette* and tell them that I'll only be in my office before eleven and after three?"

The color drained from the secretary's face, and Charles reached out and grabbed Drew's arm. Nodding in the direction of Drew's office, he said, "Can I see you a minute?"

Perplexed, Drew stepped into his office, followed by Charles who shut the door behind them and fixed Drew with a curious stare. "You haven't heard?"

"Heard what?"

"That Margaret Fenwyck was found dead yesterday. Murdered. Don't you read the newspaper, man?"

Drew dropped heavily into a chair and stared blankly at the closed door. "No, I don't have the paper delivered, and I didn't buy one this morning. What happened? Who did it? Why?"

"Those are the same questions the police are asking. She apparently was killed Tuesday night, the night before she was supposed to come here to meet you. She'd been dead almost two days when they found her."

"My God, that's awful," Drew muttered. "I never got the chance to meet her. Did you know her?"

"Not real well. She'd only been in town a few months. Moved here from Atlanta, I think. I met her at a reception the school had for parents of incoming freshmen back in August, and saw her around town now and then."

"What a shame," Drew said, shaking his head. "I thought I was leaving murder and mayhem behind when I left New York to move to this quiet little college town."

Charles smiled grimly as he stood and walked to the door. "I wouldn't worry about that. This is the first murder case this town has seen in fifteen or twenty years. It'll probably be at least that long before it sees another one." He paused, his hand on the doorknob. "On the other hand, if we've learned anything at all from Paducah and Jonesboro and Littleton, it's that small towns are anything but immune to mindless violence. Maybe Smythville's just catching up with the rest of the world."

Sonnets

Sonnet No. 2

Throughout the years she blossomed like a rose
Her glistn'ing petals sacred and reserved
Until the perfect gardener she chose
To snip the fragrant flower he deserved

She gazes at the one who comes to teach
Her thoughts engaged in chasing lustful dreams
'Tis not her mind she yearns to have him reach
When putting into play flirtatious schemes

Into his world of poetry and books
She interjects her pleading siren's voice
Conveying her intentions with coy looks
To show he is her gardener of choice

But fate decreed her sultry words be choked
Before the fires of passion could be stoked

                                        Eliot

Chapter 5

Melissa Turner sat at her desk at the *Gazette*, trying to read the typewritten page she held in her trembling hand. She found it hard to focus. The words seemed to blur and run together, as if the tears welling in her eyes were actually mixing with the letters, washing them away in a swirling current of anger and grief.

It was early Monday morning. She had been the first to arrive in the office, desperate to get out of her lonely apartment and into an environment where other people would soon be present. After spending Saturday in Atlanta, first seeing Margaret laid to rest, and then trying to console a grieving mother who was herself close to death, Melissa had spent Sunday alone. She had awakened this morning with her need for solitude satiated, suddenly finding herself anxious to be surrounded with other people who shared her sense of loss and her gnawing sense of fear. She wanted to commiserate with friends and peers who could help her get past this horrifying, seemingly meaningless tragedy, and to start the process of forgetting the lurid details of Margaret's untimely death.

But the act of returning to work, of busying herself with mindless, time-passing tasks like opening and sorting Friday's mail, ironically had the opposite effect. The very first piece of mail she opened was a stark reminder of the last few minutes she had spent with Margaret, when they had finally concluded the time-consuming process of reviewing the first batch of submissions for "Risk-A-Verse," confident that their selection was a worthy choice.

Now, she held in her hand another submission by the same poet, Eliot. This one, entitled "Sonnet No. 2," also spoke of the frustration and exhilaration of unrequited love, of passionate intentions, and "lustful dreams." It had the same proper structure and romantic imagery of "Sonnet No. 1," yet the tone seemed slightly different, more critical, and almost judgmental. And the ending couplet was decidedly more morose than that of the first poem.

Melissa still thought it was quite good for an amateur. She remembered when Margaret had first opened the envelope containing "Sonnet No. 1," one of the many submissions she had received by the Tuesday deadline, and had called Melissa over to her desk.

"Take a look at this," she had said, her eyes sparkling with excitement. "I think we have our winner."

After reading it, Melissa had immediately agreed. Not that she would have likely disputed her boss' judgment anyhow. Margaret was better read, more worldly, and a bit more sophisticated than Melissa considered herself to be. If Margaret thought this sonnet was the best submission, Melissa would certainly not argue.

She dropped the envelope into her trash can, and put the poem in a manila folder. She would have to go through the large stack of mail piled on Margaret's desk and pull out the other submissions for this week's "Risk-A-Verse." A finalist would have to be selected by tomorrow evening. It occurred to her that Eliot's poem could very well end up being the best submission this week as well. If so, she wondered if she should publish it, or pick another just to make the process and the column appear more fair and inclusive.

She supposed she would have to wait and cross that bridge when she came to it. Still, it concerned her to have sole responsibility for such a decision, and she knew better than to bother Mr. Moss with something like this. Then she remembered a remark she had made, albeit in jest, to Andrea Warren. Perhaps Dr. Osborne could help her decide. That would address two issues. First, it would impart to the selection process a sense of professionalism and impartiality. The second issue was strictly personal.

She found herself smiling despite the shroud of sadness that she wore. She had a valid reason to see Drew Osborne again. So caught up was she in her momentary daydream that she did not even consider the implications of the fact that the envelope she had just thrown in the trash, the one that had contained "Sonnet No. 2" had not been addressed to Margaret, as were all the other submissions. It had been addressed to Melissa.

Celeste Holbrook heard the sound of approaching footsteps only a split second before she felt the hand on her shoulder. She gasped, and whirled around, momentarily disoriented and frightened by the unexpected presence.

"I'm sorry, dear. I didn't mean to startle you, but the library's closing now."

Celeste looked up at the stooped, wizened form of Alice Albrecht, joked by the students of Smythville College to have been head librarian on campus since the Johnson presidency, Andrew, not Lyndon. Her library was a veritable model of order and efficiency. Books were never left out of place, chewing gum was strictly forbidden, and closing time, ten o'clock on weeknights and six on Saturday, was enforced with the unerring punctuality exhibitive of the woman's Swiss ancestry.

"Sorry, Mrs. Albrecht. I think I dozed off for a few minutes. I'll put these books away and get out of here."

"I'll take care of the books, dear. You go downstairs and phone for a member of the bicycle patrol to escort you back to your dorm. It's too late for a young lady to be walking across this campus alone."

"Yes, ma'am," Celeste said, although she had no intention of waiting around for some geek on wheels to show up and try to hit on her all the way from the library to Hollidell Hall. Besides, she did not plan to take the most direct route. She decided she would stroll past the Liberal Arts Building. You can never tell who you might bump into along the walkway between there and the parking lot, she thought. Perhaps some handsome young English professor is working late tonight, grading those quiz papers he promised to return tomorrow.

She stuffed her belongings into her backpack, bade Mrs. Albrecht goodnight, and headed for the stairs. Once outside, she set off at a brisk pace in the direction of the Liberal Arts Building, her feet crunching the dead leaves that covered the ground. A blustery wind separated even more leaves from the trees that had been their home since spring, sending them swirling through the cool, night air like a flock of frightened starlings, all moving in the same direction, but each with its own circuitous flight path.

She slowed as she approached the quadrangle, focusing her attention on one particular building. She peered above the two-storied white columns to the third floor, fourth window from the right. Her heart skipped a beat when she saw that the light was on, a beacon of desire among the dark, unoccupied offices surrounding it. He was in there at this very moment. She thought about what she would give to see his face right now, to see the smile that made her weak, and the eyes that made her think deliciously naughty thoughts.

She briefly considered going up there. It would be a unique chance to talk to him alone, without interruption from the other female students who constantly embarrassed themselves with their thinly disguised efforts to gain his attention. She could tell him how he had awakened this insatiable passion for literature, this burning love of poetry that had been locked deep inside her, waiting for someone to set it free. She could mention that she planned to change her major from marketing to English, and that she wanted to become a teacher, like him. She imagined he would be astonished to discover their common interests. He might want to engage her in frequent literary conversations, perhaps some about his own poems. He might even be inspired to write one about her.

She stopped fantasizing for a moment and told herself that she must be crazy. She argued that a man like him would never have an interest in her, and would probably be appalled to learn of her feelings. He might even laugh at her. Even worse, he might give her a piteous look, and then sit her down for a patronizing lecture about their differences in age, station, and experience. That would be impossible to bear. She knew she would sooner leave Smythville College forever and never see him again than have that scene unfold. She concluded that it was probably better to just leave things alone, better to not know and still dream, than to know a cruel truth and have one's dreams shattered. With a final glance at the lighted window, she resumed her lonely walk.

The paved walkways that criss-crossed the campus were well lit, but staying on them would require her to walk an extra three blocks—up, around, and down the other side of the Pattianne Smyth Memorial Arboretum. The century-old arbor, a memorial to the founder's mother, was over half the size of a football field, and consisted of a series of six tunnels sculpted of thick wisteria vines growing over wooden trellises and converging like the spokes of a wheel to a clearing in the center. There, an ancient covered well sat surrounded by cement benches. The well no longer held water, but probably contained enough pennies and nickels from decades of fanciful wishers to finance a new library wing.

Despite the darkness of the autumn night, especially in the tunnels where even the moonlight was blocked, Celeste crossed the street and entered the barren arbor. In the spring and summer it was glorious in its color and fragrance, an absolute must for graduation and wedding pictures. In the fall and winter, when the grape-like clusters of flowers were gone and the thick vines resembled giant, gnarled fingers stretching across the empty gardens, it was used primarily as a place for students to pursue their amorous intentions.

She had just entered one of the tunnels when she heard a sound behind her. It was not loud, just a slight rustling of the dead leaves that carpeted the path. Probably a couple of students looking for an isolated bench, or maybe a place to spread a blanket. She smiled, a tiny bit envious, and continued on.

The wind gusted through the vines, creating both sound and movement, as if Celeste were traversing the entrails of some giant, bony creature. It seemed to move about her, to whistle and groan as it held her captive in its woody clutches. She again heard something behind her, but could not tell if it was the sound of lustful students or simply the wind.

She continued through the passageway, a little slower now, listening closely for other noises behind her. She thought she heard something and froze in her tracks, scanning the darkness. She could not see anything clearly unless it was practically within arm's reach, but still she looked. She thought that if it were a couple of lovebirds, they were being particularly quiet. Maybe it was some frat pledges, trying to play a practical joke on an isolated coed. If so, it was not very funny. She heard something again.

"Hello?" she called out tentatively. There was no response.

She thought about the local newspaper woman who had been found murdered a few days ago, and shuddered involuntarily. Willing herself to move again, she crept slowly and quietly toward the center of the arbor, away from whatever was behind her.

A minute later she saw a faint glow ahead and knew she was approaching the clearing, which would at least offer the benefit of moonlight. As she stepped out and touched the brickwork of the old well, she again heard the sound of movement from the tunnel she had just exited. She quickly turned and started to run into the opposite tunnel, the one that would emerge near her dorm, and then impulsively decided to duck into another—one that would be less obvious to anyone if she really was being pursued. She went in just a few feet, enough to be hidden in the darkness, but still allowing her to see into the clearing.

She admitted to herself that she was very frightened, and she made a conscious effort to control her breathing, to be as quiet as possible as she peered out at the moonlight-dappled well. After several minutes, minutes that seemed like hours, a shadow passed by the entrance to her tunnel. She held her breath for a moment, squeezing her eyes shut and wishing the apparition away, like she had wished the monsters out of her bedroom as a little girl. It seemed to work, for when she opened her eyes the shadow was gone. But just when she was about to resume normal breathing and her journey, the entrance to the tunnel darkened again.

Celeste let out an unwitting gasp, crouched low, and started moving backward through the blackness. She had to feel her way, her hands stretched out on either side, touching the hardened vines that wove together to form the viny passage. She moved as quickly and quietly as she could, left hand touching vines, right hand touching vines. On and on she continued, one hand after the other brushing the gnarly surface, until she extended her right hand and touched nothing at all.

Startled, she reached again, not understanding why nothing was there. She turned and strained to focus her eyes in the near-total darkness, and was able to discern a sizable opening in the wall. Extending her hand in front of her she felt nothing. She took another step and still felt nothing. *If this hole continues another few feet, it should connect with another tunnel*, she thought. *I'll exit through the other tunnel and whoever is behind me will be completely unaware!*

She continued moving slowly yet steadily, her right hand probing the darkness in front of her. She progressed about five feet before she touched something, a lone vine. Then another, then several more. *Oh my God, am I trapped in here?* Bordering on panic, she tried to think what to do. *If this is a dead end, I'm stuck here. I can't go back out the way I came in. But wait, if this isn't one of the main passages, I probably won't be found. I'll just wait a while, and then creep back out when it's safe.*

Her plans changed immediately when she heard a rustling sound behind her. There was something, or someone, back there at the opening she had entered. With her heart pounding like a bass drum, Celeste started pushing vines out of her way as she struggled further into the opening. Crouching low, her legs beginning to ache, she pushed and tugged until she came to a seemingly impenetrable wall. She blindly thrust her right arm into the tangle of gnarly vines, all the way up to her shoulder, and her groping hand felt an opening. Less than two feet of space separated her from another tunnel and another way out.

No longer caring how much noise she made, she pushed furiously at the tangled barrier, creating enough of an opening for a leg and arm. She crouched lower and repeated the maneuver, pushing on the vines as if they were prison bars separating her from a life of freedom. With a desperate lunge, she finally fell through, landing on her side in the adjacent tunnel. The moonlit clearing in the center of the arbor was visible only a few yards away.

She stood on cramped legs and raced toward the opening. She could feel dozens of cuts on her face, arms, and hands, but she did not care. She would reach the clearing, cross over into the opposite tunnel, and keep running until she reached the lobby of Hollidell Hall.

She raced into the clearing, ran around the well, and entered the opposite tunnel where she suddenly collided with a taller, harder body. She emitted a hoarse scream and retreated a few steps into the clearing. She stopped when she backed against the well, and watched, frozen in horror, as a shadowy form emerged from the darkness. She could hear a strange, tinny sound, barely discernible, like a voice calling from a tunnel or a deep pit. *Is there someone in the well behind me? Is this some kind of fraternity prank, some crude staging of an adolescent ghost story? That has to be it*, she told herself. But the recent murder case still raced, unwelcome, through her frantic mind.

Sonnets

As the figure slowly reached for her, Celeste started to scream again, then breathed a shuddering sigh of relief.

"Oh my gosh, am I glad to see you! I think someone was following me."

They were the last words she ever spoke.

Chapter 6

B ernard Moss maneuvered around the desks, chairs, and filing cabinets with surprising speed and agility for a man of his considerable bulk. Every *Gazette* employee stopped work and watched him as he moved to the center of the large room and raised both hands over his head like a television evangelist pleading for divine grace.

"Listen up, everybody. I just left the police station. I stopped by to ask Chief Hennessey if they'd learned anything more about Margaret's murder, and the place was in an uproar. I managed to find out that a female student's body has been found in the arboretum well. Looks like she was strangled before she was thrown in there. They think it happened late last night."

A shocked murmur arose from the group. Moss cut it off with a wave of his hand and proceeded to bark out his orders.

"Andrea, get over there right away. Call me on your cell the minute you arrive. Find Lou Hennessey and get as many details as you can."

Without a word, Andrea Warren stuffed her phone into her handbag, picked up a steno pad, and rushed out the door. Moss continued his instructions.

"Mitch, I want you in my office. You'll write the story as Andrea feeds us information from the scene. Gwen, clear tomorrow's headlines. Everything above the fold will be devoted to this story. George, tell your boys on the presses that it's gonna be a late night. Order in some pizzas for them. Everybody else start calling anybody you know affiliated with the college—professors, students, janitors, whatever. We need the victim's name, her background, anything you can get. Mitch will be back out here in an hour or less, so make sure you have something for him."

He gave the assemblage a stern look, as if daring anyone to ask a question, then hurried back toward his office with Mitch Grannan, assistant editor, in hot pursuit. The moment his office door slammed shut, the stunned employees erupted into a beehive of activity. Everyone seemed to be talking and moving at a frenzied pace, scrambling to find some piece of information to contribute to the story. Everyone except Melissa, who sat quietly at her desk, hugging herself as she stared uncomprehendingly at the commotion around her. As the sole staff member of the arts and leisure section, she would not be expected to contribute to a hard news story. That was good, because she was too stunned to function.

Margaret Fenwyck had been the first person Melissa had ever actually known who had died from something other than natural causes. That had shocked her considerably. But the implications of another murder in the quiet town of Smythville, the second within a week, horrified her. For the first time in quite a while she regretted living alone. A roommate, even another young woman like herself, would be a comfort now. She knew that she would be jumping at every sound, and that she would probably be sleeping with the lights on for at least a week.

Realizing that dwelling on that train of thought would only feed her fear, she tried to focus her attention on the work spread out on her desk. Even though the murder would undoubtedly dominate the *Gazette's* front page for the next several days, the arts and leisure section on Thursday would still feature the second installment of "Risk-A-Verse," and it was up to her to select this week's winning poem.

She had already analyzed the submissions received so far, and would have to review this morning's mail before making her final decision. At this point, none of the submissions were nearly as deserving as the one by the enigmatic Eliot. Compared to most of the other poems—soppy, overwritten drivel with little sense of syntax and even less imagery—"Sonnet No. 2" was almost professional by comparison. Despite her confidence in her ability to recognize superior verse, Melissa suddenly had a nagging sense that something was not quite right. She read the poem again and felt the sense of doubt grow stronger, more defined, like a blurred image gradually coming into focus under a microscope, until she finally realized what was bothering her. The poem was about a student. A young, infatuated, female student. And while it did not specifically say so, it could certainly refer to a college student. To publish it the same week as the campus murder might appear to be exploitative, if not downright callous.

Damn! she thought. *I'll have to select another winner after all. Of all the dumb luck.* If only Eliot had reversed his submissions. She knew she would have had no qualms about publishing "Sonnet No. 1" this week. It was actually the better of the two and would certainly not be construed as resembling the campus killing. It was about an auburn-haired beauty who loved poetry. Margaret had been so taken with it. She had said it reminded her of . . . *Oh no! Oh, God, no! Margaret!*

She fumbled through the files stacked on her desk until she found the one containing the poetry submissions from the previous week. She rifled through the folder and found "Sonnet No. 1," her hands shaking so badly that she had to put the sheet of paper on the desk in order to read it. Having now reached her shocking conclusion, the clues seemed so painfully obvious.

Her auburn hair reflects the harvest moon.

There had been a full moon the night Margaret was killed.

By day she reads auditions to the Muse.

Margaret had spent that very day reviewing poetry submissions for "Risk-A-Verse." But it was the ending couplet that terrified Melissa the most.

And so her heart will plunge into the night
And grant her restless soul its final flight

The image of the ice pick, which the coroner said had punctured the left ventricle of Margaret's heart, caused Melissa to shudder.

She looked again at "Sonnet No. 2," its meaning now seeming so horrifyingly clear. Again, it was the closing couplet that chilled her to the bone.

But fate decreed her sultry words be choked
Before the fires of passion could be stoked

Mr. Moss said the woman had been strangled before being thrown into the well.

Clutching the two poems in her hand she hurried to the office of the senior editor, rapped twice on the door, and boldly stepped inside. Bernard Moss and Mitch Grannan glanced up at the unexpected intruder, the former with a look of annoyance, the latter with a look of disbelief. One simply did not enter this office without a specific invitation.

Melissa shut the door behind her and took a deep breath. "Mr. Moss, you need to look at these poems."

The expression on the big man's face quickly changed from bemused irritation to angry scowl. "Need I remind you, Miss Turner, that we're working on a murder story here? I don't have time to worry about any damned poems! If you want to keep your job, I recommend you march your butt out of here right now and take care of that column yourself."

Her feet firmly planted and her blue eyes flashing, Melissa thrust the two sheets of paper toward her boss. "You can fire me if you want. But first, I'm going to tell you about these poems. And you're going to listen."

Drew walked into his freshman comp and lit class on Wednesday morning, late, as usual. As he dropped his satchel on the table and stepped to the lectern, a tomb-like silence fell over the room. He studied the young faces before him, saw the fear, confusion, and sorrow in their eyes. Although he still had trouble with their names, the hundred or so faces were now familiar. Except one, that of a woman seated in the back, right corner. The lighting was poor, but he could see well enough to tell that she looked a little older than the others. Probably a graduate student checking him out before registering for one of his classes next semester.

He leaned forward, resting his elbows on the lectern, and spoke softly into the microphone. "In his poem, The Reaper and the Flowers, Henry Wadsworth Longfellow wrote:

'There is a reaper whose name is Death,

And with his sickle keen

He reaps the bearded grain in a breath,

And the flowers that grow between.'

I am sure that all of you are painfully aware of the horrible crime that occurred here on Monday night, and that one of your classmates was the victim. Celeste Holbrook was a bright, charming young woman, truly a flower among the grain, and I know that each of you, like me, is deeply saddened by her death."

The sense of grief in the room was palpable. The expressions on the faces remained unchanged, but an occasional sniffle emanated from various points throughout the lecture hall as Drew pulled a sheet of paper from his class folder.

"Dean Morrison and all the department chairmen met with the police last night, and the entire faculty has been asked to tell every class that all possible steps have been taken to assure your safety. Still, until Miss Holbrook's killer is apprehended, we need you to take some special precautions to protect yourselves."

He glanced down at the departmental memo in his hand. "Always travel in groups of three or more, especially after dark. Don't let anyone unfamiliar into your dorm building or your car, or even within arm's reach, if possible. And, until further notice, we ask that you stay on campus. The police simply cannot patrol the entire town of Smythville as effectively as they can this campus. Right now, this is the safest place you can be. Any questions?"

He slowly scanned the room. There being no response, he commenced with his lecture.

An hour later, he entered the English department office suite, stopping by Judi's desk to pick up his mail and messages.

"Dr. Ainsworthy is in the dean's office and needs you to call him right away," she said.

"Oh? Did he say what it was about?"

"No, just that you should call him the moment you got in. Here's the extension number." She handed him a slip of pink paper.

Drew went into his office and closed the door. He quickly removed and hung up his jacket, then sat at his desk. Just as he was reaching for the phone, Judi knocked softly on the door and stuck her head in. She looked awkward, nervous, as if something had changed in the thirty seconds since he had last seen her.

"Dr. Osborne," she said tentatively, "Lou Hennessey is here to see you."

"Who?"

"Lou Hennessey, our police chief."

Wonderful. His boss was sitting in the dean's office, the two of them anxiously awaiting his call—there was no way that could be interpreted as a good sign—and now some pot-bellied bubba with a badge was there, undoubtedly to ask him a bunch of questions about Celeste Holbrook's death. *Hell*, Drew supposed, *I might just find that I'm a suspect. After all, I'm new in town, and a damn Yankee to boot.*

"I have to make this call first, Judi."

"Chief Hennessey said it was important," she said, glancing over her shoulder as if making sure the officer knew that the proper sense of urgency was being communicated.

"So is this call," Drew said irritably, then lowered his voice and reached for the phone. "Have Chief Hennessey park his fat ass in a comfortable chair, and I'll be with him in a minute."

"But . . . " Judi stammered, then disappeared from the doorway as Drew, feeling distinctively uneasy, punched in the four-digit extension for Dean Morrison's office. He was greeted with a busy signal.

"Shit!" he muttered, pushing the receiver button down angrily and preparing to try again. He glanced at the number to be sure he had it right, and was about to redial when he heard the sound of a throat being cleared.

"Ahem."

He glanced up, expecting to see Judi again, but instead saw the graduate student who had sat in on his class this morning. She was tall, slender, and very attractive in her college chic attire of jeans, red turtleneck, and navy blue blazer. He knew he had never seen her before. He would have remembered. She appeared to be a few years older and a damned sight prettier than most of the other grads.

"Excuse me," she said, smiling. "Dr. Osborne?"

"Uh, yeah," he said, as he rose from his chair. "Look, I usually meet with students in the afternoon. My secretary, Judi, should be out there somewhere. Could you see her about setting up an appointment? I have a very important call to make, and someone is waiting outside to see me."

"That would be me," she said, entering the room, still smiling brightly as she extended her hand. "I'm Lou Hennessey, the Smythville Chief of Police. I don't believe I've had the pleasure of meeting our resident poet laureate yet."

"Uh, no, uh, nice to meet you." Drew shook her hand. It was warm, delicately shaped, but not particularly soft.

She was still smiling, obviously enjoying the surprised look on his face. "I know you have to make a call, so why don't I park my fat ass over here in this comfortable chair until you're done?"

"Uh, sure, have a seat," he stammered. "Look, I'm sorry about that. You certainly don't have a . . . I mean . . . please, sit down."

Her smile never faltered as she sat, nor did her eyes leave his. She clasped her hands together in her lap and watched him reach once again for the phone. This time the call went through.

"Drew Osborne, calling for Dr. Ainsworthy. I was told he's there."

A moment later, the department chairman was on the line. "Hi, Drew, I've been waiting for your call."

"I just got back from my eight o'clock class."

"Yeah, well, listen, you're going to have a visitor this morning. Chief of Police Hennessey was here a while ago, and said she was heading over to see you."

"The chief is sitting in my office as we speak," Drew said, glancing at her. She was still smiling. It was beginning to get on his nerves.

"Oh, I see," Ainsworthy said. "Well, I just wanted to let you know she was on her way over. And, it goes without saying you should provide her with any and all assistance possible. Miss Holbrook was a student of yours, and you . . . you seemed to know her pretty well."

Oh, so that's it, Drew thought. The attractive female police chief with the not-so-disarming smile had somehow been made aware of Drew and Celeste being seen together. Once at the poetry reading, and again after a morning class. Perhaps Charles Alexander had inadvertently, or perhaps even purposely, implied something more than a proper teacher-student relationship between Drew and Celeste. Drew realized that Charles had enjoyed kidding him, but hoped the man did not really think there had been anything improper going on.

"Actually, I didn't know her all that well, Dr. Ainsworthy, but I'll certainly do all that I can to help," Drew said into the phone. He hung up the receiver and looked at his visitor.

"For some reason, Dr. Ainsworthy felt I needed to be prompted to help you with your investigation," he said. "Believe me, that was totally unnecessary. I'll do whatever I can to help you catch the person responsible for Miss Holbrook's death."

"Good. I have a few questions I need to ask you."

Drew held up one hand. "Before you get started, may I ask one of you, Chief Hennessey?"

"Certainly."

"Lou?"

"Short for Louise."

"But why . . . ?"

"Would you want to be called Louise?" The corners of her eyes crinkled as she smiled.

"Well, no, but . . ."

"Me neither. Any other questions?"

"No. Your turn."

"Great," she said, and the smile disappeared. "This is your first semester here at Smythville College, isn't it?"

"Yes. I moved here right after Labor Day."

"From where?"

Drew suspected she already knew the answers to these questions, but he responded politely and promptly. It seemed an appropriate time for a little damage control. "Manhattan. Previously I taught at NYU."

"A New Yorker in north Georgia. Pretty drastic lifestyle change."

Drew noticed that Chief Hennessey had no southern accent herself. In fact, she seemed to have no discernible accent at all.

"You're not from around here either, are you?" he asked.

"No. Born and raised in Cleveland, but I lived in Philadelphia for about eight years before moving here." She flashed that smile again. "It's good to finally have another Yankee in our midst. Except for a few students, I think I was about the only one in town."

"Well, you definitely have another one now. Before I moved here, I never lived further south than Greenwich Village."

"You've published a book of poetry, right?"

Again, Drew felt she was asking questions to which she already knew the answer. "Yes, I published a collection of sonnets about a year ago."

"I should probably remember this from college, but would you please tell me what differentiates a sonnet from any other type of poem?"

"Well, actually, there are several different types. The most com-

mon is the Shakespearean sonnet, which consists of fourteen lines—
three quatrains and one couplet. The rhyming scheme is every other
line in the quatrains, and both lines in the couplet. And sonnets are
quite consistent in terms of measure."

"What is measure?"

Drew leaned back in his chair, glad to have the opportunity to
steer the conversation away from his personal life and onto a more
comfortable topic. "Measure refers to two things, the kind of metri-
cal foot, which is the term used to describe a unit of accented and
unaccented syllables, and the length of the line."

"What kind of measure would a Shakespearean sonnet employ?"

"Generally, iambic pentameter."

"Which means?"

"Iambic refers to the accentuation of the syllables. An unstressed
syllable, followed by a stressed, comprises a foot. Pentameter signi-
fies five metric feet."

"So there would be ten syllables in every line?"

"Yes."

"And that would not vary?"

"Not if the poet were being true to the classic form."

"Anything else?"

Drew shrugged his shoulders. "Well, a lot of the classic Shakespearean sonnets were written in such a way as to comprise an argument of sorts."

"An argument?"

"Yeah, the poet would state a premise, then a counter-argument,
and a conclusion in the couplet. But over the years that hasn't been
held to as rigidly as the structure."

She reached into her inside coat pocket, pulled out a folded sheet of
paper, and handed it to Drew. "Have you ever seen this sonnet before?"

He took the sheet of paper and unfolded it. It was entitled "Sonnet
No. 1." He read it quickly, and then looked back at Chief Hennessey
to find her staring intently into his eyes.

"If I'm not mistaken, this sonnet was published in the newspaper last week," he said. "In that new column."

"Yes. Margaret Fenwyck received it in the mail the day she was killed."

"Oh," Drew said, still holding the typewritten page. "I imagine she received quite a few submissions. What's so unusual about this one?"

Her eyes were still focused on his. "Doesn't anything about it strike you as being a little peculiar?"

Drew glanced once again at the poem, taking a minute to read it once more. "No," he said afterward, "I don't see anything peculiar. Actually, it's not bad."

"You don't think that the description of the woman in the poem is remarkably similar to Margaret Fenwyck?"

Drew shrugged his shoulders. "I wouldn't know. I never met her."

"But you spoke with her several times on the phone?"

"Two or three times, I guess. She had planned to come to a reading of my poems here on campus last Wednesday night, but, of course, she never showed up."

She pulled another sheet of paper from her coat pocket and extended it across the desk to Drew. "What about this one? Recognize it?"

Drew took the paper and saw it was entitled "Sonnet No. 2," and was signed with the same single name—Eliot. As he read it, the police chief's line of questioning suddenly became clear.

"You think this poem was referring to Celeste Holbrook?" he asked.

"Possibly. It just seems to be one hell of a coincidence that this quiet little town suddenly has its first two murders in nearly twenty years, and the victim in each case appears to resemble the subject of this Eliot's poems. And both times the poem was received on the very day the murder took place."

"So 'Sonnet No. 2' was sent to Miss Holbrook?"

"No. It was sent to Melissa Turner at the *Gazette*."

Drew frowned. "Now I'm confused. The first one was sent to

Margaret Fenwyck, who you tell me bore some resemblance to the subject. The second one is obviously about a young woman, a student to be precise, yet it was sent to Melissa Turner. I met Miss Turner last week. She's young, but has probably been out of school several years. I'm afraid I've lost the connection."

Lou Hennessey leaned forward, as if moving closer to Drew would allow her piercing, determined eyes to see into his soul. "That confused me at first, too. I think Eliot sends all of his poems to the *Gazette*, probably in hopes of seeing them in print. But something peculiar occurred. You see, 'Sonnet No. 1' was mailed to the attention of Margaret Fenwyck, as per the contest instructions printed in the paper."

"Okay," Drew said, the confusion still evident in his expression.

"'Sonnet No. 2' was addressed to Melissa Turner. She received it last Friday, which means it had to be mailed before noon on Thursday."

"So?"

"So, why did Eliot address this one to Melissa? It had to be mailed before Miss Fenwyck's body was even discovered, and several hours before her murder became public knowledge."

Now Drew understood. "You think this Eliot guy knew that Margaret Fenwyck was already dead, and therefore addressed his second poem to Melissa Turner instead?"

"It's a long shot, but I'm giving it serious consideration."

"Do you mean to tell me that some lunatic is writing sonnets about young women, then killing them? That's incredible."

"Both poems made oblique references to death. The first one had something about a soul's final flight, and the second referred to the subject's words being choked. It makes for a pretty compelling theory, don't you think?"

Drew also leaned forward. "And since I'm new in town and a published sonneteer, I'm a natural suspect, right?"

"I didn't say that."

"But one could certainly assume it, given your theory."

"You make your assumptions, Dr. Osborne, and I'll make mine. While we're on the subject, campus security tells me you were here late on Monday evening. Why was that?"

Drew's stomach began to knot, but he fought to keep his nervousness from showing. "I was grading quizzes. I promised my class I would get them back the next day."

"This was the class Celeste Holbrook was in?"

"Yes."

"Was anyone else here with you?"

"No, not past seven thirty or so. That's when Dr. Alexander left."

"Yes, that's what he told me." She paused a moment before locking eyes with him again. "Just one more question. Not even a question, really, more of an observation. I sat in on your class this morning."

"I know. I saw you."

"I noticed that the poem you quoted this morning, the one by Longfellow, mentioned death and flowers."

"That's right," Drew said. "It's called 'The Reaper and the Flowers.'"

"I guess it struck me as a bit of a coincidence that both Eliot's sonnet and your selection of a poem utilized the image of a flower to describe Miss Holbrook."

Drew's voice took on an edge. "Flowers are used quite frequently in poetry, Chief Hennessey, especially when referring to young women. Is there an underlying point to your question?"

"No, not at all. I just thought it was an interesting coincidence." She stood. "Well, listen, I've taken enough of your time. I'll be on my way."

Drew was surprised that she did not have any more questions, particularly any regarding his interactions with Celeste. "That's all?" he asked.

"For now," she said as she walked to the door, then turned to face him again. "I'm sure I'll think of some more questions later. In fact, I would appreciate it if you would stay in town for the next few days."

"So I am a suspect?"

"I didn't say that. It's just that I don't like being the only Yankee in town."

She smiled again, her laser-like eyes seeming to burn right through him before she walked out the door.

Chapter 7

So, Drew, did you have a nice little chat with our chief of police?"

Drew looked up from his desk to see Charles Alexander standing just inside the doorway, the pearly white teeth of his smile contrasting with ebony skin. He had the gloating look of one who knew a secret he was not supposed to know and wanted desperately to broadcast that knowledge without admitting to it.

"Yeah, I guess."

"You didn't know our Police Chief was a woman, did you?" Charles asked, still smiling.

Drew emitted a long sigh and, despite his melancholy mood, allowed himself a sad smile. "So that's why you're grinning like a Cheshire cat. Judi must have told you about my little faux pas."

"Didn't have to. I was standing right outside your door with Chief Hennessey when you said it. You should've seen the expression on her face."

"So much for making a favorable first impression on the local authorities," Drew said. Remembering the strange phone call from his boss, he locked eyes with Charles and leaned back in his chair. "I guess Dr. Ainsworthy was with you when you were interviewed by the chief."

Charles held Drew's stare for a moment before sitting in the same chair Lou Hennessey had occupied a few minutes earlier. He had a quizzical look on his face, and his dark brown eyes seemed more focused on the view outside the window than on Drew. "What makes you ask that?"

"He called me to insist that I give Chief Hennessey my full cooperation since I—let's see, how did he put it? 'Since I knew Celeste Holbrook so well.' I don't know where else he, or the chief, could have gotten such an impression."

Charles shifted in his chair, clearly ill at ease with the unexpected confrontation. "I just happened to mention that Celeste seemed to have a little crush on you, that's all. I thought that perhaps during one of your private conversations the girl might have said something that would provide a clue as to the identity of her killer."

"We had only two conversations. Murder never came up."

"There's no need to get defensive, Drew. I was just trying to provide Chief Hennessey with any leads that could help her solve this dreadful crime."

Drew inhaled a deep breath, then blew it out slowly. "I know. I'm sorry. It's just a bit disconcerting to have a police chief, even a pretty one, imply that you may be guilty of two brutal murders."

Charles leaned forward in his chair, resting his elbows on his knees. His serious expression matched his tone of voice. "Look, Drew, nobody who knows you would think you're capable of these crimes. But Chief Hennessey doesn't know you, and she has a job to do. Look at the situation from her viewpoint." He proceeded to count on the fingers of his right hand. "First, you're new in town. Prior to your arrival, there hadn't been a homicide in this town in twenty years. Suddenly there's two in one week. Second, both victims appear to be the subject of a sonnet, a fairly obscure, outdated form of poetry, and you've published a whole damn book of them. And third, you'd been associated with both women."

"I never met Margaret Fenwyck."

"Oh, that's right. She was supposed to come to your poetry reading, but Andrea Warren and that blond lady came instead."

"Melissa Turner."

"What?"

"The blond. Her name is Melissa Turner. She worked for Margaret."

"Yes, well, I'm afraid I had my attention focused on Andrea. She's quite an attractive woman, don't you think?"

Drew managed a tight smile, glad to move the topic away from his unique qualifications as a murder suspect. "I noticed you two seemed a bit chummy at the reception following the poetry reading. Do we have a little romance blooming, Charles?"

"Not really. She was amiable, maybe even a bit flirtatious, but I don't have any evidence to indicate that the attraction is mutual. Besides, I'm not sure this town is ready for an interracial couple. I imagine Lucille Chambertin and the Smythville Literary Society would call up a lynch mob if Andrea and I were seen together."

"That's a rather harsh view. I know race relations aren't yet where they need to be, but it seems to me that society has made substantial progress in the past thirty or forty years."

"Only on the surface, Drew. If you look deep enough, the old tried and true American prejudices are still going strong, especially in a small southern town like this. Equal opportunity applies to education, jobs, and housing. Not your women."

"Damn, Charles, I didn't realize you were such a cynic."

"I'd prefer to characterize myself as a realist." Charles stood. "Well, I have a ten o'clock so I'd better get going." He paused by the door. "By the way, you've never said why you gave up the glamour of the Big Apple to move down here to Smalltown, USA."

Drew shifted his attention to a stack of student essays on his desk. "Personal reasons." He looked back at Charles. "Looks like it might have been safer to stay up there."

"Well, I wouldn't worry too much about this murderer being on the loose. Chief Hennessey may look like some kind of fashion model, but I've heard that she's actually a very smart, tenacious cop. The killer won't hide from her for long."

"I'm feeling safer already."

Charles did not acknowledge the sarcasm. He simply stared at Drew a moment longer before turning and walking away.

Andrea Warren glanced at the clock on the wall as she waited impatiently for the last sheet of paper to emerge from the printer.

Three fifty. She would beat the four o'clock deadline, but not by much.

She caught the final page of double-spaced copy before it hit the tray, and stuffed it into the red folder with the words "Senior Editor Approval" stenciled in big block letters across the front. No time for even a cursory proofread. She would have to proceed on the assumption that her computer's spell-check function had caught any glaring errors, and hope that Mr. Moss would be too busy to make a federal case out of any minor ones.

Folder in hand, she hurried across the bustling pressroom to his office and knocked on the door. She waited for the gruff "Come in," before opening the door and stepping inside.

The big man glanced at his watch as the red folder was extended toward him. "Pushing the deadline today, aren't we, Andrea?"

"Sorry. I got a call from one of the college professors right before lunch and it put me a little behind schedule."

"Oh? Who?"

"Charles Alexander, from the English department. I met him last week at Dr. Osborne's poetry reading."

"Tall, bald-headed black guy with an earring, right? Did he have anything new on the murder?" Moss arched one bushy, white eyebrow. "Or was it a personal call?"

Andrea returned the smile. "Both, I think. But, ostensibly, he called to say that the police found a thread from Celeste Holbrook's sweater caught on a broken branch between two of the tunnels in the arbor. He said they think she may have become aware of being followed by someone and then tried to hide."

"Did you confirm that with Lou Hennessey?"

"Yes. She said it looks as if she hid for some indeterminate period of time, then emerged into the clearing, and was caught by the well. She said the girl's hands and face had scratches that could be explained by her crawling through the thick branches of the wisteria vines."

Moss sighed. "Maybe if she'd stayed hidden a little longer she'd still be alive."

"Maybe. We'll probably never know. Anyway, Charles said he saw that I was heading up the *Gazette's* coverage of the murder, and thought I might be interested in that new development. I mentioned it briefly in the copy."

"Was Dr. Alexander just being a friend of the press, or did he have another reason for calling? Like asking you out?"

Unlike most of the other *Gazette* employees, Andrea did not allow herself to be intimidated by her physically imposing and socially prominent boss. "Whether or not he asked me out would be of no one's concern but mine, Mr. Moss, but he did have an additional reason for calling."

Moss said nothing, but looked at her questioningly. She continued.

"He said this was 'off the record,' but that Chief Hennessey was asking a lot of questions about Drew Osborne."

"Did he say anything to indicate that she considers Osborne a suspect?"

"No, just that she had confirmed that Celeste Holbrook was one of Osborne's students, and that the poems he published were sonnets."

"So Dr. Alexander knew about the two sonnets we received here?"

"Yes. He said Chief Hennessey showed them to him, Dr. Ainsworthy and Dr. Osborne when she interviewed them this morning." Her forehead creased in a frown. "And then, almost like an afterthought, he suggested that I might want to look into Dr. Osborne's background."

Moss leaned forward, resting his meaty arms on the cluttered desk. "Why would he suggest that? Simply because the man writes sonnets and we believe that two sonnets we received for our contest may have been describing Margaret and the Holbrook girl? Or does he know something about Osborne that we don't?"

"I'm not sure. But he said he's often wondered why a native New Yorker would leave a prime teaching job like NYU to come to a small, private college in rural north Georgia. And he said that Osborne has never explained why he left New York. Just says his reasons were personal and changes the subject."

"So you think Dr. Alexander is actually suspicious of Osborne?"

"At this point I don't know if he's really suspicious or, like all the rest of us, is simply struck by the coincidence that, shortly after the arrival of a new English professor—one whose special area of expertise is Shakespearean sonnets—two murders are committed."

"And the only clues happen to be sonnets."

"Exactly. When the circumstances of these killings become widely known, Alexander won't be the only one eyeing Osborne suspiciously."

Moss stared at his local news editor, then started fumbling through his overflowing card file. He plucked out a card and handed it to Andrea. "I want you to call this man, Amos Metzger, at the New York Times. He's an old fraternity brother from Georgetown. Tell him you work for me and that you need to check out a former professor at NYU. He can help you get to the right people to learn whatever there is to know. And get a copy of Osborne's poetry book. Let's see if we can find any similarities between his work and the two sonnets we received."

"I'll get right on it." Andrea took the card. "I just hope this doesn't turn out to be a case of professional envy."

"What do you mean by that?"

"Well, it's probably nothing, but after the poetry reading last week I got the impression that Dr. Alexander is a little jealous of Osborne's notoriety on campus. He's published a book himself, a textbook, but he joked that it doesn't attract the women the way those romantic sonnets do. Maybe he thinks Osborne's popularity will make him a more desirable choice for department chairman when Dr. Ainsworthy retires in a couple of years."

"Over the years I've had a few professional rivals that I've had to muscle out of the way," Moss said, "but I've never gone so far as to implicate one in a murder case. I think there's something else going on here. If your preliminary search turns up anything suspicious about Osborne, anything at all, we'll keep digging."

"And if not?"

"Then we'll follow one of Moss' rules of investigative journalism. When you find nothing on the accused, start investigating the accuser."

Chapter 8

Select Screen Name: Eliot

Enter Password: Sonnets

Send Instant Message To: Melpomene

Eliot: Fools! This town is populated by simple-minded fools!

Melpomene: What's wrong?

Eliot: The idiots at the newspaper! How could they publish that dreadful, sentimental doggerel instead of my sonnet? Only a literary indigent would confuse that slop with poetry.

Melpomene: What did you expect? Once they made the connection between your poetry and your acts of salvation, they would naturally be reticent to publish your work.

Eliot: But why? Did they think that keeping my verse hidden would make it any less true? If so, they are worse than fools.

Melpomene: You mustn't let your anger distract you. You must learn to focus it — to use it to inspire and motivate your work.

Eliot: I know. That's the one thing I learned from that wretched bitch who tried to ruin my life. I remember how she'd listen to my dreams, feigning interest and support, all the while waiting for the perfect opportunity to use my own words against me. I can still hear her saying I'd never be a poet.

Melpomene: But she was wrong, wasn't she? I'd venture to say that your sonnets are now being read with great interest—studied and parsed like the classic verse of Shakespeare, Keats, or Browning.

Eliot: And I have you to thank for that — my Muse, my soul.

Melpomene: I merely help you to see truth, and to reflect it in your poetry.

Eliot: You've opened my eyes more than I ever dreamed possible. I imagine I knew more about Celeste than she knew herself. When she looked into the mirror she saw only the beauty and innocence of youth. But I saw so much more. I saw what she would have become.

Melpomene: I love the poetic sense of the scene — a blossoming young beauty meeting her end in an orchard of dead flowers.

Eliot: And the wishing well. If the wishes granted are commensurate with the sacrifice, all my dreams will be fulfilled. But I'm still incensed that my sonnet wasn't published.

Melpomene: Perhaps you need to make a statement.

Eliot: A statement?

Sonnets

Melpomene: A symbolic statement . . . one that even those simple minds can comprehend. They must be made to understand that truth is a thing of beauty to be shared, even revered, not hidden away in some editor's desk.

Eliot: How can I make such a statement?

Melpomene: You know how.

Eliot: Yes. I will write another sonnet.

Chapter 9

Drew awoke early on Saturday morning, intent on writing one, or maybe even both, of the two final sonnets for what he hoped would become his second published volume of verse. He had promised his publisher a draft by the first of October, a date that had come and gone amidst a whirlwind of events that included moving, starting another school year, and getting himself acclimated to a totally new environment. And unfortunately, becoming a possible suspect in two grisly murders.

It was, in fact, the lingering pall of Celeste Holbrook's death that framed his mood as he sat at his small dining table, absently watching the first rays of morning light peek timidly between the slits of his living room drapes. The notions of tender, passionate love that he needed for the work at hand seemed as foreign to his current disposition as a clown at a funeral.

After a fruitless hour wherein his only activity was pouring and drinking three cups of coffee, he abandoned his efforts and headed into the bedroom for his sweat suit and running shoes. He thought that a little exercise would clear his head and smooth the edges of his frayed nerves. If nothing else, it would get him out of the apartment. Away from the mirrors where Kate hid, materializing to haunt him at those times when his psyche was most vulnerable. Like now.

A couple of minutes later, dressed in his NYU sweat suit and Atlanta Braves baseball cap, he stepped into the hallway of his apartment building. As he walked toward the front entrance he saw a door ahead of him opening. It was apartment 1-G, occupied by a pleasant, matronly high school teacher who had brought Drew a plate of fresh-baked oatmeal cookies on the day he moved in.

"Morning, Miss Hinson," he said, tipping his hat in what he assumed was a chivalrous manner.

Apparently he startled her, for she emitted a squeaky gasp and stepped immediately back inside. He heard the lock clicking into place as he walked past her door. *Didn't she recognize me as one of her neighbors? Does the dark blue sweat suit and baseball cap make me look like a burglar?* Something about his appearance had certainly frightened her.

It all made sense when he stepped outside and noticed the *Gazette* headline that dominated the window of a coin-operated newsstand. "POLICE SEARCH FOR KILLER POET," he read. Below that, a sub-title declared "Two Murders Linked by Anonymous Sonnets." That certainly explains Miss Hinson's strange behavior, he thought.

"It's so thrilling to have a published poet as a neighbor," she had gushed one evening shortly after he moved in. "Maybe one day you could come to the high school as my guest and speak to my students."

"Don't you teach math?" he had asked.

"Well, yes," she had stammered in reply, "but I want to invite you before Mrs. Trammel in the English department does." Lowering her voice to a conspiratorial whisper, she added, "It's about time I beat that old bag to the punch on something."

Having only his money clip with him, Drew decided he would get some change while he was out so he could pick up a paper and read the article. He doubted that Miss Hinson would be the only Smythville resident to join the chief of police in erroneously connecting his poetry to that of the killer. He should at least know exactly what was being said to fuel such speculation.

The cool, crisp air and sapphire blue sky of a beautiful October morning did little to revitalize Drew's spirits as he began jogging toward the campus. The awkward encounter and subsequent discussion with Lou Hennessey continued to weigh heavily on his mind. *Can she actually consider me a suspect? What about Dr. Ainsworthy? Could that have been the reason for his strange comments on the telephone? How long would it be before my students start whispering behind my back, wondering if I'm some kind of modern-day Jack the Ripper with a penchant for poetry?*

He remembered his conversation with Charles Alexander. One particular comment stood out in his mind. "Look, Drew, nobody who knows you would think you're capable of these crimes." *But that's the problem, isn't it? Nobody in town really knows me at all.*

He had run about two miles when he passed under the arched entrance to the campus and proceeded down the street that bordered the arboretum. A group of somber-looking coeds carrying flowers was approaching the entrance to one of the tunnels, probably preparing to add to the makeshift shrine at the well. One of them seemed to recognize Drew and they all turned to watch him pass. Not slowing, Drew lifted his hand in a solemn salute. At first, no one in the group acknowledged the gesture, simply staring at him as if he were an alien from another galaxy. But as he turned the corner of the Administration Building, he glanced back to see one solitary hand, belonging to a girl he recognized from his freshman comp and lit class, raised in a timid wave.

He continued to run along the outermost streets and walkways of the campus, and emerged back onto Main Street about fifteen minutes later. The sidewalks were now crowded with pedestrians getting an early morning start on their weekend errands, so he slowed to a brisk walk past the restaurants and storefronts of the town. Remembering that he wanted to get change to buy a newspaper, he decided to stop at the Southern Style Bakery, which, ironically, was the only place in town where one could get a decent bagel.

The delicious aroma of fresh-baked rolls and muffins assaulted Drew's sense of smell the moment he walked in the door. The place was packed with its usual Saturday morning crowd, and several people were standing in line at the counter. "The Southern," as it was affectionately called by the locals, was a favorite breakfast and lunch spot, a casual setting in which to swap gossip and debate politics and college sports. Every table was taken this morning, and Drew assumed that the *Gazette* headline was the primary topic at each one.

He fished a five-dollar bill out of his sweat pants pocket as he waited patiently in line, then ordered a coffee and poppy seed bagel to go. As he pocketed his change and turned to leave, he noticed one crowded table near the entrance where a familiar, wrinkled face appeared to be making a desperate attempt to avoid his gaze. Undeterred, he made his way to the table, tipping his cap and flashing his brightest smile.

"Good morning, Mrs. Chambertin. What a pleasure to see you again."

The woman glanced nervously at her companions before looking up at Drew, feigning surprise. "Oh, yes, hello Dr. Osborne. I didn't see you come in."

Ignoring the obvious lie and noticing the morning edition of the *Gazette* lying amidst the plates and coffee cups, he nodded toward it and said, "Horrible, isn't it? She was a student of mine. A lovely young lady."

"Yes, it's a terrible tragedy. I feel so badly for her parents." She gave Drew a direct stare. "We've never had anything like this happen in Smythville before. Never."

"I know," Drew said. "It's one of the reasons I wanted to come here, to escape the crime of the big cities. But as Dr. Alexander, one of my colleagues, said yesterday, no town seems to be safe from this type of mindless violence anymore."

"Oh, yes, Dr. Alexander. He's the black one, isn't he?"

There was something about the tone of the question that made Drew think there was a hidden insinuation. Perhaps Charles wasn't such a cynic after all. "Actually, the college has several black professors, Mrs. Chambertin. But, to answer your question, yes, Dr. Alexander is black. Why do you ask?"

"Just wanted to make sure I was thinking of the right person."

Drew knew it was time to go, but not before one more little test. "By the way," he said, glancing around the table, "are you ladies also members of the Smythville Literary Society?"

"They are," their president volunteered for them.

"Well, then, I hope to see you all real soon. Mrs. Chambertin was kind enough to invite me to be the guest speaker at your November meeting. I checked my calendar, and it just so happens I'm free that evening."

Lucille Chambertin looked as if she had just been caught pilfering money from the church offering. "Uh, I'll have to get back with you on that, Dr. Osborne. Our November meeting agenda is looking pretty full. I'd forgotten we have our committee reports scheduled for that night."

"Oh, I see," Drew said. "Well, if November doesn't work out, I'm sure I can make it in December. If I'm lucky, I'll have my second book of poetry sold by then. I could read a few selections for you."

"That would be exciting," one of the blue-haired ladies said.

"I'll call you, Dr. Osborne," Lucille Chambertin said firmly as she shot the woman a stern look.

Meeting over, test failed. Drew tipped his baseball cap again and walked out the door. As he had suspected—feared—the rumors were starting. He could only hope that Lou Hennessey was as good as Charles had said, and that the "Killer Poet" would be caught soon. Or, if nothing else, that Eliot would simply stop writing sonnets.

Sonnets

Sonnet No. 3

For pleasures of the nighttime she doth wait
She gently combs her hair of fine-spun gold
Completely unaware of her dark fate
A mangled, battered body, dead and cold

Her eyes of azure sparkle as she dreams
But they have seen their final dawning day
For in the midst of muffled, tortured screams
These eyes of hers will soon be plucked away

Attempts to plead salvation will be vain
No sympathetic ear to still the flood
Of terror, dread and all-consuming pain
And raging rivers of her tears and blood

So through the night she uses each pained breath
To pray she'll soon receive the gift of death

Eliot

Chapter 10

It was Monday morning, and Bernard Moss was in a particularly sour mood. His weekend had been anything but restful. Everywhere he went, whether it was dinner at the country club or Sunday morning services at Smythville First Presbyterian Church, he had been hounded by the frightened, the concerned, and the simply curious. Do the police have any suspects? What's the deal with these poems we read about? Were the victims sexually molested? Were they tortured?

By the time he had arrived at his office this morning, grateful to be back inside his fortress where his door was guarded and telephone calls screened, Moss had reached two conclusions. First, being on the receiving end of relentless questions had convinced him that the public was justified in hating the insensitive manner in which the press often conducted its investigations. To him, having someone invade the sanctity of your dinner table and ask for details about an ice pick murder as he and his wife feasted on cherries jubilee was not much different from asking a grieving woman how it felt to lose her husband in a plane crash. There simply were times when a person's privacy should be respected.

The other conclusion Moss had reached was that, for some reason, the town seemed to be holding him personally responsible for solving the two ghastly murders that had annihilated their sense of security. Perhaps it was because he had used his significant influence to ensure the appointment of Lou Hennessey as chief of police when her male predecessor had retired after holding the post for eighteen years. More than one anxious citizen during the course of the weekend had reminded Moss that there had been no homicides in Smythville during the previous chief's tenure.

The *Gazette's* senior editor swiveled his chair around to face the credenza behind his desk and studied his schedule on the computerized calendar. Editorial staff meeting at nine, budget meeting at ten-thirty, then nothing until the layout meeting at two. *Good. I'll be able to make time for a little chat with Lou.*

He heard his office door open and knew, without looking, who it was. Only one person on the planet, including his wife, dared walk into his office without knocking.

"Put the mail anywhere you can find a space, Mildred," he said. "And I could use a cup of coffee and another donut."

"Everything is opened and prioritized except one envelope marked 'Personal,'" said Mildred Blount, his secretary of twenty-one years. "And what you could use is a can of my Slim-Fast. The French vanilla is actually pretty tasty."

He swiveled around to face her, his chair squealing like an anguished banshee. "Why do you insist on continually nagging me about my weight? My wife gave up the battle years ago."

"Because I don't want to come in here one morning with a cup of coffee and a half dozen jelly donuts to find you dead of a heart attack, that's why. I'm too close to retirement to go through the hassle of breaking in another boss." She smiled. "Besides, how would I ever find another one with such a sunny disposition?"

Moss chuckled. "I suppose that's a valid point. Be that as it may, I still want another cup of coffee and a donut, if you'd be so kind, and I want you to call Lou Hennessey and see if she's free for lunch."

Mildred turned to leave. "I'll make you a reservation at The Bistro."

"You know I hate that place, Mildred. Their steaks are tough as leather."

She didn't answer until she was outside the office and just about ready to pull the door closed. "Yes, but they have a wonderful salad bar."

"Damned insubordinate woman," he muttered.

Moss picked up the bundle of mail with the red "Priority" sticker on top. He signed a few forms, pulled out a report he would need to review prior to the budget meeting, and quickly scanned the rest. As he was about to move to the larger bundle with the blue "Routine" sticker, he noticed the unopened envelope with the word "PERSONAL" typed across the front in bold, capital letters. It was postmarked in Smythville with Saturday's date. That struck him as being a bit odd. Anyone in town would most likely send personal mail to his home address.

He tore open the envelope and extracted a single, typewritten page. He started to read it just as Mildred returned with his coffee and donut. But in the brief span of time it took her toplace the small tray on the corner of the desk, his appetite disappeared.

"Mildred, send Andrea in here. Then call Lou Hennessey and tell her we'll be in her office in ten minutes."

A few minutes later he and Andrea emerged from his office wearing grim, anxious expressions. She headed to her desk to grab her coat and purse while Moss stopped at Mildred's desk to tell her to reschedule his morning meetings. As he turned to leave he collided with Melissa Turner, causing her to drop a stack of files and splash coffee across the custom-made white shirt that covered his ample belly.

Her bright blue eyes went wide with shock, nearly filling the frames of her tortoise shell glasses, when she saw the damage she had wrought. "Oh, my God," she gasped. "Oh, Mr. Moss, I'm so sorry. I was on my way to the staff meeting and I didn't . . . I just—"

"Forget about it," he said as he tried to maneuver around her in the tight confines of Mildred's cubicle. "I was in a hurry and wasn't watching where I was going."

"But I should've been more careful. Oh, your shirt! Let me get you a wet cloth." She did not move. She simply looked around, panic-stricken, as if she expected a cloth to miraculously materialize.

"I said forget about it. I'm in a hurry. A little stain doesn't matter."

"But our staff meeting—"

"Has been postponed. Mildred will let you know when it's rescheduled."

"Is . . . is there a problem?"

"Nothing that concerns you. Now could you please move out of my way? I've got to go."

He looked across the bustling pressroom and saw Andrea waiting by the door. As he hurried toward her, he heard Melissa call out to him.

"I'm really sorry about your shirt, Mr. Moss."

He threw up his hand in a dismissive wave and continued on his way. He had more important things to worry about right now than a dumb, accident-prone blond.

"Oh, shit, here we go again," Lou Hennessey muttered, as she read the poem she held in a glove-covered hand. She looked across her desk at her two visitors. "Did you both touch this?"

"No," Moss said. "I showed it to Andrea, but no one but me has handled it since it came out of the envelope."

"Okay," Lou said, "we'll dust it for prints. And we'll need to print you, Bernie. Any fingerprints on this sheet of paper that don't match yours should belong to Eliot. The other two sonnets had been touched by so many people that we got nothing useful off of them."

"What about the envelope?" he asked. "This is the first one we've recovered."

Lou shook her head. "There's no point checking the envelope for prints. Too many people have already handled it—postal workers, office mail clerks, Mildred. But I'll send it to the FBI lab in Atlanta for DNA testing. Maybe there's some dried saliva on the flap where it was sealed."

"Do you have anything else to match a DNA profile with?" Andrea asked. "I didn't know Eliot had left any biological evidence behind at the murder scenes."

"He didn't," Lou sighed. "You'd think one of those two women would've put up a struggle. At least scratched him or something."

"Maybe we'll get lucky with the next one," Moss said, then realized how callous the remark sounded. "Shit, you know what I mean. These damn poems are driving me crazy."

"Yes, Bernie, I know," Lou said softly. "By the way, any idea why this one was addressed to you?"

"Not unless it was a move designed to taunt me," Moss said, looking tired as he massaged his temples with his fingertips.

"Assuming this really is from the killer, why would he want to taunt you?"

"Because I'm beginning to get the feeling that the people of this town are expecting the *Gazette*, and me in particular, to figure out who the killer is and put an end to this nightmare. And I think the killer is aware of that."

"Why wouldn't people hold me accountable for solving these crimes?" Lou asked, a slight edge to her voice. "Because I'm a woman?"

"Probably. Plus the fact that I have a bigger investigative team than you."

"I think there may be another reason it was sent to you, Mr. Moss," Andrea said.

The big man turned to her, one bushy eyebrow raised. "And what's that?"

"It seems to me this killer seeks recognition. Why else would he broadcast his intentions in advance of each murder? I think it's important to him to see his poems printed in the *Gazette*. Since you're the ultimate decision maker with regards to what gets printed and what doesn't, it's logical that he would send this one to you."

Moss twisted his massive bulk around in the tight-fitting chair.

"So I print the ghoulish poems of a lunatic in the hopes that he won't carry out his threat to murder some unidentified woman?"

"I doubt it would make a difference," Lou said. "Margaret Fenwyck had already decided to print his first sonnet, which appears to have been written about her, and he killed her anyway. And Celeste Holbrook was strangled before the killer had a chance to see whether the poem about her would be printed, and it wasn't. There doesn't appear to be a pattern."

"Maybe not," Andrea said. "It was just a thought. But if printing the poem had any chance at all of stopping a murder, or even buying us a little time, wouldn't it be worth it?"

"She has a point, Bernie," Lou said. "When does your poetry column appear again?"

"Thursday."

"I wouldn't wait. Why don't you print it in tomorrow's edition? If nothing else, it would serve as a warning to the public. Especially to blond females."

"Of which there must be dozens at the college," Andrea said. "If we lose another student, we'll have a real panic situation on that campus."

Lou stared directly at Moss. "If we lose another student, I'll have to shut the campus down."

Bernard Moss returned her stare for a moment, then emitted a sigh of resignation. "I hate being played as a pawn in a psychopath's chess game, but I guess I don't have a choice. Andrea, write a short column about the investigation for tomorrow's edition, and print the damned poem, saying we think it may have been sent by the killer."

"Anything else?" Andrea asked.

"Yes," Lou said. "Tell your readers to call the police if they know of anyone this poem might be referring to, or if they have any idea who may have written it. We'll set up a special hot line. I'll get you the number."

"Okay, then," Moss said, glancing at his watch. "I'll leave you

78

two to work out the details of the article and the special phone line. Are we on for lunch, Lou?"

"Are you buying?"

"Don't I always?"

"Then we're on. By the way, I'm sure it's a long shot but I asked Martha at the Holiday Inn and George at the Smythville Guesthouse to send me a list of their out-of-town guests on the nights of the two murders. Maybe there'll be a match."

"I don't think our killer is from out of town," Moss said matter-of-factly.

Lou's forehead wrinkled in an inquisitive frown. "How can you be sure of that?"

"I can't be sure, but like I told you, the buzz around town is that I'm somehow expected to do something about these murders. I don't think an outsider would pick up on that, but the killer must be aware of it or he wouldn't have addressed this last poem to me. I still think it was intended to taunt me."

"So you're convinced it's someone who lives here in Smyth-ville?" Lou asked. "Someone walking among us, listening to all the town gossip as he plans his next murder?"

"Yep."

"But Bernie," Lou said, "it's been nearly twenty years since the last homicide in this town, over six years since the last one in this county, and they were both solved. What would cause a previously law-abiding citizen to suddenly go on a killing spree?"

"I don't know. Maybe something happened in his personal life that caused him to snap." He paused. "Or maybe it's someone who hasn't been here all that long."

She held his gaze. "Do you have anyone particular in mind?"

"Yes, and I think you do too."

Andrea spoke. "I got a call from Charles Alexander in the English department at the college. He told me you were asking a lot of questions about Drew Osborne."

Lou leaned across her desk and looked alternately at the reporter and her boss, her head moving back and forth as if she were watching a tennis match. "Look, you two. It's a matter of routine in a case like this to inquire about recent arrivals on the scene. But, at this time, I do not, repeat, do not, consider Dr. Osborne a suspect. This town is already scared out of its wits, and the situation is ripe for finding a convenient scapegoat. I'm warning you—don't print anything that will contribute to that."

Moss stood and glared down at Lou, his ears burning red. "I'm not accustomed to being warned about anything, Lou. Not by the chief of police or anyone else. And my newspaper does not subscribe to yellow journalism, so the point is moot anyhow. Now, if you two will excuse me, I have to go get myself fingerprinted and then I've got work to do." He looked at Andrea. "So do you. Get back as quick as you can."

"See Sarah," Lou said. "She'll get someone to take care of you right away."

Moss acknowledged the comment with the wave of a hand and huffed out, slamming the door behind him.

Lou turned to Andrea and sighed. "Sometimes I wonder why this town goes to the trouble to hold elections. No matter who's in office, they'll still turn to Bernie Moss when there's a crisis."

Andrea smiled. "I grew up in a little town about forty miles north of here, and even there everyone knows that the Moss family runs Smythville."

"Let's get back to your conversation with Dr. Alexander. Tell me what he said about Osborne."

"Just that you had asked a lot of questions about him, and about his poetry. And he hinted that there might be something unusual about Dr. Osborne's background. But if he had anything specific in mind, he didn't say what it was. Mr. Moss put me in touch with a friend of his at the New York Times who's checking Osborne's record at NYU. I'll call you when I hear back from him."

"Do that," Lou said, then walked out with Andrea to get the number of the phone line they would dedicate to calls about the sonnet. As Andrea started to leave, Lou asked, "You sometimes work out at The Slim Gym, don't you?"

"I used to go there after work with Margaret Fenwyck," Andrea said, a distant look in her eyes. "I haven't been since . . . you know. I need to get back into the routine. I walk right past it on my way home, so I really don't have an excuse."

"Maybe I'll see you there sometime. I try to work out at least two or three nights a week," Lou said, then lowered her voice. "Listen, I'd be careful about walking home late at night, Andrea. I don't want to scare you, but you fit the profile that this psychopath seems to seek out."

"You don't have to worry about scaring me," Andrea said. "I'm already there."

That night, as Melissa Turner lay in bed, she couldn't help thinking about Mr. Moss's strange behavior that morning. She had known something was wrong, and had suspected that it was related to the murders of Margaret and that college student. Ordinarily, something like that would have preyed on her mind the rest of the day, but all she had been able to think about was spilling coffee all over her boss.

When she had bumped into him and had seen that huge, brown stain spreading across his shirt and had looked at the shocked expression on his face, Melissa had been convinced that she had reached the limits of her fear. But now, as she lay tied to her four-poster bed, choking on the pantyhose gag that had been forced down her throat and looking into those wet brown eyes that seemed to dance to the rhythm of a barely audible song, she knew she had been dreadfully mistaken.

Chapter 11

B oy, it sure is dead around here this time of night," Patrolman Art Schaeffer said, as the squad car cruised slowly down Main Street.

Howard Mullins smiled at his baby-faced partner. "Why do you think they call it the graveyard shift?"

Art yawned and rubbed his eyes. "I'll be glad when we're back on regular duty. I just can't sleep well in the daytime. I almost dozed off during the briefing."

"You might as well get used to it. Unless you're the chief, you're gonna have to work your fair share of graveyard shifts."

"Hell, even she was there tonight. I guess this lunatic poet has everybody on pins and needles. But it looks like he must be taking the night off. Nothing's been reported so far, and where's he going to find a victim in this town at two in the morning?"

The squawk of the radio cut through the silence, sounding like an angry parrot. "Car sixteen, come in. Calling car sixteen."

"Looks like you spoke too soon," Mullins said as he picked up the handset. "Patrol car sixteen, acknowledging. What's up, Sarah?"

"Go to 1204 Beasley Lane," the female voice said. "It's a duplex. Mr. Jacobson in the A-side said he's been hearing some bumping noises in the other apartment. It belongs to Melissa Turner, the gal that works at the *Gazette*."

Mullins laughed. "Bumping noises coming from a pretty young woman's apartment, huh? Does old man Jacobson suspect foul play, or is he just jealous?"

"The chief's not in the mood for jokes, Howard," the voice on the radio said. "Better get over there, pronto."

"We're on our way," Mullins said. "We'll report in once we check it out."

Five minutes later, the two officers walked up the steps of the wide porch and approached the door on the right, the one with the big, brass "B" mounted on its center panel. The doorbell elicited no response, so Mullins began to knock loudly on the door as Art walked around to the side of the building, shining his flashlight on the curtained windows.

After a moment the door to the left opened, and a tall, lanky man who appeared to be in his mid to late sixties stepped out, moving tentatively. Upon seeing the blue police uniform, he appeared to relax a bit, and cast an embarrassed glance down at his right hand, in which he clutched a golf club.

"Mr. Jacobson?" Mullins said.

"Yeah, I'm the one who called."

"I'm not getting a response over here. Are you sure someone's home?"

"I don't know about now," the man said, "but there was definitely someone there earlier. The missus and I both heard something like bumping or knocking going on. At first, we didn't think much of it, but after a while I got suspicious, what with all this stuff about a killer being on the loose, and I tried to call Melissa. That's the young lady who lives there. Melissa Turner. But I didn't get an answer."

"About what time was that, Mr. Jacobson?"

"One thirty. A few minutes, later I heard another noise and that's when I called you fellas."

Art came walking back to the front porch. "Nothing unusual

around there, Sarge. All the windows are secure. Looks like a couple of lights are on."

Mullins suddenly had that bad feeling again. "Mr. Jacobson, you wouldn't happen to have a key to this unit, would you?"

"Sure I do," the old man with the golf club said. "I'm the super. Hold on and I'll get it for you."

He returned shortly and handed Mullins a single key. "Fits both the doorknob lock and the deadbolt."

"Thanks, Mr. Jacobson. Why don't you go back inside with your wife? I'm sure she's a little nervous. We'll let you know if we need anything."

"You think the Turner woman's in here, Sarge?" Art asked, his voice shaky.

"I sure as hell hope not," Mullins said as he slipped the key into the door lock and turned it. The door swung open. The deadbolt was not engaged.

"You know, when we found that other woman, that was the first dead person I'd ever seen," Art whispered. "It just caught me off guard."

"That's nothing to be embarrassed about, kid. Unfortunately, it's something you get used to."

"Oh, I'm not worried about it now. I saw that Holbrook girl's body when they pulled her out of the well and I didn't feel sick at all."

"Hold on a sec. Let me call the station and tell 'em we're going in."

He detached the radio from his belt and pressed the transmit button as they walked through the door. They found themselves standing in a small living room. It was dark, but there was light coming from a room down the hall. Art started moving slowly toward it, his hand resting on the handle of his service revolver.

"Go ahead, Howard," the radio crackled.

"We got no response, so Mr. Jacobson let us into Miss Turner's apartment," Mullins said as he watched his partner step into the lighted room. "We're now in the process of—"

He suddenly heard the sound of violent retching. "Oh, shit, Sarah. Send Lou."

Drew was having the dream again. As if from the vantage point of a hovering bird, he watched each sad, familiar scene unfold. The arrival, the lovemaking, the walks on the beach. The red flags rippling in the wind as he and Kate raced into the water—the clear, blue-green, life-stealing water.

Once again, he actually felt the suffocating sense of panic, followed by a tiny sliver of hope which gradually dissolved away, like salt in warm water, until only the bitter, briny taste of grief remained. As the dream progressed steadily and unmercifully toward the scene in the morgue, he could actually feel his heart racing and his body sweating. As he watched himself approaching the table, seeing the sheet being slowly pulled back to reveal the death mask that had replaced Kate's lovely face, he willed himself to wake up. As he saw himself staring at the bloated lips and the bruised, milk-white face, he tensed his body, trying to shut out the horrible conclusion to the recurring nightmare, yet wanting it to go ahead and happen so he could wake up.

Strangely, inexplicably, it did not occur. The eyes did not open. The lips did not move. Instead, he watched as the sheet was placed back over her face, and then found himself at the cemetery in Albany standing next to Kate's weeping mother as the coffin was gently lowered into the ground. The minister was reading Scripture, something from the Book of Matthew, and everything else was deathly silent.

Then, he heard the knocking. He turned to Kate's mother, but she simply stood there with a tissue pressed against her teeming eyes. The knocking grew louder, and he looked around wondering why no one else seemed to notice. It became faster, almost frantic in nature. And it was coming from Kate's coffin.

Was he the only one who could hear it? It continued, louder and louder, incessant. Why couldn't anyone else hear it? He had to do something! He had to get her out! Oh, God, they were shoveling dirt onto the coffin even as the knocking grew louder, more furious. *Stop! She's in there! Stop!*

His eyes flew open and he immediately knew where he was, knew that it had been a dream. *But why did it change?* he thought. *I've never dreamed about the funeral before. What could have caused—?*

The pounding resumed, startling him so much that he suddenly found himself on his feet beside the bed, yet he had no recollection of moving. He heard it again and was on the verge of screaming in terror when he realized it was coming from his front door. He flipped on the light and looked at his alarm clock. Four fifteen. *Who the hell would be pounding on my door at this hour of the morning? Is there a fire in the building?* He pulled on a pair of jeans and hurried out of the bedroom and across the living room to the door.

He closed one eye and looked through the peephole. The image on the other side was distorted but immediately recognizable. He opened the door. "Good morning, Chief Hennessey. It's a little early for a social call, don't you think?"

The look on her face caused Drew to suspect that this was an occasion where humor might not be appropriate. The look on the faces of the two police officers with her—a man who appeared to be in his mid forties, the other looking as if he'd just graduated high school—confirmed it.

"May we come in, Dr. Osborne?" she asked.

"Sure," he said, stepping aside as they filed by, the older officer eyeing him suspiciously and stepping just a little too close to Drew's bare feet.

Drew closed the door and turned to face them. "Would you like to sit down?"

"We'll stand, thanks," Lou Hennessey said, her expression still grim.

"Do you mind telling me what this is about?" Drew asked. "It's four in the morning."

The Smythville Chief of Police did not acknowledge his question. Instead, she looked Drew over from head to toe, and then stared intently into his eyes. "Have you been exercising at this odd hour, Dr. Osborne? Or did you just step out of the shower?"

"What?"

"Your T-shirt is wet."

Drew suddenly noticed that the faded gray shirt from the New York City Athletic Club was indeed splotched with perspiration. "No," he said, more than a little embarrassed, "I was asleep. I guess I had too many blankets on."

"Have you been home all night?"

Drew had a bad feeling about where this was heading. "Yeah, since around nine. Why do you ask?" He then noticed the younger cop walking around the living room and dining area, studying everything, yet touching nothing. "Hey, officer, if you'll tell me what you're looking for I'll be happy to help you find it."

"No thanks, just browsing," said the boyish policeman. Drew noticed he had a piece of food or something stuck to his chin.

His patience starting to wear thin, Drew turned back to the tall, attractive woman who, under other circumstances, he might feel quite differently about having in his apartment at four in the morning. "I'll ask you again, Chief Hennessey, what's this about?"

She handed him a sheet of paper. "There's been another murder."

Drew looked at the page, an apparent photocopy of another sonnet by Eliot. Despite his nervousness, he forced himself to quickly read it. When he handed it back to her, he noticed that she held it by the edges, not touching the areas he had touched, as she refolded it and carefully tucked it in the inside pocket of her blazer.

Drew took a deep breath. "Are you here to ask for my help with interpreting this poem, or to confirm my whereabouts for the last several hours?"

Once again, her eyes locked with his. "Both. But let's take it one step at a time. What are your thoughts on the poem?"

Sonnets

"Well, I read it pretty quickly, but the first thing that struck me was that the tone was dramatically different from the other two, yet he still held to the exactness of the form."

"Meaning?"

"The structure is still precisely that of a Shakespearean sonnet—three quatrains, one couplet, iambic pentameter, all that stuff we talked about before. But his use of imagery is drastically different."

"Can you elaborate?"

"Come on, Chief, you don't have to be an English professor to pick up on that. It's a hell of a jump from gardeners and glistening petals to eyeballs being plucked out." He paused, looking at her, then at the older policeman, who appeared to be warily watching his every move. "Please tell me the eyeball thing was a metaphor."

She spoke softly but with a sharp edge to her voice. "They were on the bedside table. Right next to her glasses."

"Oh, shit." Ignoring the others in the room, Drew sat heavily on his imitation leather sofa. "Another student?"

"No. Melissa Turner."

Drew suddenly felt as if his whole body was crumbling, like a building being demolished by strategically placed bundles of dynamite. His shoulders sagged, his head dropped, and his arms hung limp and useless into his lap. It took a few seconds for him to realize that Lou Hennessey was speaking.

"I said, you mentioned to me in your office last week that you knew her," she repeated.

"Yes. I met her once, the night of my poetry reading on campus. She seemed very nice, so cheerful and full of life. What kind of animal could have done such a thing?"

"You were here alone all night, Dr. Osborne?"

The implication was clear and Drew was suddenly overcome with rage. "Look," he said as he rose to his feet, "you do one of two things. Either you get your crime lab people or the FBI or somebody who knows what the hell they're doing to come over here and gather whatever forensic evidence you need to prove that I've been in my bed for the past five hours, or else I want you and your two goons to get the fuck out of here and leave me alone."

"I'd advise you to sit back down, sir," the older officer said sternly.

"Yeah, well, while you're at it, you'd better go ahead and advise me of my fucking rights if you intend to stay here and make these preposterous allegations."

"You want me to cuff him, Chief?" the youngster said, edging cautiously toward Drew.

"No," Lou Hennessey said quietly. "Not yet."

Drew realized he had to calm himself, or else he would indeed find himself under arrest, but the smirk on the young cop's face had him seething. He shot him a quick glance and again saw the small glob on his chin, then noticed a streaky film on the toes of his spit-polished shoes. "Are you the one who found the body?"

"Why do you ask that?" the boy asked, the smile fading fast.

"Because you still have vomit on your chin."

The young cop's face turned beet-red, and the older one looked like he was on the verge of planting his nightstick against the side of Drew's skull.

"That will be enough!" Lou Hennessey shouted in an authoritative tone that seemed totally inconsistent with her decidedly feminine appearance. The room fell silent. She looked at her two officers, then back at Drew, as if to assure herself that there was no longer any threat of confrontation. "Would you object to us taking a quick look around your apartment, Dr. Osborne? Or would you prefer to wait until we have a search warrant?"

Drew returned to the sofa. "Turn the place upside down if you want."

"That won't be necessary." She nodded to the two officers, one of whom headed for the kitchen, the other for the bedroom. She then sat in a chair across the room. For a couple of minutes, neither one spoke, the silence between them awkward and palpable. Finally, she cleared her throat. "I'm sorry, Dr. Osborne. I know this is very uncomfortable for you, but I have a job to do."

"Uncomfortable? That's the word you'd use to describe how it feels to have three police officers come banging on your door at four in the morning, and accuse you of murdering and mutilating a lovely, innocent young woman? Uncomfortable doesn't even begin to describe how I feel right now."

The two policemen returned to the living room. "Nothing unusual in the kitchen," said the young one, his face still flushed.

"Bed's been slept in," the older one said, checking out Drew with a sideways glance. "Dirty clothes in the hamper, but nothing peculiar."

"Shower?" asked Hennessey.

"Dry."

"Okay," she said, standing. "Dr. Osborne, if you don't mind, I may give you a call later in the week. I'd like for you to take a closer look at all three sonnets. Maybe we can find some kind of pattern or something."

Drew walked across the living room and opened the door. "I'll be glad to help in any way I can."

As the three law officers filed out, Drew locked eyes with the young one. "Listen, I'm sorry about what I said. If I'd seen what you saw tonight, I doubt I'd even be able to walk."

"Walking's no problem," the boy in blue said. "I just think I'm gonna have nightmares the rest of my life."

"I know what you mean," Drew said. "Believe me."

Chapter 12

It seemed to Drew that the morning dragged on forever. He found himself simply going through the motions of teaching his classes and attending an English department staff meeting. It was as if he were on automatic pilot—he was physically there but not mentally engaged. At one point during the staff meeting his lack of attention actually prompted Dr. Ainsworthy to ask if he were feeling all right.

"I didn't get a good night's sleep," Drew offered by way of explanation, eliciting a few unwanted and misguided snickers. In reality, he was not sure whether it was the lack of sleep, the shock of having another person he knew being savagely murdered, or being accused, or at least suspected, of the crime that had him so shell-shocked. Probably a combination of all three. The cumulative effect was one of him staring absently into space while his colleagues argued politely, but aggressively, for the projects they needed to fund in the coming year.

Drew spent his lunch hour behind the closed door of his office, drinking cup after cup of coffee as he tried to make some sense of his predicament. Losing Kate had pushed him right to the brink of what he could tolerate without going mad, and he had realized that his only chance of restarting his life would be to continue it somewhere away from the daily reminders of her. He had accepted the position at Smythville College, far away from New York City in a multitude of ways, and had moved there with the hope that a dramatic change of scenery would allow him to escape the dreams that had turned his bed into a psychological torture chamber. But Kate had followed him, and she showed no signs of ever allowing him to break free of the grief, guilt, and regret.

Ironically, he now found that his new life had, to some small extent, supplanted his dark obsession with the loss of the only woman he had ever loved. Ironic in that his life had become an even greater nightmare, an infestation of his days as well as his nights. He could hardly fathom the depths of his misfortune. Within weeks of his arrival in a town that had not suffered a homicide in nearly two decades, there had been three particularly brutal ones. And of all the distinctive calling cards that a serial killer could employ, this one had chosen to use a form of poetry that was not only relatively rare but also happened to be Drew's specialty. Add that to the fact that he had some degree of interaction with all three victims, and he could not help but feel there must be some sinister, cosmic conspiracy at work.

But the most recent assault on his fragile karma by these unseen forces of evil provided the most bitter irony of all. In the past eighteen months, he had met only one woman who appeared to possess that rare combination of beauty, intelligence, and inner fire that could put her in the same league as Kate. And that woman not only suspected him of being a maniacal killer, she had the power to charge and arrest him for the crimes.

Without so much as a knock, his office door suddenly sprang open. Charles Alexander stepped in, wearing a look that Drew could have interpreted as either excitement, shock, or near hysteria.

"Drew, have you heard? There's been another murder. That Turner woman from the *Gazette*, the blond one you introduced me to."

Drew stared at him, saying nothing. He had known that by the time his associates went to lunch the town would be on fire with the tragic news, the restaurants and sandwich shops serving as hotbeds of hysteria. Unfortunately, he had not had the presence of mind to determine how he should respond when people spoke of it.

He now wondered whether he should feign ignorance and shock or admit that he was already aware that this deranged poet-killer had claimed another victim?

It ended up that he did not have to respond at all. Charles read him like a book. "Good God, man, you already knew! Is that why you've been so wacked out all morning?" His look grew wary. "How did you know?"

"Chief Hennessey came to see me this morning," Drew said reluctantly, wishing he had given some thought to this eventuality. He would divulge as little as possible. "She wanted some help interpreting a new poem."

"Another sonnet?"

He nodded.

"Do you mean to tell me that within a few hours of finding this town's third murder victim within two weeks our police chief had time to visit you for the sole purpose of chatting about poetry? She didn't have any other reason for coming to see you?"

Drew knew exactly what Charles was fishing for, but refused to take the bait. "Those sonnets are the best clues she has right now. She's trying to construct a profile of the lunatic who wrote them. But I probably shouldn't say anything else. Chief Hennessey has taken me into her confidence, and I have to respect the sensitive nature of her investigation."

Drew hoped he had done an adequate job of positioning himself as a consultant instead of a suspect, but he knew that Charles would draw his own conclusions, regardless of what was said. Charles murmured a hesitant "Yeah, okay," and backed out the door without another word.

The rumor factory received its next batch of raw materials that afternoon when Drew returned from his two o'clock class. Judi, looking pale and nervous, literally jumped from her chair to intercept him before he reached the door to his office. "You have a visitor," she whispered. "Chief Hennessey."

"Good, I was expecting her," Drew lied, trying to act nonchalant and hoping the sudden rush of anxiety was undetectable. As he reached for the door knob, it occurred to him that Judi apparently was not among those who suspected him of murder. Otherwise, she would not have felt compelled to give him advance warning that the chief of police was lying in wait. He turned around and gave her a weak but heartfelt smile. "Thanks, Judi."

The older woman smiled nervously. "Don't worry. This will all get sorted out."

Lou Hennessey was standing by his window, watching students scurry across the leaf-strewn campus. She had obviously showered and changed clothes since her visit to Drew's apartment nearly twelve hours earlier, but her face betrayed the lack of sleep. Her bloodshot eyes followed Drew as he walked to his desk and dropped his satchel on the floor beside his chair.

He sat and indicated she should do the same. "At some point you're going to have to get some sleep."

"This town won't be able to sleep tonight," she said, her voice thick. "Why should I be any different?"

"Any progress?"

"We're still compiling evidence. The autopsy has been completed. The crime lab went over Miss Turner's apartment with a fine-tooth comb, and the only fingerprints, other than hers, were those of a young man she dated occasionally."

Drew raised his eyebrows.

"He was in Charleston last night," she said in response to the unspoken question. "So it appears the killer wore gloves. And there was no sign of forced entry, so Miss Turner apparently let the killer in voluntarily."

Drew knew it was bad form, but he had to ask. "Am I still your number one suspect?"

"I never said you were my number one suspect, Dr. Osborne. But surely you understand that a recent arrival in town, one who has published a volume of sonnets and who knew, to some degree, all three victims, would have to be questioned."

"Yes, I understand that," Drew said, "but it doesn't make it any easier to take. My only brushes with the law have been a few parking tickets in Manhattan. It's a big jump from double parking to murder."

"I know. But if it makes you feel any better, I've come to the conclusion that, in addition to the fact that you just don't seem to be the murdering kind, it's highly unlikely that you could have killed Miss Turner anyhow."

"That's good to hear, but may I ask why?"

"I won't go into any details about the condition of Miss Turner's body, except to say that whoever killed her had to have gotten awfully bloody. You had no evidence of blood on your face, neck or arms when I arrived at your apartment, and your bathtub was dry. Miss Turner's was as well, so the killer didn't clean up there. The only way I can think of that you could've done it was to have another place to shower before going home. Either that, or you took a late night swim in the river."

Drew smiled despite himself. "It's a little cold for that, don't you think? Besides, I don't swim."

"Really? You never learned to swim?"

"I didn't say I don't know how. I'm just not very fond of the water." He noticed her staring at him, her eyes looking tired but nonetheless inquisitive. "It's a long story. For another time."

She stared at him a moment more, as if hoping her silence would prompt further explanation, before pulling an envelope from her coat pocket. "I brought copies of all three sonnets we have received from Eliot. I'd like for you to study them a little more, and call me with anything you can think of that would give me insight into the kind of person I'm looking for."

"I'll do what I can, Chief Hennessey, but my area of expertise is poetry, not psychology."

"I know. I already have the FBI working on a psychological profile of the killer. But I'd still like your input."

"Why?"

"Well, poetry is kind of like song writing, isn't it? Doesn't the poet strive to capture a certain mood, or communicate certain feelings?"

"Yes, of course."

"Well, I happen to have a little expertise in psychology, and my thinking is that Eliot develops cravings before he kills, and I think they may be reflected in his sonnets."

"Cravings?"

"Yeah, like hunger for food, or an alcoholic's thirst for booze, or someone's desire for—" She paused, and Drew thought he could detect a tiny hint of color in her cheeks.

"Sex?"

"Or chocolate," she said, her eyes smiling more than her mouth. "For some of us, the two are virtually interchangeable."

Drew found himself smiling back at her, and could hardly believe he was chatting freely and exchanging innuendoes with a woman who earlier in the day had practically accused him of murder. "I'll take a look at them and see what I can come up with," he said. "When would you like me to call you?"

She handed him a card and stood. "As soon as you can. Here are my office and pager numbers. Don't worry about calling at any hour if you think of something that has the slightest possibility of being helpful."

"Oh, I don't know, Chief Hennessey. Where I come from, it's considered impolite to wake someone up in the wee hours of the morning."

She shot him a stern glance, the smile no longer visible. "Call me, okay?"

"Okay." He opened the door for her and escorted her out to the hallway. On his way back in, he saw Charles standing in the entrance to his own office, straining his neck as if trying to see behind Drew.

"Well, I don't see any handcuffs," he said, a mischievous grin on his face.

"Not yet, Charles. It's a little too early in our relationship for the kinky stuff."

Apparently having no comeback, Charles simply gave Drew a curious look before retreating into his office. But the moment was not lost on Judi, who chuckled under her breath as Drew walked by. "Christians one, lions nothing."

Andrea Warren saw her extension light up a second before the phone actually rang. She glanced at the number on caller I.D. before picking up the receiver. "*Smythville Gazette*. Andrea Warren speaking."

"Miss Warren, this is Charles Alexander. I just heard about Melissa Turner a couple of hours ago. I'm very sorry. I know she was an colleague of yours."

"And a friend, Dr. Alexander. The second friend I've lost in two weeks. I'm still in a state of shock, I guess. The reality of this hasn't quite sunk in yet."

"I can only imagine how difficult it must be for you, heading up a story that involves the tragic deaths of two friends."

"Yes, it's very hard. But I'm trying to maintain my professionalism, not to mention my sanity. In some way, I feel I owe it to Margaret and Melissa to make certain that the stories of their murders are told properly, and to do whatever I can to help find the killer."

"I suppose Miss Turner's family hasn't had time to make funeral arrangements yet."

"Actually, I just found out that the service will be at the Methodist church on Thursday morning. Eleven o'clock."

"I didn't know Miss Turner that well, but I'd like to go. Perhaps I'll see you there." He paused for a moment before continuing. "Maybe we could have a cup of coffee afterwards. I'd still like to help with your story in any way I can. It looks as if the same maniac was responsible for Celeste Holbrook's death, and that investigation is still active on campus."

"Uh, sure, Dr. Alexander, that would be nice. Have you seen anything new going on with the Holbrook case?"

"Not really. But Chief Hennessey was here in the English department this afternoon."

"Oh? I would've thought she'd have her hands full with the investigation of Melissa's murder."

"She was here to see Drew Osborne. Ostensibly to solicit his help interpreting the latest sonnet."

"Ostensibly? You think there may have actually been another reason for her visit?"

He paused a moment before answering. "I don't know, really. But Drew was acting real strange all day, and I found out later that the chief had visited his apartment real early this morning. He's either working on the case with her, or—" Another pause.

"Or Chief Hennessey's keeping real close tabs on him."

"Could be either, or a little of both," Charles said. "By the way, did you ever find out anything unusual about his tenure at NYU? Like I mentioned before, he doesn't like to talk about it."

"My contact in New York is still doing some checking, but he called this morning and told me he thinks he's discovered why Dr. Osborne left."

"Really?"

"Yeah, it seems he was seriously involved with a stock broker. She drowned about a year and a half ago while they were on vacation in Cancun. I don't have a lot of the details yet, but it looks like it happened right in front of Osborne. According to one of his friends, he blamed himself for her death. The word around NYU is that he came pretty close to having a nervous breakdown."

"That could certainly cause one, all right," Charles said, then added softly, "or maybe even manifest itself in other aberrant behaviors."

"Like what, Dr. Alexander? Murder?"

Sonnets

"Oh, I wouldn't know about that sort of thing, Miss Warren. You're the investigative journalist. I'm just trying to be a friend."

Shortly after noon on Thursday, Bernard Moss walked into his office and removed his coat. He was doing something that he did only rarely—he was skipping lunch. Melissa Turner's funeral had left him depressed and numb, and what he needed right now was some isolation. He knew he would be accosted by frightened towns-folk wherever he went, and he had decided he would rather be alone and hungry than to pay that price for a midday meal.

He sat at his desk and began to absently sift through his mail. He saw the unopened envelope almost immediately. It was addressed to him, with the word "PERSONAL" typed in bold capital letters right above his name. Remembering the content of the last such envelope, he tore it open with trembling fingers.

Using tweezers, he carefully removed a newspaper clipping. It was the article written by Andrea for the Tuesday edition, the one in which she had printed "Sonnet No. 3" and asked readers to call the special police hot line with any information they could provide to help determine Eliot's identity. The poem was circled in red ink. Attached to the clipping was a small, yellow sticker with a short, typed message—two words that made Moss feel as if he had just swallowed a tablespoon of acid.

"Thank you."

Chapter 13

Select Screen Name: Eliot

Enter Password: Sonnets

Send Instant Message To: Melpomene

Eliot: I believe I have their attention now.

Melpomene: Perhaps the good people of Smythville will finally recognize they're dealing with a unique poetic talent.

Eliot: I hope so. I'd be saddened to think that my experience with Melissa was wasted.

Melpomene: Wasted? You have regrets?

Eliot: Oh, heavens no! It's just that I invested so much of myself into her sonnet—and into its realization.

Melpomene: So it was a good experience?

Eliot: Glorious! Right before my eyes she played out the full range of human emotion, like a music student playing scales on a piano. Trust—surprise—shock—terror—anguish—despair—surrender. And then back to trust. For in the end she trusted me once again, this time to do what she needed to be done, what she truly desired. It was so touching when she finally realized, after hours of suffering, that it had been there the whole time.

Melpomene: Like Dorothy in Oz, all she had to do was ask.

Eliot: Exactly. You know, it seems ironic that the realization of the sonnet progressed so perfectly to its conclusion.

Melpomene: Ironic? Why?

Eliot: Because writing it was such a struggle—as if the words were purposely evading me, taunting me. I think the writing is becoming increasingly difficult.

Melpomene: And the realization of the verse?

Eliot: Oh, that part is becoming easier. And more sensual.

Melpomene: Do not cheapen your work with such base comparisons. Cheapen your poetry and you cheapen yourself. And me.

Eliot: No, I didn't mean that!

Melpomene: Just remember your responsibility—our responsibility. You're not merely a writer of truth, but a provider as well. Only a superior talent can write a timeless tribute to a future occurrence—and make it come true.

Eliot: And yet there are those who are committed to stopping me.

Sonnets

Melpomene: Are you surprised? They are the ones who are accustomed to being in control. They cannot bear the thought of relinquishing their power. And they don't yet understand what you are doing for them—ridding them of those cheap, sluttish parasites who were destined to use their God-given beauty for evil. Left to do their bidding, they would break hearts, destroy families and shatter the dreams of the young.

Eliot: I know. I have been a victim.

Melpomene: And I have transformed you from victim to victor. All I ask in return is that you not shy away from your responsibility.

Eliot: I won't. Please believe me when I say that. As long as you are here to guide me, to teach me. I only wish that the writing were not so hard.

Melpomene: I know it's hard, but you must write before you act. For neither the writing nor the actions alone make the poem. They must be combined.

Eliot: I understand. I just need your inspiration. Send me words. Speak to me the truth. Inspire another sonnet.

Chapter 14

It was Monday morning, and Drew had just dismissed his eight o'clock class five minutes early. He could have kept them a little longer, perhaps soliciting some additional observations about the life and works of e. e. cummings, but what was the point? The death of Celeste Holbrook had taken something out of this group of students, something irretrievable. And their unspoken suspicion of Drew—a suspicion that he hoped, but seriously doubted, was a figment of his imagination—had taken something out of him.

He waited around for a couple of minutes, just on the off chance that one of the students had a question about their assignment, but no one did. Like him, they seemed to be merely going through the motions, looking forward to the day when the fall semester, and this daily reminder of a woeful tragedy, was finally over. He headed upstairs to his office.

His phone rang just as he sat at his desk. He picked up the receiver and cradled it between his head and shoulder, keeping his hands free to finish unpacking his satchel while he talked. "English Department. Drew Osborne."

"Well, hello darling. I haven't heard that sexy voice of yours in quite a while."

Drew smiled. "Hi, Barbara. How are things in New York?"

"Things in general are fine, sweetie. Things for Troutman Publishing would be much better if I had a new book to sell. Started on that novel yet?"

"No, but my new collection of sonnets is coming along. All I have to do is write two more and do some final editing and I'll have something to show you. Maybe by the end of the month."

"What kind of shape can you have it in by the end of the week?"

Drew stopped shuffling papers and moved the phone to his other ear. "What's so special about the end of the week?"

"What's so special? Why, the chance to have dinner with me, darling. There's a Romance Writers Symposium in Atlanta, this weekend and a couple of my writers are going to be there. None who show as much potential as you, dearie, but I still have to support them. I thought you could spend Friday night in Atlanta and we'd have a nice dinner and a little strategy session. I've been thinking that another volume of love poems may be just the thing to set the stage for a hot new romance novelist. What do you say?"

Drew was unsure how to respond. He was not sure that Chief Hennessey would let him leave Smythville at this point, but he had no intentions of telling his publisher that he was a possible suspect in a series of brutal murders. But Hennessey had said she no longer suspected him, that he was "not the type," plus the fact that she did not think he would have had the opportunity to clean himself up after the Turner murder. Still, Drew felt he would need to check with her before committing to Barbara.

"Listen, Barb, I have plans for the weekend, but I may be able to change them. Can I get back to you in an hour or two?"

"Plans, huh? If she's pretty I'll be jealous."

"She's beautiful, but you know I'd rather spend Friday evening with you. Let me see what I can do."

"Why don't you bring her along? I've always wanted to meet a real, live southern belle."

"Uh, it's a little early in the relationship for me to ask her on an overnight trip. In fact, it hasn't really even reached the relationship stage yet. I'll check with her and call you back as quick as I can."

"You do that, darling. I'll be in all morning. Please try to make it, okay? I'd really love to spend some time with you, and I can't wait to take a look at your new poems."

The moment he got off the phone with Barbara, Drew dialed the Smythville police station and asked for Lou Hennessey.

"The chief's on another call right now," the woman on the other end of the line said. "Who's calling, please?"

"Drew Osborne, at the college. Would you have her call me, please? As soon as she can."

"Yes, sir. I'll give her the message."

Drew hung up the phone and leaned back in his chair, thinking about Lou Hennessey. When she had said she did not consider him a suspect, he had desperately wanted to believe her, but had not known how to test her honesty. Now he had his test. He only hoped she would pass it.

"Hold on a sec, Andrea," Lou Hennessey said, as she picked up and read the message slip that had just been placed on her desk. Son-of-a-gun, she thought. Talk about timing.

"Listen, I have to run, but thanks a lot for the call."

"I just thought you might be interested since you've spoken to Dr. Osborne a couple of times," Andrea said. "I'm glad to share all of my information with you." She paused before adding, "And I'm sure you'll remember me when the time is right."

"Everything about everybody is of interest when you have three unsolved murder cases on your hands. I had a routine police record check done by the NYPD, but I didn't know anything about his girl-friend drowning."

"Well, it probably has no relevance whatsoever to these murders. I've met Dr. Osborne only once, but he certainly didn't strike me as being capable of crimes like these. But, then again, they say Ted Bundy was a real charmer."

"That's what I've heard," Lou said. "So you make sure you're very careful, Andrea, even around people you know. By the way, have you been back to The Slim Gym?"

"No, but I was thinking I'd go after work on Thursday."

"Great. Why don't we meet there? We could work out together, then maybe grab a bite to eat afterwards. I haven't had a night off in three weeks."

"Sure, I'd like that. What time?"

"Around seven?"

"Perfect."

"Okay, see you Thursday. In the meantime, don't hesitate to call me again if you come up with any ideas about these murders. I think the people in this town are expecting some results real soon, and I can't say that I blame them."

"I agree," Andrea said. "If I hear anything, I'll call you right away."

Lou thanked her again, then hung up the phone and picked up the pink message slip. She had been waiting to hear from Osborne. Maybe he had picked up on something useful as a result of studying the three sonnets she had left with him. She dialed his number.

He sounded surprisingly chipper. "Good morning, Chief. How are you?"

"Okay," she said, "but I'll be a lot better if you have any new insights for me."

"Well, I do have some observations, or maybe assumptions is a better word. Anyway, I think I've picked up an emerging pattern in the sonnets. Not anything that would necessarily help you identify Eliot, but perhaps some thoughts that could help you develop a better profile of him."

"Anything at all would help at this point."

"And, uh," he hesitated a moment before continuing. "I have something else I need to speak with you about."

"Maybe we should get together. Do you have any free time this morning?"

"I have an eleven o'clock class, but I'm free until then. Want me to come to the station?"

"Why don't we meet for coffee? How about the Starbucks on Main?"

"Why, Chief Hennessey," he said, his voice conveying feigned surprise, "are you asking me on a date?"

Lou smiled to herself. "I don't date suspects."

Her comment had the intended effect—the man of words was speechless. After a long silence he finally responded, his voice lower, less confident. "I thought you said I was no longer under suspicion."

"I said I didn't know how you could've done it. I never said it wasn't within the realm of possibility. There's a difference."

"Oh."

"Starbucks in ten minutes. Can you be there?"

"Sounds like I don't have much of a choice."

Lou hung up the phone and reached for her jacket. Osborne sounded like he might have some fresh ideas. She hoped so. She needed something to work with. Anything. Anything, that is, except another mutilated body.

Drew was just about to reach for the small ceramic pitcher of cream on the table when he noticed that Lou Hennessey was drinking her coffee black. Not about to chance having his machismo questioned by the beautiful police officer, he reached for a napkin instead.

She looked more rested than the last time he had seen her, but still had dark circles under her eyes. Nonetheless, in her seemingly standard uniform of turtleneck sweater and blazer, today accentuated by a pair of pleated khakis, she looked gorgeous. Intense, but gorgeous.

"So," she said, "you've had a few days to study those poems. What do you have for me?"

"It may not be anything you haven't already considered," Drew said, trying not to stare at her, "but something you said in my office last week got me thinking along a certain track."

"What was that?"

"Remember our discussion about cravings?"

She smiled, and he noticed for the first time that only her left cheek dimpled. For some reason, that struck him as being sexy. But, then again, so did the fact that she breathed air and walked on two legs.

"I remember you talking about sex and me talking about chocolate," she said.

"Well, we all have our preferences. Anyway, I kept in mind the thought of Eliot's poems being motivated by cravings. Which would mean, of course, that the murders were too."

"That seems logical, but I'm afraid it's nothing new. As you said, I'm already working under that assumption."

"Yes, I know. But when I read the sonnets again and thought of them as being inspired by Eliot's cravings, it struck me that his moods, his poems, and the murders were all following a parallel pattern."

Her forehead wrinkled, a gesture that Drew could have interpreted as either intense concentration or complete disapproval. "What kind of pattern?"

"A pattern of increasing volatility," he said, as he reached into his coat pocket and pulled out the three sheets of paper. "All three sonnets are structurally correct, but the imagery and tone reflect three clearly distinct moods. Here in "Sonnet No. 1" his description of the auburn-haired woman, whom we assume was Margaret Fenwyck, was quite typical for a classic, Shakespearean sonnet—romantic, admiring, almost spiritual."

"The old 'he worshipped her from afar' theme."

"Exactly. And her death, while brutal, was not only quick, with no prolonged suffering, but was also romantically symbolic. A pierced heart."

"Okay, I'm with you so far."

"I knew you'd be a good student," he said, hoping for an amiable reaction. No such luck. He continued. "Now look at "Sonnet No. 2." The difference in tone is subtle, but nonetheless distinct. Instead of worshipping the subject from afar, Eliot seems almost disdainful of her. He speaks of her schemes, her pleading, her coy looks. And then consider the way Celeste Holbrook was killed—chased, strangled, then thrown down a well, like disposing of garbage or something."

"The evidence would certainly indicate that Miss Holbrook suffered more than Miss Fenwyck."

"And less than Melissa Turner." He extended the third poem across the table, several key words and phrases circled in red ink. "Which is to be expected when you read the sonnet about her. It states in rather graphic, unpoetic terms what her death would be like. There hasn't been a lot of details in the newspaper about the condition of the body, but I'd be willing to bet your next cup of coffee that the evidence indicated a slow, excruciatingly painful death."

"You wouldn't believe what that poor woman went through." The pain of the recollection shone in her eyes. "So what's the key takeaway here?" she asked. "That Eliot's becoming more and more brutal with each sonnet he writes?"

"Yes. But there's more to it than that, I think. Let me ask you something. What kind of psychological profile have you constructed so far?"

She pushed aside her coffee mug and leaned forward. "I've been working with a profiler from the FBI office in Atlanta who has a lot of experience in serial murder cases. He and I believe Eliot is a white male in his early to mid thirties. He's highly intelligent, probably some kind of professional, well educated, and articulate. And seriously disturbed. Perhaps schizophrenic."

Drew frowned. "I can understand the intelligent, articulate part, but what makes you so sure that he's white and in his thirties? For that matter, how can you even be sure Eliot's a he?"

"We can't be absolutely positive about any of these things, but the FBI's extensive statistics support this profile. First of all, most serial killers select victims of their own race."

"Why is that?"

"Because when they kill they are usually acting out some depraved sexual fantasy, and the vast majority of Americans have relationships with members of their own race."

Drew thought about Charles Alexander's infatuation with Andrea Warren, an obvious exception to this generality, but decided not to mention it. "So that's your reason for thinking he's white?"

"That, and the fact that the majority of serial killers on record have been white tends to push the statistics pretty heavily in that direction."

Drew closed his eyes in concentration. "Now that you say that, most of the ones I've read about or seen on the news have been white."

"And male," Lou said. "Female serial killers are extremely rare. You see women killing their own children, and there's been a few cases of a nurse or nursing home worker committing what appeared to be mercy killings, but selecting and brutally murdering strange women seems to pretty much be a male thing."

"Okay, so you think Eliot is a white male in his thirties, some kind of professional, and highly intelligent and articulate." He smiled sadly. "I guess I should take your suspicion of me as a compliment."

Her tone suggested she did not find his joke amusing. "You can kid about that if you want, but you match the profile almost perfectly."

"Except that I'm not schizophrenic, and I'm not a murderer."

She stared at him, but said nothing.

"So," Drew continued, disappointed that she had not acknowledged his denial, "you also think Eliot is a local?"

"Do you mean a Smythville resident? Yeah, probably."

"Which means he's somehow been able to hide his emotional state, not to mention his demented cravings, from the people around him."

"Of course."

"Well, I don't think he's going to be able to continue the Jekyll and Hyde routine much longer."

She raised her eyebrows. "Why would you say that?"

114

"Because if his sonnets are indeed reflective of his moods, his cravings appear to be getting stronger, more violent, more consuming. I think we have someone who is steadily progressing toward a mental explosion. A big one."

She nodded. "He's decompensating."

"What?"

"That's the technical term for coming unglued. It happens to most serial killers. That's usually when their behavior becomes so bizarre that people start to notice. It's also the time when the violence tends to escalate significantly."

Drew pointed to the poems Lou held in her hand. "Based on the patterns I see in those, that's where I think this guy is heading." He let out a long breath, and added, "Like a freight train."

Lou folded her arms and leaned back in her chair. "So, Dr. Freud, do you have any suggestions?"

"Yeah, two. First, I would try to find some way, without causing a panic, to get the people in this town to be on the lookout for unusual changes in the behavior of family members or co-workers, especially on the part of your better educated, professional types."

"What's the second suggestion?"

Drew looked into her eyes. "The second suggestion is that you brace yourself. "Sonnet No. 4" is going to be a real ass-kicker."

They were silent for a moment, the implications of Drew's hypothesis having a sobering effect on both of them. Then Drew brought up the other subject that was on his mind. "Chief Hennessey, I need to ask you something."

She snapped out of her trance-like state. "Yes?"

"I seem to keep getting mixed signals regarding my status as a suspect in these murders which, I have to tell you, is extremely disconcerting. Be that as it may, I need to know if there's any reason why you would object to me making a trip to Atlanta this weekend. My publisher will be in town and wants to get together Friday night."

"I guess I don't have a problem with that. Where would you be staying?"

"Why do you ask? So you can keep track of my movements?"

She smiled. "Don't be silly. Nothing like that. It's just that if we receive another sonnet from Eliot I'll want you to have a look at it as quickly as possible."

"Well, I guess I'll stay at the Marriott Marquis. It's near most of the other downtown hotels, so it'll be easy to get to wherever my publisher will be staying. I spent a couple of nights there when I was here interviewing for my job a few months ago."

"Great. Just be sure you let me know if you change your mind about where you're staying." She paused, then asked nonchalantly, "By the way, whatever prompted a sophisticated New Yorker like you to move down here to a small town in Georgia?"

Drew's smile faded. "Personal reasons."

"Anything you feel like talking about?"

"Not unless I have to."

"Why would you have to? I was just curious, that's all."

Drew glanced at his watch. "Look, I have to go. If there's anything I can do to assist your investigation, give me a call. I'll be here until around noon on Friday, then back from Atlanta sometime Saturday afternoon."

"Thanks, but unless we receive another poem, I can't think of any reason I'd need you."

"I'm sorry to hear that," Drew said, then left her to interpret his meaning as he hurried out the door.

Back in her office, Lou pulled a card out of her files and dialed the Atlanta police headquarters. "Chief Collins, please," she said when the call was answered. "Chief Lou Hennessey from Smythville calling."

Thirty seconds later, Atlanta Chief of Police Beverly Collins was on the line. She and Lou had first met when they had served on a special task force on hate crimes for the governor, and then had started running into each other at police conventions and various law enforcement seminars. Beverly Collins was an attractive, petite, black woman, but could be as tough and ornery as any man when the situation called for it.

"Lou, how's it going? I hope you're calling to tell me you're coming to Atlanta. We can have ourselves a real good time in this town, you know."

"No, Bev, I'm afraid not. I've got my hands full here in Smythville right now."

"I've heard about those murders. Having any luck finding the killer?"

"Not yet, but I'm pulling out all the stops."

"Let me know if I can help in any way."

"You can. That's why I called. I need a favor this weekend."

"Sure. You know I'll provide whatever help I can."

"I need a man."

Beverly laughed. "Don't we all, honey? Don't we all?"

Lou could not help but chuckle too. "That's not what I meant. There's someone I'm watching, and he's coming to Atlanta on Friday. He'll be staying at the Marriott Marquis. I need you to assign a man to watch him from the time he checks in until the time he leaves."

"Is he involved in those murders?" Beverly asked, her tone serious.

Lou sighed. "I don't know, Bev. I'm praying he's not, but I just don't know."

Chapter 15

Everyone at the *Gazette* who was involved with the "killer poet" story breathed a sigh of relief when the Thursday morning mail did not include another sonnet from Eliot. It was the first time in three weeks that one of his poems had not been received along with the other submissions for the weekly "Risk-A-Verse" column. In fact, the number of entries received this week was down dramatically. Apparently, given the circumstances surrounding the recent murder epidemic, few Smythville residents were anxious to draw attention to any poetic ability. Most people around town were going out of their way to claim they did not even like to read poetry, much less write it.

Andrea Warren was in the process of packing up for the night when her phone rang. The voice on the line was distinctive and familiar.

"Good evening, Miss Warren. How are things in the newspaper business?"

"Fine, Dr. Alexander. Every day we go without another sonnet from this Eliot character is like a reprieve."

"I suppose that's a mixed blessing, though. Unless the police are finding some new leads, you're probably running out of things to write. Have they come up with anything newsworthy?"

"Not really, but believe it or not, I don't care. I actually miss the days when our biggest story was a local kid making Eagle Scout. This murder stuff is just too much for a small town girl like me. I don't mind telling you that I get a little nervous walking home at night, and it's only three blocks."

"That's why I called, sort of. After Miss Turner's funeral, we said we'd get together one evening for a drink. I know it's short notice, but how about tonight? I'll make sure you get home safely."

"Thanks for asking, but I'm afraid I already have plans. Give me a rain check, okay?"

"Oh, sure. The important thing is that you'll no doubt have some big, muscular hunk protecting you tonight."

Andrea laughed. "Why, Dr. Alexander, do I detect a trace of jealousy?"

"Perhaps a touch. But I won't let it get me down."

"You shouldn't. It's actually going to be a girls' night out. A workout at The Slim Gym and a bite to eat afterwards."

"I guess I'll have to wait then. By the way, do you think I could persuade you to dispense with the formality and call me Charles?"

"Sure, as long as you drop the 'Miss Warren.'"

"Great. So, have a good workout, Andrea. Perhaps I could call you next week."

"I'm counting on it, Charles. Bye." She hung up the phone and smiled. Bernard Moss had been right after all. The tall, dark, and handsome professor really was interested in being more than just a "friend of the press." No problem, she thought. I can deal with that.

She glanced at her watch. Six thirty. She decided she would go ahead and walk down the street to the gym and get a head start on her workout before Lou Hennessey arrived. It had been nearly three weeks since she'd been there, and her muscles would undoubtedly need some loosening up.

A half-hour later, she was working up a sweat on an inclined treadmill when she saw Jackie Phelps, owner and operator of The Slim Gym, walk by, picking up loose towels and wiping down the equipment.

"Hi, Jackie, how's it going?" she asked, puffing heavily.

"Fine, Andrea. Where've you been lately? Haven't seen you in a while."

"Where do you think? This damned Eliot story has had me working sixteen hour days."

"God, it's awful, isn't it? I've lived here all my life, and I've never seen anything like this before. I bet poor Lou Hennessey is going nuts. The whole town is gonna turn on her if she doesn't find this guy soon. I guess that's why I haven't seen her in here either."

"Stick around and you will," Andrea said, as she turned off the machine and slowly rode it to a stop. "She said she'd meet me here tonight, unless she got caught up in something at work."

"Actually, I was just about to leave, so tell her 'hi' for me, okay?" Jackie smiled. "I'm heading over to Antonio's to see if any cute guys are hanging out at the bar."

"Be careful, Jackie. You don't know who this Eliot could be."

Jackie laughed as she walked away, flexing her well-conditioned biceps. "I'm in better shape than most of the women in this town. If the sucker tries to take me on, he'd better be ready for a helluva fight."

Alone again in the large workout room, Andrea decided she would put in another ten minutes on the treadmill. The timer had clicked off eight minutes when she looked up to see Lou stroll in, looking athletically chic in a purple leotard and gray sweatpants.

"Getting a jump on me, huh?" Lou said, smiling. "That's not fair."

"I figured I needed it," Andrea said, as she mopped her face and neck with a towel. "I've been away too long. Give me another two minutes on this thing and I'll be ready for the weights."

"Fine. I'll be over here stretching."

Andrea joined her in front of a mirrored wall a couple of minutes later, doing deep knee bends as Lou finished her leg and abdominal stretching routine. Afterwards, they moved over to the Nautilus equipment, where Lou worked smoothly and rhythmically with eighty pounds of weight. When it was her turn, Andrea increased the weight to one hundred pounds.

"Do you always work with that much weight, or are you just trying to make me look bad?" Lou joked.

Andrea laughed. "I just worked up to this much weight a couple of months ago. Once I reach a certain level, I never go back."

"Are you trying to add some bulk?"

"Nah, just definition," Andrea said, checking herself out in the mirror. "I want to make sure I look as good with my clothes off as I do with them on."

They punished their bodies for another hour, until Lou finally sat on a bench and threw up her hands. "Enough. You win. I say it's time for us to hit the showers, then go grab some dinner. What are you in the mood for?"

"I'm in the mood for a big cheeseburger and an order of onion rings, but I guess I'll settle for some pasta. How about Antonio's?"

"I'll probably just have a salad, but Antonio's is fine. Let's get out of here before you try to talk me into another round on the ab-cruncher."

"Well, you know what they say, Lou—no pain, no gain."

"Then you must've endured a lot of pain, my friend, because you seem to be in fantastic shape. If we're going to continue working out together, I've got some catching up to do."

"A girl has to be able to take care of herself, especially these days," Andrea said. "And in that regard, you have one big advantage over me."

"Yeah? What's that?"

"You get to carry a gun."

The two women waved to Jackie, who was snuggled closely to a tall man with his back to the room, as they walked past Antonio's bar to a secluded booth.

"By the way, Jackie told me to tell you 'hi,'" Andrea said.

Lou glanced toward the bar and smiled. "I owe her a check for last month's dues, but she doesn't look like she wants to be disturbed right now. I guess I'll get to hold onto the money another week—unless I see a pair of shoes I like."

A few minutes after they were seated, Andrea looked around the half-full restaurant. She leaned across the table and whispered to Lou. "Have you noticed a lot of the people staring at us?"

"Yep, I've noticed," Lou said without looking up from her menu.

"What's the deal? Haven't they ever seen two attractive, superbly conditioned women having dinner before?"

"Well, that plus the fact that they're probably wondering why their chief of police is in here having a relaxing evening instead of out there chasing down the so-called 'killer poet.'"

"Come on, Lou, you said this was your first night off in three weeks. I think you deserve a little R&R."

Lou shot a quick glance around the room, catching another table in the act of staring at her as they whispered amongst themselves. "I know that, and you know that. The question is, do they know that? More to the point, do they really care? I'd better come up with something soon, or I could see the mayor getting pressured to call a special city council session, and I'd find myself out of a job."

They chatted constantly throughout dinner, stopping only when their waiter returned to remove their plates. Andrea had ordered pasta primavera and a glass of Pinot Grigio, but Lou had been true to her word, having only a small dinner salad and a bottle of sparkling water. But when the waiter returned a minute later with a dessert menu, she literally ripped it out of his hand and began scouring it as if it were the police record of an arrested felon.

"Did you have anything particular in mind, madam?" the amused waiter asked.

"Anything with chocolate."

"Our tortufo is quite nice, but a bit rich."

"Sold." She handed back the menu. "What about you, Andrea? You can't just sit there and watch me make a pig out of myself."

"Make it two," Andrea told the waiter, then turned back to Lou and lowered her voice to a whisper. "So what do you do now? Do you have any plan to flush this Eliot out so you can identify him?"

"That's something I wanted to talk with you about. I had Drew Osborne review the three sonnets we've received so far, and he thinks they reflect a gradual deterioration in Eliot's mental state. He suggested I find some way to warn the public to be on the lookout for sudden mood swings or any aberrant behavioral patterns on the part of friends or co-workers."

"You mean, asking the people in town to spy on each other? Like in some police state?"

"Desperate times call for desperate measures," Lou said solemnly. "But I do have to give a lot of thought to how it could be done. I don't want people calling the police every time their boss loses his temper or some salesman gets depressed over losing a big contract. But at the same time, I'd hate like hell for more women to get butchered, and then have someone come forward after we catch the creep and say they'd noticed him acting real weird ever since his wife left him, or something like that."

"I see your point," Andrea said. "So look, why don't I see if I can draft an article for the *Gazette* that strikes the right balance between cautious observation and paranoid suspicion? You could take a look at it and, if you think it'll help, I'm sure I could persuade Mr. Moss to print it this weekend."

Lou managed a weak smile. "Thanks. I'd appreciate that."

Their desserts arrived, and Lou quickly peeled away and devoured the chocolate shell, leaving the ice cream virtually untouched.

Andrea laughed. "You ordered a five dollar dessert just to get two ounces of chocolate?"

Lou smiled. "Yeah, I guess it would've made more sense to stop at a convenience store for a Hershey bar. But hey, money's not important when you have a craving to satisfy."

"I guess." Andrea continued to savor her own dessert, ice cream and all. "So you think Eliot is someone who, thus far, has shown no outward signs of being a killer?"

"Not enough to arouse suspicion, at least. And maybe he never will. People who worked with David Berkowitz, the Son of Sam killer, described him as a quiet, polite, conscientious guy. His crimes were the number one topic of discussion in New York at the time, and nobody who knew him, even those who had engaged him in conversations about the shootings, ever suspected a thing."

"So you think it's someone here in town who seems perfectly fine on the surface, but who just snapped three weeks ago and decided to kill Margaret? And then liked it so much he decided to kill two other women?"

"I don't know, Andrea. Maybe this person has a dark past that's been haunting him for years, or maybe some big, traumatic event in his life pushed him over the edge."

"Like the drowning of a girlfriend?"

The two women looked at each other for a moment, then Lou sighed. "There's no denying he fits the profile."

"Well, like I told you, my source at the Times said Dr. Osborne apparently came real close to having a nervous breakdown. Maybe he really did have one, of sorts. One that doesn't manifest itself in his everyday behavior."

"I know I have to consider that possibility, and it does explain a comment he made to me about not liking the water. Still, he just doesn't seem the type."

A muted double-ring emanated from Lou's coat pocket. She pulled out a thin cell phone and opened it up. "Hennessey here," she said softly.

She listened for a moment, and then shot a glance toward Andrea. "I'll be there in five," she said, then closed and pocketed the phone. "Someone called in a disturbance in the College Heights subdivision. I've got to get over there fast, just on the off chance that it could be our guy." She stood. "I was going to give you a ride home. Why don't you call a cab, just to be safe?"

"Nonsense, it's barely two blocks from here. You get going. I'll be fine. And I'll cover dinner. You can buy next time."

"Thanks. I'll give you a call if this turns out to be anything news-worthy."

"I'd appreciate that," Andrea said as she fished through her purse for a credit card. "And I'll have a draft of that article for you tomorrow. But right now, you'd better get going."

When she looked back up, Lou was already out the door.

Andrea came out of the restaurant and turned left, walking briskly along the well-lit sidewalks of Main Street. She had gone only half a block when she took another left onto Audubon. Her apartment, the second floor of a beautifully renovated Victorian house, was only another two blocks. The streetlights along Audubon were farther apart than on Main, and the stores and boutiques along the way were closed for the night, leaving the street virtually deserted. Still, Andrea continued her brisk pace, cautious but relatively unconcerned about safety.

When she was about halfway down the first block she thought she heard footsteps behind her. Without slowing, she turned to look but saw nothing. But by the time she reached the intersection of Audubon and Elm, she heard it again. This time she stopped and turned completely around, straining to see in the darkness. She thought she caught a glimpse of movement in front of the hardware store, but could not be sure.

She crossed the street and continued one more block. All she had to do was walk another block, cross Truman Street, and she would be home. She slowed her pace, trying to listen for the sound of shoes on concrete. Hers seemed to echo down the empty street, and she wished she had put her sneakers back on after her shower and carried the heels in the gym bag instead of the other way around. If there really was someone behind her, he would be able to gauge her pace by the loud click-click of her hard soles on the sidewalk. She briefly entertained the notion of removing her shoes and walking in her stocking feet, but it was too cold for that. Besides, she did not want to ruin a perfectly good pair of pantyhose if it was only her imagination.

The unmistakable sound of footsteps hurrying across Elm Street a half block behind convinced her that it was not her imagination at all. She abandoned her efforts to listen, and increased her speed. There was someone behind her, and he was either hurrying to get out of the glow of the streetlight at the intersection, or to close the gap between them. Or both. She reached into a side compartment of her purse and extracted a small cylinder. If the son-of-a-bitch gets too close I'll make sure he gets a good snort of pepper spray.

After another minute that seemed much longer, she approached Truman Street and could see the dim, yellow porch light of her house. As she started crossing the intersection, she transferred the pepper spray to her left hand and thrust her right hand into her purse. Fishing for her key chain as she glanced over her shoulder, she could now see a dark figure, a distinctly male figure, walking briskly toward her. She focused on the approaching form just a second too long, and her left foot caught the curb on the far side of the street. Before she could even extend her arms to break the fall, she found herself sprawled on the sidewalk less than twenty feet from her front steps.

Momentarily stunned, she sat upright and forced herself to take a deep breath. She had fallen hard, and her left knee felt like it was scraped. But in the fraction of a second it took for the pain to register, her senses also detected the sound of footsteps becoming more rapid, louder, and closer.

She grabbed her purse and gym bag as she scrambled to her feet, and saw a few items spill out of the open purse and onto the concrete. She picked up her keys, not caring about anything else, and bolted for her door. She reached the steps and hurried onto the porch. In the dim yellow light, she isolated the right key, quickly inserted it into the lock, and pushed the door open. She was so intent on getting inside that she almost left her keys dangling in the lock, but remembered to grab them just as she slammed the door closed.

She turned the lock from the inside, then hurried up the stairs to her apartment. The only access to her floor of the house was through the door she had just entered, so she rarely locked the one at the top of the stairs. But once inside she did just that, engaging both the deadbolt and the flimsy chain lock.

Her knee burned and her shoulder ached from the fall, but she would worry about first aid later. At the moment, she had a much more urgent priority. Without turning on a light, she hurried to her bedroom window and pulled back the curtains, intently scanning the dark street below.

From across the street, protected by the shadows of a giant oak, he waited and watched. Even though the second floor of the house remained engulfed in darkness, he was able to see the curtains part and the dim outline of a figure peering out. He did not move until they had been closed for several minutes, and an inside light was finally turned on.

Feeling there was little risk of her opening the curtains again for another look outside, Charles Alexander then stepped out of the shadows and began to walk briskly toward the distant lights of Main Street.

Sonnets

Sonnet No. 4

Narcissus calls her name and she complies
She steps before the mirror, proud and vain
The sculpted form that stands before her eyes
Is surely worth the hours of toil and pain

She struggles to make stronger and defined
The contour and arrangement of each part
A body that is perfectly aligned
To please the eyes and captivate the heart

But beauty on the surface covers lies
Beneath her skin an evil soul conspires
Her judge will show no mercy when she cries
And carries out the sentence Truth requires

For one can't reconstruct a wretched soul
By gathering the parts that make a whole

                                    Eliot

Chapter 16

It seemed to Lou Hennessey that every single resident of Smyth-ville, with the possible exception of the kids in school, went out for lunch on Fridays. It appeared to be some kind of town tradition, an end-of-the-week celebration combined with a sort of community fellowship function. It was the day that everyone, whether profes-sional, laborer, retiree, housewife, or some combination thereof, headed to their favorite haunt to exchange news, opinions, recipes and, most importantly, gossip.

For that very reason, Lou generally ate her Friday lunch in the blessed solitude of her office. Besides allowing her to avoid both the crowds and the obligatory handshaking, back-slapping role of a local public official, eating in had led to the discovery that the Friday noon hour was actually the quietest time of the week at the police station. Mainly because everyone else, with the exception of a couple of unfortunate souls manning the phones, was out to lunch.

Today, however, Lou had decided she needed to get out of the office. For one thing, she thought it would be a good idea to make herself visible to the people, to make her presence known and felt in this time of fear and uncertainty. The other reason was that she had a vicious craving for one of The Bayou Biscuit's infamous fried oyster "po boy" sandwiches. The small salad she had eaten for dinner the night before had been metabolized away by the time she had gotten home after mediating a domestic quarrel in College Heights, and she had gone to bed hungry. Breakfast this morning had consisted of coffee and a banana, so now she was ready for some real food.

One of the advantages of being chief of police was that she seldom had to wait for a table, even during Friday lunch hour. She placed a quick call ahead to say she was coming and that she was "in a bit of a hurry," and ten minutes later, she walked in and was seated immediately. Not even needing to consult a menu, she had placed her order as she slid into the tight confines of a small booth, and was now anxiously awaiting its imminent arrival.

She was reading a small, tabletop placard regaling the spicy history of Cajun cuisine when the fluorescent ceiling lights were suddenly eclipsed. She looked up from the placard to find herself in the looming shadow of Bernard Moss.

"The gal at the station told me you'd be here," he said breathlessly. "I figured it was better to walk on over here than to call you on your cell phone."

Lou had a bad feeling, one that she did not even want to acknowledge. "Sit down, Bernie," she said. "I'll let you buy me lunch."

Moss squeezed into the seat opposite her, the edge of the formica table disappearing into the fold of his ample belly. "I've been in meetings all morning," he said.

"Me too. Budget meetings. Don't you just hate those?" She knew she was only making small talk in an attempt to postpone the inevitable message that Moss had come to deliver. But his sense of urgency was not to be denied.

"I just got back into my office a few minutes ago," he said, extending an opened envelope across the table. "This was in my mail."

With great reluctance, Lou accepted what she had dreaded receiving, what she had prayed would never arrive. A moment later, her lunch was placed before her. She pushed it aside. She had lost her appetite.

From his car, Drew could see the Atlanta skyline. In fact, he was not sure but he thought he knew which of the tall, stylish buildings on the darkening horizon was the Marriott Marquis. Probably a forty-five minute walk, maybe less. And certainly no more than a five or ten minute drive, even in traffic. But the traffic would have to be moving for that to happen, and it had not moved more than a few feet in over an hour. Less than a half mile in front of him, a Greyhound bus and a minivan had overlooked a fundamental law of physics—two objects cannot occupy the same space at the same time.

Frustrated, angry, and in dire need of a rest room, he glanced at his watch. He was going to be late, and he had no way of reaching Barbara to let her know. One of these days, he knew he would have to break down and invest in a cell phone. He had put it off because he spent the majority of his waking hours either in his apartment or at the school, and he had phones at both places. The only justification he could think of for having a cell phone was to make personal calls. Since he had no one to call anyway, he felt he could use the money for other things.

He had planned to check in at the Marriott and have enough time to freshen up before heading over to the Westin to pick up Barbara for dinner at Pano's and Paul's, supposedly one of Atlanta's finest restaurants. Now, unless the bus that lay sprawled across all four lanes was uprighted soon, he would not make it to the Westin on time even if he headed straight there. Barbara would be standing in the lobby waiting for him, wondering what had happened to her usually punctual poet.

He looked to his left and noticed a man leaning against a black BMW as he chatted on a cell phone. The man was laughing. Apparently, he was accustomed to this type of traffic snarl because it certainly did not seem to have the same effect on him that it was having on Drew. A couple of minutes later, the man put the phone in his shirt pocket, folded his arms across his chest, and started to whistle.

"What the hell?" Drew muttered to himself. "It won't hurt to ask."

He got out of his car and walked around the front of the BMW. The man noticed him approaching and tensed visibly. Then, seeming to take note of Drew's nice car and clean-cut appearance, he smiled and said, "This is a damned mess, ain't it?"

"Sure is. Any idea how much longer we'll be stuck here?"

"I just heard a radio report that said they've gotten all the injured folks into ambulances, and they've got wreckers on the scene to move the bus. I'd guess we could still be here another thirty or forty minutes."

"That's what I was afraid of," Drew said, shaking his head. "Listen, I'm late for an appointment and I need to let someone know. Would you be willing to let me pay you to make a quick call on your cell phone?"

The man stared at him, a shocked expression on his face. "No, I wouldn't be willing to let you pay me but I'd be happy to let you use my phone." He pulled it from his pocket and handed it to Drew. "Call anybody you need to."

"Thanks," Drew said. "I really appreciate this."

He reached into his shirt pocket for the scrap of paper on which he had written the Westin, Marriott, and restaurant phone numbers, as well as his reservation details. He dialed the Westin and asked for Barbara Troutman's room. She answered on the first ring.

"Hi Barbara, it's Drew."

"Hello, darling, are you here already? Couldn't wait to see me, huh?"

"Well, you're half right. I can't wait to see you, but I'm not there yet. I'm stuck in a major traffic jam a few miles away."

"Oh dear, what a pain. Thanks for letting me know, sweetie. Do you want me to just wait here in my room until I hear from you?"

"Yes. And please call the Marriott and make sure they don't give my room away."

He gave her his hotel confirmation number and also asked her to call the restaurant and explain that they might be late for their dinner reservation. As he ended the call and handed the phone back to the smiling owner of the BMW, he noticed tail lights ahead of them coming on. People were restarting their engines, so traffic was apparently getting ready to move again. Still, he knew it would take a while to unsnarl the logjam and get past the crash scene.

He could not help but smile at the irony. He had looked forward all week to getting away from the tragic and horrifying situation in Smythville, never dreaming what awaited him in Atlanta. All things considered, it probably would have been more relaxing to stay at home this weekend. The traffic jam had reminded him that there were advantages to the quiet lifestyle of a small town.

It was midnight. Lou reached into her desk drawer for the bottle of Maalox and took a big swig. She had not eaten a bite of her lunch at The Bayou Biscuit, and had not even thought about food this evening. Countless cups of strong, black coffee were now taking their toll, and the acid swirling around in her empty stomach felt as if it were burning a hole in her gut.

It was agony sitting there in her office, helplessly waiting for the phone to ring, knowing that somewhere in this town a woman would die tonight, or maybe was already dead. Another dead woman in a town that Lou had taken an oath to serve and protect. She had certainly not done an adequate job of protecting Eliot's previous three victims. And even though she had mobilized every member of the police force, fire department, and even the paramedic squad, she knew in her heart that the odds of preventing another murder tonight were slim.

She stared at the sheet of paper Bernie Moss had given her, and tried for the hundredth time to crack the poetic code and get at its underlying meaning. She thought of Drew Osborne, and wished he was not out of town. If he were in Smythville, he might be able to tell her more about the latest sonnet's meaning. She also found herself thinking that if he was with her and there was no murder that night, that might tell her something too. It would lead her to a conclusion that she preferred not to reach, but at least it would be a conclusion.

At the moment, she had nothing to go on. Osborne had not checked into the Marriott Marquis, so the undercover cop assigned by Beverly Collins was still cooling his heels in the hotel lobby. Lou had faxed a short note and a copy of "Sonnet No. 4" to the hotel, to be given to Osborne when, or if, he checked in. But, so far, he had not.

She read the sonnet again and tried to think. *What does it tell me about the intended victim? That she is narcissistic, or at least perceived to be by Eliot, tells me that the victim was probably young and attractive. The references to her "sculpted form" and to the "contour and arrangement" of her body indicates she is someone who worked out. The "hours of toil and pain" reinforce that notion. But hell, this is a college town. There are hundreds of beautiful, athletic coeds running around. Swimmers, tennis players, cross-country runners, members of the girls' basketball and soccer teams. And, on top of that, how many women routinely work out at The Slim Gym? Dozens. And some of them work especially hard on improving muscle strength and definition. Like last night when I saw . . . oh no, oh shit!*

She leapt from her chair and ran out to the radio dispatch station. "Sarah," she said breathlessly, "who's patrolling Main and its side streets?"

"Mullins and Schaeffer," Sarah said. "I just talked to Howard a few minutes ago. He said it's all quiet downtown."

"Get him on the radio."

"Sure." She pushed a couple of buttons, and then spoke into her headset. "Car sixteen, come in please. Calling car sixteen."

A moment later she said, "Hold on a sec, Howard," and looked up at Lou. "Okay, he's on."

"Put him on the speaker," Lou said tensely.

Sarah pushed another button, and then Lou reached over and held a green button down as she spoke. "Howard, it's Lou. Where are you?"

"Truman Street. Is something going on?"

"When were you last on Main?"

"Five, maybe ten minutes ago. Everything looked fine, Chief."

"Go there now. Park in front of The Slim Gym."

"Roger that. We'll be there in less than two minutes."

After about that much time his voice came through the radio again. "Okay, Chief, we're here. Now what?"

"Does anything look unusual?"

"No. Looks like somebody left a light on in the back, but sometimes Jackie does that."

"Stay there," Lou said. "I'll meet you in five minutes." She turned to Sarah. "Call Jackie Phelps at home. If you get her, tell her to meet me at The Slim Gym right away. And call me and tell me whether you reached her."

She ran into her office, grabbed her coat, and hurried out into the night. She did not turn on her siren for fear of alarming the town over what she hoped would turn out to be a false hunch, but she broke every speed limit and traffic law imaginable in her four minute race down Main Street.

Just as she whipped into the parking space next to the squad car, Sarah's voice came over the radio. "Jackie didn't answer, Chief.

She must be out bar hopping or something. I left a message on her machine."

"Thanks, Sarah." Lou suddenly wished she had brought her Maalox. She got out of the car.

Art Schaeffer took a step toward her and spoke in a hushed voice. "The door's secure, Chief. No sign of any trouble."

"Open it," she said.

Mullins now stepped over. "But Chief, if we force this door open it'll set off the alarm system. By the time I get back to Jackie's office to shut it off, we'll have every squad car on the force heading over here."

"Open it," she repeated. She shot a glance at Art Schaeffer. The color was already draining from the young officer's face.

At the same time, Drew was stepping up to the front desk of the Marriott Marquis. It was late, and he was dead tired. The food at Pano's and Paul's had been everything it was cracked up to be. So was the wine list. He knew he wouldd have a four-star headache in the morning.

The lobby was empty, except for one man who sat in an armchair reading a newspaper. Drew wondered why someone would be hanging out in the lobby at this time of night. Insomnia, he supposed. He certainly did not think he would be having any trouble getting to sleep tonight.

The clerk behind the desk was a cute young thing whose nametag identified her as a trainee named Shannon. She was awfully perky for someone who had to work the graveyard shift, but she seemed efficient, and Drew was on his way to the elevators in less than two minutes.

In reality, young Shannon may have processed Drew's registration as efficiently as a veteran hotel clerk, but she made a mistake common to many trainees. She had done a splendid job of cheerfully giving the tall, handsome guest his keys for the door and mini-bar, and had even remembered to ask if he would need a wake-up call. What she had not done was check the computer to see if Dr. Osborne had any messages waiting for him. Had she done that, she would have informed him that Chief of Police Lou Hennessey of Smythville had called four times, and needed to hear from him as soon as possible. And she would have known to give him the two-page fax, marked "URGENT," that was in the drawer right beneath her computer.

Bone-weary and depressed to a depth she had not reached since her divorce two years earlier, Lou gazed out the store front window of The Slim Gym and saw the first gray light of dawn. It had been a long, agonizingly sad night, and her worst fears had been realized. Eliot had claimed another victim, right under her nose.

Poor Jackie had managed to turn a mediocre career as a competitive body builder into a wonderfully successful business enterprise. Never allowing herself to use steroids, she had not bulked up the way other female body builders did, preferring the lean, defined look of an athletic woman instead of the manly, muscle-bound appearance that others pursued. She had not won many titles, but discovered she had a look that other health and appearance conscious women wanted to emulate. As a result, Jackie had been able to earn enough money as a personal trainer to rent the space, and buy the equipment to open The Slim Gym. It had taken eighty-hour workweeks, and had cost her a marriage, but she seemed to be happy and justifiably proud of her accomplishments.

And now she was dead, the subject of a morose sonnet and the victim of a psychopathic serial killer—one who seemed to enjoy taunting the press and the police with advance clues in his macabre poems, clues that did not reveal their true meaning until it was too late.

Lou walked back into the weight room. The coroner was finishing up, preparing to take Jackie away. The crime photographer had finished his job an hour earlier. It had taken more film than usual.

Lou walked to the far end of the large, rectangular room and knelt beside the chalk outline on the floor. The fingers of Jackie's left hand were outstretched, as if reaching for help that had never arrived. Lou touched the fingers. They were cold and stiff. Rigor mortis had set in.

Lou prided herself as a professional—a stoic, determined police officer. But as she held the fingers of her friend, she felt a tear run down her cheek. She wiped it away. Then she grasped Jackie's hand, walked to the center of the room, and gently placed it inside the body bag with all the other parts.

Chapter 17

For someone who had been so kind, considerate, and loving while alive, Kate's sense of cruelty in death was seemingly without bounds. In the early morning hours, shortly before dawn, she came to visit her tormented lover in his Atlanta hotel room, and she brought with her the slideshow images of their last day together. She brought the dream. At least, it started out as the dream.

The beaches with sand like crystalline sugar, the water a rolling, blue-green playground, and the music a cheerful, cleverly disguised Spanish dirge. There were the images of Drew and Kate making love, Drew and Kate walking on the beach, and floating in the water. And then the images of Drew alone—crying on the shore, savoring Kate's lingering scent on the sheets in their hotel room, and riding through the festive streets of Cancun in the back of a Mexican police car.

And inevitably, the image of Drew walking slowly, reluctantly, into the morgue and stepping to the table, dreading with all his shattered heart the moment that had to come, that he would have to somehow endure. Forcing himself to watch as the fat man in the white lab coat grasped the corner of the sheet and pulled it back. But instead of Kate, there was the dead, bloated face of a man Drew had never before seen.

Suddenly, Drew was in the lobby of the Marriott Marquis in

downtown Atlanta. He was standing at the registration desk, handing over his credit card to a perky young trainee. He noticed a figure in a man's suit and hat sitting in a chair, his face hidden behind a newspaper. Only the hands holding the paper were visible. The fingernails were painted fluorescent pink.

Drew stared at the solitary figure as he walked toward the elevators. He saw the newspaper start to lower just as the elevator doors closed, right before the face would have been revealed. He looked out through the clear walls of the glass box as it glided silently toward the top of the towering hotel atrium. He saw the top of the hat as the figure rose from the chair and moved slowly toward the elevator banks.

Suddenly he was lying in the darkness as the figure in the suit and hat rode to his floor. He heard the soft sounds of wingtip shoes on pile carpet outside his room. He heard the door open, and saw the sliver of light from the hallway cut a thin slice from the darkness, and then seal it back up as the door was gently closed. He heard the footsteps, and sensed the presence. He felt the slight weight of the hat as it was dropped onto the bed at his feet, and then felt the other side of the bed sink beneath the weight of the faceless figure as it slipped beneath the covers next to him.

He reached for the lamp switch, knowing, yet not knowing, who the light would reveal. Turning on the lamp, he looked at the back of a head, a head of long, blond hair, rich and sun-streaked. He felt so happy to have his long-lost lover back in bed with him. He reached to gently touch her shoulder, watching as the blond head turned slowly toward him. He looked into dead, sightless eyes, and saw bloated lips moving slowly, making no sound.

Drew bolted upright, and flung his arm wildly at the bedside lamp, knocking it to the floor. He rolled out of bed and landed on top of it, crushing the fragile shade, and then fumbled for, and finally found the switch. He turned it on, and was temporarily blinded by the sudden flash of light. The king-size bed was empty.

Only the covers on his side, now soggy with his sweat, were turned down.

His head was throbbing. He got up from the floor, put the damaged lamp back on the bedside table, and walked slowly to the bathroom. He fished around in his shaving kit for aspirin, and took three. He turned on the water in the shower, adjusted the temperature until it was as hot as he thought he could stand, and stepped into the tub.

He stayed there a good ten minutes, scrubbing himself furiously, as if trying to remove the stench of death. When he finally turned off the water and stepped out onto the floor mat, the bathroom was filled with steam. He grabbed a hand towel and wiped the mirror above the sink, looking at his drawn, bleary-eyed reflection. And seeing in the fog behind him the floating image of Kate, purple lips silently mouthing the question that continued to haunt him.

There were only a few people milling around the hotel lobby when Drew stepped off the elevator at six thirty, but he could have sworn that one of them was the man with the newspaper. Telling himself that he was simply the victim of an overactive imagination brought on by the mental and emotional strain of the dream, he walked across the lobby and out the revolving door.

The early morning air was crisp but not particularly cold for the first week in November. Certainly not by New York standards, anyway. The honk of an occasional horn, and the scream of a siren in the distance reminded Drew that he missed the sounds of the city. Saturday morning in downtown Atlanta was significantly quieter and less boisterous than any hour in Manhattan, but it was better than the ghost-town tranquility of Smythville. Despite the exasperating traffic jam, and the simultaneously frightening and depressing nightmare he had experienced since arriving, he still felt that the change of scenery had been good for him.

He turned to his left and began walking briskly, searching for what he had come to believe was on just about every street corner in the Atlanta metropolitan area. Sure enough, he had to walk only three blocks before finding one. He stepped inside the Waffle House restaurant and waited to be seated.

A few minutes later, he had a roomy booth and the Saturday edition of the Atlanta Journal-Constitution all to himself. A forty-ish-looking waitress with the hairstyle, make-up, and hemline of a woman half her age made sure his coffee cup stayed full. So friendly and chatty was she that she somehow let it slip out that she was currently single and got off work at noon. Not wanting to take a chance of losing the booth or the direly needed refills, Drew humored her as best he could, even lying that he might stop back in for an early lunch around eleven thirty or so.

His crafty charm worked, and he held onto the booth for nearly two hours, despite the fact that the place had people waiting for tables by the time he finally got up to leave. He left his waitress a generous tip, and she rewarded him with a sexy wink, and a preview of their lunch menu. He thanked her, smiled suggestively, and stepped out into bright sunshine.

He felt like walking, not only to work off a bit of the greasy Spanish omelette he had consumed, but also to clear the cobwebs from his wine-soaked, sleep-deprived brain. He did not head anywhere particular, but simply strolled along, taking in the sights and sounds of the city, and making sure the big Marriott sign was always in view.

There were a couple of times when he had the distinct feeling of being watched, and noticed one particular man with a dark suit and gray fedora on a couple of different streets. He found himself wondering if it could be the same man who had been sitting in the hotel lobby the night before. He could not remember what he had really seen and what had just been part of his dream, but he was becoming convinced that he was being followed.

By the time he got back to his hotel room it was a few minutes past ten. He turned on the television as he began packing his bag, more for background noise than anything else, and could not help but be amused when he found himself viewing a commercial extolling the delicious food and friendly service at the neighborhood Waffle House restaurant. He chuckled to himself as he went into the bathroom to brush his teeth, but was not laughing when he walked back out a few seconds later.

A serious-looking news reporter was speaking dramatically about a breaking story. "The north Georgia town of Smythville, home to the exclusive, private Smythville College, is the scene this morning of its fourth grisly murder in as many weeks. Jackie Phelps, owner of a popular health club, was found dead just after midnight last night. Details have not yet been released, but News Eleven sources in the town say that . . ."

Drew continued to stare at the television screen, but did not hear anything else that was said. *Shit, another murder. Lou Hennessey must be going out of her mind. Has Eliot sent another poem to the Gazette? If so, why hadn't Chief Hennessey called me?* He turned to look at the phone and, sure enough, the red message light was blinking.

The hotel had a guest voicemail message system. It told him a message had come in at 7:05 this morning. He pushed the button on his phone that would play the message, and heard Lou Hennessey's tired but nearly frantic voice. "Dr. Osborne, where the hell have you been? And why haven't you returned my calls or acknowledged my fax? Call me, dammit."

He hung up the phone, and then picked it back up and called the Smythville police station. He was told that Chief Hennessey was in a meeting with the mayor and could not be disturbed. He tried to explain that he was returning the chief's call and that it was urgent, but the woman on the other end of the line held firm.

"Then please give her a message. Tell her I was just now made aware of her messages and fax, and that I'm on my way back to Smythville. I'll be there in about three hours."

He threw the rest of his belongings into his bag, and hurried downstairs to the front desk. He made quite a stink when the clerk checked and then informed him that she did indeed have four phone messages and a fax for him, all received prior to his arrival and check-in. The assistant manager came out and apologized profusely, but Drew was not in a forgiving mood.

Indignantly, he told them to have the valet service bring his car around, if they had not misplaced it, and then stormed across the lobby toward the front door. It was then that he saw the man with the gray hat looking at some tourist brochures near the concierge station, positioned in such a way as to have an unobstructed view of the front desk.

Knowing that he had no real proof that the man had been following him, but not being in a frame of mind to care, Drew strolled briskly over to the man and stepped right in front of him. "I'm heading back to Smythville now. You can go home and get some sleep."

The man made no pretense of shock or confusion. He simply smiled and said, "Drive carefully."

Chapter 18

Drew returned to a town under siege. The shops and restaurants along Main Street, typically filled with customers and leisurely browsers on a Saturday afternoon, were virtually empty. Many places of business were closed. A notable exception was The Slim Gym, which appeared a virtual beehive of activity. Drew saw a couple of uniformed police officers, but most of the men and women streaming into and out of the site of Eliot's latest crime wore dark jackets with either FBI or GBI, the Georgia Bureau of Investigation, stenciled on the back. The cavalry had arrived.

A few minutes later Drew pulled into the parking lot of the police station, in back of City Hall. The scene inside was like a stirred up anthill—everybody scurrying around busily, but in no logical pattern discernible to an outside observer. He grabbed the arm of a man in a rumpled suit who was hurrying past with what appeared to be a large stack of photographs. "I'm Drew Osborne. I need to find Chief Hennessey."

The man barely slowed. "The chief's busy. You're gonna have to come back later."

"Wait . . ." Drew stammered, but the man was gone.

Looking around desperately for someone who might be able, or at least willing, to help him, Drew suddenly saw a familiar face. He hurried over to a battered gray desk where an adolescent-looking officer was talking on a telephone as he jotted down notes on a legal pad. Looking up and seeing Drew standing in front of him, he said, "Hold on a minute," and then covered the receiver with his hand. "Dr. Osborne," he said with a grim nod.

"Officer Schaeffer, I need to see the chief right away. I see you're busy, so could you just point me in the right direction?"

"Her office is over there," he said, pointing to a far corner of the large, cluttered room. "But you won't be able to get in there unless you're escorted. Let me wrap up this call, okay?"

"Sure, thanks," Drew said, and waited another two or three minutes as Schaeffer finished writing his notes, thanked the person on the other end of the line, and hung up the phone. When he looked back at Drew, the redness in his eyes and the dark circles under them gave a pretty clear indication of the kind of night the young officer had been through.

"Looks like this may have been Eliot's worst one yet," Drew observed.

Schaeffer suddenly had a faraway look in his tired, bloodshot eyes. "You wouldn't believe it if I told you," he said, as he stood. "Come with me."

They waded through a multi-coursing stream of bodies until they reached the entrance to Lou Hennessey's office. There they found a group of people standing tightly packed together, listening as Lou and a stern-looking black man Drew did not recognize talked and pointed to a city map covered with red and green plastic pins.

As Officer Schaeffer pushed his way through the crowd, clearing a path for Drew, Lou saw them. Locking eyes with Drew, she pointed to a short filing cabinet in the corner and barked an order that left no room for compromise. "Sit."

Drew did as he was told, and Schaeffer disappeared back through the crowd. The black man waited until Drew was seated before continuing.

"The profile that Chief Hennessey and I have constructed is that of a white male, early to mid thirties, a professional of some sort. Possibly an academic, but not necessarily so—just well read and articulate. We've gotten no fingerprints from any of the four poems received, so he's smart enough to wear gloves. He was even too clever to lick the envelopes. He apparently used a sponge wet with distilled water to seal them."

A man wearing an FBI jacket raised his hand. "Any matches on VICAP?"

The black man shook his head. "For those of you who might not know, VICAP stands for Violent Criminal Apprehension Program. It's an FBI database of repeat killers. To answer the question, there are plenty of unsolved cases involving attractive, young white women, but nothing where the murders were presaged by a poem. Besides, Chief Hennessey is convinced that Eliot is a local. It appears we have a brand new killer on our hands."

He looked around the room. "Any more questions?"

There being none, the packed assembly was dismissed. The room slowly emptied, leaving only Lou, the black man, and Drew, who noticed the man staring at him questioningly.

"Frank, can you give us a minute?" Lou asked quietly.

The man looked at her, then back at Drew. "Sure. I have to make some phone calls anyway."

The room was deathly quiet for a moment after the man named Frank closed the door. Finally, Drew broke the silence. "I read the sonnet you faxed me. The last line would seem to imply . . . " He was not sure how to say it. "Did he . . . was she . . .?"

"Yes."

Drew stared at her and saw something in her eyes that went far beyond weariness and fear. She looked shell-shocked, like a soldier who had just returned from a fierce battle, having witnessed for the first time the unspeakable horrors of war. But then her eyes focused on him like twin laser beams, and she sat in the chair behind her desk.

"Do you mind telling me just where the hell you've been for the past twenty-four hours?" Her voice was as hard and flat as slate.

"Ask your guy in Atlanta," Drew said, an edge to his voice that he immediately wished was not there. "The only time I was out of his sight was when I was in my hotel room. But then, you probably had the room bugged."

If she was surprised that Drew had spotted the tail, she did not show it. "You left here around one thirty yesterday afternoon. You didn't check into the Marriott, where my man was, until after midnight. Where were you in between?"

Drew took a deep breath. He could feel his anger and frustration rising, and he fought to keep his emotions under control. This was definitely not the right time for a confrontation. "I arrived in the city limits of Atlanta a little after four, then sat for an hour and a half in a traffic jam on 85 South. I'm sure you can confirm that there was a bus accident with multiple injuries. I picked up my publisher, Barbara Troutman, at the Westin Hotel around six fifteen, and we had dinner at Pano's and Paul's in Buckhead at seven. We got back to the Westin at eleven, had a drink in the lobby bar, and then I drove to the Marriott. Any more questions?"

"You can document all this?"

Drew felt the pressure building inside. "Our waiter's name was Henry. I paid for dinner and the drinks at the Westin with my American Express card." He pulled out his wallet, extracted two pieces of paper, and slapped them down angrily on the desk in front of her. "Here are the receipts. Miss Troutman can corroborate that I left the Westin at about eleven fifty, and I'm sure the Marriott and your guy with the gray hat can confirm that I checked in shortly after midnight. So unless you can explain how I managed to get all the way back here to Smythville, chop up a woman, then return to Atlanta in a fifteen-minute timeframe, I'd appreciate it if you'd dispense with your annoying, insulting and baseless insinuations."

Her nostrils flared and her eyes burned into him. "I will ask you as many questions as I want, Dr. Osborne, and you had damned well better have an airtight answer for every one of them."

"Well, has it occurred to you that if you hadn't been so obsessed with wasting your time trying to implicate me, maybe you could've done something worthwhile, and that poor woman would still be in one piece?"

The moment the words left his mouth, he knew he'd gone too far.

"Get out," she said between clenched teeth.

"I'm sorry. That was way out of line. It's just been so—"

"Get the fuck out." She started to rise from her chair.

"I said I'm sorry. We've both been through a lot."

"Get out of my office before I have you arrested." She reached for the phone on her desk.

"Dammit, Lou, listen to me! I'm sorry. I had no right to say such a thing, and I'm terribly sorry. I'd give anything to take it back, but I can't, so you're just going to have to cut me some slack." He glanced through the glass window into the squad room and saw that several people had stopped their work and were staring warily at him. He had been shouting. "This entire ordeal has been horrible for you, I know," he said softly. "And for me, too."

She stared at him for a moment before speaking in a tired voice that was little more than a whisper. "So now we're on a first name basis, are we?"

"If we're going to work together to find this damned psychopath, we should be, don't you think?"

"Yes," she said. "I suppose I do."

A few minutes later there was the sound of a commotion right outside Lou's office. Just as Drew turned to look, the door opened and a booming voice cut the silence like the roar of a cannon. "I don't need an appointment to see the chief of police, or anyone else in this town, young lady. Make sure you remember that."

Drew had never been formally introduced to the infamous Bernard Moss, but recognized the big man from seeing him around town.

He also recognized Andrea Warren, who seemed to be favoring her left leg as she walked into the office behind her boss.

"You've got to quit hiring these damned outsiders, Lou," Moss bellowed. "They don't know who's who in this town."

"She won't make that mistake again, Bernie," Lou said, with what could almost pass for a smile.

"I hope not," he answered gruffly.

Drew stood and extended his hand. "Mr. Moss, we haven't met. I'm Drew Osborne. I'm on the faculty at the college."

Moss shook hands, but eyed Drew suspiciously. "I know who you are, Dr. Osborne." He shot a quick glance at Lou, and then focused on Drew again. "If you'd be so kind as to excuse us a minute, Miss Warren and I have an urgent matter to discuss with the chief."

Drew was about to leave when Lou spoke. "Bernie, is this about the murders?"

Moss looked at her as if she had lost her mind. "What the hell do you think it's about, Lou? Fixing a damned parking ticket?"

"If it's the case you're here to talk about, Dr. Osborne should stay," Lou said in a matter-of-fact tone. "As of this afternoon, I have officially engaged him as an advisor to our investigation."

Moss stared at her for a moment, and then cut his eyes to Drew. "I don't know, Lou. This is of a fairly personal nature."

"Dr. Osborne has been very helpful in providing additional insight into Eliot's poems," Lou said, emitting a weary sigh. "And we might as well get all the cards out on the table. He was in Atlanta at the time Jackie was killed."

Moss seemed as taken aback as the others by that remark. "That may be, Lou, but there's still the confidential nature—"

Andrea interrupted her boss in mid-sentence. "Since it's about me, Mr. Moss, I don't mind Dr. Osborne staying if that's what Chief Hennessey wants."

"About you?" Lou asked.

"Andrea thinks she may have had a close encounter with Eliot," Moss said.

Sonnets

"What?" Lou gasped. "When?"

Andrea rubbed her hands together nervously. "Thursday night, on my way home from Antonio's. I think someone was following me. No, wait, I know someone was following me, I just don't know if whoever it was intended to harm me. Or if it was Eliot."

She then related the story of her late night walk down Audubon Street. She told of the sound of footsteps in the darkness behind her, her fall when crossing Truman, and the items spilling from her purse. She concluded by telling them of rushing up the stars, locking the door, and running to the bedroom window to scan the street outside for signs of her pursuer, but seeing nothing.

"Why didn't you call here to report this?" Lou asked, her voice angry. "You, of all people, Andrea, know what's at stake here. You write the newspaper articles warning everyone else in town to be careful, then you just overlook an episode like this?"

Andrea looked down at her hands, as if in shame. She spoke softly, almost in a whisper. "I guess I didn't want to admit to myself that I might have been in danger. In fact, by yesterday morning I'd pretty much convinced myself that the whole thing was just a case of letting my imagination get the best of me. You and I had talked so much about the murders during our workout and over dinner that I guess I was primed for seeing Eliot behind every bush."

"What changed your mind?" Lou asked. "Something must have, or you wouldn't be here now."

"On my way to work yesterday I stopped to look around the area where I fell," Andrea said. "I found a couple of credit card receipts and a ballpoint pen from my purse. But there had been a lipstick in my purse too, and it was missing. I know I'd had it earlier in the evening, because I remember reapplying some after dinner, while I was waiting for the waiter to bring the bill. When I got into my apartment and checked my purse to determine what had spilled out, it wasn't there. So I checked the area where I stumbled, checked the street and the nearby grass thoroughly, but it just wasn't there."

"And you think whoever was following you picked it up?" Lou asked.

"I don't know. It just seemed strange that I found the other items right where I expected them to be, but couldn't find the lipstick."

"And that's what convinced you that you should talk to Bernie about this?"

"No, not really. It was a combination of things, I guess." Andrea was looking like she might cry. "When Mr. Moss showed me the latest sonnet yesterday, I didn't make a connection. But I must've read the damn thing a hundred times last night, and started thinking maybe it could have been written about me."

No one said anything. Andrea reached into her purse for a tissue and began to dab at her eyes. "I had everything all locked up, and there's only one way into my apartment, so I felt safe. But I didn't sleep a wink. And then, this morning when I heard about Jackie, I guess I just lost it. I kept thinking it really could've been me, that if Eliot knows the regulars at The Slim Gym, he'd have to know me too. And maybe he really had been stalking me on Thursday night. Maybe it was actually me that he intended to kill. And—" She buried her face in her hands, her shoulders shaking. Lou walked around the desk and knelt beside her.

"It's okay," she whispered. "It's okay to be scared. We all are."

Moss turned to Drew. "You're an advisor on this case. What do you think?"

Drew cleared his throat. "Well, first of all, Andrea, if it really was Eliot following you on Thursday night, I don't think you were in immediate danger."

"What?" Moss bellowed. "Do you know what this maniac does to women?"

"Yes," Drew answered evenly. "But I also know that so far he hasn't killed without advertising it first, with one of his sonnets. Since "Sonnet No. 4" probably wasn't dropped in the mail until Thursday morning, I don't think there's any way Eliot would have claimed another victim that night."

"But he could have followed Andrea home to see where she lives," Moss said. "Isn't it possible he intended her to be the woman he described in this last sonnet?"

"I don't think so," Drew said. "Eliot seems to know a lot about each of his victims. Personal details, like the fact that Celeste Holbrook had a crush on a teacher, which appears to have been me. No, I imagine that "Sonnet No. 4" was written specifically about Jackie Phelps and no one else."

Andrea looked up, her eyes wet. "So I'm not in danger?"

Drew glanced at Lou who, seeming to know what he was thinking, gave him a subtle nod. He turned back to Andrea. "We can't assume that. Like I said, Eliot's sonnets reflect a knowledge of personal details about his victims."

"Then why would he have followed her the other night?" Moss asked.

Drew leaned forward and locked eyes with Andrea. He wanted to make certain she understood the implications of what he was about to say. "It's what we writers call the 'research phase.'"

Chapter 19

Select Screen Name: Eliot

Enter Password: Sonnets

Send Instant Message To: Melpomene

Eliot: Oh, the irony. To achieve recognition, yet live in anonymity.

Melpomene: But think how fortunate you are to be able to walk freely among the people and hear their uncensored comments about your work.

Eliot: I am the talk of the town, especially now that Dr. Osborne is no longer under suspicion.

Melpomene: Is that a concern?

Eliot: Not really. No one has any reason to suspect me, so I'm no more vulnerable than before. Actually, I found it a little insulting that anyone would confuse his lovesick drivel with my timeless statements of truth.

Melpomene: Yes, your gift is truly unique.

Robert K. Brown

Eliot: My only fear now is whether I can sustain it. Where do I go from here? What will be my inspiration?

Melpomene: If you look for inspiration, you will find it.

Eliot: It's the words I'm talking about. Sometimes it takes an entire night to write a single line. The verse once flowed so freely. Now it seems as if my ability has been dammed and the flow reduced to a mere trickle.

Melpomene: For a true artist, that is enough.

Eliot: It's what follows the writing that sustains me—making the words come true.

Melpomene: But first you must write. Otherwise, there is no truth, and your work is no different than that of a common murderer.

Eliot: Then tell me where to look. Where will I find my inspiration?

Melpomene: You say you have suffered. Look within. What haunts you the most?

Eliot: You know.

Melpomene: Tell me again.

Eliot: The memories of her—laughing and ridiculing me when I talked of becoming a poet. When I close my eyes I still see her painted face and provocative shape, which she used to lure men who also ridiculed and debased me.

158

Sonnets

Melpomene: Until?

Eliot: Until I wrote a sonnet about her burning in the fires of hell. And made it happen.

Melpomene: Exactly. So now you know what you must do to find your inspiration.

Eliot: No . . . what?

Melpomene: Find one like her.

Chapter 20

Sunday was a quiet day in Smythville. The police activity at The Slim Gym had ceased late Saturday night, and most of the shops along Main Street were routinely closed on Sundays. A couple of downtown restaurants were open, but customers were scarce. Even though every one of the half dozen churches in town had been filled to capacity that morning, people had not gone out for lunch afterward, choosing instead to go directly from the sanctity of God's house to the safety of their own. Even the college campus seemed devoid of its usual hustle and bustle.

Barbara had called Drew's apartment late Sunday afternoon, furious that he had spent an entire evening with her without mentioning what had been going on in Smythville.

"I know I have an unsettling effect on men, darling, but I can't believe you were so bewitched that you forgot to mention that Smalltown, USA had become the murder capital of the world. And the killer writes sonnets, no less! Why didn't you tell me?"

"It's been disturbing. One of the victims was a student of mine. I guess I just wanted to forget about it for a while. But on Saturday morning I got a message from the chief of police that there'd been another murder, so I left Atlanta in a rush. I'm sorry I didn't call you to say goodbye."

"You're not a suspect, are you? I mean, come on, not a lot of people write sonnets these days."

Drew let out a long breath. "Not anymore. My dinner with you established a pretty airtight alibi. In fact, I'm now an official advisor on the case to the Smythville Police and the FBI."

"Wonderful! I'm glad the chief had the good sense to bring you into the case instead of arresting you. He must be a pretty astute judge of character."

"Actually, she's a woman, and yes, she is."

Barbara was uncharacteristically silent for a moment. "It's her, isn't it? She's the woman you told me about when I called you last week."

Drew sighed. "Yes, but please don't make anything more out of this than there really is. I was a suspect because I write sonnets, and now I'm an advisor for the same reason. That's all there is to it."

"You play it down as much as you want, darling, but I smell a book here. A bestseller, maybe. Beautiful female police officer, handsome poet helping her solve the case, and it's true to boot. I love it!"

"You've got it wrong. Smythville's just a quiet, southern college town going through a dreadful time. This will soon be behind us—the sooner the better—and I'll be back to giving boring lectures and writing soppy poems."

But Monday dawned on a far different world than the tranquil, country setting Drew had described. Even as the sun began to climb out from behind the pine-covered hills that formed the eastern horizon, the Atlanta television news crews were rolling in. The restaurants that had not served enough meals to cover the light bill on Sunday found themselves turning away their regular customers on Monday morning in order to feed the story-starved press. Residents who were accustomed to ten-minute commutes sat in snarled traffic for up to an hour. There were video crews outside the homes of the three local women who had been killed, outside Hollidell Hall and the arboretum on campus, and on virtually every corner on Main Street. And nearly every passerby was asked the same inane question. "In your opinion, who is Eliot?"

After a night of fitful tossing, Drew had given up on sleep nearly two hours before he normally rose. Anxious to get out of his apartment, he managed to miss the major traffic logjams, and was parked in his usual spot on campus a little before seven. Having an hour to kill, he decided to stroll across the street to Starbucks for coffee and a muffin before his eight o'clock class. To his surprise and dismay, the line of customers extended out the door of the coffee shop, so he kept walking, hoping to find another place where he could get some breakfast without having to wait an hour. It did not take long for him to realize his search would be futile.

He continued along Main Street, actually having to step out into the crawling automobile traffic in order to get around the crowd gathered outside The Slim Gym. At least half a dozen reporters, microphones in hand as they stared into the blinding lights, jockeyed for position in front of the "CLOSED UNTIL FURTHER NOTICE" sign in the window. Drew made his way around the throng of news crews and curious onlookers, and was stepping back onto the sidewalk when he heard his name being called from somewhere behind him.

"Dr. Osborne, wait a minute."

He turned to see Andrea Warren emerging from the jostling crowd. She looked frustrated, but less tense than she had looked Saturday at the police station.

"So, what do you think of our media circus?" she said, turning to again survey the frenetic scene behind them.

"It's crazy," he said. "Like the carnival rolled in while we were asleep."

"Good analogy," she said with a contemplative nod.

"So, what will you write about now that the Atlanta TV stations are covering this? By the time your next edition comes out, these people will have broadcast all the latest developments a dozen times in a dozen different ways."

"Believe it or not, that's actually one of the advantages we have in the print media. We have deadlines to meet, but can usually take the time to get our facts straight."

Drew gestured toward the street. "Are you saying they don't?"

"In a situation like this, the man or woman standing next to you sets a new deadline every time they step into the lights with a microphone. So when you get something, you report it. Your primary goal is to get on the air with it before your competition does. Accuracy becomes a secondary consideration."

Drew looked at her and smiled. "That's a pretty cynical view of your brothers and sisters in the television press, don't you think?"

Her voice was curt. "Not really. Just the truth. There'll be just as much misinformation as facts broadcast on the morning news shows today. As if I didn't already have enough to do, now I'll have to spend the day sorting fact and fiction so we can give our readers, the people who are most directly impacted by all this, the real story once the media blitz has packed up and left town in search of their next sensational event."

"So your job today will be to cover the coverage?"

She smiled, her ire seeming to fade. "Exactly. I'll cover the coverage. You're very perceptive, Dr. Osborne."

"Why don't you call me Drew?"

"I'll be happy to. After all, I'm already on a first name basis with one of your colleagues."

"Oh?"

"Yep. Charles Alexander called me last week and asked me out for a drink. Unfortunately, I already had plans to meet Lou Hennessey. That's the night I thought I was being followed. Anyway, Charles said he'd call me back this week."

"I'm sure he will."

She cut her eyes at him and smiled demurely. "Think so?"

"I'm sure of it. Charles may have a couple of screws loose, but there's no arguing that he's a man of impeccable taste."

"I'll take that as a compliment."

Sonnets

"It was intended as one."

Andrea stared at the crowd of news crews and onlookers for a moment, and then turned to face Drew again. "May I ask you a personal question?"

Drew looked at her. "Is this Andrea the journalist or Andrea the fellow citizen of Smythville?"

She laughed. "I'm always Andrea the journalist. But, for the moment, let's talk off the record."

"Okay, shoot."

"Based on Lou Hennessey's comments in her office on Saturday, you're clearly not a suspect in these murders, despite the fact that you're new in town, and that you write the same kind of poems as Eliot. But prior to your trip to Atlanta, did you feel you were under suspicion?"

"By Lou Hennessey, or the citizens of Smythville?"

"Either."

"Yes on both counts."

Andrea appeared contemplative for a moment, watching a female broadcaster struggle through her third take as others waited impatiently for their chance to tape directly in front of The Slim Gym sign. She cocked her head toward Drew. "I won't deny that I harbored similar suspicions. But now that we know they were groundless, I'd be happy to help you tell your side."

Drew studied her face. "What do you mean?"

"I mean that I would be happy to interview you, and publish a story that sets the record straight. You know, one that positions you as someone who is not a suspect, and who is actually helping the police with the investigation."

Drew pursed his lips and let out a deep breath. "Thanks, but no thanks. I think the less said about it, the better. People will find out soon enough that I was in Atlanta when this last murder was committed, and they'll come to the correct conclusion on their own."

"You're a private person, aren't you?"

"I've never really thought about it, but yes, I guess I am. I know you journalists must hate people like me."

"And vice versa," she said, smiling. "Well, I guess I'd better climb back into the eye of the storm. All these people will be out of here by ten o'clock, so whatever I'm going to get, I'd better get now."

"Good luck," Drew said. "I suppose I'll head over to my office. I don't think I'll be getting any coffee out here."

They said goodbye, and he made his way across Main Street and headed toward the Liberal Arts Building. The campus was coming back to life. Students on foot, and on bicycles rushed past, not sharing Drew's luxury of being able to arrive late for class.

He thought about his conversation with Andrea, especially the part about him having been suspected of being Eliot. As bad as he felt about Jackie Phelps being murdered, he could not deny that it was a relief to have the situation unfold in a way that cleared him of suspicion. Perhaps now his students would open up with him again. And perhaps he would no longer catch his peers, especially Charles Alexander, staring at him when he turned his back.

He turned down the narrow street that ran the length of the arboretum. A couple of television crews were still at work, filming the location of Celeste Holbrook's murder. For some reason, it saddened Drew even more to see the pretty young woman's death sensationalized to such an extent. It cheapened the dignity of her memory. It seemed to Drew that the whole town had taken on the atmosphere of a low-budget slasher movie.

Just as he thought he was being too cynical, his eyes focused on something that stopped him in his tracks. On a brick archway at the entrance to one of the arbor's tunnels, right below the engraved plaque dedicating the garden to a woman who had died a hundred years ago, he saw something that justified his jaundiced view. Written with red spray paint was a message that was as indisputable as it was repugnant—"Eliot Rules."

Andrea let out a sigh of exhaustion when she finally walked away from her desk and out the door of the Gazette. Her day had been a mind-numbing marathon.

She had reviewed nearly a dozen videotapes of Atlanta morning news programs before following up with Lou Hennessey on the status of the Jackie Phelps murder. She had then walked all over town capturing the reactions of local citizens to the morning's press onslaught, and had finally struggled to align her observations in what she hoped was a compelling headline story. She was proud of what she had accomplished in the past twelve hours, but felt as if her brain had been cracked open and scrambled.

She was not really in the mood to be sociable, but she waited patiently on the sidewalk outside the office, scanning the passing traffic. After a few minutes, she heard the beep of a horn as a car pulled to a stop right in front of her. Recognizing the driver, she stepped briskly to the car and got in.

"Good evening, Andrea. You look beat. Beautiful as ever, but beat."

"You're correct on at least one count, Charles." She stifled a yawn. "I'm definitely beat."

"Is this a bad night to do this?" he asked, as he merged back into the flow of traffic. "I could tell when I spoke with you this afternoon that you were having a rough day. I can just give you a ride home if you prefer."

"Thanks for your consideration, but I'll be fine. I'm just a bit frazzled. And definitely in need of that drink."

"Have you had anything to eat?"

"Not since a doughnut at about eight this morning."

Charles smiled, his eyebrows arching. "Well, we'd better get some food into you. If I take you out for drinks on an empty stomach, you might get the impression I'm trying to take advantage of you. What are you in the mood for?"

She returned his smile and spoke in the throaty voice of a sultry soap opera vixen. "You mean, in addition to being taken advantage of?"

"Yeah. Pasta? Seafood? Salad bar? I know you're very health conscious."

She arched her back and stretched her arms and legs. "You want to know what I'm really in the mood for?"

He took in the view of her long, taut frame for a moment before turning his eyes back to the road. "Yeah, tell me."

"I would love a cold beer and the thickest, greasiest, most cholesterol-laden cheeseburger we can find."

He chuckled and shook his head. "Then I know just the place. Do you mind a little ride? Ten or fifteen minutes at the most."

"If the burgers are worth it, that's no problem."

"They are, indeed, madam." He pointed the car toward the city limits. "First stop, Bert's. Second stop, the cardiac lab at Smythville General."

Twenty minutes later, they were seated at a Formica table with a pitcher of beer in front of them, sawdust on the floor, and Vince Gill crooning a sad song from a genuine Wurlitzer jukebox. Bert's Roadside Bar & Grill sat all alone on County Road 501, about ten miles south of Smythville. Andrea said she had never heard of it before, but it looked as if everyone else had. The place was packed.

After a few minutes their waitress came back to the table to take their order. She wore the standard uniform for Bert's female employees—cowboy boots, a short, tight denim skirt, and a low-cut, billowy white blouse that left little to the imagination. Bending low over the table directly in front of Charles, she allowed him, and nearly everyone else in the place a clear view of her ample, unfettered bosom. "See anything you like, big fella?"

Charles closed his menu and looked at Andrea. "I recommend medium rare. If you're going to trash your body, I say go all the way."

"Works for me," Andrea said.

"We'll have two Bert's Supremes, medium rare, an order of fries, and an order of onion rings," he said, looking at the waitress. "And be sure you don't let us run out of beer."

"Oh, I'll be keeping my eye on you," she said with a suggestive wink. "But you be sure to call me over here if you need anything, okay?"

"Sure," Charles said. "What's your name?"

"I'm wearing a nametag, sugar."

Charles darted his eyes at the view she was still providing. "I can't see it."

"Really?" she said, feigning puzzlement, then stood upright and looked down at her blouse. "See, here it is. Jesse."

"Okay, Jesse, we'll let you know if we need anything."

"Now I know why you like this place," Andrea said as Jesse sashayed away, hips swinging in time to the jukebox like a human metronome. "Is the food actually good?"

"Just like our waitress," Charles said, smiling. "Hot, cheap, and definitely bad for your health."

She laughed. "I think this is just what I needed tonight. The last few weeks have been a nightmare, and today was the icing on the cake."

"You've really been burning the candle at both ends, haven't you?"

"As long as Eliot's busy, I'm busy."

Charles finished his beer, reached for the pitcher, and refilled their glasses. "Aren't the police making any progress? They've got the feds and the Georgia Bureau of Investigation on the case. Surely they must have some suspects in mind."

"If they do, they damn sure haven't shared them with anybody at the *Gazette*. Lou Hennessey has promised me I'll be kept in the loop, and I haven't heard a thing."

Charles glanced around, and then leaned toward her, resting his elbows on the table. "I guess she's decided that Drew Osborne is no longer a suspect."

"I'm not sure he ever really was. Does that disappoint you?"

His eyes widened with a look of surprise. "Disappoint me? Why would you think that?"

"Call it female intuition, but I got the impression that you don't quite trust him."

He smiled. "If everybody I didn't trust was a murderer, this town would be awash in bodies."

"Are you saying you don't trust anybody, Charles?" she asked.

"No," he said. "I'm just saying that I'm selective. Very, very selective."

They chatted casually until their food arrived, then pounced on it like lions on a gazelle. Afterward, Andrea mentioned that she had another early day coming up, and Charles called for the check. Jesse made a point of bending low when she placed it in front of him. "I hope you'll be coming back to see me," she said.

"You can count on it," Charles said, then winked at Andrea as they stood to leave. They talked about music, literature, and life in a small town during the ride back to Smythville. Discovering that they shared a passion for classical music, Andrea proceeded to review the extensive collection of CDs in a case at her feet. The next thing she knew, Charles brought the car to a stop and turned off the engine.

"Here we are," he said.

Andrea looked up from the CD case and was surprised to see her own front porch, dimly lit by the single yellow bulb. "How... how did you know where I lived?" she asked quietly.

"Smythville's not a very big town," he said, smiling. "There aren't that many people to keep up with."

"You make it a point to know where everybody in town lives?"

"No, not everybody. Like I told you, I'm very, very selective."

Chapter 21

E unice Pemsley was an observant woman. Many people in town would be more apt to use the word nosy, but Eunice would argue that. In fact, Eunice would argue just about anything with just about anybody, the position she was taking on the subject at hand being essentially irrelevant. She did it for the mental exercise. She was convinced that it was paying attention to details, and engaging in verbal jousting with her friends and neighbors that had kept her so sharp for all her seventy-one years.

As currently written, the city by-laws mandated retirement from her position as Smythville Postmaster on her next birthday. She had held the job for the past forty years, and was convinced that the U S Postal Service would collapse into chaos without her. She was pushing hard on the mayor to introduce a by-laws amendment to the city council later in the month. He would probably oblige, not wanting to incur the same level of wrath he had suffered when, shortly after his election, he had referred to Eunice as Smythville's Postmistress. "I ain't never been anybody's mistress, young man," she had admonished, "and I'm as much a master at running this post office as any man you'll ever meet. If you want to keep getting your mail, you'd best remember that."

At the moment, Eunice was not concerned with either her job

or her title. She was focusing her eyes on the license plate of a dark blue car as it pulled out of the post office parking lot. The fading afternoon light, combined with the distance, made it hard to read all the characters, but the first number was a "4," and the last two letters were "GF." Her memory was good, but she scrawled the information on a slip of paper, just to be safe. This could be important, and therefore not the time to let personal pride get in the way of accuracy.

The object of her concern was the man driving the car. He had walked into the post office right before closing. Not anticipating any more customers for the day, Eunice had emptied the "LOCAL DELIVERY" bin a few minutes early. She had carried the mail to the back to be sorted first thing in the morning for tomorrow's rounds when she heard the front door open, followed by the clunk of a letter as it hit the bottom of the empty bin. Her post office guaranteed next day delivery of all local mail deposited by four o'clock on weekdays, and it was still two minutes till, so she had hobbled back over to pick up the solitary envelope. As was her habit, she had also glanced at the address. *The Smythville Gazette.*

It could be anything, of course. A subscription payment, a letter to the editor, maybe an ad for the classifieds. On the other hand, there was no return address. Eunice had peeked through the mail slot to see who had dropped the letter in. All she could see was the figure of a man wearing sunglasses, a baseball cap pulled low over his face, and a raincoat with the collar turned up. This struck her as being strange because it was not raining. It had been a sunny, unseasonably warm day. The sunglasses made sense. The raincoat did not.

The man appeared to be in a hurry to get back to his car, and Eunice had to run, bad hip and all, to get to the window in time to see it. Eunice could tell the color but not the make, and only three of the six characters on the Georgia license plate. She thought that would probably be enough for the Smythville police and those FBI agents who were still hanging around town if they were interested in following up on it. She thought it was possible that they might not see anything unusual about a man wearing a hat, sunglasses, and a raincoat as he mailed a letter on a sunny day. Eunice knew that she might not either, were it not for the letter's destination. Everyone in town knew about the poems that had been mailed to the *Gazette* recently, and what happened shortly after each letter was received. If this envelope contained a poem, as Eunice suspected, the police might be very interested in chatting with the strangely dressed man.

After watching the car pull from sight, Eunice scanned the empty parking lot and locked the front door. Grasping the slip of paper, she then hurried back to her office and picked up the phone.

Lou Hennessey was meeting in her office with FBI Special Agent Frank Clay, reviewing the frustrating lack of progress on their case, when they were interrupted by a frantic knock on the door. She turned to see Art Schaeffer, his baby-faced cheeks flushed with excitement, standing in the doorway. He looked like a balloon about to burst.

"Chief, I just got a call from Eunice Pemsley at the post office," he said, seeming to be having trouble catching his breath. "She said a strange man was just in there mailing a letter to the *Gazette*. She thinks it could've been Eliot."

Despite her sense of skepticism as to the value of such a lead, particularly when considering that the source was such a cantankerous old busybody, Lou felt a sudden surge of adrenalin. "Why would she think it was Eliot?" she asked, struggling to keep her voice level.

"He came in right at closing time, when there were no other customers around, and he was sort of disguised."

"Disguised?"

"Yes ma'am. Eunice said he had on sunglasses, a baseball cap, and a raincoat with the collar turned up. And she said he was acting funny. Like he was in a hurry to get out of there without being seen."

"Did she see his car?" Frank Clay asked.

"Dark blue sedan. And she got the first number and last two letters of his license plate." Art handed Lou a slip of paper with his notes from the call.

Lou looked at it, then handed it back. "Get on the computer and get me a listing of every car in the state that's a possible match. Sort the owners by county of registration. One of the Georgia Bureau Boys out there can help you if you need it."

"Yes, ma'am." He ran out the door.

"Come on, Frank," Lou said as she strapped on her shoulder holster, and put on her blazer. "Let's go see what our Postmaster has to show us."

"Wouldn't that be Postmistress?" he asked as he rose from his chair.

Lou smiled. "You may be right. Be sure you ask her that when you meet her."

They emerged from her office into a squad room that was suddenly teeming with activity. News of a possible lead had spread quickly, and the atmosphere was electric. Lou walked over to Art Schaeffer, seated in front of a computer with several onlookers gathered around, and put her hand on his shoulder. "Call me the minute you have that list," she said. "Any time within the next half hour will be fine."

The young officer started to laugh it off as a joke, but thought better of it when he saw the look in her eyes. "You'll have it," he said.

Ten minutes later, Lou and Frank were screeching to a halt right in front of the post office door. Eunice Pemsley was standing just inside, clutching an envelope. She eyed the black man suspiciously as she watched them step inside.

"Eunice, this is Special Agent Frank Clay from the FBI," Lou said. "Frank, meet Eunice Pemsley, our Postmaster for—how long, Eunice—forty years?"

"Forty years come July."

"It's a pleasure, ma'am," Frank said with a polite nod.

"What do you have for us, Eunice?" Lou asked.

"It may be nothing, but this man I didn't recognize came in a minute or two before closing time and mailed this letter. As you can see, it's addressed to the *Gazette*."

"You're sure this is the one he mailed?"

"Yep. I had just emptied the bin, so it was all by itself when it dropped through the slot."

"And you told Officer Schaeffer that the man was dressed kind of strangely?"

"Yep, he had a cap pulled down over his face, and he was wearing sunglasses. And he had on this raincoat with the collar turned up, so I couldn't see his hair, his face, nothing. It's been warm and sunny all day, so I thought it kind of peculiar that somebody'd be wearing a raincoat."

"Can you tell us any physical characteristics about the man?" Frank asked. "For instance, was he Caucasian?"

Eunice looked at him for a moment, as if not sure she should answer questions for anyone besides Lou. Then she shook her head slowly. "I don't really know. I didn't see anything but his back as he was walking out. I saw him get into his car, but with the shadows and his collar turned up, I never got a look at his face."

"What about his hands?" Frank asked.

"They were in the pockets of his raincoat until he got out to his car. I never saw them."

Lou extended her hand. "May I have the letter?"

Eunice suddenly had a pained look on her face, as if she had only now considered the possibility of turning over a piece of mail that had been entrusted to the U S Postal Service. "Oh, I don't know, Chief Hennessey. I really shouldn't without a warrant. Mail tampering is a federal offense."

Lou's face flushed with anger and she took a deep breath. Before she could speak, Frank reached out a gloved hand and grasped the letter, but did not attempt to pull it loose from the woman's bony fingers.

"Miss Pemsley, I'm a federal officer. I have the authority to confiscate U S mail that may be relevant to a criminal case."

Eunice studied him with wary eyes. "Are you sure?"

"Yes, ma'am, quite sure."

She released the envelope and Frank handed it to Lou. "No reason to worry about fingerprints," Lou said, tearing the letter open. "If this is from our guy, he always wears gloves."

Despite her own statement, she gingerly extracted a single sheet of paper from the envelope and handled only its corners as she unfolded it. The typeface was different from the others, but the title and single name at the bottom were enough to make her shudder. "'Sonnet No. 5,'" she said to Frank as she held it up for him to see.

She pulled her cell phone from her coat pocket and unfolded it. "Eunice, where's a fax machine?"

"My office," the old woman said. "Follow me."

Lou punched in a speed-dial number as she and Frank followed Eunice behind the counter and toward the back of the building. She put the phone to her ear and heard it ring twice before being answered.

"English Department," the female voice said.

"This is Lou Hennessey. I need to speak with Dr. Osborne, right away."

He was on the line in a matter of seconds. "Hi, Lou. How's the investigation going?"

"We may have a break," she said quietly. "Give me your fax number, and go stand by the machine. I'm sending you a sonnet."

She punched in the number on Eunice's machine as Drew recited it, and then hit the "Send" button. "Okay, it's on its way. Study it carefully, and call me as soon as you have any observations. I'll call you back immediately."

She disconnected, dialed the police station, and asked for Art Schaeffer. "What do you have for me, Art?" she asked, her voice urgent.

She listened for a moment. "Eighty-seven? Shit!" She glanced at the elderly woman and covered the phone. "Sorry, Eunice." Turning her attention back to Schaeffer, she then asked, "How many in Smythville?"

She listened intently before pulling out a pen and a small spiral notepad. "Give me all three."

She wrote as she listened, and then locked eyes with Frank.

"Okay, Art," she said into the phone, "nice work. Frank and I will check on these three. I want you to follow up on the other four in the county and call me if you turn up anything."

She folded the phone and put it back in her coat pocket.

"Eunice, I can't commend you enough for your observation and your prompt action. I'll be sure to call you and let you know if this leads anywhere."

The Smythville Postmaster started walking back toward the front door. "That's fine, but don't call after nine o'clock. I go to bed early."

When they got to the door, Frank removed the latex glove and extended his hand. "Miss Pemsley, I will take personal responsibility for this piece of mail, and I will send you a certified release form in the morning. Do you want me to do anything else?"

She looked at him as she grasped his hand, an expression of grim determination on her face. "Yes. If my lead allows you to find this Eliot character, please do me a favor."

"Yes, ma'am. What would that be?"

"Shoot the bastard."

It took slightly more than an hour to eliminate two of the three possible license plate matches in Smythville. One car belonged to an elderly woman who said she had not been out all day. A quick check under the hood confirmed that the engine was cold. The second was registered to Lou's insurance agent, but driven by his sixteen-year-old son. It was in the body shop getting the front bumper and grill replaced.

"Second fender-bender that kid's had since he got his license four months ago," the man had said. "Good thing I'm in the insurance business."

The third possible match looked more promising. Lou and Frank had driven by the man's address, an apartment in the Camellia Commons complex, but had not seen the car outside. They had parked and waited for about fifteen minutes before Lou got a message on her radio. The blue sedan had been spotted by one of her patrol cars. It was parked downtown on Audubon Street, just off Main.

Within ten minutes, Lou sat parked across the street, while Frank and three of his agents strolled casually along the sidewalk, strategically positioned so as to allow quick access to the dark blue Buick. It was almost six o'clock, and there was a lot of foot traffic as people were heading home from work or were making a quick stop in one of the downtown stores before they closed.

Lou studied the faces of the people walking by, looking for the man she had met once before. Her pulse quickened every time someone slowed in the vicinity of the blue car, but so far, no one had approached it. She jumped when her cell phone buzzed, and quickly glanced at the number being displayed. It was Drew Osborne.

Keeping her eyes focused on the people outside, she opened her phone. "Hi, it's Lou. I'm in the middle of something, so talk fast."

"Okay," he said. "I've studied this sonnet and compared it to the others, and I've come to the conclusion . . ."

"Wait," she said suddenly, as she saw a man wearing a baseball cap and carrying a paper bag walk out of the hardware store and approach the Oldsmobile. As he reached into his pants pocket for his keys, Frank stepped up beside him and said something. The man looked down for a moment, threw the bag at Frank's face, and turned to run out between the cars of the slow-moving traffic. He appeared to be heading straight for Lou's car, but before he could make it across the street, one of the other FBI agents tackled him from behind. They struggled briefly, but the man gave up the fight the moment he looked up and found himself staring into the barrel of Frank's Walther PPK.

"I have to go," Lou said into the phone, and then dropped it on the passenger seat as she reached for the door handle. She could hear a voice screaming through the phone, and in her hurry to get to the suspect, she almost ignored it. But seeing that the situation that had unfolded right outside her window was under control, she picked the phone back up.

"Lou, listen to me," Drew was shouting. "He's not Eliot! Do you hear me? He's not Eliot!"

It was almost nine o'clock that night when Drew was escorted into Lou's office. He waited until the uniformed officer walked out, and then placed a small, gold box on her desk. "I figured you could use a drink. Since you're on duty, I thought this would be the next best thing."

She looked down at the Godiva chocolates and smiled. Without saying a word, she pulled off the red elastic ribbon, removed the top, and popped a cherry cordial into her mouth. She closed her eyes as she chewed, as if experiencing sheer ecstasy, and let out a long, sensuous sigh.

"Damn," Drew said quietly, "you really do equate that stuff with sex, don't you?"

"It's better," she said. "Chocolate will never break your heart. And it always seems to pick you up a little when you're feeling as low as I feel right now."

"I'm sorry I had to be the bearer of bad news, but it was just too obvious that this sonnet was not written by the same person that wrote the other four. The style was different, the syntax was forced, and the imagery was amateurish by comparison. Eliot may be a psycho, but he's not a bad poet."

"I know," she sighed. "I should've picked up on that myself, but I knew that if there was any possibility at all that the man in the post office had been Eliot, we had to work fast."

"Who is he?"

"Brad Sutton. He's a lawyer, a defense attorney. I met him in court about two years ago when I was a detective, and he was defending a burglary suspect I had collared. Evidently he's an alcoholic, and the booze has just about destroyed his practice, in addition to his marriage."

"What made him decide to try his hand at poetry?"

"He said he found out last week that his wife was having an affair. She moved out a couple of days ago, and said she was filing for divorce. Apparently, Mr. Sutton was planning to kill her."

"And pin it on Eliot?"

"So it seems. He claims he would've never been able to go through with it, but he had just bought some nylon rope, a roll of duct tape, and a hunting knife at the hardware store when we grabbed him."

"In that case, it sounds like you really did prevent a murder. You should feel good about that."

"Yeah, I know." She selected a chocolate covered cashew from the box and held it up to the light, as if inspecting a diamond. "We prevented a potential copycat murder, but the real McCoy is still out there, and he's preparing to strike again."

She put the piece of candy in her mouth and chewed it slowly, then looked at Drew. "He's ready for another kill. I can feel it."

Sonnets

Sonnet No. 5

She flashes her intoxicating smile
She captures hearts and holds them in a cage
Until she can bedevil and beguile
And ransom those hearts for a sinful wage

She tempts the soul with glimpses of her flesh
'Tis her desire to make a weak man yearn
And dream that their two bodies will enmesh
To satiate that evil, lustful burn

But now the time has come to stop her lies
That started in her days of reckless youth
I'll taste her fear and hear her anguished cries
And purify her with the fire of truth

And thus her wretched longings I will quell
Condemning her to feel the flames of hell

                                        Eliot

Chapter 22

Drew was excited when he walked into his eleven o'clock class on Thursday morning. The class was a small one, only eight students, all post-graduates. One, Jennifer Alsop, was a doctoral candidate, and extraordinarily bright. What Drew liked most about this class was that he really did not have to teach it. He would merely show up with a provocative question about a work they had been assigned to read, and they would debate the answer for an hour. Often, he felt that he learned more from these students than they learned from him.

Today, they would be discussing his all-time favorite romantic poem by the undisputed father of the English sonnet, William Shakespeare. Drew considered the opening line of "Sonnet 18"—Shall I compare thee to a summer's day?—to be the ultimate pick-up line. It had certainly worked the night he met Kate. The thought had actually occurred to him on the way to class that Shakespeare's sonnets represented to him what chocolate represented to Lou—the epitome of sensual delight.

He was only about fifteen minutes into the class, the discussion just beginning to get insightful and lively, when there was a tentative knock on the door. Drew turned as the door slowly opened, and his heart sank when he saw Judi. She would never interrupt his class unless it was something terribly important. And these days, terribly important was synonymous with dreadfully wrong.

"Yes, Judi?" he said, his voice polite but concerned.

She walked into the room wearing a nervous smile. "I'm so sorry to interrupt your class," she whispered, as she handed him a pink message slip. The handwritten note confirmed his fears. Call Chief Hennessey—Urgent. It could mean only one thing.

He turned to his students, noticed the expectant looks on their faces, and tried his best to muster a smile. "Sorry, folks, but I have to step out for a bit. Jennifer, can you moderate, or should I say referee, the discussion? If I don't make it back before noon, you all know your assignments for tomorrow."

He grabbed his satchel and hurried out to the hallway with Judi. "How long ago did she call?" he asked, as he walked briskly toward the stairs.

The short, middle-aged woman had to almost run to keep pace with Drew's long, urgent strides. "No more than five minutes ago," she answered breathlessly. "I came right down."

He opened the door to the stairwell, and turned to look at her. "You know what this is about, don't you?"

She swallowed hard. He could tell she was trembling. "Yes."

"Will your husband be home tonight?"

"No, he's in Orlando on business. He'll be back tomorrow."

"Okay, Judi, listen to me. I don't care what your workload is, you're leaving early today. I want you inside your house with all the doors locked before dark. And don't open them back up until tomorrow. Not for anything. Got it?"

She looked at him questioningly. "But haven't all his victims been young, beautiful women?"

He smiled and gently squeezed her shoulder. "Yes, which is precisely why you have to be so careful."

He ran up the stairs two at a time, and was breathing heavily when he picked up the phone in his office. He dialed the police station and identified himself to the gruff-sounding officer who answered. Lou was on the line in a matter of seconds.

"Can you get over here right away?" she asked.

"I can be there in ten minutes."

"Good. We're waiting for you in my office. We got another sonnet, Drew. And there's no doubt about this one. It's real."

It occurred to Drew during the short drive to the police station that he did not know who Lou had been referring to when she said "we're waiting for you in my office." His question was answered when he was escorted in and found her sitting at her desk, surrounded by a half dozen stone-faced people.

"Drew, you know Andrea and Bernie. They just brought me this." She handed him a sheet of paper. It was "Sonnet No. 5."

"This is Special Agent Frank Clay of the FBI," she continued, pointing to a black man Drew remembered being in her office when he had arrived from Atlanta on Saturday.

"Next to Frank is Lieutenant Bill Witherspoon, on loan from the Georgia Bureau of Investigation," she said. Drew nodded at a rugged looking man with short gray hair and a military bearing.

"And I believe you've met Officers Mullins and Schaeffer," she said, with a trace of a smile. "They have more experience with this case than anyone else on my force."

Schaeffer smiled and nodded, but the older Mullins just shot Drew a brief, hard look.

All of the chairs in the room were taken, so Drew utilized the low, metal filing cabinet he had sat on when first arriving back from his Atlanta trip. He immediately began reading the poem. It was only when he had finished that he noticed the room was completely silent. Everyone was staring at him, and he realized they were waiting for his assessment.

He looked at Lou. "This sonnet was definitely written by the same person who wrote the other four. I don't know exactly what it means yet, but it seems to be a continuation of the trend toward increasingly graphic depictions of a violent, probably torturous, death."

Lou nodded quietly, then stood and gestured to the city map on the wall behind her desk. "All four of Eliot's previous murders have been committed the night following delivery of one of his sonnets. If he remains true to form, we can expect him to make another attempt tonight. These red pins mark the location of each crime. You can see that, so far, he's operated within a pretty tight area. We can't necessarily assume that his intended fifth victim lives within this area, but we have only so much manpower, so we're going to focus it within a five-mile radius."

She picked up a black marker pen from her desk and drew a circle on the map, its epicenter at the town square. She then drew lines to divide the circle into three roughly equal sections. Ironically, the result looked like a peace symbol.

She pointed to the left-hand section. "This area will be patrolled by the GBI. Bill, you'll have nine men, including yourself, in five cars, right?"

"Right," he said.

She pointed to the right side. "The eastern section will be patrolled by Frank and his FBI team in four cars. Our goal is to spread out and cover each street as frequently as possible.

"The Smythville police will cover the southern section which, as you can see, includes the college. Jake Crenshaw, head of campus security, is on his way here now. He's canceling all night classes this evening and imposing an eight o'clock curfew. Anyone other than members of his bicycle patrol will be detained and questioned, then escorted to wherever they are supposed to be. Howard, you and Art will be patrolling this area, from Main Street to County Road 501, and I want you to make a drive through the campus on every loop. At least twice an hour. Clear?"

"Clear," Mullins said.

"Our other six cars will cover the rest of this section," Lou said. "The Highway Patrol will have roadblocks on the three main arteries coming into town. There are a lot of back roads, but we have limited resources, so the rest of us will just have to spot-check them as we make our rounds in our assigned areas. Questions?"

Drew looked up from the sheet of paper he continued to study. "Other than trying to make some sense of this poem, what do you want me to do?"

She sat in her chair and rubbed her eyes, obviously still drained from the stakeout and arrest of Brad Sutton the night before. "I'm going to float through all three patrol sections in my car, and I'd like you with me, just in case something occurs that could provide you with more insight into the identity of the intended victim. It'll probably be an all-nighter. Are you up to it?"

Being close to her all night would have ordinarily thrilled him, but the sense of anticipation was more than offset by the dread of what he might be forced to witness before the sun came back up. Still, he knew there was only one acceptable response.

"I'll be here at six."

"Good. Thank you," Lou said quietly, as she turned her chair to again face the map. "We know from unfortunate experience that Eliot is a brutal killer, and we know from the incredible lack of physical evidence left behind that he's shrewd and cunning. But unless he's got built-in radar, I think we have a very good chance of nabbing him tonight." She turned back around to face them. "Any more questions or suggestions?"

The room remained silent.

"Okay," she said. "We've got a lot to put in place before it gets dark. Let's get to work."

The four law enforcement officers stood up and filed out the door, each preparing to meet with his respective team and work out the details of their area of responsibility. Andrea and her boss also stood. "I'll be home all night," Moss said. "Call me if anything develops."

"Sure, Bernie," Lou said. "Thanks for getting the poem over here so quickly."

She looked at Andrea. "This sonnet doesn't seem to describe you, but we can't take any chances. Why don't you spend the night in a cell here? It's not the most comfortable bed you've ever slept in, but it would guarantee your safety."

"Thanks," Andrea said, "but I'll just make sure I get home before dark and that everything is all locked up. I'll be fine."

"You're sure?"

Andrea exhaled heavily. "I'm sure."

They left, and Drew was alone with Lou. As she continued to stare at the map, he studied her face, noting the dark circles beneath bloodshot eyes. "You should get some rest this afternoon," he said. "Like you said, it'll most likely be an all-nighter."

"Too much to do. I'll have plenty of time for sleep once we catch this bastard."

Drew followed her eyes to the map. "It looks like you have a good plan. This town's going to be sealed up tight as a drum. What else can you do?"

She turned to look at him, her expression solemn and resolute. "Whatever I have to. Eliot's already claimed four victims on my watch. I'll be damned if I'll let him take a fifth."

The invading darkness brought a cold, blustery night. Winds from the north blew dark, fat clouds across a ghostly white moon, creating a lunar peek-a-boo game that had the effect of an on-again, off-again nightlight. Barren tree limbs seemed to come alive with each gust, reaching toward the south like the bony fingers of a thousand spectral hands.

By midnight, the town of Smythville had become somberly quiet, like a saddened household trying to sleep the night before a funeral. Over a dozen cars patrolled the deserted streets, and tired, eager eyes scanned the darkness for signs of any peculiarity. There had been a couple of false alarms—a dog making the mistake of cornering a prowling raccoon, and a teen-age boy caught slinking through backyards to rendezvous with his girlfriend. For the most part, the radio frequency to which the roaming night watch was tuned had remained disquietingly silent. The mood inside the cars was a mixture of tense frustration and unadmitted relief.

Drew sat in the passenger seat of Lou's car, his sixth cup of coffee in his left hand, a penlight in his right, and a copy of "Sonnet No. 5" in his lap. He had spent the entire afternoon and most of his evening with Lou trying to decipher the poem's meaning. He had focused most of his attention on the first two quatrains, believing they held the key to the intended victim's identity. But he had been able to come up with only one explanation, and Lou had repeatedly disputed its feasibility.

He read the eight lines once more, and then turned to look at her classic profile silhouetted in the darkness. "Okay, if you persist in denying the existence of any form of prostitution in your fair town, which I still find incredibly hard to believe, tell me who has the reputation of being a 'loose woman.'"

She turned her head in his direction. Her eyes reflected the dim light from the dashboard, seeming to magnify it into uncommon radiance. "Are you still working on the sonnet, or is this pertinent to your personal agenda?"

He smiled. "Unlike you, I occasionally have needs that can't be satisfied by a candy bar, but I'm asking because of the poem."

"Well, we have a few women in town who have been reputed to pursue the pleasures of the flesh," she said. "Most are single, but a couple are married. Brad Sutton's wife, for example. Why?"

"Eliot is obviously describing a flirtatious, seductive woman. And he refers to the 'fire of truth' and the 'flames of hell.' Maybe he's planning to burn some woman's house down, with her in it."

She looked from left to right at the houses on either side of Truman Street. "By the time a neighbor smells smoke or sees flames, and calls the fire department, it would be too late."

"And with the distraction and confusion created by a house fire, it would be easy for Eliot to make his escape."

"But what am I supposed to do?" Lou asked, the anger and frustration clearly evident in her voice. "Go knocking on random doors, waking people up and asking if everything is all right?"

"You obviously can't do that, but you could take some of the randomness out of it if you had someone call the women with, shall we say, blemished reputations. It's a long shot, but better than waiting for the sound of a fire engine's siren."

"I suppose I could have Sarah and a couple of others at the station make a list and start calling. They could say a neighbor reported seeing someone outside, or something like that. And we could send one of the patrol cars to any house in their patrol section where there's no answer. What do you think?"

Drew did not reply. His attention was again focused on the sonnet. "On second thought, I'm not so sure he's describing a promiscuous single woman or a cheating housewife," he said quietly, almost as if talking to himself. "This reference to a 'sinful wage' indicates some type of payment. And the second quatrain speaks of a man 'dreaming' about being with the woman, not actually having it happen. So I don't think this is about a prostitute either."

"Then what do you think it's about?"

"A stripper, maybe. Are there any topless bars around here?"

"In Union County? Are you kidding? I understand the Baptists almost revolted when the people voted to no longer be a dry county ten or twelve years ago. There's no way they'd tolerate a girlie bar. If someone wants that kind of action, they have to drive to Atlanta."

"But a stripper or nude dancer would sure seem to fit this poem."

"Keep looking. It has to be something else. The most risqué thing a man around here can do is guzzle beer and eat greasy food while checking out cleavage at Bert's."

"What?"

"There's a cowboy bar about ten miles south of town. The waitresses wear miniskirts and really low-cut blouses. Since Bert only pays them minimum wage, they try to get the guys drunk and tease them with a view so they'll leave big tips."

Drew's mind was suddenly racing. Booze—"intoxicating smile." Tips—"sinful wage." Cleavage—"glimpses of her flesh." He looked at Lou and, even in the darkness, could see the realization and fear as it registered on her face.

"Shit!" She turned on the flashing blue light, made a screeching U-turn, and raced down Main Street toward County Road 501.

Jesse Kirkpatrick's head was spinning wildly. She felt like she was going to vomit. Her mouth was dry and cottony, and she was having trouble swallowing. It took her a moment to realize there was something in her mouth causing her to gag. She tried to speak, but could not move her tongue. Something was blocking the way, something bulky and scratchy, held in place by a tight knot at the back of her head.

She felt as if she were slowly rising out of a deep, dark well. Her head throbbed, and a lingering, familiar odor permeated her nostrils. It reminded her of high school, of biology class. Of the time they had put a mouse in a jar of cotton and watched as it gradually stopped squirming and went to sleep. They had put the mouse to sleep so they could pin it to a board and cut it open and study its beating heart. And Jesse had gotten sick, just like she felt she was going to do right now.

Regaining her senses enough to realize that she had been gagged, and that if she got sick she would probably choke to death, she fought to control the nausea. The air was cold, and her hair kept blowing across her eyes. She thought she caught a brief glimpse of a white light—the moon, perhaps—but then it seemed to disappear again.

The nauseating spinning sensation continued, but seemed to be slowing a bit. She could make out the tops of trees in the distance, black branches contrasting with ink-blue sky. Occasionally she heard a strange, muffled sound—a song, sounding as if it were coming from far away. And there was someone nearby who kept moving into and out of her field of vision like a dark apparition, putting things at her feet that pricked her bare legs when she moved against them. They felt like tree limbs.

Jesse tried to move her arms, but they were tied to something that was cold and cutting. Every time she flexed her hands she felt sharp, stabbing pains at multiple points from her wrists to her shoulders. Her arms were stretched out to her sides, and she suddenly realized they were bound to strands of barbed wire. She was tied to a fence.

How did I get here? She tried to think back, but all she could remember was leaving work a little after midnight and getting into her car. After that she had a faint memory of that biology lab smell, but nothing else until waking up gagged and tied to a fence in what appeared to be a field. *But why? Why would someone tie me to a barbed wire fence and build a mound of tree limbs around my legs?*

Jesse could hear the song again, louder now, and turned her head in that direction. The dark figure was close, and she could feel something wet and cold splashing on her legs. She tried to speak through the gag, and then her nostrils detected the familiar smell of the liquid as it splashed around and on her. Suddenly she understood.

The posted speed limit on County Road 501 was forty-five miles per hour. Lou was doing nearly twice that as she reached for the radio handset and pushed the button. "Come in, Sarah."

"I read you, Chief," the voice on the radio replied.

"Do you know what time Bert's Roadside Bar & Grill closes?"

"Midnight, except on Saturdays. That is, unless Bert's got one of his after-hours poker games going."

"Call and find out. If you don't get an answer, send Mullins and Schaeffer to his home. Tell them I want them to get a list of Bert's waitresses, and I want every one of them called tonight."

"Got it. You onto something, Chief?"

"Just a hunch at this point, Sarah. But I've got to play it."

Drew spoke. "Ask her if the fire department has received any calls."

"Any fire alarms, Sarah?" she asked. Calls to the fire department also rang at the police station, allowing officers to be dispatched immediately. If the situation sounded serious, the police usually arrived before the fire truck.

"Uh, yeah, funny you should ask," Sarah said. "Just a minute or so ago, George Willowby out on Old Church Road called in. Said it looks like there's a brush fire in a field across from his house. Someone leaving Bert's must've thrown out a cigarette and caught the grass on fire."

"Old Church intersects with 501 about a mile past Bert's, right?"

"Yeah, a mile, maybe two. I don't get out that way very much."

"Is Willowby's place east or west of 501?" Lou asked, mashing even harder on the accelerator now.

"West, he said, about half a mile."

"Call Frank Clay and tell him to meet me out there," Lou said. "And send an ambulance, Sarah. This isn't just a hunch anymore."

Within three minutes, they sped past Bert's on the left. It looked dark, and the parking lot was empty. A minute later, they ignored a four-way stop sign and took a right onto Old Church Road on two wheels.

Almost immediately, Drew could see a faint glow in the distance, ahead and to the right. "There it is," he said. His heart was pounding like a jackhammer.

Lou brought the car to a screeching halt on the side of the road, almost running down a stooped, old man wearing pajamas and a tattered flannel robe. "Are you Mr. Willowby?" she shouted, as she got out of the car and ran to the trunk.

"That's me," he said. "I'm the one who called this in. Is the fire truck coming? If this wind keeps up, these flames could jump the road and set my place to burning."

Lou opened the trunk and pulled out a fire extinguisher. "It's on the way," she said, and then abruptly felt the metal cylinder being pulled from her grasp.

"Give it to me," Drew shouted, and then broke into a run toward the wind-whipped flames.

Lou sprinted after him. The fire looked to be about fifty or sixty yards from the road. Some of the flames were six feet high, as tall, dry pine seedlings and clumps of sawgrass combusted like powder kegs.

She saw Drew twenty yards ahead of her, appearing to jump through a wall of flame in front of a fence. Seconds later, she heard him yell, "Over here!" as the whoosh of the fire extinguisher competed with the crackling sound of the burning field.

When she reached him he was bending over a foam-covered form that was tied to a post, arms spread out on barbed wire—a smoldering crucifixion. Drew had waded through a barrier of burning tree limbs. The cuffs of his pants were smoking but he did not seem to notice. He was untying something from the woman's head. He put his fingers against her throat and turned to Lou.

"She's alive," he said.

"Thank God," she muttered. "We finally saved one."

Chapter 23

T he rain that had darkened the windswept clouds throughout the previous night began to fall in a steady, cold drizzle about an hour before dawn. The fire had long been extinguished, but patches of scorched grass and smoking tree stumps, bathed in the sterile glow of the investigative team's spotlights, lent a surreal quality to the scene. At times, it reminded Drew of old black and white photographs of World War I battlefields. At other times, when the bright yellow rain parkas, such as the one he was wearing, provided the only color in an otherwise gray picture, it looked like a scene from a science fiction movie.

Drew was wet, cold, and bone-achingly tired, and he assumed Lou Hennessey was too. Still, she moved among the other investigators with a quiet air of authority that he knew was not entirely contingent upon her position. She was a female equal in a world dominated by men. An expert one minute, an eager student the next, she never seemed to let her pride stand in the way of getting the job done. She endured every hardship, every discomfort, and every gruesome bit of evidence that everyone else endured. She seemed to Drew the quintessential leader. He certainly knew that he would be willing to follow her anywhere.

To his profound surprise and delight, she walked over to him and slipped her arm through his. "I have a couple of forensics guys heading back to the station. They'll give you a ride to your car. But right now I just need you to stand here a minute and hold me up. It would be bad form for me to collapse from exhaustion in front of all these men."

Drew noticed that she was indeed leaning heavily on him, and he was afraid that if he walked away she would fall to the ground like a mortally wounded soldier. "I'll stay as long as you need me," he said.

"You've already contributed more to this case than I had a right to expect," she said, still resting against him. "That woman's going to live because of your intellect and your brave, decisive actions."

"I'm not just talking about the case," he said quietly.

She stood up straight and released his arm. She looked at him, smiling weakly. "You're tired. Go home and get some rest. I'll call you later and bring you up to date."

Drew was suddenly embarrassed. He felt as clumsy as a lovesick boy on a school playground. "I'm sorry, I shouldn't have said that. It was inappropriate."

She looked into his eyes. Her own eyes seemed to smile, despite their obvious weariness. "Sometimes there's an issue of appropriateness, sometimes one of timing. This is simply a case of the latter."

His mood brightened. "So you're saying it's not a lost cause?"

"Let's just say that poets and cops share a common trait—perseverance."

"But even a poet can only worship from afar for so long. Sooner or later, his urges get the better of him."

She reached into the pocket of her parka, and then placed something in his hand. "That's why God invented chocolate."

A man came trotting toward them. "Chief, Greg and I are heading back to the station now. Is this the gentleman who needs a ride?"

"This is the gentleman who saved that woman's life," she said. "You take him anywhere he wants to go." She turned back to face Drew. "I can't thank you enough. Maybe the mayor will award you some kind of medal, or something."

Sonnets

"No," Drew said, rather abruptly, then smiled and looked down at his feet, feigning sheepishness. "Shucks, ma'am, it warn't nuthin. Just tryin' to help out."

He told her goodbye, and then proceeded across the soggy, smoldering field with the officer, being careful to avoid the numerous stumps and fallen limbs that littered the charred, gray landscape. When he reached the car, he paused to look at what Lou had placed in his hand. He smiled, peeled off the foil, and popped the Hershey's Kiss into his mouth.

By the time Drew got back to his apartment and took a long, hot shower, it was seven o'clock. He thought briefly about canceling his eight o'clock class—he had not had time to prepare for it on Thursday afternoon—but decided he would show up and just ad lib it. He was too keyed up to sleep anyway, so he thought he might as well earn his paycheck.

Fueled by equal measures of caffeine and adrenalin, he got into his car and headed for the campus. His ankles hurt, the result of numerous second degree burns he had noticed for the first time during the course of his shower. There were also blisters on his hands. He did not recall feeling the injuries at the time he sustained them, or during the aftermath as he wandered around the crime scene with Lou. Among her many other attributes, the woman apparently had the power to soothe pain. Drew wondered if she could also heal with the laying on of hands. He decided it would be worth almost any affliction to be the subject of that test.

He managed to muddle through his class with some modicum of purpose, primarily by enticing the students to do most of the talking. At one point, he visualized Celeste Holbrook sitting in the room, smiling prettily as she flirted with her eyes, and found himself hoping that she somehow knew they had stopped her killer from claiming yet another victim. It was little consolation for her loss, but it seemed that finding and stopping Eliot was the only thing he could still do for her.

Judi seemed surprised to see him when he limped into the office a little after nine. His ankles were throbbing now.

"Drew! Oh, my God, have you heard?" she exclaimed. "Eliot tried to kill another woman last night. Tried to burn her alive. At least, that's what a friend of mine just called and said she'd heard. Is it true? Were you working with the police last night? Do we have someone who can identify him?"

Drew stopped at her desk and spoke in a tired whisper. "Yes, it's true he tried to burn someone and, yes, I was there. I don't know much else. Could you do me a big favor and keep my involvement under your hat for the next couple of hours? I haven't had any sleep, and I've got to plan something for my eleven o'clock class. Think you could screen my calls, and guard my door for a while?"

She seemed pleased to have been taken into his confidence. "Sure, Drew. Do you want me to bring you some coffee?"

"Please. Lots of it. And could you also get me some ice?"

He went into his office and closed the door. Judi did her job of keeping the curious at bay, as Drew spent the next hour drinking coffee and holding ice to his blistered ankles while he struggled to devise a compelling debate topic for his graduate students. A little after ten, Judi buzzed him on the intercom.

"Sorry to interrupt, Drew, but I thought you'd want to take this call," she said. "It's Chief Hennessey."

"Thanks, Judi," he said, pushing the flashing button on his phone console. "Hi, Lou, you still wading around in the mud out there?"

"No, thank goodness, I'm back in my office. Soaked to the bone, but at least getting warm again."

"When are you going to get some sleep?"

"I was about to ask you the same thing."

"I have a class in about an hour, then I'm heading home."

"Good." She paused, and Drew could hear her take a deep breath. "Listen, I just want to tell you again how much your help last night meant. Having you figure out that poem was everything I had hoped for, but putting yourself at risk to save that woman from the fire was way beyond the call of duty. It was a very foolhardy thing to do . . . but thank you."

A little embarrassed by the unexpected acclamation, Drew was not quite sure how to respond, so he deftly maneuvered the conversation in a different direction. "Who is she?"

"Jesse Kirkpatrick, a waitress at Bert's."

"What's her condition?"

"Her legs are pretty badly burned, but the doctors think they're salvageable. Needless to say, she was in severe shock. As soon as they can get her stabilized, she'll be airlifted to Emory in Atlanta."

"That's good news."

"Yes, it is. The jury's still out as to whether she'll ever walk again, but at least she's alive. Two things saved her—your heroics, and Eliot's mistake."

"Mistake?"

"Yeah, he tied her up and built the fire on the wrong side of the fence. The south side. The wind was blowing from the north, and actually blew the flames away from her. Eventually, of course, the tree limbs closest to her would've caught fire and those flames would've been fatal in a minute or two. Apparently, you got to her right before that happened."

"Yeah, some of them were starting to burn when I first reached her."

"Well, if the fire had been built on the other side of that fence, there wouldn't have been enough of her left to identify. Like I said, she got lucky."

Drew sighed wearily. "I guess. It's not exactly the kind of luck I'd want to have, but I suppose it's better than being dead. How do you think he got her there?"

"Her car."

"How do you know that?"

"The FBI found it in Bert's parking lot. The back door on the passenger side had been jimmied open, and there was a chloroform-soaked rag left on the floorboard. Apparently, Eliot was hidden in the back seat when Miss Kirkpatrick left work. He put her out with chloroform, and then drove her car to the field."

Drew was silent for a moment, trying to arrange the jumbled memories of the distressful night into chronological sequence. "But wait a minute, Lou, we didn't see any cars in Bert's parking lot when we drove by. I remember looking."

"I know. It looks like Eliot could have been nearby when we arrived. Maybe watching us from further down the road. My theory is that when he saw it was safe, he drove back to Bert's, parked the car, and then walked back to some nearby spot where he had his own car hidden. If we can find that spot, maybe we can get some tire tread prints, but with all the rain we had this morning, that's doubtful."

"He sure does a thorough job of covering his tracks, doesn't he?"

"No doubt about that," she said. "He's very smart, and obviously very meticulous with his planning. But now we know that he's capable of making mistakes, which means we'll catch him. God only knows when, or how many more lives he'll claim first, but we'll catch him."

"Do you think Miss Kirkpatrick saw his face? Maybe she can describe him."

"That would be a huge break, but I'm not hopeful. One of Frank's FBI agents is at the hospital, and will accompany her to Atlanta. He'll speak with her as soon as the doctors okay it, but I was told that, so far, she's only mumbled two words—'black' and 'fire.'"

"No question about what she meant with the second word. What do you think she meant by 'black?'"

"I don't know. It could just be her memory of waking up in a totally dark field, or it could be that Eliot was dressed in black. We'll just have to wait until someone can ask her."

"You'll keep me posted, won't you? I'll be home all weekend."

"Are you kidding me?" she asked in a wearily cheerful voice.

He could picture her smiling, with her left cheek dimpling. "You're my number one case advisor. I have to keep you informed, because I never know when I'll need your services again."

He laughed. "I never thought of myself as a crimebuster, but I stand ready to provide my expert assistance on a moment's notice."

"Don't downplay your importance to this investigation, Drew," she said, her voice serious again. "We have a slim chance of learning something about Eliot's identity, thanks to you."

"I'm not fishing for praise, Lou. I just want this bastard to be caught."

"Well, you'd better get used to it," she said. "It's all over town that you saved Jesse Kirkpatrick. Andrea Warren and a *Gazette* photographer arrived at the field just as I was leaving, and she said that you'll be the headline story in tomorrow's edition."

"Oh, great."

"Hey, what are you complaining about?" Lou said. "It's better being a hero than a suspect, isn't it?"

When Drew walked out of his office to head downstairs for his class, Charles Alexander and Dr. Ainsworthy were standing by Judi's desk. Although trying to appear nonchalant, they obviously had been waiting for him to come out.

"Ah, the reluctant hero emerges from his solitary refuge," Charles said with dramatic flair.

"Congratulations, Drew," the department chairman added. "You're the talk of the town."

"That's for sure," Judi said, nodding vigorously. "Andrea Warren from the *Gazette* and people from both local radio stations called requesting interviews."

"Tell Andrea I'll give her a call around noon," Drew said. "Then I'm going home to get some sleep."

"What about the radio stations?"

"If they call back, tell them I won't discuss any details about last night until I get clearance from Chief Hennessey. At this point, I don't know what's public knowledge and what's classified police evidence."

He glanced at his watch. "Uh-oh, I'm late for my class. See you folks later."

Charles followed him outside. "Seems like you had quite a night."

"I've certainly had better."

"Well, I'm sure it was unpleasant, but you've undoubtedly earned the respect and gratitude of every resident of Smythville. Except one, of course."

"Oh? And who would that be?"

"Eliot. In fact, I'd imagine he's quite pissed."

Chapter 24

T he ringing of the telephone woke Drew from a sound sleep. Eyes still closed, he groped for the lamp switch, but then opened his eyes and realized that the room was not dark. It was morning. He glanced at his bedside clock, which read eight thirty, and reached for the phone.

"Hello?" he said in a froggy voice.

"Sounds like I woke you. I'm sorry." It was Lou.

"No . . . well, yes, but it's okay. I've been asleep over twelve hours. What about you? Did you get finally get a decent night's sleep?"

"Yeah, not quite twelve hours, but enough to keep me going."

Drew lay back on his pillow and tried to wipe the sleep from his eyes. "So, what's up?"

"I'm leaving for Atlanta in a few minutes. Jesse Kirkpatrick is conscious and alert enough to talk. Frank Clay and I are driving down to question her."

"That's great! Maybe you'll be able to get a description of Eliot."

"I doubt it. One of Frank's agents is over there and spoke with her briefly this morning. It appears she never saw his face. Still, we're hoping to learn something useful."

"Is there anything I can do?"

"That's why I called. I'd like to fill you in with whatever we find out when I get back this evening. With your insight into the mind of a poet, maybe something she tells us will click with you. Maybe you'll be able to provide us with something else to look for."

"Sure. What time?"

"How about dinner?"

Drew sat up in bed. "Why Chief Hennessey, are you asking me on a date?"

She laughed. "I don't date fellow caseworkers."

"I'll resign."

"Not until I catch Eliot, you won't. So this dinner will be strictly business, compliments of the city."

"In that case, let's go somewhere expensive."

"That's probably not a good idea."

"Why? Is the city on a tight budget these days?"

"The city is always on a tight budget, but that's not the reason. As a result of all the town gossip, bolstered by today's headlines in the *Gazette*, you and I are Smythville's number one topic of conversation. I stopped at Starbucks for coffee this morning and was almost mobbed."

"So, what do you suggest? Disguises?"

She laughed again. "No, I was thinking I could pick up some takeout and meet you at your place. Do you like Chinese?"

"Do you?"

"Adore it."

"What a coincidence. Me too. What time should I expect you?"

"Let's say around seven. I'll call if it looks like I'll be much later than that."

"Sounds good. See you then. Good luck in Atlanta."

"Thanks. Bye."

He hung up the phone and bolted out of bed. He had a lot to get done. He would need to do the shopping for wine and a dessert, and his apartment could use a thorough cleaning. A clean shirt might also be a good idea, he thought, eyeing the huge pile of dirty laundry on the floor by his closet.

He hurried into the bathroom and turned on the shower. He suddenly felt well rested and refreshed, and he had pretty much forgotten the pain in his swollen ankles. That changed the moment he stepped under the hot water.

His doorbell rang at 6:59. Drew decided that he would have to add promptness to Lou's seemingly endless list of attributes.

He limped to the door on bare feet. He did not have a pair of shoes into which his swollen feet would fit comfortably. Even socks hurt.

He opened the door. She stood there smiling, her one dimple sexily creasing her left cheek. She was holding what appeared to be enough food for half a dozen people. "I didn't know if you preferred Szechuan or Cantonese, so I got both," she said.

"Good choice," he said, then craned his neck and peered out into the hallway. "Just you this time?"

"You're never going to let me live that down, are you?"

"No, it's just that, with all this food, I figured you must have brought Starsky and Hutch with you again."

"Their names are Mullins and Schaeffer, and they're only a phone call away if I decide I need them."

He smiled and stepped aside, extending his arm in a gesture of welcome. "I don't think that will be necessary. I'm in a law abiding mood tonight."

She walked in and handed him the aromatic bags of food. Noticing his bare feet, she smiled again. "Are you always so Bohemian, or did I arrive before you could finish getting dressed?"

He looked down at his feet and wiggled his toes. "Fits the image of a poet and academic, don't you think?"

Despite his attempt to conceal it, she noticed his limp when he carried the food into the kitchen. "What's wrong with your feet?" she asked, her smile gone.

"Oh, nothing really. Just a little blistered around the ankles."

"Let me see."

"It's no big deal. Since we're eating in, I decided I'd give them a rest from shoes."

This time, her tone left no room for debate. "Let me see."

He limped back to the dining area and pulled out a chair. She knelt in front of him and gingerly lifted the cuff of his pants.

His ankles had the look of roasted chicken.

"Dammit, Drew, these are second degree burns! Have you seen a doctor?"

"No, but I put some Neosporin on them."

"These burns should be covered. Do you have some sterile gauze?"

"I don't think so."

She stood and headed for the door. "Don't move. I have a first aid kit in the car. I'll be back in a minute."

She returned with a large metal case that appeared to contain the medical supplies for virtually any kind of trauma a police officer might encounter, from gunshot wounds to automobile crashes. She gingerly swabbed his burned skin with antiseptic, applied a soothing analgesic cream, and loosely wrapped the area with gauze.

"You need to keep the area moist with antiseptic. Neosporin is fine. Some of these blisters are open, so keep fresh gauze on here to protect the area from dirt, as well as from being irritated by your pant cuffs."

When she finished, she readjusted his pants legs and fixed Drew with a stern look. "That'll hold you until you can see a doctor at the hospital. Tomorrow. Capisce?"

"I didn't know you were Italian. Hennessey sounds Irish."

"My maiden name was Andretti," she said, standing.

"As in Mario Andretti, the race car driver?"

"He's out there on the family tree somewhere, along with quite a few lesser known Andrettis who, like me, take it personally when their instructions aren't followed."

Drew raised both hands in a gesture of surrender. "I get the picture. I'll go to the doctor tomorrow. And speaking of burns, what's the latest with Jesse Kirkpatrick? How bad are her legs?"

"Better than originally thought. She'll need skin grafts, but the doctors think she'll regain full use of both legs."

"That's terrific. What else did you find out?"

She cocked her head to the side and smiled. "Would it be rude of me to ask if we can talk while we eat? I skipped lunch and I'm famished."

"Sure," Drew said, standing up gingerly. "The table's set. I'll get the food and pour us some wine."

"Uh, no wine for me. One glass and I get real mellow; two and I'm ready for bed. I could get called back to the station at any time. You go ahead though."

"Okay, if you're sure you don't mind. By the way, if I have two glasses, will you tuck me in later?"

She did not respond, but Drew caught her smiling as he brought the food back out from the kitchen.

Over dinner, Lou brought him up to date on the status of the investigation, as well as her discussion with Jesse Kirkpatrick. The woman had been unable to remember much more than getting into her car, and then waking up tied to the fence as tree limbs were being piled around her. She had been woozy and nauseous from the chloroform, but remembered seeing a tall figure dressed in black, moving in and out of her field of vision. She had never been able to see the face, and thought he may have been wearing a ski mask or some type of hood. She had watched the figure moving around, and had tried to scream at it, to plead for mercy, when she realized she had been doused with gasoline. Once the match was thrown, she had no more recollection of the dark figure, only of the terror and the pain as the flames burned closer and closer. Mercifully, she had then passed out, and had not fully regained consciousness until she was being airlifted to Emory.

"That's it? She couldn't remember anything else?"

"She's not sure, having been so woozy from the chloroform, but she thinks she remembers hearing a song."

Drew put down his fork and stared across the table. "A song? Eliot was singing?"

"No, she said it sounded muffled, like it was coming from far away."

"A car radio, perhaps?"

"Maybe. The car was left near the road, so the distance and the sound of the wind would've made it seem muffled, I guess. We're still mulling that over."

"Then what do we know that we didn't know before, except that he's tall, dresses in black, and listens to music?" Drew smiled. "Why don't you just drive over to Nashville and arrest some Johnny Cash impersonator, and we'll be done?"

"Ha, ha, very funny." Lou leaned back in her chair. "What we do know now is that his victims, except for all being young and attractive, don't seem to be connected in any way."

"Had you thought they were?"

"We had considered the possibility of a connection. Margaret Fenwyck worked with Melissa Turner, who had met Celeste Holbrook, and all three had worked out at Jackie's gym. But Miss Kirkpatrick didn't recall ever meeting any of them. She had seen Margaret and Melissa's names alongside newspaper articles they'd written, and knew Jackie Phelps when she saw her, but didn't know any of them personally. And she'd never even heard of Celeste until she read about her murder in the *Gazette*."

"Speaking of the *Gazette*, I bought a copy when I was out today. Andrea did a good job of relating the facts as I told them to her yesterday afternoon, but the article still had a bit of a comic book hero feel to it."

Lou sighed and shook her head. "I think the whole town is so elated to see us win one against Eliot that they're forgetting he's still out there, and that next time we may not be so lucky. They're desperate for the sense of protection that a couple of heroes, real or otherwise, can provide. I think Andrea was just playing to that."

She pushed her chair back from the table and reached for her purse. "Where's your bathroom? I need to powder my nose."

Drew smiled. "Your nose looks fine."

She folded her arms across her chest and glared at him playfully. "And I have to pee."

"In that case, around the corner to the right."

By the time she returned, Drew had cleared the table. "Have a seat in the living room," he said. "We'll have dessert in there."

"Let me help you," she said. "It hurts me to watch you walk."

"Okay. You can take this and put it on the coffee table." He handed her a platter of sliced fresh fruit—apples, bananas, pineapple and strawberries.

"Wow," she said, bestowing an admiring smile. "You're quite the little homemaker, aren't you? And so health conscious."

"That's me, all right," he said. He followed her into the living room where a fondue pot filled with rich, dark chocolate was simmering over a burning can of Sterno.

She placed the fruit platter on the table, and then sat on the floor. Her eyes reflected her approval. "He writes poetry, chases criminals and feeds me chocolate. The man is definitely a hero."

"Just trying to impress you with my romantic side."

"Do you really want to do something romantic?" Her eyes seemed to catch and magnify the light from the fire beneath the fondue pot.

"Of course. What do you have in mind?"

She handed him his book of sonnets from the corner of the coffee table. "Read to me while I eat."

He was surprised, and felt more than a little ill at ease.

"You like poetry?"

"I like yours. Read the last one."

"Mourning Light."

"Yes, it's my favorite."

"When have you read it?"

"I bought a copy of the book right after I met you." She smiled. "Of course, at the time I was simply collecting evidence on a suspect."

"Thank God we've gotten past that." He sat on the sofa on the opposite side of the coffee table, and opened the book to the last page. As Lou slowly stirred the bubbling chocolate with a strawberry on the end of a long fork, he began to read.

"On starlit nights she hastens to my side
Her long, blond tresses, sparkling and fine
I hold my breath and open my heart wide
And wait to feel her supple lips on mine

Her kisses take me back to days of joy
To nights of passion, wild and full of fire
To when the whole world seemed our private toy
And life was simply fuel for our desire

She takes me to a place of pure delight
A place not spoiled by daylight's heartless glare
A place where I escape, for just a night,
The cold, hard truth my heart can hardly bear

On wings of dreams her memories are borne
To soothe my soul 'til I awake to mourn"

When he looked up, she was staring at him, the chocolate-covered strawberry poised an inch from her mouth. "That is so beautiful. It's haunting."

"Thank you. That's what I was going for."

"Tell me about her."

Drew took a deep breath, and the pain that stabbed his heart seemed as sharp as that day on the beach in Cancun. "Her name was Kate. She was a stockbroker, one of those tough-as-nails wheeler-dealers who also happened to have a love of poetry. She was a graduate of NYU, where I taught, and I met her at an alumni fundraiser where I read a couple of my sonnets that had been published in a magazine. She introduced herself, I fell head-over-heels in love and, after putting into play every romantic notion in my arsenal, finally got her to love me too."

"And she died."

Drew swallowed hard, and his mind began to replay the movie-frame images of that fateful day as he continued his story. "We were on vacation in Cancun. We went swimming. She loved the water, and was a very strong swimmer. She had been on the women's swim team at NYU. Anyway, for some reason we paid no attention to the red flags on the beach. They signified hazardous conditions, in this case a strong undercurrent."

"A riptide?"

"Yes. After we'd been out there a while, she challenged me to a race back to shore. She gave me a head start." He paused to smile. "She always had to spot me a few yards because she was so much faster. But when I made it to the shore, she wasn't there. The next time I saw her was that night, when I had to go to the morgue to identify . . ."

He did not think he could finish the sentence without his voice breaking, so he left the words unspoken. As a child, he had believed that if you left bad things unsaid, they would not come true. As he grew up, discovering that was not the case had been one of his harshest lessons in reality.

"Does Kate visit your dreams, like in the poem?" Lou asked. Her voice was soft and caring.

"At first she did. That was the inspiration for the poem. It got to the point where I hated the daytime with all its reminders of the fact that she was gone. I would look forward to going to bed at night, hoping I would dream of her, hoping to experience the sensation of holding her again. But, at about the time that I moved here, the dreams changed."

"Changed? How?"

"She began to haunt me. Instead of reliving our intimate times, our happy times, I keep reliving the day she died. Every horrid detail. It's like she had a change of heart, deciding she would no longer comfort me. She tortures me now, as if she blames me for her death."

"Drew, it was an accident. What makes you think she's blaming you?" Lou seemed to have lost interest in the chocolate. She put the fork on her plate. "Do you have these dreams often?"

"Often enough."

"I'm sorry. You must have really loved her."

"I did. I still do. But she's gone, and I have to get on with my life." He popped a slice of apple, sans chocolate, into his mouth and chewed slowly, contemplatively. "So, what's your story?"

"My story?"

"Yeah, how did you come to trade your Italian name for an Irish one?"

"Oh, that one," she said. "Not too dissimilar from your story, I guess, except it was the love that died, not the partner."

"You fell out of love with the guy?"

"Actually, he fell out of love with me."

"I find that very hard to believe."

"Believe it," she said.

"What happened?"

"I met John when I was getting my masters in criminal psychology at Temple. He was a professor, about ten years older than me, and everything I'd been unable to find in relationships with guys my own age. Shortly after I got my degree, he was offered the departmental chairmanship here at Smythville College. He asked if I'd come with him, I said yes, and he said a small, private college might frown on a department chairman living in sin. So he asked me to marry him."

She picked up another strawberry and then continued. "Things were good for a while. I did some consulting work for the police department on a serial rapist case, and Chief Bodell liked my work so much he suggested I go to the police academy. He promised to make me a detective when I graduated, which he did. When he announced his retirement a year or so later, Bernie Moss talked me into going for the job. I won the city council's approval, but lost John's."

"He didn't want you to work, or didn't like the high profile you'd achieved?"

"Both, I suppose. Anyway, I worked long hours, the relationship started to deteriorate, and John was offered a higher paying position at the University of Oklahoma. He accepted without even discussing it with me, moved to Oklahoma, and sent me the divorce papers in the mail."

"He was probably just jealous of your celebrity status in town."

"Maybe. Because he was older, he had always seemed to be the one in charge, and I was so dependent upon him. I guess he saw that had changed."

Drew smiled. "Did I ever mention that I am totally lacking the capacity for jealousy? I think it's a genetic thing."

She laughed. "No, I think I would've remembered that."

They were interrupted by a muted buzz coming from Lou's coat pocket. "Hold on a minute," she said, extracting and opening the small phone. "Hennessey here."

She listened for a few seconds, locking eyes with Drew. "I'll be right there." She closed the phone and stood.

"I hate to eat and run, but I have to go to the station. Frank said they have a partial tire tread print that could possibly be from Eliot's car. We'll have to track down sales of that particular tire. I'll let you know if it leads to anything."

He rose to his feet and limped toward her. "What am I supposed to do with all this leftover food?"

"You can do whatever you want with the Chinese food, but if you throw out this chocolate I'll arrest you."

He smiled as he opened the door for her. "I'll save it for you." They simply stared at one another for a moment. An awkward moment, but a pleasant one.

"I'd better get going." She turned to leave. "Maybe this clue will lead us somewhere. God knows none of the others have."

"I hope so," he said. "Good night. And good luck."

After taking a few steps down the hall, she paused, turned back to him, and smiled. "Sweet dreams," she said softly, and then disappeared around the corner.

Chapter 25

Drew was amazed at how much the mood of an entire populace could change in the course of a weekend. The town that had seemed under siege just a few days earlier now projected an aura of liberation, as if the evil force that had held the people hostage was vanquished, not just temporarily at bay. The sense of optimism created by the headlines in the Saturday *Gazette* was further fueled by Sunday's headline—"Heroes Capitalize on Eliot's Mistake." The "heroes," of course, were himself and Lou, yet Drew realized that their success in saving Jesse Kirkpatrick from a fiery death had more to do with luck than with heroism. He knew that, and Lou knew that. And so, he had to assume, did Eliot.

Not having a personal physician in Smythville, and knowing that even if he did, he would never be able to schedule an office visit on a Sunday, he had followed Lou's orders and gone to the Smythville General emergency room to have his burns checked. The receptionist behind the desk had treated him with typical hospital indifference until he handed back the clipboard with his medical history and insurance information. Her eyes going wide when she saw his name, she had ushered him past a man with a sprained back and a little boy with a broken arm, and the nurses and attending physician had treated him as if he were the President. They would not even let him pay for his care or medication, despite his protestations that the costs would be covered by his medical insurance. It occurred to him how fickle public opinion could be. A week earlier, these same people had probably wanted him arrested.

The next illustration of his newfound celebrity status came on Monday morning when he walked into his eight o'clock class. On the previous Friday, when he had been emotionally and physically exhausted, had no lesson plan, and would have gladly welcomed any diversion, the students had been as quiet as a roomful of deaf-mutes until he literally dragged them into a discussion. Today, they all rose as one, clapping and cheering loudly the moment he entered the hall. The standing ovation lasted nearly a full minute, an embarrassingly long time for Drew who knew nothing else to do but smile and wave.

When the students finally quieted down and took their seats, Drew stepped to the podium, a big grin on his face. "Gee, I knew you would enjoy your weekend reading assignment, but I never expected a response quite this favorable."

Again, they stood in unison. This time, laughter mixed with the cheers and applause, and the ovation lasted nearly as long as the first one. His carefully constructed lesson plan never made it out of his satchel, but he did not care. These students had been mentally disengaged since Celeste Holbrook's murder. This morning, they had cause to return from their self-imposed emotional exile, and Drew was happy to provide that reason. He entertained their questions, and accepted their accolades for nearly a full hour, saving just enough time to give them another reading assignment before dismissing the class a few minutes before nine.

He received essentially the same treatment everywhere he went. Dr. Ainsworthy called a special staff meeting to officially congratulate and thank him, and Drew received a phone call and a letter of commendation from Dean Morrison. His graduate class also got in on the act, saluting him with a hilarious yet ardent parody of "The Charge of the Light Brigade."

But perhaps the single most telling example of the change in public sentiment was what he saw when he went out to run some errands at noon. As he was passing by the arboretum, he noticed that the spray painted graffiti he had seen the week before had been edited. The message beneath Pattianne Smyth's commemorative plaque now seemed to reflect the new conventional wisdom on campus and around town. Drew could not help but smile when he read the bold, red words—"Eliot Sucks."

Andrea needed a break. She had been on the job almost constantly since Friday morning, including both days of the weekend, overseeing the Jesse Kirkpatrick story. The *Gazette's* coverage had been compelling, and had sold every copy printed, yet Andrea felt that the line between news journalism and public relations had become a bit blurred. Bernie Moss wanted the most positive spin possible on the story, and Andrea believed that his directive had as much to do with vindicating his choice of chief of police as it did with calming the public's fears.

Right now, she just wanted some fresh air and a change of scenery. She had brought a sandwich for lunch, anticipating another twelve straight hours at her desk, but decided she would go out during lunch to run some overdue errands, and would eat in the car. At a quarter past noon, she grabbed her sandwich and her purse and slipped out the door before anyone could notice.

She walked around the corner to the parking lot. Succumbing to the insistence of Bernie and Lou, she now drove to the office every day, even when, like today, the weather was nice. She missed the brisk four-block walks from her apartment to the *Gazette* in the mornings. They had always provided just enough exercise to clear her head and get her energized. She had to admit to herself that at the end of a long day, when it was cold and dark, she appreciated having the car there. The disturbing incident during her walk home a couple of weeks earlier was still fresh in her mind.

Her car was dirty. After inspecting some of the grime on the hood and top, she unlocked the door, climbed behind the wheel, and eased into the flow of midday traffic on Main. After dropping off some dry cleaning, she filled her car with gas, bought a bottle of Evian water to wash down her sandwich, and drove to the south end of town where she pulled into the Jiffy Job Car Wash and Detailing Center. It was the only car wash in town where the work was done by real people instead of a drive-through machine, and Andrea had a few areas that required some of the special attention that a five-dollar tip would ensure. After paying for a deluxe wash and telling the two teenage boys what she needed and what would be the tip for a satisfactory job, she sat on a concrete bench in the sunshine to eat her lunch while she watched the two youngsters eagerly attack her filthy car.

She had only been there a few minutes when, suddenly finding herself sitting in a shadow, she looked up to see it was being cast by the towering figure of Charles Alexander. "Mind if I join you?" he asked, a big grin on his face.

"Hello, Charles. Sure, have a seat."

He nodded in the direction of the two boys vigorously scrubbing her car with large, soapy sponges. "Looks like you're getting the works."

"It was long overdue. Plus, I like to get a good coat of wax on it before winter sets in."

Charles sat beside her, leaning forward and resting his arms on his knees. "I guess you've been pretty busy these last few days. I see your name on all the stories about the latest murder attempt. Seems like Eliot gets more coverage when he fails than when he's successful."

She was not looking at him. Her eyes remained fixed on the activity around her car. "Well, that's what the people want to read about."

He was silent for a moment, also watching the working boys, and then turned his head to look at her. "You seem distracted, preoccupied. Is something wrong?"

"No. Like you said, I've just been real busy. I'm a little tired,

I guess."

"You need a break from work once in a while, you know. How about dinner one night this week? This time, I'll take you somewhere a little more upscale."

She turned her face toward him and looked into his eyes. "You realize that Jesse Kirkpatrick, the woman Eliot tried to burn to death, was our waitress last week, don't you?"

"Was she really? All the waitresses out at Bert's are pretty much the same, so I guess I missed that." He grinned. "Of course, my eyes were focused on someone else that night."

She didn't respond.

"So?" he asked.

"So what?"

"So, would you like to go to dinner one night this week?"

She turned her head back to stare in the direction of her car. "Thanks, but I don't think so. I'm really tied up at work. If I get a chance to leave the office at a decent time, I need to just go home and get caught up on my rest."

Charles' disappointment registered on his face and in his voice. "Okay. Maybe some other time?"

"Sure. Some other time."

The ensuing silence between them stretched on for about a minute, becoming strained and awkward. It was finally broken by Charles, who appeared to be the only one interested in conversation. "Are you planning any more interviews with our two local heroes?"

"I don't know. Like everyone else at the *Gazette*, I do what Moss tells me. If he wants more interviews, I'll do more interviews. Why do you ask?"

"Well, I just can't help thinking that Drew, and Chief Hennessey too, for that matter, have perhaps been placed on a higher pedestal than the circumstances warrant. While it's true they managed to reach that woman before the flames engulfed her, the fact of the matter is that Eliot is still out there, and they are no closer to identifying him than they were before. Am I correct?"

"Yes, I think that's right."

"I mean, if that Kirkpatrick woman had gotten a good look at Eliot, and then their efforts made it possible for her to live to tell about it, the citizens of Smythville would be justified in feeling more secure. As it stands, the score is Eliot four, police one. To me, it looks like he's still in charge."

"You sound like you actually admire Eliot."

Charles raised his eyebrows in a look of incredulous surprise. "Admire a killer? Nothing could be further from the truth." He paused for a moment. "Still, you have to admit he's managed to be remarkably elusive thus far."

"Yeah, well, he's certainly that." She stood. "Listen, I need to point out a couple of things to my guys out here. I'll see you later, Charles."

He seemed a bit disconcerted by her coolness, but said nothing about it. "Okay. Goodbye, Andrea."

As she walked away she recognized his car parked by the side of the building. While not exactly spotless, it did not look particularly dirty either. Certainly not dirty enough, she thought, to justify driving all the way out here when there were less expensive car washes at half a dozen gas stations in town. She turned back to face him. "You getting your car washed too?"

He smiled. "Of course. Why else would I be here?"

She supervised the application of the paste wax on her car, inspected the finished work, and surprised the two boys by tipping them two dollars more than she had originally promised. Their faces beamed as brightly as her freshly polished car as they repeatedly expressed their appreciation.

As she turned onto the road and headed back toward town, she saw that Charles had pulled his car up to the spot previously occupied by hers. He was chatting with the two boys, but noticed her looking back in his direction. He waved as she drove away.

Chapter 26

Select Screen Name: Eliot
Enter Password: Sonnets
Send Instant Message To: Melpomene

Eliot: This time they've gone too far!

Melpomene: What do you mean?

Eliot: The fools are saying that since the whore survived,
my sonnet was untrue. Are they really so blind?

Melpomene: How can you expect them to understand? Let
them worship at the altar of false hope—it will serve our
purposes well.

Eliot: Still, it galls me to have them think I made a mistake. Had I built the fire and tied the slut on the other
side of the fence, the flames would have killed her in a
matter of seconds. I wanted it to be slow, to give her
time to reflect on her corruption, her worthlessness.

Melpomene: They need to believe they are capable of out-
smarting you. They need to believe in your fallibility.

Eliot: I know. But to say her sonnet didn't come true like my others is absurd. It actually achieved a level of truth that transcends my original intentions.

Melpomene: Of course. Not only did she feel the fire that night, but by living she is condemned to feel it for all her days. Even when the pain has diminished she will see the scars—and she will remember.

Eliot: But there's still the insult to my work.

Melpomene: Yes, you cannot let that go unpunished.

Eliot: Especially the bitch who perpetuates this illusion of my fallibility.

Melpomene: Actually, I think she's created the perfect stage for your next sonnet. What could be more poignant than shattering the fragile faith of the people by destroying the false prophet who created it?

Eliot: She will pay a high price for her sins against me.

Melpomene: Her fate should befit an apostle of lies.

Eliot: Yes, I know what I will do to her.

Melpomene: But first you must write it. First the sonnet, then its realization. That is the way it must be.

Eliot: But the writing has become so hard—tedious.

Melpomene: Concentrate. Think of what you want your poem

to say.

Eliot: I want to speak of my need for vengeance.

Melpomene: Then speak. You are an artist, and words are your paints.

Eliot: The taste of sweet revenge will . . . .

Melpomene: Will what? What will the revenge do? What will it taste like?

Eliot: I don't know. I can't find the words.

Melpomene: Try.

Eliot: The taste of sweet revenge will . . . I can't! Where are the words? I can't find the words!

Melpomene: Calm yourself. I will help you.

Eliot: What if I can't write anymore? What if I can't continue my work?

Melpomene: You'll be able to continue as long as you listen to me. As long as you do as I say.

Eliot: I will, I promise. Just help me, please.

Melpomene: That is why I'm here—to help you. That is why I'll always be here.

Eliot: I know.

Melpomene: Don't be afraid. I'll take care of you.

Eliot: I love you, Mother.

Chapter 27

Lou spent Wednesday afternoon huddled in her office with Frank Clay, Bill Witherspoon, and Howard Mullins, but neither the FBI, the GBI, nor her own police force had developed any substantive leads on the Jesse Kirkpatrick case. They had been able to get enough of a pattern from the partial tire tread print found in a clearing near Bert's to narrow it down to one of two Goodyear models. Unfortunately, they were Goodyear's two top-selling tires, and came standard on a wide variety of American-made cars. Identification of a specific vehicle was highly unlikely.

They had interviewed everyone who worked at Bert's, and many of the restaurant's regular customers, but no one seemed to have noticed anyone acting strangely or showing up with unusual frequency over the past couple of weeks. If Drew had been correct in his assertion that Eliot conducted "research" on his victims before writing about and killing them, he had done so with considerable discretion.

The "research" aspect was beginning to weigh heavily on Lou's mind. Eliot's ability to carry out so many carefully planned, almost flawless murders in such a short period of time made sense if he were systematically sequencing his victims, and learning about one as he finalized his lethal plans for another. That theory lent special significance to Andrea Warren's incident two weeks earlier. Lou knew that if Eliot had Andrea in the queue, her number could be coming up soon. Maybe within days.

Her concerns about Andrea were raised to a new level around six thirty when Sarah stuck her head in the door. "Bernard Moss on line four, Chief. He said it's urgent."

Lou picked up the phone and pushed the button for line four. "What's up, Bernie?"

"This may be nothing, but I'm not taking any chances," Moss said. "Andrea left a little before six. Said she had to run a few errands on the way home. She just came running back in here a couple of minutes ago, scared out of her wits. She thinks a car was following her."

Lou was rising from her chair as she spoke. "Keep her there, Bernie. I'm on my way."

Ten minutes later, Lou was parking in front of the *Gazette* office. She tried to open the door but it was locked, which was customary once business hours ended at five thirty. Under ordinary circumstances, the only people in the building past six were the operators of the printing presses in the basement, and they had their own entrance from the alley in the back.

She pushed the buzzer. The door was opened a few seconds later by Moss, exuding his usual charm. "Get in here quickly. If you don't make an arrest soon, I can't afford to be seen with you."

"Et tu, Brute?"

"Well, what do you expect, Lou?" he growled, as he led her through the deserted pressroom to his office. "You know how short the half-life of public support is. They're only interested in what you've done for them lately. At the rate Eliot's been working, we can expect another sonnet any day now. And the people in this town know that."

Sonnets

"Tell me something I don't already know," she said, as they entered his office, and Moss wedged his massive frame into the worn leather chair behind his desk. There was no one else in the room.

"Where's Andrea?"

"Ladies room. She wanted to splash some water on her face and try to get her nerves back under control." He paused a moment before speaking in a hushed tone. "Do you think it really could've been him?"

"Possibly," Lou said, also speaking low. "Andrea's had a lot of exposure in the newspaper recently. Her name's been on almost every article about Eliot. If he loves to read about himself as much as I think he does, Andrea's probably been on his mind."

Moss sighed, which actually sounded more like a low growl. "So you think he could have her picked out to be his next victim?"

"I think we'd better have a plan ready, just in case."

"Just in case what?" Andrea asked from the doorway. Her eyes were glistening, as if she'd been crying, and her normally firm chin seemed to have a slight quiver. Her eyes were not focused on the two people in the room, but downward toward the floor, as if she were more embarrassed than frightened.

"Are you okay, Andrea?" Lou asked.

"Yeah, I'm all right. In fact, the more I think about it, the more I'm convinced it was just my imagination playing tricks on me again."

"Before we come to that conclusion, why don't you tell me what happened?" Lou said.

They both sat in chairs opposite Moss' desk. Andrea took a deep breath and exhaled slowly. "I left here about a quarter to six. When I pulled out of the parking lot, a car pulled out behind me. I didn't think anything about it until I turned into the parking lot of the cleaners to pick up some things, and it pulled in there too. It parked way over by the bowling alley, in kind of a poorly lit area. I noticed it parking

227

there, but still didn't think it was anything unusual. But when I came back out of the cleaners and started to drive away, its lights came on and it pulled onto Main going in the same direction I was headed."

"What kind of car was it?" Lou asked.

"I really didn't get a good look at it. It's hard to tell much when you're staring into headlights, you know? But it was a mid-sized car, and it was a dark color. That's all I was able to tell."

"Then what happened?"

"I headed home. I was going the back way instead of coming all the way up to Audubon on Main. I turned onto Claridge, followed it to Truman, and turned right. Those same headlights were right behind me the whole time. I was beginning to get a little suspicious, so I didn't turn onto Audubon and into my driveway. I kept going, zigzagging through the neighborhood, and that car followed every turn. I got scared about going home, so I came back here."

"Did it follow you here?"

"Until I turned into the parking lot. It slowed down, but kept on going. I ran back in here and told Mr. Moss, and he said he'd call you. I didn't really want him to, but he insisted."

"He did the right thing," Lou said. "We can't afford to ignore anything that has even the remotest possibility of being related to Eliot. Do you remember what Drew Osborne said when you told us about that other episode? He thought if it actually was Eliot following you that night, you were safe at the time because he was just doing research. I've become convinced that he does exactly that. It's the only explanation for how he can write such personalized sonnets, and commit his crimes with such frequency. While he's getting his plans together for his next victim, he must be simultaneously learning about two or three more."

"But we don't know for sure that it was Eliot following me either that night or tonight," Andrea said.

"But we also can't be sure that it wasn't," Moss said.

Andrea's eyes danced back and forth between her boss and Lou. "So what are you saying?"

"What we're saying," said Lou, "is that we have no choice but to consider the possibility that it really was Eliot following you that night, and again tonight. And that if he really does research his victims in advance, the way Drew suggested, you could be next."

"If that's the case, we'd know as soon as we saw the next sonnet, right?" Andrea asked.

"We wouldn't be completely sure, because his meanings are often a bit nebulous," Lou said. "In retrospect they always seem clear, but I don't want us figuring out that you're the subject of his next sonnet in retrospect."

Andrea spoke in a hushed, shaky voice. "What do you propose we do?'

"I propose we develop a contingency plan," Lou said. "If the next sonnet bears even the slightest resemblance to you, I want to take you into protective custody. We'll lock you up where Eliot can't get to you. And we'll disguise a female FBI agent to look as much like you as possible, and use her as a decoy. Flush Eliot out in the open."

"Where would you put me? One of your jail cells?"

"I'll make it as comfortable for you as possible."

"But what if it ends up that it's not me he's after? Are you going to put all your eggs in one basket?'

"Of course not. We'll still have all our teams combing the town, looking for anything suspicious, and ready for a rapid response to any report of trouble. And we'll try to determine who else the sonnet could possibly refer to." Lou paused, and stared pointedly at Andrea. "But you are the only potential victim that I'm aware of who has reason to believe she was followed by Eliot, so I think that even the most extreme precautions on your behalf are clearly warranted."

Andrea seemed lost in thought for a moment, and Lou gave her time to mull it over. It was a lot to digest, and the implications were enough to fill even the stoutest heart with terror.

Finally, Andrea looked back at Lou and spoke in a barely audible whisper. "I think your precautions are probably justified, but I don't think I should stay in your jail."

"Why?" Lou asked. "I grant it's no Ritz-Carlton, but it will be comfortable and clean, and you'll be surrounded by cops."

"That's it, what you just said," Andrea replied evenly, appearing to have cast her emotions aside, and to have replaced them with cool, calculated logic. "I'd be surrounded by people."

"Yeah, cops and other law enforcement personnel. So?"

"We don't know who Eliot is. He could even be a cop, for all we know. Or a friend of one, or the husband of one. There must have been over two dozen people in the police station when I was last there. That's too many people knowing where I am. Too many chances of a leak, which would spoil even the most carefully designed plan."

Lou's face flushed and her voice was stern. "I can assure you, Andrea, that Eliot is not a cop. For one thing, I knew the location of every cop on the force last Friday night. They were all partnered and they all had to report in on a regular basis. It would have been impossible for one of them to sneak away long enough to abduct and set fire to Jesse Kirkpatrick."

"Okay, I'll give you that. But I still contend that two dozen people is about twenty-three too many to keep a secret plan a secret."

"She has a point, Lou," Moss said. "There's no telling who Eliot is, or who he talks to, or what he's capable of finding out. He's certainly proved to be awfully damned cagey so far."

Sonnets

Lou emitted a long sigh of resignation. "So, do either of you have a better idea?"

"Yes," Andrea said. "I can go stay with my mom in Milton. It's about forty miles north of here. I wouldn't tell anyone other than you two where I was going. You could still use your decoy, or whatever else you thought would work. If Eliot doesn't make a move that night, I can stay there indefinitely."

"I don't know," Lou said. "You'd only be safe if Eliot didn't find you. If he did, you'd be unprotected."

"Send one of those FBI agents with me." Andrea smiled. "Preferably a cute, single one."

It took Lou a moment to respond to the last remark. Her mind was racing as she considered the pros and cons of Andrea's suggestion. "Actually," she said, "I think I should go with you. At least for that first night."

Andrea looked surprised. "What? And not be in on the action here?"

"If you're the target, our best chance of nabbing Eliot will be with the decoy, and Frank's FBI team is much better trained and equipped for that sort of takedown. I'd only be in the way, and if Eliot recognized me, might even scare him off. Besides," she said, her eyes again locked with Andrea's, "Eliot seems to have this uncanny ability to figure things out, and anticipate our moves. I don't want to scare you any more than you are already, but I'm betting that the action will be wherever you are."

Back in her office, Lou placed a call to Drew's apartment. If, as she feared, Andrea really was on Eliot's list of victims, and especially if she was next in line, Drew's role would be different from the last time. Lou wanted him to be prepared. In fact, she wanted every conceivable element of her plan to be locked in place. Andrea was her friend. She did not intend to lose her.

"Hi," Drew said. "How's the investigation coming along?"

"Not so well," she said with a sigh of frustration. "We really don't have any more to go on than we did before his attempt on Jesse Kirkpatrick."

"What about that tire tread print? You don't think it was from Eliot's car?"

"Actually, we do. It was taken from a little clearing in the woods on the north side of Bert's parking lot. The car had to be parked there during the night Jesse was abducted, because there were pine needles and small branches all around a relatively clear area. You remember how strong the winds were that night. Unfortunately, the rain started not long after the car was moved, so our print wasn't as decisive as we'd hoped it would be."

"So you didn't learn what type of tire it was?"

"Oh, yeah, we know that it's one of two specific Goodyear all-weather radials. And based on the size of the area that was relatively clear of pine needles from the wind, we know that the car is a mid-sized model. Furthermore, the space between the tire tracks indicates a General Motors make."

"Okay, now we're getting somewhere," he said, pretending to be excited. "A mid-sized General Motors car. What color?"

"Smart ass."

Drew chuckled. "I'm sorry. It's just so damned frustrating that you either have to laugh or cry, and real men don't cry."

"Listen, I could write a book about frustration. And I feel a lot more like crying than laughing."

"You really sound down. That's not like you."

"Andrea Warren thinks she was followed again tonight."

"What?" Drew's voice was suddenly serious. "She wasn't walking home again, was she?"

"No, she was driving. She didn't get a good look at the car, but she said it was a dark color. And it was mid-sized."

"Oh, shit."

"My sentiment, exactly. Listen, this thing you said about Eliot doing research on his victims. That's the only way I can figure out that he's been able to keep up such a pace. He must be working on two or three women at a time, making plans to kill one while gathering information on the others."

"I agree," Drew said.

"So if we go on the assumption that Eliot was researching Andrea on both nights she was followed, it's possible she could be next on his list."

"So what do you intend to do, have her leave town?"

"After we receive the next sonnet, that is precisely what I intend to do. And I'm going with her."

"Where will you go?"

She paused, and for a moment seemed to have not heard the question. When she answered, her voice was tentative. "I can't tell you, Drew. It's on a need-to-know basis."

He did not respond.

"Look," she said, "don't take it personally. It's not that I don't trust you with the information. This has nothing to do with trust. It's about control, and in a situation like this, control is paramount."

Drew sighed. "Okay, I understand. What do you want me to do? Anything?"

"Of course. You're absolutely critical to this investigation. As soon as another sonnet is received, I'll need you to study it immediately. If you conclude there is any possibility at all that it's about Andrea, we'll initiate our plan, and I'll have you work with Frank

Clay of the FBI while I'm gone."

"You know I'll do whatever I can, Lou."

"And I can't tell you how much that means."

"So, what do we do in the meantime?"

"We do the hardest thing of all. We wait."

Sonnets

Sonnet No. 6

The taste of sweet revenge will please my tongue
I'll savor her despair and anguished cries
I'll send her to her grave, so fair and young
This celebrated architect of lies

She thinks me like Cassandra, unbelieved
My prophecies no longer to come true
But now she is the one who's been deceived
And I will soon collect the payment due

No mortal has the power to forestall
The fatal truth my timeless sonnet locks
For she cannot ignore the siren's call
Nor flee her fate of crashing on the rocks

The earth will bid farewell without a sound
This wretched bitch whose grievous lies are drowned

Eliot

Chapter 28

T he dream started like all the others. Drew and Kate making love, sharing a room service breakfast, running like children across the hot, white sand toward the glistening water. Touching, caressing, kissing. For the last time.

He saw himself screaming at the lifeguard, frantically pointing in the direction where he thought he'd last seen her, yet knowing it would serve no purpose. He saw himself crying on the beach, crying in their room as he clutched the bed sheet to his face. Savoring her smell, her presence, her nearness. For the last time.

He watched himself answer the door, walk through the bustling hotel lobby, and climb into the back of the police car. He saw the glittering lights, and heard the happy strains of mariachi music as the streets of Cancun passed by his window like scenes from a movie. A sad movie. A horror movie.

He was walking into the squatty, white building. The morgue. He saw the fat man in the white lab coat, followed him to the table where she lay, as cold and still as a statue. He watched as the sheet was slowly pulled back to reveal the face he had loved more than life, yet now feared more than death. Dreaming, yet aware he was dreaming, he screamed at himself to wake up, to end this senseless torture.

Unable to avert his eyes from the corpse on the table, unable to erase the indelible image of death forever seared into his brain, he steeled himself for what would come next. But the eyes did not open, and the lips did not move, nor could he obey his subconscious rantings and wake up. Instead, he saw himself walking into the funeral home in Albany, moving toward the flower-draped coffin as if being carried by invisible hands.

Other people were there, peering into the coffin, crying silent tears as they shook their heads mournfully. Kate's mother stood nearby, supported by her two brothers as she accepted the condolences that Drew could not hear, but knew were being spoken. He tried to move toward her, needing to comfort her, and be comforted himself, but the invisible hands propelled him steadily toward the coffin. And as he moved through the crowd he saw Kate's mother lift her grief-bowed head to look at him. Saying nothing, she raised her hand and pointed at him. Slowly, everyone in the room followed suit. Men, women, and children, all pointing their fingers and staring at him with cold, unfeeling eyes. Dead eyes.

Drew was now standing at the open coffin, turning his head from the accusing fingers to the accusing face of his beloved Kate. Instead, he saw his own reflection. The coffin contained no body. Only water. Strange water, inky dark and suddenly swirling, as if part of a raging current. A current from nowhere, going nowhere. A watery grave.

He stared at the water, simultaneously bewildered and entranced. It seemed infinitely deep, as if it were not bound by the finite dimensions of the coffin that contained it. He felt a strange compulsion to touch it, to thrust his hand into its murky depths and to feel its cold embrace.

He looked around the room. He was confused and frightened. But he found no solace in the dead eyes that bore into him. Everyone was still pointing, and everyone's mouth was moving, yet there was no sound. Only an eerie, tomb-like silence. But Drew knew what they were saying. They wanted him to go into the water.

Sonnets

They wanted him to dive beneath the dark, swirling surface, to join Kate. To atone for the sin of letting her drown.

The people seemed to be moving toward him without walking. With every blink of his eyes they were closer. Reaching for him. To put him in the water, to hold him under, until the inky, black fluid filled his lungs. His head felt light, and the room began to spin. He bent back to escape the reaching hands, and he felt himself losing his balance. He was reeling backward, against the edge of the coffin and over the side. He was falling into the water. He was . . .

Awake. Heart pounding and arms flailing, his body as wet as if he had indeed plunged into the swirling current, he realized he had been holding his breath. He looked around his bedroom for any signs of the dead-eyed mourners. There were none, of course, so he inhaled deeply and lay back down. It had just been a dream, and he was awake now. And safe. Still, he did not close his eyes again until the first rays of the morning sun filtered between the slats of his window blinds.

Later that morning, Drew was in the process of dismissing his eleven o'clock graduate class, wishing them all a good weekend despite the four page essay he had just assigned, when he turned to see Judi standing in the doorway. She smiled nervously as she stepped aside to let the students file past. Drew was the last one out the door.

"Let me guess," he said quietly. "Lou Hennessey?"

"She wants you to come to her office, pronto," she whispered. "She sounded very anxious."

"Okay, I'll head over there right now. I'll try to get back in time for the staff meeting at three. If I can't, could you please give Dr. Ainsworthy a copy of my budget projections, and have him leave me a note with any questions?"

She responded with a nervous nod, and Drew hurried down the stairs.

As soon as he stepped outside he wished he had taken the time to go up to his office to get his topcoat. The rain that had been threatening that morning was now coming down in sheets, and he was soaked by the time he ran across the parking lot to his car.

Even with the heater cranked up high, he dried out very little in the ten-minute drive to the police station. Fortunately, he had an umbrella in the car, so he did not get any wetter going into the building.

He was immediately directed into Lou's office and found her huddled with what Drew had come to think of as her core team—Frank Clay, Bill Witherspoon and Howard Mullins—along with Bernard Moss, Andrea Warren, and a tall, attractive brunette woman he did not recognize.

Lou looked up from her desk when he walked in. "Hi, Drew. I think you know everyone here, except Jill Bartlett, one of Frank's agents. She'll be our decoy tonight."

Drew looked at the woman and gave her an admiring nod. She had to know the fate of Eliot's five previous victims, so he knew she must be a woman of uncommon courage. She smiled at him, and he could see there was enough resemblance to Andrea to fool someone from a distance. He hoped for her sake that her distance from Eliot would be maintained.

Everyone else in the room gave Drew a nod or a tense smile. Everyone except Officer Mullins, who looked straight ahead, as if unaware that anyone else had entered the room. Drew considered himself an astute enough student of human behavior to know that Mullins just did not like him. Maybe it was because of the sarcastic remark Drew had made to his young partner the night of Melissa Turner's murder. Or maybe the guy had some kind of inferiority complex when around academic types. Whatever it was, Drew was glad Lou was assigning him to work with Frank Clay instead of Howard Mullins.

Lou handed him a sheet of paper. "Give it a quick read and tell us what you think."

Sonnets

The room was silent as Drew read "Sonnet No. 6." When he had finished, he looked at Andrea. "I don't know what all of this means, but I have to assume it's you he's referring to as the 'architect of lies.' Your name's been on nearly every newspaper story about him."

"That's what we thought, too," Lou said.

"And the reference to Cassandra is pretty straight forward," Drew said.

"I vaguely remember the story," Bernard Moss said. "Wasn't she a Greek goddess who warned about the Trojan horse?"

"Actually, she was a mortal, the daughter of the king and queen of Troy," Drew said. "According to Greek mythology, she was so beautiful that Apollo gave her the power to foretell the future. But when she spurned his love, he made it so no one ever believed her prophecies, even though they were true. I think that's what Eliot's saying about you, Andrea. That you're telling your newspaper readers not to believe the predictions in his sonnets, even though they're true."

"What about the other stuff?" Lou asked. "The 'sirens' call,' and all that?"

"I want to spend some more time on that. I'll go back to the campus and do a little more research. I know that on his epic voyage home from Troy, Ulysses had to sail past a place where beautiful sirens called to passing sailors, causing them to go mad with desire and crash their ships upon the rocks. By answering the call, they were doomed. Maybe Eliot is saying that Andrea answering the call of a newspaper story, the story about him, is her call to death. And, like the ancient sailors, she's unable to resist the temptation."

"This all sounds like a bunch of academic bullshit to me," Mullins said.

It occurred to Drew that he had been correct in his thinking that the officer was not enamored of the scholarly. Not too unusual, he supposed, for the rough, tough ex-jock types frequently found in the police rank and file.

241

"That may be, Howard, but the man who writes this academic bullshit has killed four women and maimed another," Lou said, an edge to her voice. "Trying to figure out what he means is our best hope of getting out there ahead of him and setting a trap."

She kept her eyes fixed on Mullins a moment more before turning back to the others. "Speaking of the trap, let's talk about the rest of our plan. Andrea, you and Bernie are going back to the *Gazette* in a little while. I want you to leave your raincoat, scarf, umbrella, and keys in Bernie's office. At precisely four o'clock, go downstairs where the presses are, and then out the back door into the alley. I'll be waiting in my car. Get in the back seat and lie down on the floorboard. And stay down there until I tell you it's okay to sit up. Got it?"

"Yes," Andrea said, her voice a nervous whisper.

"Jill," Lou continued, "you head over to the *Gazette* around three or so. Just hang out in Bernie's office until time to leave, a little after six. Frank will call you to let you know that everyone is in position."

Frank took over the details of the stakeout. "Jill, as I've told you, you'll be wired. Use it. Don't take any chances with this guy. If anything happens in the parking lot, you yell out, okay?"

"Yes, sir," she said.

"If nothing happens there, drive to Miss Warren's apartment, park the car in the garage in the back, and let yourself into the apartment. Try to tie the scarf in such a way that your hair is covered, and keep the umbrella low. If Eliot smells a trap, it's all over."

"If I make it into the apartment without incident, what then?" Jill asked.

"Just hang out and wait," Frank said. "There will already be an agent in the apartment. It'll be Jenkins. Don't talk to him. If you have to communicate, write a note. We don't know if Eliot would go to the trouble to have bugged the place, or if he could be nearby with a remote listening device, but we can't take any chances of scaring him off."

"And I just stay there all night?"

"If necessary, yes," Frank said. "We'll be watching the perimeter, looking for anything unusual. But stay alert. This guy's very sneaky."

"Who's assigned to go with Andrea and me?" Lou asked.

"Fletcher," Frank said. "He'll be waiting in one of your unmarked cars outside of town. You and I will determine the exact place. No one else, other than him, will know it. He'll make sure you're not being tailed, then fall in behind you and follow you to your destination."

"Okay," Lou said, then turned to Mullins. "Howard, you're in charge of the patrol units tonight. Same routes as last week, except for one thing. Between five thirty and six thirty, I don't want any of our guys to go anywhere near the *Gazette* office. I do not want Eliot scared off by any blue uniforms. That takedown, if it happens, will be handled solely by the FBI. Clear?"

"Clear," Mullins said.

Lou turned to Drew. "If you come up with anything that could help us better understand what Eliot has in mind, give me a call before three thirty. After that, Officer Mullins will be your contact."

Drew could tell that his expression was broadcasting disapproval, because Lou quickly added, "Frank and his FBI team will have their hands full, and I'll be going through some areas with little or no cell coverage. You can try me, and leave a message if you don't reach me. If you need Officer Mullins, Sarah can patch you through to his patrol car at any time. Okay?"

"Okay," Drew and Mullins said simultaneously. Drew did not mean it, nor, he assumed, did the police sergeant.

Lou turned to Andrea. "Are you up for this?"

Andrea offered the hint of a nervous smile. "Do I have a choice?"

"To be honest, I'm afraid not."

"Then I'm up for it."

"Okay, then," Lou said, looking around the room, "let's nail this demented son-of-a-bitch."

Drew managed to get excused from the staff meeting. Despite the fact that it was the final review of the departmental budget request for the coming year, Dr. Ainsworthy agreed that Drew's time would be better spent dissecting Eliot's latest submission. He did get called into the meeting around four o'clock to answer a few questions about his projections, but was in and out in less than ten minutes.

The meeting broke at five, and by five thirty, Drew and Judi were the only two remaining in the department. Everyone else had apparently left to get an early start on the weekend, or else to get home and shelter their loved ones behind locked doors before Eliot once again descended on the town.

Judi came into his office to announce her departure. "Anything I can do for you before I leave, Drew?"

Drew stood. "No thanks, Judi. Come on, I'll walk you to your car."

"Oh, are you leaving too?"

"No, I'm going to stick around for a while, but it's dark outside. I'm not letting you go out there alone."

"It's kind of you to offer, but it's really not . . ."

Drew had already donned his topcoat and grabbed his umbrella. "No arguments, okay? I have some reports I'll need you to type on Monday, so I want to make sure you're able to be here to take care of them."

"And I thought you were just being chivalrous."

"I am, but chivalry can be self-serving, you know. Even the most gallant gentlemen usually have ulterior motives for their gracious gestures."

She laughed, and they walked out of the office. Drew normally took the stairs, but in deference to Judi, waited patiently for the elevator. They rode it down to the ground floor, crossed the lobby of the building, and stepped outside into a torrential downpour. Drew opened his umbrella and took Judi by the arm. "Which way?"

"Over here to the left," she said, hunching her shoulders under the umbrella. "I'm so glad those budgets are done," she continued, as they waded through the parking lot. "They're such a pain. I dread them every year."

"The process is quite different from what I was used to at NYU," Drew said. "Much more detailed. I can see why people dread it."

"They ask for so much detail that you never know what all you need to take into the meetings. I spent most of my afternoon looking for files people needed, and running them down to the meeting room. I had to make three trips for Dr. Alexander. He must've had something else on his mind, because he forgot nearly everything he needed for the meeting."

Drew gasped in mock astonishment. "Are you insinuating that Dr. Charles Alexander is anything less than the perfect administrator?"

Judi laughed as they approached a white Taurus and she inserted a key in the door. "Not only is he not the perfect administrator, but I think the man may have a bit of a kinky streak."

This time Drew was genuinely astonished. He had never heard this quintessential southern lady speak of such things. "Kinky?" he asked.

She opened the door and slipped behind the wheel of her car. "Well, the third time he called he said he needed a sheet of calculations from his desk. I had to search through several drawers to find it. Guess what I found under some papers in the top drawer."

"I don't know. Lacy lingerie?"

She laughed. "Not quite, but I found a tube of lipstick and several Kleenex tissues that smelled of perfume. What do you make of that?"

Lipstick? Drew suddenly had a mental image of Andrea Warren walking home on a dark night, followed by a figure in the shadows. He saw her falling, spilling her purse, hurriedly getting up and running into her house, and then returning the next morning to find everything she could think of that had fallen from her purse except for one item—a lipstick.

"Listen, Judi, drive safely, and be sure to lock your doors," he said. "I'll see you Monday."

"Thanks for walking me out, Drew. Have a good weekend, if you can. And please be careful."

"I will. Bye." He pushed her door shut, watched her lock it, and then ran back through the rain to the Liberal Arts Building.

This time Drew did not wait for the elevator. He ran up the two flights of stairs, and was back in the English department suite in less than a minute. Dripping wet and breathing as heavily as if he had just run a fifty-yard dash, he headed straight for Charles Alexander's office.

He did not turn on the overhead light. There was enough light spilling in from the reception area to allow him to see what he was doing. He hurried to the desk. Judi had said the top drawer. He wondered which side. First he checked on the left, hurriedly rummaging through loose papers and assorted office supplies, but trying to keep things in their rightful place. There was nothing there. He moved to the right side and did not have to look for long before he found a gold lipstick tube. He opened it. It had been used. It was a deep red. Drew could not precisely recall the shade Andrea normally wore, but this was close enough. It had to be hers.

Lou had said he could call her, and to leave a message if he did not reach her right away. He had to get this information to her and Andrea immediately, and then he would call Howard Mullins. He swung around to pick up the phone that was on the credenza behind the desk. His heart was pounding and he was still breathing heavily from the sprint up the stairs. He stared again at the tube of lipstick in his hand, and then closed his eyes for a moment, concentrating on calming himself down. When he opened his eyes, a large, black hand was reaching for the disconnect button on the phone console. The voice that spoke was a whisper, and it was so close that the expelled air tickled his neck.

"I don't think that's a good idea, Drew."

Chapter 29

T he drive along the two-lane country roads to the quiet, farming town of Milton would have normally taken only an hour, but the torrential rain, combined with the continuous speed fluctuations to ensure they were not being followed, made for a much slower trip. It had been an hour and forty minutes since Andrea had climbed into the back of Lou's car when they finally pulled into a long, tree-lined driveway that led to an old, Victorian-style house. With only her car lights and the occasional flash of lightning for illumination, Lou was able to see that the house was gray with white trim and black shutters that looked as if they could use a new coat of paint. Fletcher's car came to a stop behind them.

"The house is dark," Lou said. "Looks like nobody's home."

Andrea, still sitting in the back seat, peered through the front windshield as the wipers intermittently cleared a view. "I didn't call Mom to tell her we were coming. I figured it was better to keep it a secret until we got here. She's probably at my aunt's house down the road. She's a widow too. They sometimes stay over at each other's house."

"As much as I'd love to meet her, it would actually be better if we were here alone tonight," Lou said. "It'll make it easier to protect ourselves if we don't have anyone else to look after."

"If Mom's at Aunt Lillian's, she won't be coming home tonight.

Once it gets dark, she stays put. I'll call her when we get in, to let her know I'm here with a friend for the weekend, and that I'll see her tomorrow."

"Great," Lou said. "Let's get inside. I have to piss like a racehorse."

Andrea laughed, and then opened the car door. She stepped into the rain, waved at Fletcher in the car behind them, and sloshed her way to the front porch. After retrieving a key from beneath a clay planter, she unlocked the door and stepped inside.

Lou and Agent Fletcher reached the porch at the same time. He was wearing a raincoat and hat, and carrying a flashlight. "You go on in, Chief," he said. "I'm going to look around out here. I like to get the lay of the land before I settle in."

"Good idea. I'll check around inside. By the way, do you want me to keep calling you Fletcher?"

He smiled. He was young, handsome, and clean-cut. Vintage FBI. "Carl."

"And I'm Lou," she said. "I don't stand on formality when I'm in a field situation like this. You go ahead and check things out here, Carl. I'll get us a pot of coffee going and see if there's any food in here."

"Yes, ma'am," Carl said before disappearing around the corner of the house.

"Yes, ma'am," Lou muttered to herself. "No formality here."

She opened the screen door and stepped inside. She was standing in a dimly lit foyer with dark, flowered wallpaper. There was a living room to the right, and a dining room to the left. A light was on in the back of the house, and she heard the sound of cabinet doors opening and closing. She followed the sound and the light, and emerged into a kitchen that looked as if it had not had a facelift in twenty years.

"We have plenty of canned soup, and there's an unopened box of crackers," Andrea said.

"That'll be fine," Lou said. "What about coffee?"

"Should be some in the freezer, but I don't know if we have any milk for it."

"No problem for me. I drink it black." Lou opened the freezer compartment door and reached in for a one pound coffee can. "I can tell your mother has had this refrigerator a long time. The freezer looks like an ice cave. Do you have an icepick?"

"If we do, it'll be in this utensil drawer," Andrea said, opening a wide drawer beneath the counter. She rummaged through a tangle of electric cords, mixer beaters, and other kitchen tools. "We used to have one, but I don't see it now." She closed the drawer. "Let's get the coffee going and I'll defrost that old clunker later."

Lou laughed, and then looked around the room and sniffed. "Smells a bit musty in here."

"Yeah, it looks like Mom's been gone for a while," Andrea said. She stepped over to a phone mounted on the wall beside the back door. "Let me give Aunt Lillian a call."

"While you're doing that, I'm going to look around upstairs."

Andrea turned around to face her. "I'll give you a tour. But I have to warn you, it's not much to see."

"No," Lou said firmly. "You stay down here and call your aunt."

"Oh," Andrea said, seeming to suddenly understand Lou's intentions. "There's no way he could know we were coming here. And it certainly doesn't look like anyone's been here for days."

"I know," Lou said, then smiled. "It's a cop thing. It's called 'securing the perimeter.' I have to do it. It's in the police handbook."

Andrea smiled too, but looked nervous. "Well, go ahead then. We can't be breaking any police rules."

Lou walked back into the foyer and, once out of Andrea's sight, pulled her revolver from her shoulder holster. She flipped a switch at the foot of the stairs and a dim bulb lit her way. She climbed the stairs slowly, every step creaking loudly enough to announce her arrival to anyone inside the house.

She ascended into an unlit hallway with the same flowered wallpaper that decorated the foyer downstairs. She found a light switch and turned it on. The floor was hardwood, and wore a fine layer of dust. If Eliot, or anyone else for that matter, had been up here during the last several days, they had floated, not walked, down the hall.

Feeling a little more at ease now, Lou looked and listened. There were four doors, three of which were open. There was no sound other than that of the wind whipping the rain against the house and the barely distinguishable sound of Andrea talking on the phone in the kitchen. Lou took a step and the floor creaked. This house would definitely be a challenge to anyone trying to mount a sneak attack, which suited Lou just fine.

She opened the first door on the left. It was a bedroom, decorated with a mixed collection of Victorian and early American artifacts surrounding a four-poster bed and a heavy oak dresser. It was not a particularly large room, and was cluttered with shelves of glass figurines, a cushioned rocking chair, a freestanding, two-piece vanity mirror, and a footstool. She opened a closet, which was, by contrast, remarkably free of clutter. Several housedresses and a couple of wool suits hung neatly. A half dozen pairs of casual shoes, two pairs of heels, and one pair of slippers were aligned on the floor. An overhead shelf contained some battered luggage and some boxes, none of which looked as if they had been disturbed for quite a while. Lou could tell two things about Mrs. Warren—she was no slave to fashion, and she did not travel much.

The adjoining bathroom was clean and neat, and contained an extensive array of make-up and toiletries. Lou gave it a quick look, including a peek behind the shower curtain, and then returned to the hallway.

The door on the opposite side of the hall was open. It was a bathroom. Judging from the assortment of shampoos, conditioners, and other grooming products, it was the one Andrea used. Next to it was another bedroom, also with the door open. Unlike the master, this bedroom was Spartan in its furnishings. There was a standard double bed, a chest, and a dresser. There were no paintings on the walls, no collection of dolls or figurines, and simple Venetian blinds instead of lacy curtains. Apparently, Andrea had taken her childhood accessories with her when she went off to college or got her first apartment. The closet contained neither clothes nor Eliot, only several cardboard boxes taped shut.

Lou continued down the hall. Next to the master bedroom was another small room that had been converted into a den. There was a sofa, two freestanding bookshelves, and a television. She gave the room a cursory look, and then walked back out to the hall. Confident that she and Andrea were the only ones in the house, she then stepped into the bathroom to do what she had needed to do for the past hour.

A couple of minutes later Lou walked back into the kitchen just as Carl Fletcher came in the front door, and Andrea was hanging up the phone.

"No wonder it's musty in here," Andrea said. "Mom's been at Aunt Lillian's for over a week. She's had the flu. She was going to come home today but, with this storm, decided to stay until tomorrow. You'll get to meet her then."

"Good," Lou said. "I look forward to it. By the way, everything is fine upstairs." She then noticed a door behind her. She tried unsuccessfully to open it, then saw it was nailed shut. "Where's this lead?"

"Oh, that's the stairs to the cellar," Andrea said. "It's been nailed shut for years. We had a little fire down there and never had the money to get the damage repaired."

Fletcher removed his hat and raincoat. "Everything looks fine outside. I found a place off to the side of the driveway where I can park my car and be able to observe the house and the road."

"How about some coffee and something to eat first?" Andrea asked. "I was going to heat up some soup."

"I have a thermos in my car," Fletcher said. "If you don't mind, I'll take my soup and a cup of coffee out there and settle myself in for the watch."

"You're going to stay out there all night?" Andrea asked.

"Yes, ma'am, unless we hear from Frank that they've nabbed the guy. The Chief is armed, and so am I, but it's better to spread our eyes and our firepower out. Just to be on the safe side."

Andrea smiled, albeit weakly, and hugged herself. "Well, considering the fact that I'm a marked woman, I feel pretty safe. Let me get the coffee going. I want you two guardian angels awake and alert."

Thirty minutes later, Lou positioned a chair in front of the living room window, a steaming mug of coffee in her left hand, and her service revolver and cell phone on a lamp table to her right. The only lights on in the house were those in the kitchen where Andrea sat editing a story on her laptop computer. Fletcher had moved his car to the surveillance spot he had selected, and was invisible from the house. All the doors and windows were locked. Everyone was in place, and everything was secure, yet Lou could not shake the nagging, inexplicable feeling that something bad was going to happen tonight.

Drew took a deep breath as he stared into the dark, glaring eyes of Charles Alexander. The larger man was only inches away, and stood between Drew and the door. No one else was on this floor. In fact, as far as Drew was aware, no one else remained in the building.

Charles spoke in a soft voice, as if he were afraid of being overheard. "Ordinarily, I would ask just what the hell you think you're doing, snooping around in my desk." He nodded in the direction of the tube of lipstick in Drew's hand. "But, under the circumstances, I suppose I should put my moral indignation aside long enough to explain that."

Drew stood as erect as he could, but was still painfully aware that he was a good four or five inches shorter than Charles. "I think I already have an explanation. You've been following Andrea Warren, and this is her lipstick."

"Yes."

"You were following her so you could learn more about her. So you could develop the perfect plan . . . and write the perfect sonnet."

Sonnets

The expression on Charles' face evolved from one of intimidation to skepticism, and then to shock. "Sonnet? You think I'm Eliot?"

Drew tried to keep his eyes locked with those of his adversary but his mind raced as he strained to remember what items were on top of the desk, if there was anything he could quickly grasp and employ as a weapon. Without the added advantage of a sharp or blunt instrument, he knew he was outsized. He thought it was even possible that Charles already had his hand on a gun or a knife inside his coat pocket. Drew realized that his only chance was to stall for time and look for an opening to either strike an unexpected blow, or to flee, preferably both.

"It all fits together, Charles," he said, trying to keep his voice calm. "You're certainly literate enough to write good sonnets. And you've probably learned enough from Andrea to stay a step ahead of the police."

"This is preposterous!" Charles exclaimed, the vehemence of his statement startling Drew. "I admit to following Andrea, but there's quite a difference between being infatuated with one woman and killing four others! And, for your information, I was with other people on the night Melissa Turner was killed, and last Thursday night when that woman was set on fire. I have probably eight or ten witnesses who can confirm that."

"Then why have you been following Andrea Warren?"

Charles exhaled slowly, and then backed up a step. His eyes were focused on the floor, as if the answers were written on his shoes. "I've been taken with her since the night I met her, at your poetry reading. And I got the distinct impression that the interest was mutual, that our differences in color didn't matter. I asked her out a couple of times, but she was always busy. One night, after she had dinner with Chief Hennessey, I followed her home to see where she lived. I didn't mean to frighten her—I didn't even intend for her to detect my presence. But apparently she did, and in her haste to get to her house, she stumbled and fell. That lipstick fell out of her purse."

"And you picked it up from the street?"

"Yes, with the intention of returning it to her. But after I got home, it occurred to me that there was no way I could do that without revealing that I was the one following her. It wouldn't have been so much of a problem, except that she injured her knee when she fell and . . . well, it just got to be too embarrassing."

Drew was beginning to relax a little. The man's regret seemed genuine.

"I did persuade her to go out with me one night after work," Charles continued. "She was in the mood for a burger, so I took her to Bert's. She told me the other day that our waitress was the one who was abducted and burned, but I didn't remember her."

"You followed Andrea other times as well."

"Yes, a couple of times. Even though we seemed to really hit it off that night at Bert's, she started acting more distant, aloof. I thought perhaps the reality of a biracial relationship had finally sunk in, or maybe she'd started seeing someone. I followed her a couple of times, just to see if she were meeting someone for lunch or after work, but she never did."

"So it was you following her on Wednesday night?"

Charles suddenly looked confused. "This Wednesday night? No, I was playing racquetball on Wednesday night."

Now it was Drew's turn to be confused. "Well, someone followed her. That, combined with the episode with you, convinced Lou Hennessey that Andrea was being stalked by Eliot. And then the sonnet that came today seemed to verify that assumption."

"What?" Charles exclaimed, sounding genuinely distraught. "You believe that the sonnet you were working on this afternoon was about Andrea? Let me see it, please."

"It's in my office," Drew said.

Charles stepped aside and Drew slipped past him, still watching Charles out of the corner of his eye, poised to defend himself if there were any sudden movements. Instead, his colleague quietly followed him to the other office. Drew snatched up the sonnet from his desk and handed it to Charles, who took it and began reading. After a moment, he looked at Drew with sad eyes.

"This certainly appears to be about Andrea," he said solemnly. "She's been the lead writer on all of the *Gazette's* stories about Eliot. That explains the Cassandra reference."

"Yeah," Drew said, "it struck me as kind of odd that he would compare himself to a female mythological figure, but I guess he was just speaking metaphorically."

Charles suddenly fell silent, as if deep in thought. He had a faraway look in his eyes, his mind traveling to another place or time. "Tell me something, Drew," he said haltingly. "From whom do you think this killer borrowed his pen name? After all, I'm assuming that the police have checked out everyone around here with Eliot as either a first, middle, or last name."

"Oh, sure," Drew said. "Right after Celeste Holbrook's murder, when the connection was made between the killings and the sonnets. No, it's most definitely a nom de plume. I've always assumed he borrowed it from T.S. Eliot, one of the greatest poets of the twentieth century."

"What about George?"

"What?"

"George Eliot, the pen name of Marian Evans. You know, Silas Marner, Adam Bede, The Mill on the Floss."

"I know who George Eliot is," Drew said. "Why do you bring her up?"

"Two things," Charles said, his eyes beginning to light up. "First of all, she used a pen name, just as it appears our killer is doing. Second, if you assumed for just a moment that our killer, like George Eliot, was a woman, it would explain the self-comparison to Cassandra, a mythological heroine."

Drew was stunned. He began to speak, talking to himself as much as to Charles as he tried to make sense of this new train of thought.

"That's a possibility we never considered. It would explain so much, like how Eliot subdued so many victims without a struggle. Women would not be likely to expect an attack from another woman. They'd trust another woman, would open locked doors and invite her in. They'd turn their backs on her without even considering the possibility of danger."

Charles began to pace the small office as he thought through the implications of their new theory. "It would have to be someone known to the first four victims, because they all went down without a fight, right?"

Drew nodded. "Celeste was the only one with skin abrasions, and they were most likely inflicted when she was trying to hide in the arbor, not as a result of struggling with her assailant. It makes so much sense! And if Eliot is a woman who was known and trusted by the first four victims, she's probably known and trusted by Lou and Andrea. I have to warn them!"

Drew picked up his phone and punched in the number for Lou's cell phone, praying silently that it wasn't too late. "Keep this under your hat, Charles, but Lou and Andrea are together. If your theory about Eliot being a woman is right, they could both be in danger and not even know it."

"It's not really a theory," Charles said. "Just a hunch."

"Well, it damned sure would explain a lot," Drew said, listening to Lou's phone ring and willing her to answer it. She answered on the second ring.

"Lou, it's Drew. Are you at the house yet?"

"Yes, we just got here a few minutes ago," Lou said. "You sound all out of breath. Has something happened?"

Suddenly, Drew's brain seemed so overloaded with all the information he wanted to share that he did not know where to start. "I'm with Charles Alexander."

"Fine. Tell him hello for me. Now, what's going on?"

"First of all, Charles told me he's the one who was following

Andrea on the night she walked home. You know, when she fell."

"Oh, shit," Charles mumbled, burying his face in one hand.

"Why was he following her?" Lou asked.

"That doesn't matter right now," Drew said. "What matters is that he was not following her Wednesday night. So that may very well have been Eliot."

Lou sounded aggravated. "That's what we've assumed all along, Drew. Why is this so important right now? It doesn't change a thing."

Drew blurted out his next statement before giving any consideration to how he would explain it. "Maybe Eliot's a woman."

"What? A woman? What are you talking about?"

"Listen to me, Lou. The name—Eliot. I always thought it was borrowed from T.S. Eliot, the poet. But Charles had a different thought. Since we know that's not the killer's real name, that it's a pen name, maybe it was inspired by George Eliot, the nom de plume of the English novelist, Marian Evans."

Lou's impatience was reflected in the tone of her voice. "Just because Marian Evans used a pen name, and our killer uses a pen name, admittedly the same one, you believe that indicates that Eliot is a woman?"

"It would explain a lot," Drew said, determined to plead his case. "Like the reference to Cassandra, a female mythological figure. But more importantly, it would explain how Eliot got to the victims. If Eliot's a woman, other women like Margaret Fenwyck, Melissa Turner, and Jackie Phelps might have known her. If so, they would have let her in, and their guards would have been down when they were around her. She could've taken them completely by surprise. Thus, the lack of any evidence of a physical struggle."

Lou began to sound a little less aggravated and a little more interested. "I guess that makes sense. But still . . ."

"Look, all I wanted to do was share this with you and get you thinking about it. Plus, I wanted to make sure that, wherever you are, you don't open your door to a woman, thinking it's safe."

"Our door is guarded. By a man. A very handsome man, actually." Drew was convinced that the sole purpose of this last, ostensibly offhand, remark was to make him jealous. It worked.

"Yeah, well, I guess my point is that you can't afford to trust anyone. Including a handsome man."

She laughed softly. "I thought you said Eliot is a woman."

"I'm just trying to cover all the bases."

Her voice turned serious. "You may be right. But Andrea and I are in a safe, isolated place. She's in the kitchen working on a story, I'm armed and sitting just a few feet away from the front door, and an armed man is outside. Neither man, woman, nor beast is coming through this door. Unless Eliot is already in this house, he, or she, isn't getting in here tonight."

"Okay. Just be careful. Try to call me tomorrow, so I'll know you're both all right."

"I will. Bye."

Drew hung up the phone and sighed.

"Listening to your side of the conversation, it was hard to tell if she was buying it," Charles said.

"She was open to the idea," Drew said, "but I don't think she was convinced. Lou's the kind of cop that requires hard evidence."

Chapter 30

Select Screen Name: Eliot

Enter Password: Sonnets

Send Instant Message To: Melpomene

Eliot: It's time.

Melpomene: Are you sure? This one must be perfect.

Eliot: It will be.

Melpomene: Does she know?

Eliot: Not yet, which amazes me. It was like watching someone painstakingly climb a fortress wall, only to slip and fall just before catching a glimpse of what lies on the other side.

Melpomene: Perhaps she doesn't have the courage to face the truth. She may know, subconsciously, that all the signs point to you, yet be scared to admit the implications.

Eliot: It really was an amazing thing to watch. A few minutes ago, I heard her say, "What? A woman?" She even glanced over her shoulder at me, the only woman in her company—and the only one who, if she'd allowed her mind to pursue the thought, was capable of doing the things Eliot has done.

Melpomene: Did she go into my room?

Eliot: Yes. It's just as you left it, exactly the way it was on the day they took you away. I put everything back in its rightful place once that whore sister of yours was gone.

Melpomene: Did she notice the door to the cellar?

Eliot: Yes, but I explained that it had been nailed shut since we had a little fire down there.

Melpomene: Lillian got what she deserved.

Eliot: I am blessed with your big heart, and I could have forgiven her for the nights she locked me down there while she desecrated your bedroom. But her final sin was unforgivable.
Melpomene: I know. That's why I inspired you to write her sonnet.

Eliot: And how fitting it was for those timeless words to be the last she ever heard. She was not laughing then. Not like when she threw my poems into the fireplace. But my fear and shame turned into pure, white hate when I discovered that your poems, the only thing I had left of you, were among the pages she incinerated.

Melpomene: I knew you needed my help. That's why I came back. It was my way of repaying you for what you had done for me.

Sonnets

Eliot: But you never needed to repay me for anything. It is I who am forever indebted to you. You recognized my gift, and you nurtured it. You inspired me. And you loved me.

Melpomene: And I still do, child. I always will.

Eliot: I still have the tape, you know. Me reading my sonnet to you, then you singing your favorite hymn. Your voice is so beautiful. I always have your voice with me, to guide me, when I'm doing my work.

Melpomene: Speaking of your work . . . as you said, it's time.

Eliot: Yes, Mother. Time to reveal who I really am. And that "Sonnet No. 6" is for her.

Chapter 31

Sitting in his office, staring out the window into the darkness, Drew wrestled with a host of opposing feelings. Like Charles, who was still sitting opposite the desk as he silently studied "Sonnet No. 6," Drew's thoughts were on a woman for whom he cared deeply, but whose intentions toward him were as foggy as the night outside. He wanted her, but did not know if she wanted him. He felt she was in danger at this very moment, but did not know exactly why. He thought he should be doing something to help her, but did not know what. And more than anything else, he wanted to be with her, but did not know where she was. The rain beating relentlessly against his window served as a reminder of the only other time in his life that he had felt so utterly helpless. Charles shifted in his seat, still staring at the sheet of paper. His face wore a solemn scowl. "I have another question," he said.

"Yeah?"

"Andrea was in charge of the *Gazette's* coverage of Eliot, and wrote most of the stories herself, but it stands to reason that she mostly wrote what she was told, right?"

"Sure, I guess so. Why?"

Charles looked at him. "When I ran into Andrea at the car wash earlier this week—well, actually, when I followed her there—she made some comment about doing more interviews with you and Lou Hennessey if Bernard Moss told her to. She seemed frustrated, as if she resented the lack of editorial control."

"Well, if you've met Bernard Moss, you know he's quite accustomed to doing things his way."

"I've never met him personally," Charles said, his shaved head wrinkling as he flashed a cryptic smile. "They don't invite people like me up to the country club, you know. But I'm aware that he and Chief Hennessey are pretty tight. Most people say he's the only reason she was appointed chief of police."

"So you think that Lou, through Bernard Moss, was influencing Andrea's coverage of Eliot?"

"To some degree, yes."

"Okay, but what's your point?"

"My point is that maybe Lou Hennessey is the 'celebrated architect of lies.'"

Drew sat up straight, as did the hairs on the back of his neck. "You think this sonnet could have been written about Lou?"

"I don't know, maybe I'm reaching here," Charles said. "You're the poetry expert. But, to me, the word 'celebrated' seems more applicable to Lou Hennessey than to Andrea. Andrea's name may have been on all the stories, but you and the chief were the heroes after Eliot's last attempt. And what if the reference to the 'siren's call' was a double-entendre? In addition to the ancient Greek nymphs, what if it also referred to a police car siren?"

Drew was having trouble catching his breath. "God. It could be Lou."

"If they're together, I think they're both at risk," Charles said. "But if they knew Lou could be the primary target, it might make a difference in the way they set up their defenses."

"I need to call her again," Drew muttered, more to himself than to Charles. "I know she'll resent being disturbed again when she's on that type of assignment, but I think this is important, don't you?"

Charles sighed. "You should do whatever you think is right, Drew. I'm the wrong guy to ask. Andrea is my latest example in life of having obviously made a wrong move, and not even knowing what it was."

Drew was already reaching for his phone. "What makes you think you did anything wrong? You said she seemed interested the night you took her to Bert's."

"Well, when I saw her at the car wash, she was as cold as ice. And acting strange. She seemed totally absorbed in getting her car cleaned. She gave the two boys a hundred per cent tip for scrubbing all the pine sap off."

Drew put down the phone and stared hard at his colleague. "What did you say?"

"The boys told me her car was covered with pine sap. Being a city boy, you may not have had any experience with it, but let me tell you, it requires a lot of scrubbing to get that stuff off. I don't know how she ever got so much of it on her car in the first place. She keeps it in a garage at her apartment, and there certainly aren't any pine trees in the parking lot of the *Gazette*."

A fusillade of memories and images were triggered in Drew's head. He recalled what had Lou said about the tire tread prints the FBI had lifted in the woods adjacent to Bert's parking lot. They had determined the car was mid-sized, based on the clear area left in the midst of the pine needles and limbs blown down by the wind. And the distance between the tread prints matched the wheel span of a General Motors make. "What kind of car was she driving?" he asked.

"A Buick Regal. Why?"

"Shit!" Drew shouted, and then snatched up the phone, frantically dialing Lou's number. Ignoring Charles' questioning stare, he waited but there was no answer. He considered leaving a message, but decided that this theory required an actual conversation. He would just have to keep calling until he reached her. Unable to simply sit at his desk doing nothing while waiting to try her cell phone again, he grabbed his coat, thanked Charles for his help, and ran out the door.

Moments earlier, Lou's thoughts were interrupted by the sound of something hitting the front of the house. She had risen from her chair and moved quickly to the window to look out when she felt the vibrating buzz of the cell phone in her jacket pocket. She removed it and looked at the display—Drew again. What new theories has he come up with now? I'll call him in a few minutes. At the moment, she wanted to make sure everything was okay outside. She called Agent Fletcher and he assured her that no one was moving around out there. He had a clear view of the front of the house. Convinced that the noise she had heard was just the result of the wind and rain, Lou walked back to her chair and sat.

She pulled her phone from her pocket but did not call Drew. She needed a couple of minutes to think. Her years of training told her that the most important thing she could do right now was stay on the lookout for any sound, any movement, that indicated an intruder. If Eliot had somehow figured out where they were and planned to attack, the inclement weather would provide both darkness and noise to help ensure a stealthy approach. She also considered the possibility of Eliot arriving by boat—the banks of the Chattagua River were only a hundred yards behind the house.

In addition to the logistical issues posed by the storm, Lou was still grappling with the things Drew had said in their last conversation. Was it possible that Eliot was a woman? If so, it would answer a lot of questions that had baffled her from the beginning. On the other hand, based on what she knew about the murders, Lou knew that if Eliot were a woman she had to be one of uncommon strength and conditioning. Besides overcoming the victims with a minimum of struggling, which also indicated quickness and agility, she would have had to be capable of lifting Celeste Holbrook to throw her into the well, and of carrying Jesse Kirkpatrick from her car to the fence where she was tied.

The concept had merit, to be sure, and Lou wanted to talk with Drew about it some more. She hoped Charles Alexander was still there so she could speak with both of them. Wouldn't it be something if the riddle of Eliot's identity ended up being solved by two English professors? she thought, and then realized she did not care. She was way past being concerned with credit. Results were all that mattered now. She would recheck the locks on the back door and windows, to satisfy her concerns about an attack from the rear, and then return Drew's call.

"Ready for some fresh coffee?" Andrea asked from behind her.

"In a minute. I want to double-check the locks on the back of the house first."

"I already poured you a cup," Andrea said, walking around to the right side of the chair and extending the mug of steaming, black liquid. "Tell me what Drew had to say. What was that talk about a woman?"

Lou reached for the steaming mug of coffee with both hands.

"Oh, he and Charles Alexander have been studying the last sonnet, and the reference to Cassandra got them thinking about the possibility of Eliot being . . ." At that moment she glanced from the coffee to the face of the person offering it, and found herself looking into the most evil eyes she had ever seen.

"A woman?" Andrea said, a split second before she flung the hot brew in Lou's face.

Lou instinctively protected her eyes with her left hand and blindly groped for the gun with her right. She felt the surface of the lamp table where the gun had been, but knew she was too late when she heard the metallic click of the cylinder turning as the revolver was cocked.

Andrea's voice was as soft as a whisper, yet as intense as a primal scream. "Don't move."

Wiping her scalded face with her shirtsleeve, Lou finally generated enough tears to wash the coffee from her burning eyes. She looked up at Andrea and saw a face that was like a mask. It resembled the face of the woman she knew, that she had trusted, in every physical detail, but it was twisted into a malevolent smile that turned Lou's guts to ice.

"Andrea, you need help," she said quietly.

"No, Lou, you're the one who needs help," the sinister Andrea mask replied. "You need help seeing the truth. Fortunately for you, I'm here to provide it. That's what I do."

Lou's heart froze. "So 'Sonnet No. 6' was about me?"

"Oh, yes. And you should feel honored to be the subject of one of my works. It's your one chance for immortality. Whenever lovers of poetry read 'Sonnet No. 6,' they will think of you."

Lou tried to keep her voice steady, despite the paralyzing terror pulsing through her veins like snake venom. "You have to stop, Andrea. You won't get away with any more murders. As clever as you are, you won't be able to hide the fact that you were my killer. Too many people know we're here together. And there's an FBI agent right outside."

Andrea held the gun mere inches from Lou's chest. "I would think that by now you'd know better than to underestimate me, Chief Hennessey. Do you think we'd even be here if I hadn't planned it?"

Lou was genuinely confused. "How could you know that I would come here with you?"

"It wasn't so hard. I knew you were expecting the next sonnet to be about me, because I'd been followed a couple of weeks ago. All I had to do was fabricate another stalking episode a couple of nights before the new sonnet arrived, and I knew I could manipulate you. It was all part of my plan. Rather brilliant, I think."

"But your plan won't work this time," Lou said, beginning to rise slowly from the chair.

"Don't!" Andrea said sharply. "Keep your seat. You'll get a chance to stretch your legs later."

Lou continued to rise, her eyes locked with Andrea's. "It's over, Andrea, and killing me won't make a difference."

"What makes you so sure?"

"Drew Osborne has already figured out that Eliot is a woman. It's only a matter of time before my police, and the FBI start narrowing down the list of possible suspects. If you and I are here together and you just happen to be the only one to walk out alive, the coincidence will be too much to ignore. No matter what kind of story you've devised, it won't ring true."

"Sit!" Andrea hissed. "Do not dare to speak to me about truth. You can't even grasp the concept."

Lou was only inches from the barrel of the gun. She realized that she might not have another chance to get this close, and she did not believe that Andrea had gone to such elaborate measures to bring her there just to plant a bullet in her. She concluded that Andrea had other plans for her, and those plans would certainly be no more appealing than the comparatively quick death from a mortal gunshot wound. Feeling she was in a no-win situation where the only consideration was the relative undesirability of the various losing options, she lunged for the revolver.

Lou had heard the sound of her pistol firing hundreds of times before, but always either outdoors or muffled by earplugs when inside the underground police shooting range. In the confines of this old Victorian living room, however, it was deafeningly loud. The sound seemed to echo in her head when she flew backward over her chair as if tossed by a giant, unseen hand. Even before she hit the floor, the darkness of the night outside flowed into the house and enveloped her.

It was six thirty when Drew, dripping wet, stormed into the Smythville police station. "Where's Sergeant Mullins?" he asked the first person he saw, a bald, heavyset officer behind the chest-high counter just inside the door.

"He's tied up right now," said the uniformed man, eyeing Drew suspiciously. "Is there something I could help you with?"

"I'm Drew Osborne, from the college. I've been working as an advisor to Chief Hennessey on the Eliot case, and she told me to see Howard Mullins if I found out something important."

"What's so important?"

Drew could feel his anger and frustration rising to the boiling point. "Look, I'm here because this is what the chief told me to do. I need to see Sergeant Mullins right away."

The obstinate officer looked beyond Drew and bellowed, "Art! Come over here a sec, will ya?"

Drew turned around to see the boyish face of Art Schaeffer, its youthful demeanor marred by dark circles under weary-looking eyes, moving toward him. "I'll take care of it, Gus," Schaeffer said, then led Drew a few feet into the bustling squad room.

"What's up, Dr. Osborne?" he asked.

"Chief Hennessey told me to get in touch with Sergeant Mullins if I came up with anything on Eliot's latest poem," Drew said urgently. "I think I have something he and Frank Clay should know about. Is either one of them here?"

"The sarge is here, but he's really busy. We're sending out all the patrol units in another couple of minutes, and he's giving everybody their instructions. He's probably not going to have time for you unless it's really urgent."

"You can't get any more urgent than this," Drew said. "I have reason to believe that this last sonnet was written about Chief Hennessey."

That bombshell had the intended effect on the young officer, and two minutes later, Drew was face to face with Mullins in Lou's office. "What's this about Chief Hennessey being Eliot's latest target?" Mullins asked, the skepticism clearly evident on his weathered face.

"I think she was who Eliot was referring to as the 'celebrated architect of lies,'" Drew said.

Mullins, appearing to be more interested in the city map on the wall than in his uninvited visitor, turned and shot him a cold glance. "You're saying our chief of police is a liar?"

"No, I'm saying that Eliot is saying she's a liar. I think Eliot believes the chief influenced what was written in the *Gazette* about the failed attempt on Miss Kirkpatrick's life, trying to calm the public's fears by saying Eliot was not infallible. And I think the reference to the 'siren's call' was to a police siren."

"That's it?" Mullins asked incredulously. "That's what has you convinced that he's planning to kill the chief?"

"There's another thing," Drew continued, undeterred by the officer's sarcastic tone. "I don't think Eliot is a he. I think Eliot is a woman, and I believe it might be Andrea Warren."

Mullins looked at Drew as if he'd just said he thought Eliot was a Martian. "What? Do you have any idea how ridiculous that sounds?"

Drew fought to keep his temper. "I've been trying to figure out how Eliot was able to overcome his victims without any signs of a physical struggle. It occurred to me that it had to be someone those women knew and trusted, and that could very well be another woman. I tried to call Lou to tell her this but she didn't answer."

"Which proves only that Chief Hennessey, like me, doesn't have time for this crap." Mullins started for the door.

"Wait, you have to listen to me." Drew grabbed the other man's arm. Mullins looked at the hand on his arm, and then into Drew's eyes. Drew had the presence of mind to quickly let go.

"Please," Drew said, trying to keep his voice calm and non-confrontational, "just give me one more minute. Lou told me that the tire tread prints you got indicated a General Motors mid-sized car. Andrea Warren drives a Buick Regal, and earlier this week, she took it to a car wash and paid extra to have a lot of pine sap scrubbed off."

Mullins turned to face Drew directly. He was standing so close Drew could smell the stale coffee on his breath, and his voice was low and menacing. "Look, professor, I'm sure you think that being on a first name basis with my boss entitles you to special privileges around here. And I guess you believe that just because you got lucky last week and saved Miss Kirkpatrick from dying in that fire that everybody in town thinks you're some kind of crime-solving hero."

"Listen to what . . . ."

"No, you listen to me," Mullins said between clenched teeth. "I've been a cop for twenty-two years, and despite your fancy poetry degree from New York City, I think I know a little bit more about criminal investigations than you do. You can sometimes make a case out of circumstantial evidence, but you can't make one out of horse-shit. And what you have is a textbook case of the latter."

Drew realized he was getting nowhere. "Where are they?" he asked quietly.

Mullins looked at him with an expression Drew thought would ordinarily be reserved for something someone would scrape off the bottom of a shoe. "Did you hear a single word I just said?"

"I heard you loud and clear, Sergeant Mullins. Where are they?"

"I don't know."

"You don't know or you just won't tell me?"

"Both."

"Does Frank Clay know?"

"Probably. But as you heard this afternoon, he's on a highly sensitive stakeout and can't be disturbed." He lowered his voice to a threatening whisper. "That stakeout is probably our only chance of nabbing this guy Eliot. If you go anywhere near there, I will lock you up so tight that the chief herself won't be able to get you out. Are you clear on that?"

Drew held his gaze. There was nothing in the other man's eyes that indicated he was bluffing. "Crystal clear."

"Good. Now, if you'll excuse me, professor, I . . . ."

"Sarge! Sarge!" A young officer burst into the room. "Special Agent Clay's on the phone for you. He needs us to provide some additional surveillance. A maroon Pontiac LeMans looked like it was following Agent Bartlett from the *Gazette* parking lot to Miss Warren's apartment. It was last seen cruising around the neighborhood real slowly, like the driver was looking for something."

Mullins glanced at Drew and then said to the young officer, "A maroon Pontiac LeMans, you say? Let's see, that would be a mid-sized General Motors make, wouldn't it?"

The officer looked confused. "Yeah, GM makes the Pontiac."

"Just wanted to make sure what I'm looking for," Mullins said with a smirk, and hurried out of the room.

Drew walked slowly through the squad room and saw Art Schaeffer standing at the desk by the front door. The rookie stepped over to him and spoke in a hushed tone. "Any luck?"

"None. Does Sergeant Mullins really not know where the chief and Miss Warren are, or was he just unwilling to tell me?"

"I don't think he knows," Schaeffer said. "No one does, I don't think, except Frank Clay, and he's up to his ass in alligators right now."

"I know," Drew said. "Thanks anyway, Officer Schaeffer."

He had stepped out into the driving rain and was preparing to make a run to his car, when the door to the police station opened again, spilling light onto the puddled concrete steps.

"Dr. Osborne." It was Schaeffer again.

"Yeah?"

"There's one other person who might know where they are. But I doubt he'll tell you either."

"Who?"

"Bernard Moss."

His eyes weary from straining to penetrate the steady rain and pitch-black darkness, Agent Fletcher had been staring toward the road when he heard the unmistakable crack of gunfire. His head whipped around and he held his breath, waiting to hear if more shots were fired, but the only sound was that of the rain pelting his car. The dark form of the house, with only the dim glow of the kitchen lights visible through the leaded glass of the front door, loomed forty yards away, like a one-eyed monster beckoning him to its lair.

He pulled his Walther PPK from his shoulder holster and opened the car door. He grabbed his hat from the passenger seat and placed it on his head to keep the rain out of his eyes, giving him sharper aim.

Sloshing through the mud in a low crouch, he covered the distance to the house in a matter of seconds, approaching on the far left. He climbed over the railing onto the porch, and then crept toward the dining room window. Looking in and seeing nothing but black, he moved quickly past it, cautiously approaching the front door.

His finger exerting light pressure on the trigger of the gun, he peered in through the glass. He could see Andrea Warren bending over another form lying on the floor. It looked like Chief Hennessey. Andrea did not appear to be cowering, but rather trying to provide assistance. Acting on the assumption that a gun was not trained on her and that his entry would not put her life in further danger, he burst through the door, dropped to one knee, and quickly scanned the dimly lit room.

Andrea let out a gasp as she turned to face him, and then shouted, "She's been shot! He must have come through the kitchen. I was upstairs. I heard the shot and came running down the stairs, and he must have thought I was armed because he ran out the back door."

Fletcher moved cautiously through the foyer to the kitchen entrance and glanced into the room. It was empty, and the back door was open. Rain was blowing in. The floor was already wet. Again moving cautiously, he stepped to the door and looked out into the darkness. He knew that walking out that door would be suicidal if Eliot were lying in wait, watching the back of the house. He decided that his best bet was to exit the house through the front door and sneak around the side.

He heard a voice from behind him in the foyer. "Do you see anything?" Andrea asked.

"No. I'm gonna call for an ambulance and some back-up, then go out the front door and look for him." He picked up the wall phone receiver and held it to his ear. There was no dial tone, not even the sound of static. Eliot must have cut the line.

"The phone's dead," he called out. Then, he heard a metallic click right behind his head.

"So are you," Andrea said.

Chapter 32

The streets of Smythville were deserted, everyone apparently having yielded to the relentless force of the storm. Sheets of rain danced across the streets to the rhythm of the gusting wind, and the tops of the barren maple trees along Main Street bent toward the ground like stretching ballerinas. Along the curb, a raging river of dark water washed away everything in its path.

Drew hoped Bernard Moss would still be in his office. The FBI stakeout had apparently moved from the *Gazette* parking lot to Andrea Warren's apartment only a short time earlier, so he had reason to believe that Moss was still waiting by his phone, hoping for the opportunity to make Eliot's capture the next morning's headline.

Drew parked his car right in front of the *Gazette* door. It was locked, but there were lights on inside. He pressed the button, waited about twenty seconds, and then pressed it again.

"Who is it?" a familiar, surly voice called from the other side.

"Drew Osborne. I need to speak with you," he called back, the sound of his voice nearly drowned out by the pouring rain.

The door opened. Moss appeared to study Drew's drenched form for several seconds, as if confirming his identity, before stepping aside to allow entrance. Drew literally leapt through the door, anxious to get out from under the waterfall created by a shallow overhang a couple of feet above his head.

Moss pushed the door shut, locked it, and turned to face his unexpected guest. "You look like a drowned rat," he said.

"I feel like one," Drew replied, as he removed his overcoat.

Moss turned and started walking toward his office. "Leave your coat by the door. I don't want you dripping water all over the place."

Drew did as he was told and followed the rapidly retreating man through the pressroom. Entering the senior editor's office, he watched him squeeze his considerable bulk between the armrests of his desk chair, which squealed in protest.

"What can I do for you, Dr. Osborne?" Moss asked.

Drew wasted no time getting to the point of his visit. "I believe that Lou, not Andrea, is the subject of 'Sonnet No. 6.' And I believe that the danger she faces could come from . . . from an unexpected source."

The big man's forehead creased in a quizzical frown. "Of course it'll be an 'unexpected source.' None of us knows Eliot's identity. He could be anybody. For a while, I thought you were him."

"I know, so did Lou. But I'm not Eliot, and Eliot is not a him."

"What?"

Drew proceeded to give Moss the same explanation he had given Howard Mullins, but stopped short of divulging his theory of the killer's identity. He wanted to make sure Moss was on board with his train of thought before he took the chance of derailing it with such a bold accusation. Drew had no way of knowing whether Moss was buying his story, but he was considerably more attentive, and less belligerent than Mullins had been.

When Drew completed his narrative, Moss sat silently for a few moments, his elbows resting on the arms of his chair and his fingertips pressed together an inch from his nose. "She would have to be a strong woman to do the things Eliot has done," he finally said, "but I suppose a young, physically fit female could have done them, especially if she took her victims by surprise. And your theory about Lou makes sense too. She and I had some discussions about how to tell the story of Eliot's failed attempt in a way that would ease the public hysteria, although I don't see how Eliot could have been aware of that."

"One of the things I've learned from my involvement with this case is that Eliot should never be underestimated," Drew said. "And if my theory is true, Lou is focusing on protecting someone else when she's the one who needs to be protected. That might be all the advantage Eliot needs."

"Have you spoken to Lou about this?"

"Only the part about Eliot being a woman. I tried again a few minutes later, to tell her that I believe this last sonnet was written about her, and she didn't answer. I left right after that to go to the police station, and then I came here. Why don't you try her now? I'm worried about her."

Moss grabbed his phone and punched in Lou's number. After a few seconds he spoke into the phone. "Lou, call me at my office as soon as you get this message. Drew Osborne is here and we have some important information for you."

Moss hung up the phone and turned back to Drew. "I should hear back from her soon. Meanwhile, you should share this information with Frank Clay and Howard Mullins."

"I saw Sergeant Mullins before I came here. He didn't buy it. It seems that interpretations of a poem don't quite meet his definition of evidence."

"Yeah, I remember that crack he made in Lou's office this afternoon. But Frank Clay is a bit more sophisticated in his thinking. You should speak with him."

"He's heading up that stakeout at Andrea's apartment right now, and they have a suspicious car under surveillance. I was explicitly ordered to stay away from there."

Moss looked confused. "Then why are you here? Do you want me to speak to Mullins and demand he patch you through to Clay?"

Drew stared directly into Moss' eyes. "No. I want you to tell me where Lou and Andrea are."

Moss held his stare. "Why?"

"Because I feel very strongly that getting this information to Lou might save her life."

"And you intend to deliver it personally?"

"Frank Clay and his FBI team can't be disturbed, especially with evidence as circumstantial as this, and Sergeant Mullins thinks I'm crazy. I don't see where I have a choice."

"But Lou's armed, and there's an armed FBI agent with them. And I don't see how Eliot could know where they are. The decision was just made a couple of nights ago, right here in this office. Only Lou, Andrea, Frank Clay, and I knew where they were going. And now, of course, the agent that's with them."

Drew took a deep breath. This was where he would see if the cards he held comprised a winning hand, or if he was busted. "Remember me saying that I believed the threat to Lou would come from an unexpected source?"

Moss frowned a moment, obviously confused, before his eyes suddenly went wide. "The FBI agent? But you said Eliot was a woman."

Drew said nothing, waiting for Moss to reach the only other logical conclusion. It did not take long.

"You think it's Andrea?"

"The FBI found the spot where they believe Eliot's car was parked during the Jesse Kirkpatrick abduction."

"Yeah, I know all about that," Moss said with an impatient flick of a hand.

"Then you know their evidence indicates a mid-sized General Motors car was parked there, and that it would have been covered with pine needles and limbs blown from the trees."

"Yeah," Moss said, looking less certain now, as if he knew that what was coming would force him to admit the feasibility of Drew's theory.

"Andrea drives a Buick Regal. Earlier this week, Charles Alexander ran into her at the car wash just south of town. He said she paid a big tip to the boys working there to scrub a large amount of pine sap off her car."

Moss protested, but it was a half-hearted attempt. "It's not that unusual to get pine sap on your car."

"Andrea keeps her car in a garage at her apartment. And the only trees along Main Street or bordering your parking lot are maple trees."

"But still . . ."

"You agreed just a few minutes ago that the evidence indicates Eliot is a woman. A young, physically fit woman, which Andrea clearly is. And remember, the two of you were in Lou's office when the patrol routes were outlined for last Thursday night. She would have known which roads to take to get out to Bert's and back without being seen. And by the way, she and Charles Alexander had dinner at Bert's the week before Miss Kirkpatrick was taken. Guess who their waitress was."

Moss was visibly shaken, but still seemed unwilling to take that final step that Drew needed him to take. "Look, I see the logic of your argument, but I think it's too flimsy and circumstantial to convince Frank Clay, let alone Howard Mullins."

This was Drew's chance. "I agree. That's why I need you to tell me where they are. If I'm wrong, then nothing, including Andrea's reputation, has been harmed. And if I'm right, I just might be able to save Lou's life."

Moss looked pleadingly at his phone.

"If she was going to call you back, she would have done so by now," Drew said.

Moss did not reply. He opened a drawer in the credenza behind his desk and extracted a manila folder. "This is Andrea's personnel file," he said, opening it. "It lists her mother's home in Milton as her previous address. Her mother's name is Isabel. That's where they went."

He scribbled the address on an index card and gave Drew directions for the drive from Smythville to Milton. Drew thanked him, stood to leave, and then nodded at the file.

"Is there a phone number?" he asked.

Moss opened the file and looked. "It just says 'unlisted'."

"Okay, well, I'm sure there's a phone in the house. I'll call you when I get there. Give me an hour."

He was putting on his dripping overcoat at the front door when Moss called out to him. "Dr. Osborne."

Drew turned. "Yes?"

The big man was struggling to pull on an overcoat as he hurried across the room carrying an umbrella. "Hold on, I'm coming with you."

"No," Drew protested, "I think you should stay here."

"Why?" Moss bellowed, clearly angered at having his authority challenged. "Lou Hennessey is a friend of mine, and Andrea is a valued employee. I care about both of them. I'm coming with you."

"Mr. Moss, listen to me," Drew pleaded. "If my suspicions are correct, I could be walking into a trap. If you're there too, there's no one to get word to Mullins and Clay. If you don't hear from me in an hour, hour and a half tops, you call them. You'll be the only person in a position to send help."

Moss appeared to ponder Drew's argument for a moment, and then sighed wearily. "I guess you're right. Just make damn sure you call me the minute you get there. If I don't hear from you, I'm sending in the cavalry."

"That's as good a plan as I can think of right now," Drew said.

Moss stared at him a moment before speaking in a low, tired voice. "You know, Dr. Osborne, your theory makes sense. But I hope like hell you're wrong."

"So do I," Drew said, and he meant it. He knew that if his theory was right, Lou was probably already dead.

Lou's first sensation as she began to emerge from the dark depths of unconsciousness was that of a sharp, stinging odor. Then came the pain, radiating out from an epicenter in her right shoulder and extending to every nerve ending in her body. Finally, she was aware of light—brighter than what she remembered in the living room, and coming from directly above her.

"Welcome back to the land of the living," she heard Andrea say. "Even if only for a short visit. Sorry about the household ammonia, but I didn't have any smelling salts."

Lou tried to lift her head from the floor, but the resulting pain almost caused her to faint. "Where am I?" she murmured. Her tongue felt twice its normal size, and her throbbing shoulder felt tight.

"I moved you to the kitchen," Andrea said. "The light was better. I put a compress on your shoulder to slow the bleeding. I don't want you to bleed to death." She smiled. "I have other plans for you. But you know that, don't you? After all, you're a student of my poetry, and now, a subject."

It occurred to Lou that Andrea did not appear to be in any hurry, or to have any concerns about being interrupted as she sat on the kitchen floor chatting casually. She thought that could mean only one thing. She dreaded hearing the answer, but had to ask the question. "Where's Agent Fletcher?"

Andrea's eyes focused on the other side of the room. "If it's any consolation, he never felt a thing."

Despite the searing pain, Lou lifted her head to follow Andrea's gaze. All she could see was a pair of legs clothed in gray flannel slacks and muddy, black wingtips, but it was enough to confirm the young man's fate. "Oh, Jesus," she whispered, as she closed her eyes.

"My mother always says you shouldn't call the Lord's name unless you're praying to him," Andrea said.

Lou was silent for a moment, and then opened her eyes to look into the face of the devil. "I was," she said. Then, she asked the question that had first occurred to her moments before she had been shot. "Why have you done these things, Andrea?"

"It's my calling," Andrea said quietly. "I have a gift. I write truth.

I write it even before it happens, and then I make it true. And in the process, in addition to creating beautiful, compelling poetry, I rid the world of evil, vile creatures who are destined to cause great pain and suffering."

"Like Margaret Fenwyck and Melissa Turner? What was so evil about them? You worked with them. They were your friends."

Andrea's eyes seemed to be looking at something far away in another dimension, one that neither Lou nor any other sane person could see. "Friends? Maybe. Even so, I did them both a favor." She smiled. "You know, I believe Margaret actually had a crush on me."

"And that's why you killed her?"

"I killed her because she had the power to capture the heart of just about everyone she did have a crush on—man or woman. And that is a destructive power. It destroys lives."

"All of your . . . subjects . . . were young, attractive women. Is that why you killed them? Out of jealousy?"

"Jealousy?" Andrea sneered. "Don't you think I could have just about any man I wanted? And women too, if I were so inclined. But I have more than physical beauty. I have insight, talent, and power."

Lou swallowed hard, and then whispered, "Why me?"

Andrea smiled and looked into her eyes. "Do you know that you remind me of my mother?"

Drew stepped into the phone booth at the Exxon station on the outskirts of Milton. He had stopped to fill his nearly empty gas tank, and to ask for directions to Riverbank Road. The proprietor had asked what he was looking for, and Drew had told him the Warren house. The old man had dutifully given him directions, and a bit of history as well.

Drew punched in his calling card number issued by the school, and then dialed Bernard Moss at the *Gazette*. It rang several times. Just as Drew was about to hang up and call directory assistance for his home number, he heard a gruff voice coming through the line.

"Moss here."

"Mr. Moss, it's Drew Osborne. Have you heard from Lou?"

Moss said something Drew could not understand. Drew shouted. "I'm in a phone booth, and the rain is so loud I can barely hear you."

"I said no, I haven't heard from Lou, but I was just on the other line with Howard Mullins. The Pontiac they were following turned out to be a false alarm. Just some kid looking for his date's house. Where are you?"

"At a gas station in Milton. Based on the directions the man here gave me, I should be able to get to Andrea's house in another five minutes or so."

"Good. I'll stay right here until you call me back and tell me what's going on. I've been thinking about what you said, and I just don't believe that Andrea could be Eliot."

"I'm more convinced than ever that I'm right, Mr. Moss."

"Why the hell do you keep insisting on saying that?" Moss snapped. "I've known her a lot longer than you have, young man, and I'm a pretty decent judge of character."

"Just answer something for me," Drew said. "You told me that the decision to go to Andrea's mother's house was made in your office a couple of nights ago. Who suggested it?"

"Andrea did. It was that or spending the night in one of Lou's jail cells. I'd have come up with an alternative suggestion too, if it had been me."

"Did Andrea specifically say they would come stay with her mother, or just that they would stay at her mother's house?"

Moss sounded as if he were losing his patience. "What the hell's the difference?"

"There's a difference, believe me," Drew shouted over the noise of the rain pelting the glass booth. "What exactly did she say?"

"She said she'd visit her mom. Lou then suggested that she'd go with her. Why?"

"Has Andrea ever said anything to you about her mother before?"

"Well, every once in a while she'll tell me she's going home to spend the weekend with her. In fact, I heard her on her office phone with her mother just a couple of weeks ago, telling her she had to postpone a visit because she had to work all weekend. She was a little embarrassed because I don't allow personal long distance calls on the office phones. She offered to pay for the call, but I told her to forget about it. When an employee works as hard as Andrea, you don't sweat the small stuff."

Drew did not say anything. The pit of his stomach was as cold as the winter rain outside.

"What's this all about?" Moss bellowed. "What have you learned?"

Drew took a deep breath and tried to keep his voice from shaking. "The old man here at the gas station knew right where the Warren house is. He even knew Isabel Warren. And he told me she's been dead for over fifteen years."

Chapter 33

With every step, pain jolted through Lou's body like lightning flashes in the stormy night sky. Her hands were bound behind her back with her own handcuffs. The positioning of her arms had reopened the shoulder wound, and she could feel the warm, steady flow of blood down her side. The loss of blood, perhaps combined with shock, caused her to stumble frequently as Andrea led her across the open field behind the house. Despite the gun pressed against the back of her head, Lou did not fear a bullet to the brain. Andrea clearly had other plans—the turbulent rush of the rain-swollen river could be heard in the distance.

After a couple of minutes, Lou realized that they were no longer heading straight for the sound of the river, but were angling right, up a small hill. The incline was actually easier for her to maneuver than the movement down the slope had been. Her footing was surer and she was able to lean forward, relieving some of the tension on her wounded shoulder.

They reached the top of the incline, and Andrea pushed open a rickety, waist-high wooden gate. As they passed through it, a flash of lightning pierced the darkness, and Lou could see that they had entered a small burial plot. Her view of the area was brief, but long enough for her to see there were roughly a half-dozen headstones in various stages of disrepair. She was being led to one in particular.

"These are the Warrens," Andrea said, as if conducting a historical tour. "My grandparents were the first to be buried here, behind the house my grandfather built." Her voice then took on a mocking, derisive tone. "And over here is my dear Aunt Lillian, may she burn in hell." She laughed. "I got her off to a good start."

They walked a few more steps and stopped. Lou could barely make out the shape of a headstone at her feet.

"No one from my father's side of the family is buried here," Andrea continued. "I really don't know who he was. Some drifter that passed through here, working for the county fair, when my mother was in high school." She paused a moment, as if lost in thought. "I think that was the only sin she ever committed. And yet, out of that sin came her greatest blessing in life—me."

Another bolt of lightning streaked from the sky, seeming to almost reach the ground. The graveyard lit up like a football stadium during a night game for a split second, allowing Lou to read the name on the tombstone—"Isabel Warren."

"Mother," Andrea said, her voice now solemn, almost prayerful in tone, "this is Lou Hennessey, the woman I told you about. She's special. That's why I've decided she will find the truth the same way you did."

Without another word, she turned and pushed Lou back in the direction from which they had come. They exited the small cemetery through the tottering gate, and continued down the hill, away from the house. As they walked, Andrea thrust one hand into her coat pocket, and a moment later, Lou could hear a muffled voice. It sounded like a girl's voice, and it was speaking in a set rhythm broken only by intermittent sobs. At first, Lou thought it was coming from the cemetery behind them, but then realized it emanated from Andrea's coat. A tape recorder?

Lou strained to hear what was being said, but could not make out the words. After a minute or so, she heard the sound of crying again, followed by a woman's voice, soft and clear. The voice was singing, and Andrea joined in. The song was vaguely familiar to Lou, reminding her of Sunday evening church services in the tiny Ohio town where her grandparents had lived when she was a little girl.

"Yes, we'll gather at the riv-er
The beau-ti-ful, the beau-ti-ful riv-er"

Drew pulled his car about halfway up the long, tree-lined driveway and stopped. He wondered for a moment whether he should advertise his arrival by driving in, or should make an attempt at stealth. If everything was okay at the house, he feared that sneaking up on foot carried the risk of being mistakenly shot as an intruder. On the other hand, if Eliot was in control, it would be to his advantage to remain undetected for as long as possible. He decided on the covert option. He would have to trust that Lou and the FBI agent would be professional enough to identify their target before pulling the trigger.

The darkness and the torrential rain limited his visibility to a few yards. He could scarcely make out the obscure shape of the house silhouetted against the gloomy sky, and the dim light shining through the front door barely penetrated the thick, black curtain of night. It was only because of a sudden flash of jagged lightning that he saw the car parked among the trees to his left. He did not recognize it, and assumed it belonged to the FBI agent. Drew crept closer, peered in the window and, unable to see a thing, opened the driver's side door. The interior light did not come on, but he could see well enough to tell there was no one inside. He sat on the seat for a moment, reveling in a brief reprieve from the rain as he waited for his pounding heart to slow to a less dangerous rate.

As he took a deep breath, preparing to ease back out of the car and continue on his cautious approach to the house, he put his right hand on the seat. A sharp pain stung his palm and he lifted his hand quickly. Holding his hand an inch or two from his face as he delicately probed with the fingers of his left hand, he removed a small shard.

Reaching again with his right hand, he gently brushed the seat beside him. It was covered with bits of glass. He extended his right foot and heard the crunch of more glass under his shoe on the floorboard.

Confused, he quickly glanced around the car. All of the windows seemed to be intact, so the breakage did not appear to be from damage caused by the wind. Slowly, carefully, he felt along the dashboard. The gauges directly in front of him seemed fine.

But as his probing hands moved to the right, his fingers caught on a jagged edge. Having spent an evening in Lou's car, he knew what belonged in that space, and his heart froze. The police radio had been smashed.

There was no longer any doubt in his mind that this situation called for a furtive approach. He was about to enter Eliot's domain.

He climbed out of the car and, despite the covering noise of the wind and rain, eased the door shut as quietly as he could. He then turned and started toward the house, staying just inside the tree line to his left. He saw Lou's car parked near the front steps, but did not approach it. He assumed its radio had also been destroyed.

He reached the side of the porch and climbed over the railing, being careful not to put too much weight on it for fear the shaky spindles would collapse, sending him crashing loudly to the floor. Once on the porch, he crept to the window and peered in, but it was like looking at a black screen. The front door was only a couple of steps away, and the dull glow of diffused light was visible through the leaded glass panes. He realized that if he was going to see any-thing he would have to take the chance of looking in from that van-tage point, simultaneously making himself visible to anyone inside. Knowing that was his only option, he took and held a deep breath, moved to the door, and looked in.

His vision was distorted somewhat by the thick glass, but he could tell the light originated from the back of the house, at the far end of a foyer. He slowly turned the door knob, freezing every time it made a noise, and eased the door open. It creaked as it swung inward, and Drew realized that anyone on the first floor of the house would undoubtedly be aware of his presence. Knowing Eliot's murderous history, he knew he could be greeted with anything from an ax to a flamethrower. Of all the undesirable options flashing through his anxious mind, he hoped it would be something quick. He had never imagined the time would come when he would find himself hoping for a well-placed bullet, but if Eliot was lying in wait, that was exactly what he hoped was in store.

He stepped inside the house and looked to his right. It was a living room, with an overturned chair and lamp table near the window. There had been a struggle, which he thought was most likely between Andrea and Lou. A lump formed in his throat, as he wondered who had prevailed. He continued through the foyer, and then cautiously looked around the corner into the kitchen. A man's body lay sprawled on the linoleum floor, his back to Drew. The head, with a red patch about the size of a quarter just below a boyish cowlick in the back, rested in a large pool of blood.

There was no one else in the room. Drew moved to the body and knelt beside it. He thought that it had to be Agent Fletcher. He did not recall meeting him, and gently turned the body over to see if he could recognize the face. He did not, because there was no face left. The damage caused by the exit wound was devastating. Drew looked away, fighting the urge to vomit.

He stood on shaky legs, and then noticed that Fletcher's raincoat was still buttoned. There was no gun on the floor, so the buttoned raincoat told Drew that it was probably still in his shoulder holster. He quickly bent down and unbuttoned the raincoat and the suit jacket, and breathed a sigh of relief when he saw the pistol handle right below the dead man's left armpit. He removed it, realizing he knew very little about how to use it, but immediately felt more secure just by having it in his hand.

He located the safety, switched it to the off position, and was comforted by the fact that at least he could now make some noise.

Whether he could actually hit anything, or even point it at another human being, was another question.

Standing again, he noticed for the first time the wall phone dangling at the end of its cord. He listened, heard dead silence, and knew he would be unable to call Moss. Knowing that anything to be done would have to be done by him alone, he shifted his focus to the most critical question: *Where has Andrea taken Lou? Upstairs?*

There were no lights visible at the top of the stairs, nor had he noticed any in the second floor windows as he approached the house. He looked around the kitchen and saw a door. Thinking that it probably lead to a basement or cellar, he tried to ease it open, but it would not budge. Closer inspection revealed that it was nailed shut. He was beginning to panic. It appeared the two women were not in the house, yet both cars were still outside. *They have to be nearby—but where?*

It was then that he noticed the open laptop computer on the kitchen table. He walked over to it and looked at the screen. There was a heading at the top that indicated it had been used for instant e-mail messaging. His stomach knotted when he saw the sender's screen name—Eliot. He saw the other name, Melpomene, and wondered who that was. The only Melpomene he had ever heard of was the ancient Greek Muse of tragedy. Somehow that seemed eerily appropriate.

Drew's mind was being bombarded by a hundred questions. Was this Melpomene a partner who had helped Andrea with her murderous rampage? Should the police be looking for two killers? Looking around the room as he frantically tried to organize his thoughts, he noticed something else. The computer was not plugged into a phone line. Of course not—the phone line is dead. He looked again at the laptop and saw no wireless card. How could Andrea have been communicating with anybody? And why would she even be trying to communicate with someone tonight? Desperate for answers, and fighting the urge to run outside to look for Lou, he forced himself to read a few lines.

Sonnets

Eliot: It's time.

Melpomene: Are you sure? This one must be perfect.

Eliot: It will be.

Melpomene: Does she know?

Eliot: Not yet, which amazes me. It was like watching someone painstakingly climb a fortress wall, only to slip and fall just before catching a glimpse of what lies on the other side.

Drew concluded that Eliot—Andrea—was referring to Lou, indicating that the chief of police was, at that time, still unaware that the killer she was searching for was in the same room. This was confirmed when he read the next entry.

Eliot: It really was an amazing thing to watch. A few minutes ago, I heard her say, "What? A woman?" She even glanced over her shoulder at me, the only woman in her company—and the only one who, if she'd allowed her mind to pursue the thought, was capable of doing the things Eliot has done.

Drew realized he was reading an e-mail conversation that had taken place earlier that evening, at the same time that he was speaking on the phone with Lou. Still, he could not understand how the messages could have been sent or received, or who Andrea had been communicating with. Totally bewildered, he scrolled down to the bottom and got his answer to the last question. It chilled him to the bone.

Eliot: Yes, Mother. Time to reveal who I really am. And that "Sonnet No. 6" was for her.

The terrifying thought sprang into his mind before he could consciously block it—maybe Andrea has already killed Lou and is outside somewhere disposing of the body. Then he saw a blue rag on the floor under a chair. He picked it up, felt the wetness of it, and smelled ammonia. Did Andrea knock Lou unconscious, then revive her to take her outside to kill her? If so, what was her plan?

Wait! The answer has to be in the sonnet.

He concentrated on the lines he had read a hundred times that afternoon. "Nor flee her fate to crash upon the rocks"—are there cliffs nearby? But the next line—"The earth will bid farewell without a sound"—did not fit. Someone would surely scream if thrown from a cliff, unless already dead. Then it hit him. "This wretched bitch whose grievous lies are drowned." *Drowned! The house is on Riverbank Road. I didn't cross a river on my way here, so it has to be behind the house.*

Drew raced out the front door, down the steps and into the rain. He turned left and started running as fast as he could, keeping the gun pointed skyward, just as he had seen in the movies. He could see no further than a few feet in front of him, except when lightning lit up the landscape to reveal a huge field, sloping gradually downward. Not knowing in which direction to proceed, he simply headed straight back from the house, sensing that was where the river would be.

When he had gone some distance, far enough that the outline of the house was no longer visible behind him, he thought he heard something. Strangely, it sounded like singing. He could not be sure, but he thought it had sounded as if it was coming from his right. He started running in that direction, slower now, not wanting to literally stumble over someone in the pitch-black darkness.

He was so focused on the sound of singing in the distance that he did not notice a tree stump. He fell hard, but managed to hold onto the gun. As he struggled back to his feet, there was another bright flash of lightning and he saw them—forty or fifty yards ahead and to the right, moving in the direction of a wooden footbridge traversing the narrow but raging river.

He did not think they had seen him. Knowing that was his only advantage, he hurried after them, crouching low to minimize his exposure should another bolt of lightning suddenly illuminate the field. The more he closed the gap between them, the more convinced he was that it was indeed singing that he had heard.

"Gather with the saints at the riv-er"

He could no longer see them or the footbridge, so he continued moving toward the sound of the singing. He could not help but think about another reference in "Sonnet No. 6"—"the siren's call." He knew that he, like Ulysses' men, was possibly being lured into a deathtrap by an evil songstress, but he had no choice. He had seen Lou in the brief flash of light. She was alive, and he was her only hope of staying that way.

He continued along until he came to the steep riverbank. He still heard the singing to his right, and could tell he was very close now. Another flash of lightning revealed Andrea leading Lou, whose arms were bound behind her, onto the narrow wooden bridge. Andrea held a gun—which she had already demonstrated the ability to use—to Lou's neck. There was only one reason Drew could think of for Andrea to take Lou onto that bridge, and that was to toss her, arms bound, into the roiling river below.

"That flows by the throne of God"

Running as fast as his legs could carry him, Drew closed the remaining distance between them, no longer concerned with stealth. The only way he would get a clear shot at Andrea was for her to dispose of Lou, and then it would be too late. He would have to somehow talk Andrea out of going through with this realization of "Sonnet No. 6." Or die trying.

"Andrea!" he shouted as he stepped onto the wooden slats of the bridge. He was close enough to see their outlines in the darkness, but not much more.

Andrea stopped singing, and Drew could see her turning, pushing Lou between herself and him. "Why, Dr. Osborne, my most clever student," Andrea said, "I see you have successfully interpreted my sonnet." Her voice had a dreamy, sing-song quality about it which Drew found more chilling than the freezing rain.

"Don't do this," Drew said, inching forward, the gun extended in front of him despite the fact that his fear of hitting Lou precluded any possibility of firing it.

"Stay where you are," Andrea said. "And drop the gun."

"No way. If I put this gun down, you'll kill us both. You can either release Lou and let us get you some help, or you can kill her and I'll kill you. Either way, this insanity stops now."

"You'd stand by and watch the death of another woman you love? You did that once before. What kind of man are you?"

Drew's finger tightened on the trigger as he took another step. "Let her go, Andrea! Let her go or I swear I'll blow your damned face off, just like you did to Agent Fletcher."

"You can either try to kill me or you can try to save Lou, but you can't do both. Looks like it's decision time."

"What?" He froze.

"Are you still afraid of the water, Drew?" Andrea taunted, and then pushed Lou off the bridge.

Time seemed to stop for Drew. He watched as Lou went over the side, as if in slow motion, and thought he could see a look of pleading in her eyes. As another bolt of lightning lit the sky, he saw that Andrea had extended her arm and was pointing the gun at him. And in that same brief period of light, he saw her finger starting to squeeze the trigger.

Drew realized that everything he had said to Andrea had been a bluff. He had only one choice. Hearing the loud crack of the gun and the sound of the bullet whistling past at the exact spot his head had been a fraction of a second earlier, he leapt off the bridge and plunged into the swirling black water.

Chapter 34

Because Drew was already drenched from the rain, he did not think the river would be much colder, but he was wrong. The shock of hitting the water almost caused him to gasp as he went under, but he managed to hold his breath until he broke the surface. He heard the distant crack of gunfire again, and realized not only he had lost Fletcher's gun, but that Andrea was still shooting at him. He glanced behind him, preparing to dive beneath the surface, but quickly saw that was not necessary. The swift current had already carried him so far that he could no longer see the footbridge. He hoped that if he could not see it, then Andrea could not see him.

Struggling to control the speed and direction of his motion lest he pass Lou in the darkness, he scanned the turbulent surface for any sign of her. "Lou!" he shouted, but his call went unanswered. At the rate the current was moving, the two or three seconds she had hit the water before him could make the difference of several yards. He stroked furiously to catch up with her, knowing that her bound arms would prevent her from keeping her head above the surface for very long.

After every few strokes, he would stop to look around and shout her name. He was freezing and his arms already ached with fatigue, but he was determined that he would not, for the second time in his life, go to a morgue to identify the body of the woman he loved. The only way he would leave this river alive was if he was carrying Lou.

Frantic, he swam a few yards, shouted her name, and then swam a few more. The current was incredibly strong and swift. Even if he had wanted to, he was not sure that he would be able to get out. Not that getting out was an option. He called her name again, his voice less urgent but more pleading in nature. "Lou! Please, Lou, answer me!"

At first, he thought it was only a wishful indulgence of his imagination, so faint and whispery that it could have been the sound of the wind. Then, he heard it again. "Drew!"

His heart nearly exploded in his chest as he whipped his head from side to side. "Lou! Shout again! I can't see you!"

"Drew . . . here!" he heard behind him and to his left, and immediately swam in that direction. Making progress against the current was nearly impossible, but he pushed himself to the limit of his endurance, kicking and stroking with every ounce of strength he possessed. Just when he was about to shout again, he saw her holding on to a fallen tree limb at her back. Because the limb was near the surface and her arms were extended straight behind, her body was forced forward, and she was struggling to keep her nose and mouth above the rushing water. He doubted she would be able to maintain her grip much longer.

He wrapped his arms around her, and she gasped in pain. "What's wrong?" he shouted. "Are you hurt?"

"I've been shot," she said, her voice weak, barely discernible over the noise of the rain and the churning river.

"Okay, try to hold on to me," he said. "I'll get you out."

As soon as he spoke those words, he realized he did not have a clue how he would fulfill that promise. The tree limb to which Lou clung was too flimsy to support them both, and the rock-lined shore was too steep to climb out at that point anyway. They would have to go back into the current and try to stay afloat as they sought a suitable spot to climb ashore.

"Are your hands tied?" he asked.

"Handcuffed," she gasped, spitting out water. "There's a spare key in a pouch on my shoulder strap, just above the holster."

He reached his hand under the water and felt along her left side. "Found it," he exclaimed, as his probing fingers located a snap about three inches above the empty holster.

"Be careful, it's small," she said.

He carefully unsnapped the pouch and probed inside with his fingers. He felt a thin, cylindrical strip of metal. Slowly, gingerly, he extracted it.

"Got it," he said, grasping it tightly in his right hand.

"The lock is in the bulge on the inside of my wrists," she said. "There's a notch at the bottom that matches a lip on the key. You'll have to go under water to do it, so just try to get one side unlocked. We'll undo the other when we get on land."

He put his left hand under her chin and gently lifted her face above the water. "Can you keep your head above water while I do this? I won't be able to see anything, so it could take a couple of tries."

"I think so. Just please hurry."

Drew inhaled deeply and dipped beneath the surface. They were apparently near the shoreline because his feet touched bottom when he submerged. He estimated the water was about seven feet deep at this point, and knew that was plenty deep enough to drown in.

He moved around behind her, and followed her arms with his hands. He could not see a thing. He felt the handcuffs and tried to stick his head above the surface to gulp more air, but the branches of the fallen limb prevented him from getting more than the top of his head out of the water. He would have to try to get the job done with the air he had in his lungs.

He felt the place where the metal of the handcuffs widened, and located the keyhole with his thumb. He was at an awkward angle to get his right hand close enough to insert the key. He lowered himself about six inches deeper into the water, thinking his best bet would be to get the handcuffs positioned directly above him. It took a couple of attempts to work himself into the appropriate position, and by then, his lungs seemed ready to burst. He exhaled the remaining air as he pushed off from the bottom of the riverbed and arched his neck back as far as he could. Just as he finished emptying his lungs, his face broke the surface of the water. Jagged edges of the tree limb cut into his face and a sharp point stabbed his forehead, narrowly missing his left eye, but he managed to suck in air before he went back under.

He lowered himself into his previous position and reached above his head with both hands. He located the metallic bulge, the keyhole, and then the notch, and carefully positioned the key in his right hand. He had to move the thumb of his left hand out of the way, causing him to miss the precise location of the keyhole, but on the third try he felt it go in. He turned the key one way and nothing happened. He reversed direction and was exhilarated when he felt the mechanism give way.

With his left hand, he opened the clasp around her wrist, but as he tried to move her arms forward, the open cuff caught on the limb. So desperate was he to free her that he made the mistake of using his right hand to unsnag the cuff. The key slipped from his grasp and disappeared. He told himself that it did not matter. The important thing was that Lou's arms were now unbound.

Making certain the open end of the handcuffs was free of entanglement, he moved in front of her and surfaced inches from her face. She was in a more upright position now, and she immediately draped her left hand, cuff dangling, around his neck.

"Are you okay?" he gasped, gulping in air.

"Much better," she said, but her voice was weak and she seemed to be putting all of her weight on him.

"I lost the key."

"Just get me out of this water."

They moved slowly at first, Drew holding her around the waist with his right hand as he stroked with his left. When they hit the current again, they took off like a canoe shooting the rapids. At least with the water doing the work of carrying them, Drew did not have to swim. He could devote all of his waning energy to just keeping them afloat.

He tried to scan the shoreline for a suitably flat area to climb out of the river, but he could only see when there was lightning, and even then he saw no viable exit point. Then, he saw a four-foot long log caught in a tangle of tree limbs. It took considerable effort to keep from being swept right past it, but he managed to grasp hold of a branch and pull the two of them over to the log.

"At least we'll be able to stay afloat," he said.

Lou murmured something unintelligible, and Drew realized she was going into shock. He had to find a way to get her out of the freezing water and into some place warm, or drowning would not be the only threat to her life.

He carefully lifted her wounded right arm, and draped it over the log. Her other arm was still wrapped around his neck. Holding tightly to her waist and grasping the log with his other arm, he used his legs to propel them back into the raging current.

It seemed they had been adrift in the angry river for hours, but it had probably been no more than ten or twelve minutes when Drew spotted a faint glow ahead and to his left. He immediately began angling toward it. With such a swift current, waiting until they were close enough to see more clearly would be too late.

Turning the log and kicking furiously, he positioned them at a slight angle to the current. The distant light gradually became brighter, and he could see that it emanated from multiple points. It was a big building, and the lights indicated someone was there. He could get help. Most importantly, he could find a way to get Lou warm before she died of hypothermia.

As they drifted closer, Drew could see the dark outline of the building. It was too big to be a home. *A factory?* he wondered. *Doesn't matter. If they have lights, they have heat, and most likely a phone as well.* He kicked his weary legs even harder.

He tried to steer them straight toward the lights, but the current was carrying them faster than Drew had anticipated. Just as it looked as if they would be swept right past the building, his foot snagged on something. It was some type of post submerged in the water, and when he tried to locate it with his left foot again, he touched bottom. He planted both feet and found that the water depth was about five feet, just up to his shoulders. Holding tightly to Lou, he struggled up the gradual incline. When he had reached the point where the water was only waist-deep, he released the log that had served as their flotation device. It shot away and was out of sight in a matter of seconds.

Both hands now free, Drew shifted Lou around so he could get his left arm across her back and his right arm under her knees. Carrying her like a child, he stumbled the final few steps out of the rushing water and muttered a prayer of thanks when he finally felt grass beneath his feet.

He hurried through the rain toward the closest light, and as he got nearer it seemed to be multi-colored. When he was within a few feet of the building he saw why. He was looking at stained glass. They had reached a church.

He had to find a door. He took a chance and turned left, following the side of the building and passing another window before he turned a corner and stepped from slippery grass to concrete. There was an expansive open area to his left, probably a parking lot. He turned another corner and found himself on a covered walkway that connected the first building he had seen, apparently the sanctuary, with another, less stately building that he imagined housed offices or classrooms.

The doors to both buildings were locked. He pounded on them and screamed at the top of his lungs, but elicited no response. No lights were visible in either building, but the lights he had seen on the other side of the sanctuary had to mean someone was in there. Stepping out from under the cover and back into the driving rain, Drew continued along the side of the building, hoping to find the main entrance. Reaching another corner, he struggled through a sparse hedgerow and emerged onto another walkway. To his right he could now make out wide concrete steps and massive white pillars.

He had found the entrance.

He carried Lou up the steps and approached the tall, ornate double doors. They were locked. Releasing Lou's legs so that her feet dangled helplessly beside him and holding her around the waist with his left hand, he pounded on the door with his right. For what seemed to him an eternity, there was no response. He continued hammering the door and shouting furiously. Finally, he saw a sliver of light appear through the crack between the two doors. Someone was coming.

Holding tightly to Lou, Drew took a step back and waited. He was scared, cold, and every muscle in his body ached. He had spent so much time in the dark, murky clutches of the rain-swollen river that he had begun to believe he would die there. Now, as one of the huge doors before him finally swung open, revealing the splendor of warm light dancing off marble floors and polished brass fixtures, he felt as if he were standing at the gates of heaven.

"Who are you?" asked a mountain of a man with crew-cut hair and greasy coveralls.

"My name is Drew Osborne. This is Lou Hennessey, the Smythville chief of police. She's hurt. We need help."

The man craned his neck to look down at them. "Lou's a man's name." His voice was deep but had a simple, child-like quality.

"I know," Drew said impatiently. "Can we come in? She's been shot and she's half frozen. I need to call an ambulance."

"Reverend Porter, he says women dressing in pants and acting like men is the work of the devil." He seemed oblivious to Drew's plea for help.

Realizing the huge man was mentally deficient, Drew tried a different tact. "What's your name?" he asked.

"My name's Nate."

"Nate, the devil's been after us tonight. We've got to come in and get warm."

"Reverend Porter, he says I'm not to let anyone in when I'm working. He says I should keep the doors locked."

"I think Reverend Porter would want you to let us in, Nate. He wouldn't want us to be left out here at the mercy of the devil, would he?"

Nate pondered that a minute, then moved his massive frame aside. "No, I suppose not. The devil's name is Satan. I hate Satan. He makes people do bad things."

"You don't know the half of it," Drew muttered, as he carried Lou past the immense man-child. As he stepped inside, a wide table laden with flowers and big brass collection plates stood against the wall directly in front of him. Embroidered in gold on the white linen tablecloth was "Riverside Baptist Church."

He looked for a place to put Lou down where she could be reasonably comfortable while he found a phone and called an ambulance. To his left, he saw a door labeled "Choir Room."

"What's in there?" he asked.

"Just robes," Nate said. "That's where the choir puts on their robes for the service. They walk right down this aisle during the last hymn. It's kinda like a parade."

"I'm sure it's very impressive," Drew said, as he carried Lou to the door and tried the handle. It was locked. He spied the large ring of keys dangling from Nate's belt. "Does one of those keys fit this door?"

"Sure," Nate said, beaming with obvious pride. "I've got a key to all the doors. I'm the caretaker here. That means I take care of things."

"Please open it," Drew said.

"But nobody's supposed to . . ."

"Please," Drew shouted, "She's going to die if I can't get her warm!" Noticing the look of hurt and confusion on the man's face, he added quietly, "And if she dies tonight, the devil will take her soul. You and I can't let Satan do that, Nate."

That was all the rationale the huge caretaker required. "Oh, no. We can't let him do that. I hate Satan."

Nate unlocked the door, and Drew carried Lou in. He flipped on a light and saw two long rows of red robes hanging neatly. On the floor in a corner were several cloth laundry bags, presumably for sending the robes to the cleaners. He used his foot to bunch several laundry bags together and gently laid Lou on top of them. He started unbuttoning her blouse and said, "Hand me one of those robes, Nate. A small one."

Nate looked through several robes before selecting one and reluctantly putting it in Drew's outstretched hand. When he looked over and saw what Drew was doing, he let out a horrified gasp. "Oh, no! You can't take her clothes off, mister. Not unless you're married to her. Reverend Porter, he says you ain't supposed to see somebody naked unless you're married to 'em."

"Don't worry, we're married," Drew said as he pulled the robe over her head and put her left arm through the billowing sleeve. He looked at the puckered wound in her right shoulder, beginning to ooze blood again, and left that arm resting against her side. "Now, give me a larger robe."

He put the larger robe on over the first one, trying to create layers that would warm her. He then removed her soaking wet slacks and quickly covered her bare legs with several more robes. The thin cotton material was not as absorbent and warm as a wool blanket, but it would have to do for now.

Drew stood, his own body trembling violently from the cold.

"Nate, where is there a phone in here?"

"Oh, there ain't no phones in the sanctuary. I was just in here cleaning the baptism pool. I scrubbed it real good, and filled it back up. It's all ready for Sunday morning."

"That's good, Nate, but I need a phone. Where can I find one?"

"All the offices are in the building next door," Nate said. "They have phones. But all the doors are locked."

Drew looked at the man's belt. "But you have all the keys, Nate. Show me which one will get me into the other building, and which one will get me into an office."

Nate stared at him for a moment, and then started unhooking the bulky key chain from his belt. "You can't use the pastor's office, though. Reverend Porter, he says nobody can go in his office 'cept him. He's got holy stuff in there that can't be bothered."

"Okay, I'll use another office. Just show me the right keys."

Fortunately, each key was labeled. The large one with the blue "Admin" sticker on it was for the other building, and the one with the red "Music" sticker was for the Music Director's office.

Knowing it would be faster to go outside and retrace his earlier steps, he told Nate to stay with Lou.

"Try to keep her warm, okay?" he said. "Put some more robes on her. If she wakes up, make her stay still. Tell her I've gone to call for help. Got that?"

"Yep, I do," Nate said confidently. "I keep her warm and tell her that her husband has gone to call for help."

"That's fine," Drew said, and then muttered to himself, "She'll probably be delirious anyway."

"I can sing for her," Nate suggested cheerfully. "Reverend Porter, he says I've got a real good voice, but he won't let me sing in the choir, though."

"That would be nice, Nate. Just keep her still and warm, and sing to her. I'll be back in just a few minutes."

As he turned to walk out of the small room, Nate sat on the floor facing Lou and began to sing. His voice was a surprisingly clear and pleasant baritone. Drew smiled, but felt the hairs on the back of his neck spring to full attention when he recognized the lyrics.

"Yes, we'll gather at the riv-er
The beau-ti-ful, the beau-ti-ful riv-er"

Moments later, Drew snatched up the phone in the Music Director's tiny office and dialed the operator. "I need the Milton Police. It's an emergency," he said.

She obediently connected his call, and Drew heard a male voice on the other end of the line. "Milton Police. Officer Curry."

"My name is Drew Osborne. I'm at the Riverside Baptist Church. I'm with Lou Hennessey, the Smythville chief of police, and she's been wounded. I need help right away."

"Were you at the Warren place earlier?" the officer asked.

"Yeah, how'd you know?"

"The sheriff got a call from Bernard Moss at the Smythville *Gazette*. He said there was trouble at the Warren place. The sheriff went over there, and just called me and said there's a dead man in the kitchen. Do you know anything about that?"

"Yes," Drew said impatiently. "I can tell you everything you need to know. He was killed by Andrea Warren, and she's the one who shot Chief Hennessey, and tried to shoot me. But right now I need you to get an ambulance over here. Please hurry."

"Okay," Curry said. "We'll get you an ambulance, and I'll radio Sergeant Mullins of the Smythville P.D. He's on his way over here. I'll tell him you're at the church."

"Tell anyone you want. Just hurry. And try to find Andrea Warren. She's the one who's been killing all those women in Smythville."

"Holy shit!" Drew heard the officer exclaim as he slammed down the phone and hurried out of the office. He had to get back to Lou. If he could keep her alive until the ambulance arrived, everything would be all right. He had done everything in his power to save her—he was not going to let up now.

He raced through the rain and arrived back at the front entrance to the sanctuary. Rushing inside to the ornate vestibule, he headed toward the choir room. He immediately sensed that something was not right. He could not hear Nate singing, and the door was closed. He distinctly remembered leaving it open.

He tried to open the door, but something was blocking it from swinging all the way in. It was Nate.

"Nate, move over so I can get in," Drew shouted, but there was no response. He pushed harder on the door, allowing him to stick his head into the room. And to see a sight that made his heart sink—an empty bed of choir robes.

He leaned heavily on the door, opening it enough to slide in. Nate's head was a bloody mess, and the marble floor was slick with the shiny red fluid pulsing from a hideous gash. Drew knelt beside him and felt for a pulse. Nate was breathing and his eyes were fluttering rapidly.

"Where is she?" Drew shouted frantically. "Where is she, Nate?"

But Nate did not answer the question. He simply muttered the same word over and over again.

"Satan."

Chapter 35

T he river. That had to be where Andrea was taking Lou—to finish the job she had started. She had probably known that the church would be the first level, unwooded area they would reach, and that, if they had not drowned, is where they would most likely emerge. And, Drew reasoned, the same area that had allowed emergence from the river would allow unencumbered access to the river.

Drew quickly fashioned a pillow of laundry sacks to cushion Nate's battered head, and then bolted from the choir room and out the front doors of the sanctuary. Although he knew there might be a shorter route to the river than the one by which he had arrived, he decided he could not risk the chance of getting turned around or running into a dead end in the nearly total darkness. Retracing his previous path, he sprinted between the two buildings, turned the corner, and raced toward the area from which he and Lou had emerged only fifteen minutes earlier.

He did not slow until his feet were splashing in the eddying current along the flooded shoreline. He could not be positive, but he was pretty sure this was the spot where he had waded out of the river. He stood still and listened intently, hoping to hear something that would indicate Andrea and Lou's location, but the only sounds were the wind, the rain, and the rushing water.

He turned to his left, planning to run the length of the church grounds as he continued his frantic search along the river, when a tremendous bolt of lightning tore a jagged hole in the dark sky and flooded the area with blue-white light. Drew could see all the way to the edge of the woods a hundred yards away, as well as the entire lawn that sloped up to the church. There was no sign of anyone else along the river. He was alone.

For the first time since he had walked out of Bernard Moss' office a few hours earlier, Drew felt defeated. Throughout the terrifying ordeal he had persevered in his attempts to save Lou and, even during the harrowing time in the river, had steadfastly maintained his belief that he would prevail. Now, it seemed hopeless. How could he save her if he could not even find her? Andrea's intentions were clear—she was going to drown Lou. *Where else could they be but somewhere along the river?* he wondered, panicked. *Maybe she carried Lou off in a car, planning to drive to another location to perform her demented baptism ceremony. Maybe—wait! That's it! The baptism pool. They're still inside the church!*

Cursing himself for overlooking the obvious, Drew sprinted back across the grassy slope to the sanctuary. Around the building, through the hedgerow, and up the front steps he raced, knowing that seconds counted. He burst through the doors into the marbled vestibule and looked down the long aisle toward the ornate pulpit. Below Reverend Porter's Sunday morning rostrum was a railed altar. Behind it, there was a large choir loft, and above, looming like a giant window to eternal life, was the baptism pool.

Drew had been raised in the Methodist Church where baptisms were performed, usually on infants instead of older children or adults, with a mere sprinkling of water on the head. He was familiar enough with this denomination to know that they performed the rite in the tradition of John the Baptist—total immersion—with the congregation viewing the ceremony through the window-like opening. He saw no one up there, but could hear the sound of Andrea's voice. She was singing again.

Sonnets

They were apparently in one of the stairwells behind the altar that led up to the pool. Drew had been to enough Baptist services to know that the minister usually emerged from one side, and the newly saved from the other, so there would be a stairwell on either side. The eerie voice seemed to be coming from his left. He ran out the sanctuary door on the right.

He located the stairwell immediately. Moving as quickly and quietly as he could, he climbed the winding stairs two at a time. The singing became louder as he approached the top. He pushed open a door and stepped around the corner. Andrea was already in the water, holding Lou in both arms. When she looked up and saw Drew she let go of Lou's legs and brought her right hand out of the water. It was holding Lou's gun.

"Stay where you are, Drew," she said calmly. "You can't stop the truth. It's already been written."

Drew was out of breath, his chest heaving. "No, Andrea," he gasped.

"But you can't stop me, don't you see?" She pressed the barrel of the gun firmly under Lou's chin. "Once the truth is written, it must be fulfilled."

Drew stood perfectly still, afraid that the slightest flinch would cause her to pull the trigger. "But if you shoot her, the truth won't be fulfilled. I've studied your poetry, Andrea, and I know what "Sonnet No. 6" means. 'This wretched bitch whose grievous lies are drowned.' If she dies in any other way, your sonnet is a lie. Just a childish rhyme that people will laugh at. The only way it becomes truth is if she drowns. You can't shoot her."

Andrea's eyes flashed fire. "No, but I can shoot you."

She pointed the gun in his direction and pulled the trigger before Drew had a chance to move a muscle. The empty, metallic click when the gun misfired echoed through the cavernous church like a greeting shouted in a canyon. Unwilling to take the chance that the waterlogged revolver would fail again, Drew screamed in fury and dived at her.

The gun fired when Andrea pulled the trigger the second time, but the bullet whistled past Drew, and thudded into the wall behind him. Before she could squeeze off a third shot, he had landed on top of her, knocking the gun loose from her hand. It sank out of sight beneath the battle-churned water.

Even though he knew Andrea was physically fit, he was stunned by her strength. She swung and clawed with savage ferocity, delivering punishing blows to his head, and ripping painful gashes in his face. Despite his exhaustion, Drew fought with equal intensity, and managed to get his hands around her throat. Turning his head to avoid her furious efforts to claw his eyes, he saw Lou floating face down in the water behind him.

He had no choice but to release his chokehold on Andrea and reach out to grab hold of Lou's hair, lifting her face out of the water. He heard her take a gulping breath of air just as Andrea attacked him from behind, screaming maniacally as she tried to push him aside to get at the subject of her poem. Drew held onto Lou's hair with his right hand, extending his arm as far away as possible from the flailing psychopath on his back. But with only one hand free to fight, he quickly lost whatever advantage he had held. His head was shoved under the water, and he felt two strong hands pushing down on his shoulders, separating him by mere inches from life-sustaining air. Andrea positioned herself on top of him, holding him under with one hand and the weight of her body as she stretched the other hand toward Lou. Desperate, yet determined, Drew held the woman he loved above the surface and out of the killer's reach, even as he realized he would soon be unable to continue the fight.

After only a short time under the water, his chest burned as if on fire, and his head felt like it would explode. The battle above him raged on, and he could feel his strength ebbing. Even if he released Lou, his oxygen-deprived body was no longer capable of preventing Andrea from holding him down. He had done his best, but he had failed Lou, as he had failed Kate. At least this time he would share his loved one's fate.

Determined to make one final, desperate effort, he managed to get his right leg under him. Planting his foot on the floor of the pool, he pushed with all his might as he exhaled the remaining air from his lungs. But the strength of one leg was not enough. Andrea maintained her dominance. Eliot had won again.

Drew's vision began to blur, and a million flashes of light seemed to explode like fireworks before his eyes. The noise above him continued, including a booming sound that seemed muffled and distant. The light began to grow dim, as if the sun were setting after a bright summer day. The water seemed to turn red, and then everything faded to black.

Drew heard shouting and sensed movement. He saw bright lights, and then darkness. He felt chest pain, rhythmic pressure, and forced air. He felt something deep inside, climbing and pushing to get out. Then, he saw the bright lights again.

He suddenly felt as if he were exploding. Hands rolled him over roughly as he vomited what seemed like gallons of water. Again and again he retched, until his throat felt raw. Still feeling nauseous, he lifted his face out of the foul-smelling puddle, and strong hands lifted him to a sitting position.

It took him a couple of minutes to get his bearings and to be sure that the peristalsis had subsided. Suddenly realizing where he was and why, he struggled to get up, but the strong hands held him down.

"Sit still, Dr. Osborne. Here, you need to breathe some of this."

A plastic cup was placed over his nose and mouth, and his head began to clear almost immediately. His vision came back into focus and he saw the smiling face of Art Schaeffer, the rookie cop from Smythville. "Feeling better now?" the baby-faced officer asked.

Drew pushed the oxygen mask away. "Where's Lou? What have you done with her? Is she alive?"

Schaeffer put a hand on each shoulder to hold him down. "Relax, she's right downstairs. The paramedics are getting her ready to go in the ambulance. She lost a lot of blood, and swallowed quite a bit of water, but I think she's going to be okay."

Drew sank back down on the floor. He grabbed the oxygen mask and took several deep breaths. He had never known that the simple act of breathing could feel so good. He could only vaguely remember his struggle in the baptism pool, like it was a long-ago dream. Actually, more like a nightmare.

"What happened?" he finally asked. "Where's Andrea?"

A cloud seemed to pass over Schaeffer's face and, for a moment, his eyes seemed to age thirty years. "I had to shoot her," he said quietly.

"Is she dead?"

"No, but I don't know if she'll make it or not. They took her away in an ambulance just a minute or two ago."

Drew stared at the young man, knowing that despite everything Andrea had done, and what Schaeffer had seen, he was wrestling with the remorse of using deadly force on another human being. "You had to do it," Drew said. "She didn't give you a choice. Trust me, I know."

Schaeffer said nothing. He stood and stared through the window of the baptism pool, down into the sanctuary.

"There was a man downstairs in the choir room," Drew said. "The caretaker. He was hurt pretty badly."

"He's still alive," Schaeffer said. "They took him in the ambulance too. Now it looks like it's the chief's turn."

"Help me up," Drew said.

"You really need to sit here and rest, Dr. Osborne."

"Help me up. Now," Drew repeated urgently as he struggled to his feet. He felt a little wobbly, but thought he could walk. Despite Schaeffer's protestations, he pulled open the door to the stairwell and, holding tightly to the rail, wound his way down to ground level.

Reaching the bottom, he pushed through the door and stumbled into the sanctuary. He could see two paramedics rolling Lou's stretcher into the vestibule, heading for the front door. "Wait!" he shouted weakly, and ran on shaky legs up the carpeted center aisle.

Sonnets

Appearing not to hear him, one paramedic opened one of the large front doors as the other pushed the stretcher through it. Drew stumbled to his knees, stood back up, and continued running, bracing himself on the corner of each successive pew he passed. When he finally made it through the vestibule and pushed the front door open, the paramedics were already lifting the stretcher into the back of an ambulance parked near the steps.

"Wait!" Drew shouted, as he ran out into the rain.

One of the paramedics met him at the bottom of the steps. "I'm sorry, but you can't go with us, sir. It's against regulations."

"No, you have to let me!" Drew pleaded. "I have to go with her."

"Sir, I'm sorry, but it's not . . ."

"Let him go with her," a stern voice behind Drew said. He turned to see Howard Mullins standing in the downpour.

The paramedic started to protest. "But we're not allowed . . ."

"I'll take full responsibility," Mullins said firmly. He looked at Drew, then back at the paramedic. "You do anything Dr. Osborne says. If it weren't for him, you'd be taking that woman to the morgue instead of the hospital."

Drew said nothing. He just looked at Mullins for a moment, and then crawled into the back of the ambulance. The young paramedic climbed in behind him and closed the door. Drew knelt on the floor by the stretcher and looked at Lou's face beneath the oxygen mask. She was pale, bruised, and cut, but he could tell by the rhythmic rise and fall of her chest that she was breathing. To him, that was all that mattered. He reached for her hand and held it in both of his as the ambulance, lights flashing and siren screaming, cut a path through the dark, rainy night.

Epilogue

Warm, tropical breezes blew their hair and caressed their skin. Powdery white sand crunched like sugar beneath their bare feet. Blue-green waves beckoned, rhythmically rising and falling like the chest of a sleeping giant. The happy music of Cancun, hanging in the air like gliding seagulls, was accompanied by a chorus of laughing children.

The scenes of his dream played before him, like a movie he had seen a hundred times. Progressing steadily, deliberately, toward the same tragic ending. An ending which, unlike a movie, was real. The heroine would never be cast in another role. There would be no sequel.

The pain, the sorrow, and the crushing sense of loss were as strong as ever. Tears fell on white sand, on hotel room sheets, and on the stainless steel table where her lifeless body was revealed. The grief was palpable, but the feeling of horror, of dread, was gone. The pain was still real, but it was more like the pain of healing than that of new wounds being cut.

Now, he was walking into the chapel, moving slowly toward the flower-draped coffin. This time, her family and friends did not stare at him with dead eyes as they pointed accusing fingers. Instead, they politely stepped aside as he made his way to the prayer altar by the open lid. He found solace in the tender embrace of her mother, and sensed rather than heard the words of consolation. He turned away from his fellow mourners and lowered his knees to the cushioned rail.

Through tear-filled eyes he gazed once more at the soft, blond hair, the long, dark eyelashes, and the full, supple lips. Her face was that of an angel—peaceful, pure, perfect. She was at rest.

He closed his eyes and prayed that she would have a special place in heaven, a place of laughter, joy, and poetry. A place where she could spend eternity in the company of other souls whose beauty was so rare that they had made an indelible impression on the world they left behind. Just as she had.

He opened his eyes and rose to his feet. He reveled in her beauty one last time, and then leaned forward and gently kissed her cool lips. He gave his head a subtle nod, and the coffin lid was lowered. He watched with an aching heart as it slowly closed, hiding forever the lovely face he knew he had just seen for the last time in this life.

Kate would haunt him no more.

It was Friday, exactly one week since their horrifying ordeal in Milton. The ache in Drew's muscles, and the discoloration on his battered face were beginning to fade, as was the underlying sense of fear that had continued for several days after the incident. He parked his car outside of the North Georgia Psychiatric Hospital, and then opened his door and stepped out into bright sunshine. He squinted his eyes against the solar glare, causing pain in his right cheekbone, which had suffered a hairline fracture in his fight with Andrea.

He walked around to the other side of the car and opened the passenger door for Lou. Her face also still bore the telltale signs of a violent struggle, and her right arm was in a sling. The bullet had passed cleanly through her shoulder, missing bone, but tearing some ligaments. The damage had been repaired by a two-hour surgical procedure and she would have six weeks of physical therapy to look forward to, but all in all, she considered herself lucky just to be alive. She could deal with a little pain.

Sonnets

They had an appointment with the doctor treating Andrea. She would recover from the gunshot wound inflicted by Officer Schaeffer, whose uniform now sported a medal of commendation presented by the mayor. Once Andrea recovered sufficiently, she would undergo a battery of psychological tests. There was no doubt that she was crazy. It was simply a matter of degree. The question of whether she would be put on trial for multiple homicides would have to await the outcome of those tests. She would either face lethal injection, or decades of psychiatric incarceration. Either way, Eliot's reign of terror was over.

Lou had called Drew this morning to say she was making the ninety-minute trip to the facility, and to ask if he would like to be her driver. He had jumped at the opportunity. The only downside to the Eliot case being resolved was that he no longer had a ready excuse to see Lou every day. He had visited her each of the three days she had been in the hospital, smuggling chocolates in under his coat, but had not seen her since her release. All of her time had been spent either wrapping up the details of the case or resting at home, trying to regain her strength.

Without talking, they climbed slowly and carefully up the long flight of steps to the front door of the hospital. They had spoken very little during the drive from Smythville, their silence not due so much to any sense of awkwardness with each other, but rather to the nervous anticipation of again coming face-to-face with the psychopath who had nearly ended their lives. Although she had not spoken about it, Drew was convinced that Lou was punishing herself for missing what she now, in retrospect, considered to be so many obvious signs about Andrea. He knew it was important for her to somehow get beyond the point of holding herself personally responsible for allowing a deranged killer to wreak havoc on the town she was sworn to protect. Drew felt he could help her—he knew a little something about harboring guilt.

Entering the hospital promptly at noon, they were met by a nurse who escorted them to the office of Dr. Jonathan Bain, the hospital's chief of staff. The doctor was a plump, pleasant-looking man in his late forties, a man who looked more suited to run a neighborhood candy store than an institution for the criminally insane. He greeted his two guests cordially, asked about their numerous injuries as if he really cared, and then invited them to sit down in his small but comfortable office.

Seated behind his desk, Dr. Bain removed his glasses and massaged the bridge of his nose with the thumb and index finger of his right hand. "As I told you on the phone, Chief Hennessey, cases like this have to be handled very carefully from a legal perspective. I can share what we've managed to learn about Miss Warren's background and her current psychological state, but I can't divulge anything she might have said about any of the crimes of which she's accused."

"I understand, doctor," Lou said. "Those questions will be answered in the competency hearing. My interest is more in the area of . . ." She paused for a moment, as if unsure of how to continue. "More in the area of how all this came to happen. How someone I thought I knew could be carrying around demons that could cause her to do these things."

Dr. Bain studied Lou's face, as if diagnosing the most serious wounds she had sustained at Eliot's hands, the ones beneath the skin.

"Okay, well, as you're probably aware, most serial killers commit their first murder very close to home, in an environment that is familiar to them."

"Yes, I'm aware of that," Lou said.

"Miss Warren's first time was actually in her home." He looked at his audience, as if preparing them for what he would say next. "At the age of twelve, Andrea killed her mother."

"Oh, my God," Lou muttered. "Why?"

"Because her mother asked her to," the doctor replied. "Isabel Warren had ovarian cancer that was diagnosed much too late to treat.

It had spread to her spine, most of her abdominal organs and, near the end, her brain. She must have been in excruciating pain a lot of the time."

"What a terrible thing for a twelve-year-old child to witness," Lou said.

"Yes," Dr. Bain continued, "particularly when they were so close. From what I've been able to piece together, Andrea was not what you would call a popular girl in school. She was tall, gangly, and exceptionally bright. She was more comfortable secluded in her room writing poetry than playing with other children her age."

"Did the other kids ridicule her?" Drew asked.

"Probably," Dr. Bain said, "but Andrea seemed well enough as long as her mother was alive. They wrote poems together, read Greek mythology, basically just lived for each other."

"So the knowledge that her mother was dying of cancer must have devastated her," Lou said.

"Undoubtedly. But not nearly as much as what her mother asked her to do." Dr. Bain paused, as if expecting questions at that point. There being none, he continued.

"She finally prevailed upon Andrea to help her end the suffering. They staged it to look like an accidental bathtub drowning. In reality, it was a carefully orchestrated ceremony. Andrea wrote her mother a final poem—a sonnet—and read it to her as she sat in a tub full of water, surrounded by candles. Then her mother sang her favorite hymn."

"*Beautiful River*," Drew said.

Dr. Bain looked at him. "Yes, that's right. Then Andrea pushed her mother's head beneath the water and held it there until she drowned."

"And she recorded this ceremony," Lou said, now understanding what she had heard as Andrea was leading her from the cemetery to the river.

"Yes," Dr. Bain said. "It was Andrea's way of holding onto her mother's memory. These memories became increasingly important over the next five years while Andrea was being raised by Isabel's sister, Lillian."

Lou shuddered, remembering the scene in the small cemetery behind the house.

"Apparently Lillian was quite an attractive woman, but a promiscuous alcoholic," Bain said. "She probably resented having the responsibility of raising an adolescent thrust upon her, and was abusive toward Andrea. Whereas Isabel had always praised Andrea's poetry, Lillian ridiculed it, and even ridiculed the girl herself. Called her ugly, gawky, et cetera. That is, until Andrea began to change."

"Change?" Lou asked. "In what way?"

"She began to mature, physically. What looks tall and gangly for a twelve year old girl can be stunning for a seventeen-year-old woman. According to Andrea, her aunt, and her aunt's numerous male callers, began to look at her differently—in ways that made Andrea uncomfortable and confused."

"Uh-oh," Drew said with a sigh. "I think I see where this is going."

"Exactly," Bain said. "One night, after consuming God-knows-how-much gin, Lillian apparently made an improper advance. When Andrea reacted with disgust, Lillian flew into a rage and threw a stack of Andrea's poems into the fireplace. Included among them were several poems written by Isabel—the only physical possessions of her mother that Andrea owned."

"So Andrea killed her, too," Lou said wearily.

Bain put his glasses back on and referred to some notes on his desk. "She said her mother made her do it. She told me that her mother said that killing Lillian was another 'act of mercy,' an act that would save Lillian from continuing a life of unabated sin, while also ridding the world of her 'wicked impurity.'"

"This was seen as another accident?" Lou asked.

"Yes. Given Lillian's reputation for drinking, spilling gin on her dress and setting herself on fire while burning trash in the cellar incinerator seemed tragic but logical. Since Andrea was about to turn eighteen, she was allowed to live on her own after that. She worked her way through the University of Georgia, double majoring in English Literature and Journalism, and appeared to be reasonably normal. At least, on the surface."

"And beneath the surface?" Drew asked.

"A time bomb," Bain said. "She wrote poems to her mother constantly, then started writing letters to her, and finally got to the point of staging one-sided phone conversations with her."

"Bernard Moss told me he had heard her having a phone conversation with her mother," Drew said. "Now we know she was just imaging her mother's side of the conversation. Just like she made up her mother's responses when Instant Messaging on the computer."

"Exactly," Dr. Bain said. "None of her friends at school, or later at the newspaper, had a clue that her mother was dead."

"Where there any unsolved murders at or near the university during her time there?" Lou asked.

"We're checking on that," Bain said, "But apparently not. She seems to have been delusional with regard to her mother's presence, but not prone to violence. That is, until a woman she worked with at the newspaper in Smythville came on to her."

"Margaret Fenwyck," Lou said. "That must have triggered memories of Lillian's come-on."

Bain shifted in his chair. "I, um, think this would be a good place for me to stop. Everything from this point on would be inappropriate for me to discuss without her legal counsel being present."

"I understand," Lou said. "At least, I'm trying to. I'm not sure what I understand anymore." She locked eyes with Bain. "I'd like to see her."

"I'm afraid I can't let you speak with her," Bain said, his tone almost apologetic. "She's pretty heavily medicated, and not fully responsible for what she might say. In fact, she's probably asleep.

They give her a pretty big dose right after lunch."

Lou swallowed hard, and inhaled deeply. "I don't want to speak with her, Dr. Bain. I just want to see her. Please."

Bain stood. "Well, I guess there's no harm in that. But I'll need to be there with you."

"No problem," Lou said, shooting a glance at Drew as she rose from her chair. "The more the merrier."

They exited the office and started down a long corridor, past nursing stations and cheerfully decorated patient rooms. It looked like virtually any other hospital—nurses in white uniforms, muscular orderlies pushing trays, and doctors studying charts. Only the bars on the windows and the electronic locks on the reinforced steel security doors indicated the contrary.

They took an elevator, activated by the doctor's key, to the top floor and emerged near a door with a uniformed Georgia State Trooper sitting outside. Dr. Bain whispered something to him, and the officer preceded them into the room. Before they could follow, Bain touched Lou's arm.

"I obviously can't divulge what I intend to say at the competency hearing," he said quietly, as he stared into her eyes, "But I will tell you this. In my professional opinion, based on what I've learned about this patient, no one, not even an experienced psychiatrist, would have noticed anything unusual about Miss Warren's public behavior."

Lou stared back at him, but said nothing.

"You had no way of knowing," he added. "No way at all."

"Thank you," she whispered, "That helps." She clutched Drew's arm and walked into the room.

In a private room on the sixth floor, Andrea lay in bed, her arms and legs restrained. An armed guard was posted just outside the open door, and he accompanied the nurses and doctors when they came in to care for her. Fluids flowed into the veins of both arms, an oxygen tube was positioned in her nostrils, and a drainage tube protruded from the wound in her chest.

The doctors had kept her heavily sedated for the first few days, primarily to ease her pain, and to keep her from thrashing about as she tugged at the restraints, but were beginning to ease back on the dosages. Her head was slowly starting to clear and, even though she still slept a lot, she was more lucid and alert when awake. She knew she was in a hospital, but they would not tell her which one. She also knew that not all of the doctors who frequented her room were there to heal her body. One of them, a pleasant man named Dr. Bain, was there to explore her mind.

He came into her room frequently, and always talked with her for as long as she was willing. But he never pressured her. He was gentle, patient. He asked a lot of questions about what she remembered of the days leading up to her arrival here. At first her memory had been fuzzy, but as she focused her thoughts it had all started coming back. Like the various shapes and colors in a kaleidoscope, jumbled and random at first, and then gradually melding into an organized pattern.

This morning, Dr. Bain had said now that she was better, he would need to talk with her more often. He and others would need to ask her a lot of questions, some of which might seem abstract, even pointless. It did not really matter to her. She felt she had nothing to lose by answering their questions and taking their tests. In fact, she looked forward to it. There was so much to tell about Mother, about Aunt Lillian, and a childhood of ridicule and shame. About ridding the world of evil, about revenge. About truth.

Dr. Bain had just been in her room again. Even though she had been on the verge of falling asleep, she had heard the telltale squeak of the guard's shoes. The squeaky shoes always preceded the arrival of visitors. This time, the visitors who came in with the guard and Dr. Bain were not hospital workers, nor were they strangers. Andrea had not opened her eyes, pretending to be asleep, but she had sensed the presence of Lou Hennessey and Drew Osborne. *So they had both sur-*

vived after all. What a pity. So close to the truth. I did my best. That was all I could do. The world will just have to go on with them in it.

Even as the narcotic-induced sleep threatened to overtake her, she could feel the rage starting to swell up inside her. She felt her fists clinching, her teeth grinding. And then, just as quickly as it had risen, the tide of fury began to ebb. The tension flowed from her muscles, her racing pulse began to slow, and a feeling of peace and calm enveloped her. Someone else was in the room.

She knew that no one was allowed in without the guard, and she had not heard the distinctive squeak of his rubber-soled shoes. Yet she could sense that someone was there, standing by her bed. Someone with the power to calm her—to put her tortured mind at ease.

Ever so slowly, ever so cautiously, she opened her eyes. A vague form loomed at her side, standing quietly, and looking down at her. Gradually, as her eyes began to focus, her face transformed. The furious, murderous scowl was replaced by the gentle smile of a little girl as she opened her mouth to speak.

"Hello, Mother."

"It's certainly a beautiful afternoon," Drew said, offering a hand to help Lou down the hospital's steep front steps.

She took his hand and shifted some of her weight to him as she slowly and carefully maneuvered each step, one at a time. "Yes, it is, isn't it? A bit brisk, but that sunshine feels wonderful."

"Sure does," Drew said, and then stopped walking so he could look into her eyes. "Did you accomplish what you came here for?"

"I suppose," she said. "I'm not really sure why I came. Just to get some answers, I guess. But there's so damn much that I don't think I'll ever understand."

Drew smiled. "What's to understand? Eliot is in custody, and we're alive. From where I stand, that's about all that matters right now."

"You have a point," she said. "In fact, I was thinking of having a little celebratory dinner party at my place tomorrow night. Are you free?"

Sonnets

"Why Chief Hennessey, are you asking me on a date?"

"Yes, I am."

It was the answer he had hoped for, but not the one he expected. "Okay," he managed. "I'd love to come. What can I bring?"

"Do you know much about wine?"

"Sure. I can tell the difference between a white and a red, even with my eyes closed."

She laughed. "Good, then you're in charge of the wine."

"Do you have anything specific in mind?"

"I'm very partial to Bordeaux. A nice Margaux would be great."

"I can handle that. How much do we need?"

"Well, not too much. Like I told you before, one glass and I get mellow, two and I'm ready for bed. A bottle ought to do it."

Drew gave her a sidelong glance as they reached the bottom of the steps. "Just one bottle? Are you sure? How many people will be at this dinner party?"

She looked into his eyes and smiled. "Two."

Drew's heart fluttered like the wings of a sparrow taking flight. "Oh, I see. Well, I think I know just the right wine."

"Good. Why don't you come over at seven?"

"Okay." Reluctantly, he released her hand.

She immediately took it back, intertwining her fingers with his. "I think you'd better let me hold onto this. I'd hate to fall and re-injure my shoulder."

"Hold on as long as you like. That's why I'm here."

Hand in hand, they walked slowly across the hospital parking lot. It was, indeed, a glorious November afternoon. The cloudless sky was a brilliant blue, and a gentle breeze stirred the crisp, mountain air. A flock of Canadian geese flew overhead, the tip of their V-formation pointing due south. They moved their wings in synchronized cadence, as perfect and predictable as the rhythmic measures of a sonnet. Like the two people below them, they were on a journey to some place warm—seeking a haven in an uncertain, sometimes brutal, world.